Praise for the Novels
of Kathari[illegible]

East H[illegible]

"Katharine Davis has written an utt[illegible] novel, suffused with the special light and clarity of Maine. A book about second chances and real love, with characters as complicated as we really are. I couldn't put it down."

—Lee Smith, author of *The Last Girls* and *On Agate Hill*

"A warm and gentle journey on the long road between loss and hope. The writing and characters are as crisp and clear as the Maine setting in this moving story about the transforming power of forgiveness and letting go."

—Karen White, author of *The Memory of Water* and *The House on Tradd Street*

"*East Hope* is a charming love story, delightfully old-fashioned with a very modern twist. Katharine Davis captures Maine not just as a setting but as the character it is."

—Lily King, author of *The English Teacher*

"Katharine Davis's captivating novel of loss and recovery follows a forty-four-year-old woman from a long-settled life into one that is anything but certain. The author's clean prose suits the spare setting. . . . Her keen sensitivity to the people and countryside in that remote place vividly evokes its power to reshape her character's life."

—Kathleen Maloy, author of *Every Last Cuckoo*

continued

"Katharine Davis has created an elegant and compelling tale about loss, love, and, of course, hope. Her characters are rich, her story is gripping, and her prose beautiful and effortless."

—Joanne Rendell, author of *The Professors' Wives' Club*

Capturing Paris

"The layered experience and sensibilities of Americans in Paris are captured marvelously in this haunting and evocative novel by Katharine Davis. Reminiscent of William Maxwell's *The Chateau*, *Capturing Paris* is an impressive debut."

—Katharine Weber, author of *Triangle*

"In this graceful and atmospheric first novel, Katharine Davis explores a question that fascinates us all: What if I had chosen differently, when I still had my choices to make? Through Annie's reinvention of herself in a time of flux, we see anew the consequences of deciding to be who we are, and the consequences of questioning all that we have been."

—Carolyn Parkhurst, author of *Dogs of Babel*

"In *Capturing Paris*, we meet Annie Reed, poet and wife, navigating through a year of upheaval. Through it all, her adopted city of Paris glows, with its abundance of charm, quirks, and moods, all beautifully captured in Katharine Davis's sensitive observations."

—Leslie Pietrzyk, author of *A Year and a Day*

"Dreamy and sentimental, readers with a soft spot for the City of Light will want to give this a look." —*Publishers Weekly*

East Hope

KATHARINE DAVIS

NAL Accent
Published by New American Library, a division of
Penguin Group (USA) Inc., 375 Hudson Street,
New York, New York 10014, USA
Penguin Group (Canada), 90 Eglinton Avenue East, Suite 700, Toronto,
Ontario M4P 2Y3, Canada (a division of Pearson Penguin Canada Inc.)
Penguin Books Ltd., 80 Strand, London WC2R 0RL, England
Penguin Ireland, 25 St. Stephen's Green, Dublin 2,
Ireland (a division of Penguin Books Ltd.)
Penguin Group (Australia), 250 Camberwell Road, Camberwell, Victoria 3124,
Australia (a division of Pearson Australia Group Pty. Ltd.)
Penguin Books India Pvt. Ltd., 11 Community Centre, Panchsheel Park,
New Delhi - 110 017, India
Penguin Group (NZ), 67 Apollo Drive, Rosedale, North Shore 0632,
New Zealand (a division of Pearson New Zealand Ltd.)
Penguin Books (South Africa) (Pty.) Ltd., 24 Sturdee Avenue,
Rosebank, Johannesburg 2196, South Africa

Penguin Books Ltd., Registered Offices:
80 Strand, London WC2R 0RL, England

First published by NAL Accent, an imprint of New American Library,
a division of Penguin Group (USA) Inc.

First Printing, February 2009
1 3 5 7 9 10 8 6 4 2

LIBRARY OF CONGRESS CATALOGING-IN-PUBLICATION DATA:

Davis, Katharine.
East Hope/Katharine Davis.
p. cm.
ISBN 978-0-451-22587-0
1. Widows—Fiction. 2. Booksellers and bookselling—Fiction. 3. Maine—Fiction. 4. Conduct of life—Fiction. I. Title.
PS3604.A967E17 2009
813'.6—dc22 2008024547

Set in Garamond Three • Designed by Elke Sigal

Printed in the United States of America

For RPD

Acknowledgments

I would like to thank my agent, Katherine Fausset, for her enthusiasm, support, and quick replies to all my questions. Many thanks to Ellen Edwards, my editor, for her careful reading and wonderful insights. I am fortunate to be able to work with such dedicated women who are both so generous with their time.

Thanks to E. J. Levy, C. M. Mayo, Ann McLaughlin, Carolyn Parkhurst, Leslie Pietrzyk, and Amy Stolls for reading the novel in its early stages and giving me excellent advice.

I am always grateful for the love and support from my family. A very special thanks to my sister Carroll Charlesworth, for her reading and listening to the novel, often on her porch on the Kennebec River, and giving me invaluable suggestions. And thanks to my sister Mary Harding, for introducing me to so many beautiful places Down East, and showing me the real Hope, Maine. And, most of all, thanks to my husband, Bob Davis, who is always willing to listen—the greatest editor of all.

"Hope" is the thing with feathers—
That perches in the soul—
And sings the tune without the words—
And never stops—at all—

—EMILY DICKINSON

I

Caroline Waverly wished that she hadn't accepted the invitation for dinner. She glanced again at the street, then pressed the doorbell and waited.

Pete opened the door. "How's my favorite redhead?" He smiled.

Caroline stepped into the air-conditioned house. Pete drew her into a hug, his fingers pressing into her back through the fabric of her raincoat and silk shirt. He kissed her lightly on the cheek, and as they drew apart the scent of his aftershave mixing with a whiff of bourbon reminded her of Harry's funeral. There had been a reception with cocktails after the service.

"It's nice of you to have me." She tucked a strand of hair behind one ear, feeling its weight more than usual in the humid evening. "I thought you might have given up after my saying no so many times."

"I'd never give up on you," he said. After twenty-five years in Washington he hadn't lost his South Carolina drawl.

"I'm not sure I'm up for this," she said.

"It's just us and the Cummingses." He slipped Caroline's raincoat from her shoulders and she shivered in the cool air. Her skin was clammy, her coat too warm for the humid evening. The hot weather in Washington—unusual for early May—had taken everyone by surprise.

Caroline's husband, Harry, had died at the beginning of November, exactly six months before. She still found it difficult to be with people—the mere exchange of pleasantries with her neighbors made her feel awkward, as if she didn't know who she was anymore. Forty-four years old and a widow, a fact that still filled her with disbelief. On this May evening, when the world around her was lush in the newness of spring, she felt ancient.

Pete Spencer, Harry's business partner and best friend, and his wife, Marjorie, had invited her to their home. She had been indoors all day, but despite the threat of rain she'd decided to walk to the Spencers' house, less than a mile from her own. The fresh air, she thought, might do her good. Mostly she just needed to get through this day, marking yet another month since her husband's death.

"Do you believe this heat?" Pete asked.

"I probably should have driven," Caroline said. "It looks like we might have a storm."

Pete nodded. The partially lowered lids of his dark eyes made her think of blinds tilted against the late-afternoon sun. "Red, you look great. You really do."

Caroline looked away. Pete had given her this nickname when they first met. During the winter, when he'd helped her go through Harry's papers at the office, he'd started calling her that again.

"Come on back and join the others," he said, and guided her to the sunroom. He was the sort of man who gave a firm handshake, patted the backs of his buddies, and kissed his women friends. After months alone, Caroline was alert to the sensation of his hand on her waist.

The familiarity of touch had vanished from her life. Even during the last months of Harry's life, when he had grown remote, when they had quietly retreated from each other, there had been moments of contact—a brief kiss, a light hand on her shoulder, the unconscious gravity that pulled two bodies together deep in slumber. Unbeknownst to her, these insignificant gestures had nourished her. Pete's touch now made her think about what she had been missing.

They passed through the living room, a room possessing all the expected details of a large colonial house in this Washington neighborhood: a gilt mirror above the fireplace, a set of four English prints matted in teal, a Chinese bowl of potpourri on the coffee table. Everything was in order, tasteful and elegant. Like Marjorie. Caroline's own living room was not much different, and the thought displeased her. She stepped into the sunroom, where family pictures of children at boarding school, trips to Vail, and days on sailboats filled spaces in the bookshelves.

"Well, well. Here she is at last," Arthur Cummings said with theatrical enthusiasm. Arthur, recently retired, had been chairman of Harry's investment firm. He gave Caroline a robust, fatherly hug. She sensed they'd been talking about her from the quick glances that passed between Arthur and his wife, Julia.

Julia Cummings stood and leaned forward to kiss Caroline on both cheeks, releasing wafts of Chanel No. 5. "You look wonderful, dear," Julia said. She was a woman in her sixties, with the perfectly highlighted hair, polished nails, and trim figure required of women in their circle. The sudden thought that she might one day be just like this woman, twenty years her senior, was unsettling to Caroline.

Julia reached for Caroline's hand. "Come sit with me on the sofa; I want to hear how you've been. I don't think I've laid eyes on you since Harry's funeral."

"Margarita?" Pete asked. "It's that kind of night."

"I think I'll stick to white wine. Thanks," Caroline said.

Arthur inspected his glass and joined Pete to freshen his own drink. No sign of Marjorie. She would be in the kitchen putting the final touches on a dinner that would be something from the latest *Gourmet* or *Bon Appétit*. Pete took Arthur's glass, and Arthur asked him what he thought of trends in the European bond markets.

Julia held the salt-rimmed glass of one of Pete's infamous margaritas. She gave a small shrug, seemingly accustomed to her husband's tendency to talk about business. "How are you coping?" She spoke softly, as if about to share womanly confidences. "Is it getting any easier?" Julia appeared sincere in her concern, though there was a weariness in the lines around her eyes, a woman tired from the weight of continual thoughtfulness and attention to propriety.

Caroline shifted on the soft cushions. She had feared that the conversation might go this way. "Nothing's the same since Harry died, but . . ." Julia always had a way of making her feel inept, an ingenue at the functions that they had attended over the years. And here she was now, an ingenue in the realm of grief. If only she had the energy to get up and leave, maybe make some excuse of a headache coming on.

"I can certainly imagine," Julia said. "We all think it's time you got out and started seeing people." Julia sipped her drink. "You're still young. It's not good to go through life alone."

"I have Rob," Caroline said. She thought of her son at college, his first year. Rob had become more withdrawn since his father's death. His silence worried her. Tonight, Sunday, was when she usually called him. He had not e-mailed at all this past week.

"Come on, dear. I'm not talking about children. You should go out. Meet someone."

"I don't want to meet anyone." This came out more sharply than Caroline intended.

Arthur laughed loudly at something Pete had said. Julia said, "Well, of course, I know it's too soon. Still . . ." She glanced up at Pete and Arthur, now coming to join them.

"I'm doing fine," Caroline said. "I'm keeping busy, and I'm editing another book for Vivien."

A look of annoyance crossed Julia's face. "But that's work." The wrinkles on her forehead deepened. "You shouldn't spend all your time working. Anyway, you can't need the money."

Caroline felt her face redden. Obviously Julia had no knowledge of her financial affairs. She wondered if Pete had told Marjorie about the mess she was in. Before she could reply, Pete handed her a glass of white wine. She took a long sip. It tasted woodsy, like spring. She leaned back into the soft sofa cushion. A dull exhaustion lingered in her bones.

Julia turned her attention to their host. "Pete, a girl could get in trouble drinking this concoction."

Pete grinned. "Not you, Julia." He pulled a chair closer to Caroline and sat down. "Here's to Caroline. She's been incredibly brave, a real trouper." He looked at his friends. "To Harry."

Pete, Julia, and Arthur raised their glasses. Pete clinked his glass against Caroline's. She sipped the wine, and, feeling the familiar tears threatening, she sipped again and swallowed.

"I still remember how beautifully you spoke at Harry's service, Pete," Julia said. "You captured all his remarkable traits."

Pete and Harry had been close friends in business school as well as partners at the firm for almost twenty years. Their friendship was somewhat unexpected; Harry, the proper Bostonian, quiet, diligent, was the opposite of Pete, a party boy with dark-haired good looks and an easy grin. Pete was known for being a tough, hard-driving businessman, not afraid of a fight to close a deal. Yet, when he had helped her this winter, Caroline had witnessed his kinder side, his patience with her endless questions, his willingness to give her his full attention not just as a business adviser, but also as a friend.

"I miss him," Pete said. "We all do." His gaze slid to Caroline. She sipped her wine and set the glass down.

Arthur cleared his throat. "Harry was remarkable," he said. "Never missed a day at the office. Stayed on top of everything, a perfectionist." Arthur's silver hair, silk tie, and blue blazer exuded authority.

Caroline tried to smile. Arthur was probably unaware of the full extent of Harry's business dealings, his disastrous encounter with Sunil Gava and Avistar, the biotech start-up. Maybe Pete hadn't told him everything. Caroline didn't want to disappoint Arthur, a man so comfortable in his predictable world. He had helped nurture Harry's career. What good would it do to tell him that even a hardworking perfectionist had made terrible mistakes?

Caroline eased forward on the sofa. She reached for her wineglass and stood, seeing the concern in Pete's eyes. "I'll go give Marjorie a hand in the kitchen."

In the dining room she paused, recalling one of the awful conversations she'd had with Pete in his office after Harry had died.

"You knew nothing about this?" Pete had stared at her across his desk, all glass and chrome. Harry's old office, just down the hall, had been traditional, with mahogany furniture, a leather chair, and photographs of Caroline and Rob on the desk.

"I knew he was excited about Avistar." She admitted her ignorance about Harry's work beyond that.

"He'd had several bad years and knew he had to turn it around. Most of his older clients were loyal, but I'm afraid his performance was all there in black and white."

"But he worked so hard," Caroline said.

"Some of it's luck." Pete turned away. He seemed embarrassed.

"I've been through everything at home. There's almost nothing. Just the shares in Avistar."

"They went belly-up in September."

"Just like that?" She was breathless. Harry had told her nothing.

"It was actually a slow downhill spiral. Harry insisted it would turn around." Pete looked so annoyingly vital.

"What about his shares in the firm?" Caroline's voice quavered. She swallowed. "He's been here for so long."

"He'd been cashing out. He took the last of it in September." Pete came around the desk. He put a hand on her shoulder. "He must have said something."

Caroline's mind raced. She recalled flashes of Harry's anger when she'd asked about his work. How long had it been like that? This entire situation was so trite. She felt like the idiot wife who'd lived her pretty life, being a good mother, working in her garden, cooking, writing about food.

She hunched forward. "There's still money in our checking account," she said.

"That's not going to last long. I can help you." Pete crouched beside her and placed his hand on her back. She lowered her head. "I've got a client who might be interested in buying your house," he said.

"You want me to sell my house?"

He withdrew his hand and stood. "You're going to need the money."

"It's Rob's house. It's where he grew up."

"We can invest the profits. You can get something smaller."

"I just don't think I can do that." She looked around for her handbag, wanting to get away from him, not wanting to hear any more.

"Let me help you, Red."

"I'm going to be fine." She found her handbag on the floor. "I'll work things out." At that moment she had been overcome with anger, though not at Pete. He had only been trying to help.

"There you are, Caroline, darling." Marjorie, a pretty, dark-haired woman wearing a crisp linen dress, came through the swinging door into the dining room bearing a white ironstone soup tureen. "You've been hiding away far too long," she said, a little too loudly. Marjorie placed the tureen at the head of the table, removed the lid, and smiled with satisfaction.

❦

During dinner, Pete kept Caroline's wineglass filled. The strains of a violin concerto trickled into the candlelit dining room above the hum of the air-conditioning. Caroline and Harry had dined at the Spencers' home many times, but tonight was the first time she had been there by herself. Everything felt strange to her, as if she had never been with these people before.

Caroline no longer fit into this world of couples. Her life was now made up of solitary rituals: breakfast in the kitchen, and after her second cup of coffee she would sort through Harry's papers and documents in hopes of salvaging something, a statement from a forgotten mutual fund, an overlooked insurance policy. The only new thing was the letter from Maine. Harry's great-aunt, who had died the previous summer, had left him her house. She hadn't shown the letter to Pete.

Most days, after lunch, sometimes with her best friend, Vivien, Caroline walked for hours on the canal towpath. More work, and then supper alone in front of the evening news. She never even went to the trouble of opening a bottle of wine. She went to bed early, still keeping to her side of the bed.

Working on the cookbooks was the only way she could escape the intolerable consequences of Harry's death. Vivien, the food editor at World Life Books, was producing a new series, Back to Basics, a kind of "clean cuisine," she called it, with the emphasis on simple recipes using fresh organic products. They were pitching it to an older, well-heeled set.

Caroline had spent the winter working on the soup book, writing an introduction to each recipe, and clarifying the accompanying directions. After Harry died, soup was the only thing she liked to eat; everything else seemed to get caught in her throat. She wrote about a velvety cream of broccoli, the virtues of a hearty pasta fagioli, and a smoky lentil soup with an underbite of curry that tasted like no other version she'd ever prepared. If it weren't for the task of cooking, tasting, and trying to make the recipes appealing and workable, she might have cooked nothing at all that winter.

Marjorie, like many who knew that Caroline was a food writer, went overboard in an effort to impress her. Tonight Marjorie was serving carrot-and-ginger soup, a roast pork tenderloin in a teriyaki sauce with new potatoes in a cheese sauce, along with asparagus in a piquant lemon vinaigrette, a menu that didn't make much sense. In truth, Caroline never minded what people cooked when she went to parties. She was happy for a night away from her own kitchen. In the last few years she liked thinking and writing about food more than cooking it. She complimented Marjorie on the soup.

Marjorie thanked her, reached for the bottle of wine at her end of the table, and began talking about the garden club's daffodil show. "Melissa didn't set up enough tables for horticulture." She glanced at her own centerpiece, a bouquet of lush peonies, their heavy blooms bowing toward the mahogany table. "Did you see Barbara's arrangement?" Marjorie asked Julia, pouring them both more wine. "The worst container you ever saw." Caroline was supposed to have chaired the daffodil show, but was excused after Harry's death.

"How's Rob doing?" Arthur asked Caroline.

"Better, thanks." She made an effort to focus. The wine was going to her head. "It's hard having him away this year, even though he doesn't say much when he's at home."

"You don't look old enough to have a boy in college," Arthur said.

The skin of Arthur's neck was slack and overflowed onto his starched collar. Harry had not lived long enough for his facial muscles to soften. His death at fifty-three had shocked everyone. He had been a lifelong runner, a fit man, not a candidate for a heart attack.

"Boys never talk about their feelings," Marjorie said.

"With girls," Julia said, "you hear more than you ever want to know." She had three grown daughters.

Caroline looked at her watch under the table. She didn't want to share her concerns about Rob with either of these women.

Julia turned to Marjorie. "Are you and Pete taking the same house in Nantucket this summer?"

Marjorie dabbed her lips with a napkin. "Just the last two weeks in August. It's appalling how the rents have gone up." Her voice sounded thick. She seemed to be drinking more than usual. Caroline took a sip of water.

Julia nodded consolingly. "We've taken the same house as last year. Lucy and her boys will join us for one week."

Caroline pushed the potatoes around her plate. It seemed too great an effort to join in the conversation. Eventually Marjorie brought in dessert, a strawberry tart glistening with a currant jelly glaze. Pete put his hand on Caroline's shoulder. "Are you okay?" he asked.

"Sorry," she said. "I'm fine." The dining room had grown warmer. Wind rattled the windows, but the air inside was still.

"Bet we're going to have a huge thunderstorm," Arthur said.

"Did you hear what the Petersons paid for that house out in Potomac?" Julia said.

"Just where does he get his money, anyway?" Marjorie asked. She filled her wineglass once again. "People are saying his company has hit hard times."

The evening continued to play out like a drawing room drama in which Caroline had a small role. She was the odd guest, the one who didn't fit in. Arthur and Julia balanced each other, their repartee easy and expected, finishing each other's sentences and offering affectionate smiles at appropriate moments. They were the couple dancing cheek-to-cheek, a two-step. Pete and Marjorie artfully avoided each other, performing a formal minuet. Caroline thought back to earlier exchanges that evening, trying to remember any shared glances between them, even a brief touch. She could recall none. Had she and Harry become like that? Her memories of Harry had clouded.

After dinner they moved to the living room for coffee. The storm finally broke. Quick flashes of lightning yielded to deep, rolling booms of thunder. Beyond the heavy folds of the curtains rain beat against the windows.

"Pete, go check the thermostat," Marjorie said. "The air-conditioning hasn't clicked on in a while." Her face was flushed. The beautifully orchestrated dinner was taking its toll. Pete looked annoyed and disappeared into the hallway.

Arthur shook his head. "I can't believe it got hot this early in the season."

"It won't last," Julia said. She turned to Marjorie. "This is decaf, isn't it?"

"Of course, Julia." The central air-conditioning clicked on with a hum, and Marjorie looked relieved. She continued to drink her wine, which she'd brought in from the dining room. Her job as hostess was almost over.

Pete came back into the room. "I reset the circuit breaker," he said. "Should be okay now." He carried a tray from the bar with a bottle of brandy and some balloon glasses that clinked together as he set it down next to the coffee service.

"Anyone care for a nightcap?" Pete lifted the bottle. "I know Arthur will join me. How about you, Julia?" He didn't offer a glass to his wife.

"It's Sunday night," Julia said, "and we need to think about heading home. Okay with you, Arthur?" It was a statement, not a question, and Arthur was adept at reading his wife's signals.

"Thanks, buddy. Julia's right. It's late." Arthur stood, and he and Julia said their good-byes along with giving the kisses and idle promises of familiar friends to get together soon. Marjorie walked into the hall with them.

Pete poured the amber-colored drink into a glass. "What about you, Red?"

"My hair is more silver than red these days."

"Hardly," Pete said. He held the glass toward her. She remembered the warmth of his hand on her back.

"No, thanks. I'll just finish my coffee." She was tired. The evening had grown late.

"I wish you'd let me help you." He spoke softly. "You're going to need money to live on."

Caroline shook her head. Marjorie returned. Her lipstick had worn off and her linen dress held deep creases across the middle. She began gathering the empty coffee cups. "Tell us about this health cookbook you're doing," she said.

Caroline put her cup down. "Thanks for asking, but it's time for me to go, too." She spoke carefully, feeling the effects of the wine. "Marjorie, it was a wonderful dinner."

"I'll drive you home," Pete said.

"Thanks, but I'm happy to walk."

Marjorie offered a tired smile. "Promise you'll come back again soon." She gave Caroline a quick hug.

"I hate leaving you with all the dishes," Caroline said.

"Francine is coming in the morning. She'll take care of everything."

Caroline had forgotten about the housekeeper.

"Come on, Red," Pete said. "I insist on giving you a ride home."

"Really, I love to walk, and the rain's let up."

"Nonsense. It may pour again any minute."

"Pete doesn't mind," Marjorie added, swaying slightly with the tray in her hands. She turned and went to the kitchen.

❦

The air had cooled after the rain. Caroline breathed in deeply, hoping to clear her head. She got into the car. The door on her side of the BMW sat heavily on its hinges. At first it didn't shut, so she opened it again and gave it another slam while Pete started the engine. The red leather seats were cracked with age. The car had an old-car smell, a mixture of oil, mold, and wax. He backed out of the narrow drive and started slowly up the wet street. The neighborhood was quiet. SUVs were parked in driveways of the well-kept homes. The doors and windows opened to the warm air earlier in the evening had been closed. The families were settled inside for the night.

Within minutes the rain began again. The windows fogged. Pete reached for the defrost switch. His hand brushed Caroline's knee. She leaned against the door. He stopped at a light. "You okay?" His hair looked damp.

Caroline nodded. "I'm sorry you have to go out in this."

"I'm not," he said. The light at Wisconsin Avenue changed to green and he drove the final blocks. The rain was coming down harder when he pulled into her driveway. The house was dark.

"Wait, I'll get the umbrella and come around," he said. His steps crunched on the gravel. Seconds later he opened her door holding a large black umbrella. Caroline reached for his arm and they walked to the front door. The rain blew sideways, making the umbrella practically useless. Pete held it over her as she put the key in the lock and pushed the door open. He followed her inside.

"I thought I'd left some lights on," she said, reaching for the switch. "Damn," she whispered, "the power's out." She peeled off her raincoat, and water pooled onto the flagstone floor.

"I think I'll wait a few minutes for it to let up," Pete said. "Do you mind?"

"Of course not." He'd been kind enough to bring her home. He was her husband's best friend.

He draped his coat over the bench in the hall. She could barely see his face in the darkness. "I can't believe I've brought you out in this awful weather," she said.

"Don't keep saying that."

She stepped into the living room. "You and Marjorie were great to have me. I know I'm not much fun these days." She knew she should go and look for candles, do something practical, but his presence alone with her in the dark was making it impossible for her to think. The effects of all the wine made her feel dreamy and loose, not at all herself.

"Come on," he said, following her into the room. "You were charming. I hate to think of you home by yourself."

"I don't mind it. It was really Harry who liked going out." A part of her wished Pete would go. She didn't want to talk about Harry, and she didn't want Pete to start discussing her financial problems again.

"You haven't called me," he said.

"I'm okay now. Really, I can manage."

"I'm not talking about that."

Caroline was aware of the bond that had grown between them. Pete knew everything about her financial worries. He had seen her vulnerable side. Now, far from the formal setting of his office, away from the presence of their friends, his wife, that connection seemed electric, different altogether. "I think I've got a flashlight in the kitchen," she said. "There's no need for you to stay. Marjorie will worry."

"She'll have taken a pill by now. Out cold. The usual routine." He lowered his voice. "She never knows when or if I ever come to bed."

Caroline folded her arms across her chest and walked to the front window. The rain pelted against the panes. Pete followed and stood behind her, so close that she could feel the heat of his body and smell his wet clothes.

"Come on, Red." His breath hit her neck. "I'm glad you asked me for help."

"Pete, no." It had been a long evening after a long winter, an unsettling spring. Maybe she shouldn't have gone to see him so often. She stepped away from him.

"Do you mean that?"

"You've been wonderful to me. Truly, I couldn't have managed without you. But—"

"Shhh." He put his hands around her waist. "I know you miss him." Pete was taller than Caroline, taller than Harry had been. For a moment she relaxed and felt the loveliness of just being held, the warmth of arms encircling her. If only she could forget about Harry for just a while, forget her worries and the struggle of getting through an evening. Why not allow herself to be comforted?

Pete bent down and kissed her neck. His hands tightened around her.

"No. We mustn't."

He didn't release his arms.

She turned to him and looked into his eyes. What was she doing? Was she going to let this happen? Harry's friend, their friend? He eased his hands under her shirt onto her bare skin. Her breath stalled, and Pete kissed her hard on the mouth. Caroline closed her eyes.

Later, the house buzzed and the lights came back on, though the bedroom remained dark. After making love, Caroline had fallen asleep in Pete's arms. The bedside clock blinked the relentless digits of twelve o'clock; it needed to be reset. She shifted slightly, still savoring the warmth of his skin against hers. The bedroom windows were open and the curtains swayed gently.

Caroline felt clearheaded in a way that she hadn't in a long time. With Pete, she had experienced the free fall of pleasure. He had given her a gift she hadn't even known she'd wanted. Pete had helped her to escape her troubles for a while, but at the same time, their lovemaking brought back her memories of Harry, and the passion they had once shared. She longed for the past, and yet, she was overcome with a distinct yearning to be once again desired, cared for, loved. In the darkness of this spring night she was all the more aware of what she had lost.

She fumbled for her watch on the bedside table. Turning on the lamp, she nearly knocked over the photograph of Rob that Harry had taken on their last fishing trip in Wyoming. It was after two. Pete stirred in the pool of light.

"It's late," she said, moving away from him and leaning back into the pillows.

Pete reached for her. "You're so lovely, Red." His arm remained draped across her. "Are you all right? I mean . . ." He stroked her face.

"I'm fine." Caroline held his hand. She looked around the bedroom. The letter from Maine was still propped on the maple dresser that was her grandmother's, the chair and ottoman still next to the window, the blanket chest still at the foot of the bed. All was the same. She stroked his arm and kissed the back of his hand lightly. His skin was surprisingly soft. Yet Pete wasn't hers. He had his own world, his own life. "You should go."

"I wish I could spend more time with you," he said. But he

pulled on his rumpled clothes and combed his hair back with his fingers. He cupped her chin.

She gently pushed away his hand. She wasn't sure what she wanted. He searched her face as if hesitant to leave, his gaze tinged with longing, the kind of look that he might have given Marjorie years ago, or perhaps the look he might give any woman now. When he turned and left the bedroom, and then the front door closed behind him and his car started and pulled away, she felt a terrible emptiness.

Gradually, cooler air filled the bedroom. In the silent moments just before dawn the vague recollection that Rob would be home soon eased the loneliness in her heart.

2

Will Harmon crossed the quad of Habliston, the small women's college where he worked as an English professor, knowing that this blue late-afternoon Pennsylvania sky was weak in comparison to the vibrant blue over an ocean. At least the sun was out. It had been a dreary, wet spring.

He was headed to a meeting with Jack Mathews, dean of the college. They were old friends. Adele, Jack's secretary, had called yesterday to set up this appointment. It was early May, and Will had just taught his final class of the semester, a survey of nineteenth-century American literature. Exams were next week. The article on Henry James that Will had submitted to the *Fairfax Review,* a prestigious academic publication, had been accepted. Jack would be pleased. Now Will would have time to work on his novel about a boy growing up on the coast. Mary Beth, his wife, was proud of his academic work, and she had been encouraging him to start a novel.

Two students had kept him after class to question him about what would be on the exam. It had been a week of interruptions. He had made a quick stop in his office to pick up a set of essays that needed grading and added them to his briefcase. The unpleasant matter of Jennifer Whitely crossed his mind again. He couldn't stop thinking about her. He wondered if this appointment had something to do with her behavior last week. There had been no opportunity to discuss the incident with Mary Beth.

Will missed his wife. She had not come home for several weeks—one of the trials of a commuter marriage. He wanted this summer to be a good one. She would be glad to escape the stifling heat of the city; New York was no place to be on summer weekends. He pictured Mary Beth sitting on the terrace behind their house, a charming fieldstone cottage a few miles from campus. He had built the patio himself the summer after they moved in. He imagined her sipping a glass of wine, her hair dark and sleek, her skin pale, her lips red on the rim of the glass. She preferred red wine, even in summer.

Mary Beth had a small, shapely body. Will loved tracing the curve of her hip with his fingers and circling her waist with his hands. In ten years of marriage her curves had not changed. She had been a senior at the university and he had been a teaching assistant when they'd met. He had called her his Snow White. She had laughed and accused him of being a hopeless romantic. Their lives had not been romantic lately, but he was determined that this summer would be different.

Will picked up his pace toward Worthington Hall, the administration building that dominated the green. The fieldstone walls reflected the sound Quaker values once so prevalent in the region. But even at this distance one could see that the painted trim was peeling and the windows carried the lingering grime of winter.

Women's colleges like this one had been struggling for years or remaking themselves into testosterone-flooded institutions by building large gymnasiums and state-of-the-art science centers, and upgrading technology in the dorm rooms and formerly musty libraries in order to attract male students. Now, in the first decade of the twenty-first century, with careful cutbacks and by lowering its once rigorous academic standards, Habliston struggled on. Two smaller dormitories had been purchased by a hotel chain to use for adjunct housing for their conference center. The portraits in Kirk Library had been sold, and the collection of Audubon prints that had graced the walls of the president's mansion had gone on the auction block last year.

Will passed a large circular bed of azaleas. The fading blooms clung to the plants, and the new growth looked anemic with pale, leathery leaves. A stand of daffodils looked similarly lackluster. He remembered his mother deadheading the daffodils around their house in Rhode Island, where they had lived a short walk from the ocean.

Lately he found himself longing to see the water. Brown, silt-filled streams wound through this Pennsylvania landscape, and Travers Lake was a thirty-minute drive from town. Will kept thinking about the ocean. He missed the tangy salt air, the ever-present sound of moving water, the vastness of sky meeting the horizon. As a boy in Rhode Island, he had loved knowing that he lived on the edge of the country, the rim, a straight shot to Portugal.

Will pushed open the door of Worthington Hall. It yielded grudgingly, swollen from the endless spring rains that had finally subsided. The building smelled of stone, polished oak floors, and institutional dust long embedded in the plaster walls and old wood. He turned left, passing the admissions office, then a warren of small rooms lorded over by Miss Amesbury, the registrar, and her two assistants, and at the end of the hall was the glass doorway to Jack's outer office. Will drew himself up straighter and stepped inside.

Adele looked up over her reading glasses. She was a round little woman with intense dark eyes. Today she wore a flowered dress with a pin at her neck. Under her outdated exterior, Will knew, lay one of the masterminds that kept Habliston afloat.

"Will. Good. You're here."

He stood close to the desk and smiled down at her. The roots of her hair were white. Maybe she was too busy to keep her hair colored these days, or maybe she had allowed herself to grow tattered like the college. "Hi, Adele." She did not offer her longtime greeting, "How's the handsome Professor Harmon, heartthrob of the English department?"

"Jack's on the phone. Go on in. He's expecting you." She reached for another folder and furrowed her brow. Apparently she wasn't in the mood to chat.

❦

"My hands are tied, Will," Jack said.

"It's a total lie," Will countered. He should have known that the matter with Jennifer Whitely was not over.

"She insists that you're flunking her because she refused your invitation to come back to your house."

"I didn't ask her to my house. My God. This is insane." Will felt as if he couldn't breathe.

"We've got a real problem here." Jack sat forward and put his elbows on the desk. His burly exterior belied his reputation as a Thoreau scholar. "The worst goddamned kind of problem we can have."

Will thought for a moment that Jack was about to lower his head onto the desk in defeat. He tried to think. "And it's her word against mine?" He got up and walked to the window. The Oriental rug that had impressed him years ago when he had accepted the job as an instructor in the English department looked faded and worn. "You know what this is about, don't you?" He looked back at Jack, whose insightful gray eyes were studying him now, as if trying to understand what could have gone wrong. "This girl hasn't done a lick of work. She's barely come to class. She flunked the midterm and hasn't handed in a term paper."

"Did you send her a warning after the first quarter?"

"Of course. I even offered to let her retake the test. She couldn't be bothered."

"She's a senior. You know she can't graduate with a failing grade."

Will tried to swallow. His mouth was dry. In his wildest dreams he could never have imagined this conversation taking place. "That's why I offered her the chance to do it over. You think I don't know who her father is?"

He had met John Whitely once at a faculty reception given by the trustees. A lawyer from New York specializing in class-action lawsuits, he made more money on one case than Will would make in a year. John Whitely, hawklike and tan, with slicked-back hair, Italian loafers, and a second wife, younger and equally sleek, looked like he was used to getting what he wanted.

"So what the hell were you doing meeting her at a bar?"

"I didn't meet her. I stopped at O'Grady's for a burger. All of a sudden there she was on the stool next to me."

"What day was that?"

"Wednesday. I stay late for office hours that day. Mary Beth was away, so I wanted a quick dinner."

Will remembered being in a hurry that night. He'd had an idea from an earlier discussion during class about *Ethan Frome* and Wharton's use of the landscape. It related to another essay he wanted to write on James. He knew that there was no food in his refrigerator at home, so he stopped at O'Grady's. That in itself was unusual. It was more of a bar than a restaurant, and the place was loud and popular with the seniors, but it had been a long day and O'Grady's was on his way home.

Will was halfway through his dinner and drinking a beer when Jennifer slid onto the empty stool next to him.

"Professor Harmon, hi." She wore a tight scoop-necked T-shirt. "Can I call you Will?" She spoke loudly. The television above the bar roared on a sports channel, and most of the tables were filled with noisy students.

"Jennifer." He swallowed. She had caught him with his mouth full.

"I know, I know. I still owe you that paper."

"You also need to set up a time for the midterm." Her plump lips had an unnatural purplish sheen.

"Come on," she said softly. "Please give me a break." She tossed her hair back over her shoulder.

"I'm sorry," Will said. This wasn't the place to talk about an academic matter.

She smiled again, cocking her head to the side. He sensed that she'd had a lot to drink.

"I just need a C."

There was a burst of laughter behind them. He turned and saw two girls who had been in his lit class that afternoon. "Jennifer," he said, wondering if they were putting her up to this, "you've got to do the work for this class." The words tumbled from his mouth.

"Come on, Professor." She licked her lips. "I heard your wife's not around much."

Will felt the pressure of her thigh against his. "Wait a minute. What's going on here?" He could hardly get the words out. "If you want to talk about your grade, come see me in my office." And he had pushed back his stool, handed a twenty to the bartender to cover his dinner, and fled to his car.

Now, looking across at Jack, he realized that he should have reported the encounter right away. Had she flirted with him earlier? Should he have seen this coming? At the very least he should have stayed on her case—insisting that she get her work done. He had been remiss in not alerting Jack.

"Listen, Jack. She solicited me."

"Nobody's going to believe you."

"Why the hell not?" Will felt anger pulsing at his temples.

"She's young. She's the student."

"Don't I have any credibility? I've been here ten years. There's never been a problem."

Jack leaned forward, elbows on his desk, and rubbed his eyes as if trying to erase this entire conversation. "Don't you get it? You're in a bar with your student. Her friends saw you."

Will stood and gripped the back of his chair. "You've seen that girl. She's spoiled, lazy. She doesn't give a damn about anything but herself."

"Like a lot of these students," Jack said.

"For God's sake, I've never gone after a student."

"Mary Beth?"

"Give me a break, Jack. I'm married to her. She's my wife."

"That's exactly the kind of thing they'd bring up."

"First of all"—Will swallowed and tried to calm down—"we may have met when she was an undergraduate, but we didn't date until after graduation. Please. You've got to back me up."

"With what? Do you think this place has money to put into lawsuits?"

"You mean you're not going to do anything?" A knot was forming in the small of his back.

Jack looked away, and Will could see he hated every moment of this discussion. He and Jack had become close friends over the years, going out for a beer after faculty meetings, commiserating about the declining abilities of the students, the lack of funds for symposia, the decreased enrollment. But they had also shared success stories: students accepted for graduate work, the pleasures of bringing literature into young women's lives, getting articles published in academic reviews.

Will took a deep breath. "What happens next?"

"Give her the C. Submit your resignation. They won't proceed further."

"My job?" He leaned on Jack's desk. "Jesus. You can't let them do that."

Will collapsed back into the chair. In a matter of minutes his academic career was over, turning him into what? A man without a job, without a profession, a failure at the age of forty-one. Facing Jack across the desk, Will felt as if the air had been sucked out of the room.

"So that's it?" Will clenched his fists.

"You know what I'm up against."

"Well, I'm up against a whole lot more. I'm not going to stand for this." Will forced his shoulders back. "I'll get my own lawyer. I'm going to fight this, Jack." No sooner had he said those words than he thought of Mary Beth. She would know whom to call. Some New York guy. Someone who was used to these kinds of fights.

Jack remained slumped in his chair, his face gray against the golden light pouring in over his shoulder. Will grabbed his briefcase and slammed the door behind him.

❦

That night Will sat alone in his study. He barely remembered stalking out of Jack's office, past Adele, down the hall, and to his car. Somehow he had driven home. First he had tried to call Mary Beth. His anger reignited when her secretary told him that Mary Beth was on a plane for the West Coast. She wouldn't arrive in LA until midnight eastern time.

Now, as Will sipped his second Scotch, the room grew dark. He wasn't much of a drinker, a beer or two if he was on his own at the end of the day, or a glass of wine with Mary Beth at dinner. He didn't have the energy to fix something to eat, and he wanted the alcohol to calm him down, to help him think. Had she told him about this trip? His mind was growing fuzzy. It was Thursday. She was supposed to be coming home to Pennsylvania tomorrow. At this very moment a plane was taking her in the wrong direction, away from him.

Will grew more anxious as he waited. Recently Mary Beth had been putting more pressure on him to give up his teaching job at Habliston and move to New York City. She had taken a job in pharmaceutical sales right after business school. This part of Pennsylvania was in her territory, and she was able to travel for her work from here. She was successful from the start, and after the first few years she became head of the regional division and, soon after, one of the top producers on the East Coast.

By the third year Mary Beth's salary was twice Will's, and they bought their house. It had been her idea to live in the college town. Neither of her parents had gone to college, and she had grown up in a New Jersey suburb. The conflict came two years ago when her company wanted her to take a job in management and move to New York.

Will loved his work at Habliston. His schedule at the college allowed him time to write. He was slowly making a name for himself among Henry James scholars. Mary Beth had been thrilled when he'd been offered department chair. The academic market was flooded with PhDs, and the chance of his finding a comparable job in New York was extremely slim. When Mary Beth had taken the job in New York, she said she wouldn't mind commuting back home on the weekends. She told Will that he could use the time alone to work on his novel. She had the unrealistic notion that every English professor had a novel in him, and that once Will sold it he could give up his job and join her in the city.

Will picked up the framed photo of Mary Beth that he kept on his desk. He squinted at it in the darkness and tried to make out her face, that sweet, perfectly oval face that could also become so hard and determined. They had had a terrible argument at the first of the year. There had been a faculty party on New Year's Eve, and the next morning they both awoke to aching heads, hungover, out of sorts. While sipping coffee in the kitchen Mary Beth had announced that she was buying an apartment in New York, where her future was.

"It's your turn to commute," she had said.

"You know I hate the city." As he said this he could hear the rush and clamor of traffic pounding into his head.

"Do you think I like hauling myself out here every weekend?" She glared at him. Her fleece robe, some shade of dark purple, made her look pale.

"What about our house?"

"We can sell the house. If you insist on keeping this job, you can rent a small place near the college."

Will put down his coffee. "This is so sudden."

"Sudden? Will, you are so lost in your clouded academic world. Do you know how many times I've driven out here? You think it's easy to fight through the traffic?"

He stared at her, baffled at first, and then fearful of what she was saying.

"Well, I've lost count. That's how many, and I'm just sick of it."

"I know it's been hard."

"Hard." She began to shout. "We rarely talk these days. That's hard, Will." She went to the sink and banged down her coffee mug. "I make enough money for both of us now. New York is exciting. There are hundreds of colleges there. I love you. I want you with me."

When she turned around he saw that her face was streaming with tears. What was happening? What had brought them to this point? He remembered taking her in his arms, trying to console her. It was only fair that he commute for a while. He said he'd look for an apartment, sell the house. Only he didn't want to give up his job.

Will turned on the light and looked at the clock. He must have dozed off. It was still too soon to call Mary Beth. Her plane would not have landed yet. He poured himself another drink and reached for the copy of *Down East* magazine on the shelf near his desk. One birthday Mary Beth had given him the subscription to the magazine about Maine.

The painting on the cover depicted a yellow canoe on still water with dark fir trees silhouetted against the sky. He and Mary Beth had gone to Maine on their honeymoon, and they had talked about buying a vacation home there someday. He flipped through the pages, thinking again of that landscape so different from this one. After his third glass of Scotch, Will stretched out on the sofa. Within minutes the magazine slipped to the floor as he fell asleep.

❦

The next morning he awoke feeling rotten from the night on the couch. It was five a.m. in LA. Mary Beth would be awake, her body clock still on East Coast time. His clothes were rumpled and his mouth was dry, but he went immediately to his desk to find the information on her hotel. First he tried her cell. Her voice mail came on, requesting that he leave a message. He studied the paper where he had written the number and dialed the hotel. An efficient clerk with a flat California accent said that Mrs. Harmon had checked in and connected the call to her room.

The sun poured into Will's study. There were dust motes in the air. Three rings. Will pictured the vast country that lay between them: the broad plains of the Midwest, the Mississippi, the jagged peaks of the Rocky Mountains, the desert, and finally the sprawl of LA. A fourth ring. Will rolled a pencil back and forth across the surface of the desk. *Come on, Mary Beth, pick up.* He waited three more rings and redialed.

The same neutral voice answered. "Sir, I connected you to Mrs. Harmon's room. I'll do so again. An automated voice mail will activate after ten rings." Will carefully counted out the ten rings. He left no message. Where the hell could she be? Even Mary Beth didn't have business meetings at five in the morning. Had something happened to her? He ran his tongue over his dry lips. Slowly the worry turned to anger. Why hadn't she told him about this trip? He shouldn't have to call her secretary to track her down. Will put down the receiver and snapped the pencil in half.

After a few minutes he got slowly to his feet and went to the kitchen for a glass of water, realizing that for the last few minutes he had completely forgotten about his problem at Habliston, the problem that caused him to call her in the first place.

❦

Will was in his study sorting books on Saturday morning when Mary Beth arrived home. He was calmer now. They had not spoken, but Mary Beth had sent an e-mail telling him when to expect her. She had often complained that he kept too many books, that she was always tripping over them, and that the piles on the floor made it impossible to clean. Why did that matter when she had hired a cleaning service anyway? He had telephoned a real estate agent that morning to arrange to sell the house, something he was supposed to have done in January.

"Will?" she called from the hall.

He heard her approach and kept his back to the door. He reached for a handful of paperback novels and lowered them into the box.

"I flew all night to get here." She sounded raspy, as if she were losing her voice. She came over to him and started to put her arms around him. He pulled away. "What's the matter?"

He picked up another book. "You never told me you were going to LA."

"It was a last-minute trip. I was in a terrible rush." She stepped away and studied him, as if assessing his mood. "This isn't a very nice greeting. I took the red-eye to get home for the weekend."

"I called your hotel. You didn't answer." He met her gaze.

For a moment she looked puzzled. "When was that?" She looked as if she were trying to remember something.

"Five in the morning. So where were you?" Will was aware of his tone, like the jealous husband's in a melodrama.

She hesitated, then came to his side. "I was probably on the way to the office." She looked into his eyes, her lips pressed together as if defying him to argue.

"At that hour? Shit, Mary Beth. I was frantic with worry. I started to wonder."

"Well, you can quit wondering." She lifted her chin. "I've been asked to work on an acquisition in Japan. This is a huge deal. Drew wants me to lead a team."

"Christ. Now you'll be traveling more than ever. Who's Drew?"

"You don't have to be so angry. Come on, Will." She reached up and put a hand on his cheek. He didn't react to her touch, and she lowered her arm and turned away. "Drew Kramer is the head of the LA office. Aren't you going to congratulate me? It means another promotion. That's what I wanted to talk to you about this weekend." She sat in the armchair by the window and pulled a tissue from her pocket. "I've got this awful cold. What were you calling about, anyway?"

Will studied his wife. Pale, with smudges of fatigue beneath her eyes, she could still look so soft and vulnerable. He sank into his desk chair and tried to summon the courage to tell the entire sickening story. He kept his voice level. Having Mary Beth home and listening to him as he explained made him feel stronger, more capable of moving forward.

"I'm going to fight this thing."

"What did Jack say?"

"That the college can't afford a legal battle. Especially since it involves a trustee."

She sighed. "Will, how could you have let this happen?"

"Let it happen? The point is, I'm not going to let her get away with it."

"Jack's right. It's her word against yours. You'd never win." She leaned into the cushions, looking more disappointed than sympathetic.

"I shouldn't be kicked off a faculty because of some student's lie. I want to hire a lawyer. Maybe someone in your company would know someone."

"Darling, just do what Jack told you. Give that girl the C. Take some time off. People will forget about it. You can just slip away and it will all die down."

He stared at his wife, hoping to hear a little more sympathy. "But I won't forget. I don't want to give up my job."

She leaned forward. "Wait. Don't you see? You can come to New York. Start over."

"We're talking about my career. You expect me to walk away?"

"You're resigning. You're not being fired. Jack will give you a good recommendation."

"You have no idea what the job market is like. I'll never have a job like this one."

"You might eventually. And we'd be together again. If that matters to you." Mary Beth stood and turned to the window.

Will came behind her and put his arms around her; he bent down, resting his chin on her shoulder. Her hair was soft on his face. Her clothes smelled faintly smoky. "Of course it matters," he said, "but giving up here is wrong. It's my integrity that's on the line."

"Will, please accept it. Think of the time, the expense. I know it's hard. You can do other things—write, maybe find an editing job. You don't need to teach."

"What?"

Mary Beth turned to face him. "Think about us. Do you really want to take on the financial toll of a lawsuit? The emotional toll, too?" Her lower lip trembled and she started to cry.

He stared down at her.

"Sorry," she said. "I'm tired." She wiped her face with the backs of her hands. "I've got a lot going on. I promised Drew I'd be back in LA on Monday."

"You're going to the West Coast again?"

"Come on. We can make this work. It's not the end of the world. Please. I've missed you." This time she put her arms around him and pressed her face into his shirt.

"I don't know," he whispered. Will stepped free of her arms, thinking that at the very least she might have been more understanding. She seemed oblivious to all he was giving up. "I need some air," he said.

He left the study and went out to the back porch and sat on the top step. The warm spring sun on his back offered no relief. His entire body ached as if bruised. The exquisite morning seemed an affront. He shielded his eyes from the sun.

He remembered sitting on the back steps of his childhood home, breathing in the salt air, anticipating the long, light-filled days of summer. Life had been so much simpler then. He thought again of Maine. He had wanted to take Mary Beth there as a surprise to celebrate their tenth anniversary. Now she would be making even more trips to the West Coast. Nothing was going the way he had hoped.

Why had their lives become so complicated? Will stared out at the yard. He stretched out his legs and kicked away a pebble on the bottom step, trying to think what to do.

3

The day after the dinner party Caroline escaped into her garden. Pete's presence seemed to linger in the house. Outside, lifting her face toward the sun, she breathed in the sweet, cooler air. Fortunately May had returned to normal, with a gentle breeze and scattered clouds. She rolled up her sleeves and savored the softness of the air on her bare arms. Only hours ago she had slept in Pete's embrace, his breath warm against the back of her head. He had made her feel alive again. What would it be like the next time she saw him? Now that they had had sex, everything would be different.

This morning the real world loomed. There was lots to do in the garden. The wind started to pick up and the sun went behind a large cloud. Caroline had clipped her hair back to keep it from blowing in her face. She pulled on her gardening gloves, wet from last night's rain. They felt dank and cumbersome. Harry used to chide her for leaving her tools out. She yanked the gloves off and stared at her hands.

Beautiful hands, Harry had said once. It had been at her sister Darcy's wedding reception, and Harry had been an usher. Caroline had been amazed that Harry Waverly, older and working at his first job in New York, had seemed to take an interest in her when she was only a senior in college. At the time his compliment had struck her as odd, perhaps something that an older person might say. She drew the back of one hand to her mouth. It was cool against her lips. Since Harry had died her body had felt like a husk, dry and hollow, like the dead stalks of the plants.

This spring she'd worked in her garden only sporadically. Early morning was her favorite part of the day. She had missed spending more time out-of-doors. Today she began by raking the winter debris from the perennial border along the fence. The top layer of leaves came easily, but she had to kneel and use a small hand rake to gently lift the wet leaves that clung to the base of the plants. Using her favorite pair of red pruning shears, she clipped back the dead stalks and took them periodically to the compost heap behind the garage. The pruning shears had belonged to her father, and she could maneuver them easily through the stems of the Rudbeckia that she'd left intact for the birds to enjoy during the winter. Pale shoots peeked through the crown of the plant.

Later, after bagging the rest of the debris, she started working in the shade garden on the other side of the yard. The French lilac bush, now fifteen years old, anchored the far corner. Beneath it she had planted a sweep of hostas, hellebores, ferns, and white astilbes. She loved their frothy blooms that came in June, pristine and virginal against the rich green leaves and dark soil.

Gradually, feeling warmer, she sat for a few moments on the back steps. The phone rang. Caroline didn't go inside to answer it. It might be Pete. She leaned forward, resting her elbows on her knees. As the sun seeped into her back, she pictured what the future might hold with Pete. Hushed phone calls, plans for a weekend away, perhaps at an inn on the eastern shore, or in another city where they knew no one, where they could be alone together. Did she want that? Could she ever love Pete?

And later, months from now, perhaps an entire year, how would they feel? Would it be the end of the affair, remnants of shame, pathetic apologies, or the start of something more? She imagined talk of divorce, whispered glances at the garden club, Marjorie, hurt, indignant, inconsolable that her husband of so many years was throwing her over for someone else, for Caroline Waverly. Whoever would have thought?

And, of course, Rob. Silent, brooding, the loss of his father freshly etched across his face, he would never forget, nor would he understand his mother turning to someone else. Rob would never accept that. Caroline groaned audibly and got up. Sleeping with Pete had been a mistake. Being with him made her think more of Harry; it was as if their lives were inextricably woven together. Pete would keep her caught in the past. She needed to find a way to move forward.

She returned to the shade garden and worked carefully, not wanting to injure the new growth. The previous strangely hot days had lured some of the plants prematurely out of hiding. Spring was a tricky time of year. While it was a season of promise, there was still the likelihood of more cool nights, sudden storms, the unexpected weather that could wreak havoc on the young plants.

Caroline reached the end of the bed and stepped closer to the lilac, the heady scent still filling the air. The flowers were beginning to fade after the recent warm spell. The edges of the purple blossoms were tinged with brown. She fingered the rough bark. The shrub was large now, a mature bush. It seemed impossible. Fifteen springs ago her father had planted it when her baby, Grace, had died. Grace, who had lived only a day. The other great sadness in her life.

Her parents had come from Connecticut and stayed a week. Her mother, practical and efficient, had stocked the house with groceries, made casseroles for the freezer, and hired a woman to come clean once a week. She had taken Rob to his preschool, and in the afternoons the two of them had gone to the zoo, the children's museum, and the Air and Space Museum, his favorite.

The house had buzzed with activity, but her father had stayed outside most days, spending his visit in the garden. It had been early spring. Her father had started what became her garden for Grace. Less showy than the wide border of sun-loving perennials, these plants were quiet and restful, a peaceful part of the garden.

After Grace's death Caroline had had a difficult time resuming her life. Her mother had called it a breakdown. The doctor had said that along with her grief she suffered from postpartum depression. The pills prescribed for her made her feel as if she were wrapped in cotton batting.

On a morning like this one Harry had come and sat beside her on the steps. He held Rob in his arms.

"Our boy needs you, Caro." Harry had caressed her cool cheek with one hand and gently touched her lips, as if to coax them to a smile. Then he took her arm, bone white and wrapped around her waist, and pulled it away from her body, creating a space on her lap. Caroline remained quiet and still as Harry lowered Rob, sleepy, just up from his nap, onto her legs, firmly placing her arm around their son.

Harry drew his own arm around them both, protective and insistent, as if telling her to let go of the pain, willing her to be happy again, because after all, in spite of everything, they were a family. Caroline had looked down, staring at her hands cradling her living child. They seemed to be the hands of a stranger, lifeless and fragile-looking, with the cuticles picked ragged, hands she had trouble recognizing as her own. This beautiful, healthy child had sat in her lap, and she had not been able to feel the softness of his hair or the delicate bones of his back as he leaned against her. Her Rob.

How long had they sat like that? Harry had been so in control then, and always, she thought. His shirt had probably been clean and pressed, his khakis neatly creased—his regular weekend attire, nice enough to go down to his office for a few hours late in the afternoon. Harry had been able to continue on with his life as if nothing had happened, whereas Caroline had fallen apart. In photographs of her that first year after Grace had died, Caroline had looked like a walking unmade bed, her clothes loose and baggy from her having lost so much weight. Her hair, once the golden red of a sunset, had become dull and listless. There were pictures of Rob too, toddling on sturdy legs with dimpled grass-stained knees, always smiling, ignorant of the pain his mother bore. Harry had remained steadfast in the belief that she would get better.

On the first anniversary of Grace's death Harry had given Caroline a teak bench for the shade garden. Now, all these years later, Caroline sat on that bench looking once more at the lilac. She brushed back the tears rolling down her face: tears for Grace; tears for her father, who had died a few years later; tears for Harry, who had kept his financial problems and his sorrows to himself. She thought of Grace and tried to imagine the girl she would have become. Grace, who would have been fifteen now.

Harry had been right: Caroline had gotten better. Now her grown-up Rob, her remote, silent son, would be coming home from college next week. A breeze ruffled the branches. The phone rang again inside the house. She gave a final glance at the garden and hurried inside.

❦

Several days later, Caroline went to see her best friend, Vivien.

When Caroline and Harry moved to their big house in Chevy Chase, they had made other friends right in the neighborhood. Harry used to go jogging with Phil Larsen at the end of the block, and Phil's wife, Jill, and Caroline had formed a playgroup for their little boys, along with another mother on the block behind them. Phil and Harry swapped tools as they each tackled small home improvements.

Harry and Caroline's closest friends had been right next door, Marsha and Sam Greene. They often shared a babysitter and went off to the movies together or out for dinner. The Greenes' daughter was the same age as Rob. Marsha had been pregnant with her son, Thomas, when Caroline had been pregnant with Grace. The two mothers spent long hours together talking about their young children, their pregnancies, and coping together at "arsenic hour," the chaotic time at the end of the afternoon when the children were especially fussy, while husbands worked long hours downtown.

After Grace's death, Caroline could hear Thomas's healthy cries through the open windows all that spring and into the following summer. Her own house felt horribly silent to her, despite Rob's cheerful babbling. Marsha, seemingly sensitive to Caroline's sadness, kept her distance for a while. Once Caroline got over her depression, she tried to resume her friendship with Marsha, but seeing the growing Thomas was a constant reminder of her loss. When Sam Greene took a new job in Charlotte and the family moved away, Caroline had been relieved.

Vivien lived in the Palisades neighborhood in a charming bungalow forever in need of painting. She also had an office downtown. Vivien was not in a garden club or a book club and, having no children, had never been caught up in chatter about soccer games, carpool arrangements, college admittance, and the ongoing concerns of Caroline's neighborhood friends. Instead, Vivien talked about food, book projects, illustrators, photographers, and publicists. Thanks to Vivien, Caroline had a small part in that other world, and she spent less and less time with the local mothers.

"Honestly, Caroline. I'm worried you're going to turn into some kind of weird recluse, one of those oddball women who talk to themselves and never answer the phone." Vivien looked accusingly at her across the pot of tea, though she spoke in a familiar joking way. They sat in Vivien's kitchen, a chaotic room painted tomato soup red, every surface cluttered and an entire wall covered with shelves full of cookbooks. They had met at the Cuisine Academy. Rob was in preschool then, and Caroline had decided to take a class on the art of French cooking. Vivien had encouraged Caroline to write a dining-out-with-kids column for a community newspaper and later hired her to write for the cookbook division of World Life Books.

"I called you back, didn't I?"

"Three days later."

Caroline shifted in her chair. "I know. I don't deserve you, Vivien. You've been so patient."

"Enough of that." Vivien smiled and reached over to pat Caroline's arm. Her hands were broad and strong, good hands for kneading bread, though Vivien spent more time molding words than dough. "Sure you're okay? You look different."

Caroline shook her head. "Same old me. But I do have some news."

"Let me guess." Vivien picked up the earth-toned ceramic teapot and poured. "The all-perfect Marjorie shared some savory bit of gossip with you. How was her dinner party, by the way?"

Vivien seemed to have a sixth sense about things, as if she knew Caroline better than Caroline knew herself. Caroline shifted uneasily and lifted her mug. Wafts of smoky Lapsang souchong steamed into her face, too hot to drink. She set it down.

"It seems that I've inherited a house. Well, Harry did, and as the lawyer explained, now it's mine." She handed Vivien the letter from East Hope, Maine.

She blew across her tea and sipped it slowly while Vivien read the typed pages from Hollis Moody. Vivien, in her mid-fifties, looked no different than when Caroline had met her twelve years before. Tall, big-boned, she wore the colorful loose clothes that reminded Caroline of an art teacher. Her dark hair was swept into a topknot and held in place with two large pins resembling chopsticks. Her husband, Roger, a research scientist at the National Institutes of Health, was her exact opposite, quiet and slight, and all but disappeared in a crowd. Both were devoted to their work.

"This Lila was Harry's aunt?"

"Great-aunt, actually. She died last summer. Ninety-one years old. I took Rob there for a week the summer after Grace died. Harry wasn't able to come. Lila was lovely to us. That was the last time I saw her. We exchanged Christmas cards over the years, but nothing more than that."

Vivien's dark eyebrows drew together. "Any idea what the house is worth?"

"Not really. But selling it would certainly help."

Vivien knew about Caroline's financial worries. She had also been urging Caroline to sell her house in Chevy Chase.

Vivien looked up and waved the letter, then passed it back to Caroline. "This is great. I hope you told the lawyer to sell it."

"It's not that simple."

"How do you mean?"

"I spoke to Mr. Moody. He sounded sweet. I think he's an older man, a friend of Lila's. Anyway, he suggested I come up there and clean out the house first. He thinks that having the exterior painted would help too. I'd get a better price."

"Are you responsible for that?"

"Lila didn't have much family," she said. "There are a few distant cousins, as well as Richard, Harry's dad. Lila apparently always wanted Harry to have the house. She never had children. Once her husband, Francis, died, Lila gave up her teaching job and moved to Maine full-time. Harry used to spend summers with her when he was a teenager."

"There must be some money in Lila's estate that could be used to paint the house."

"When I called Mr. Moody, he said there wasn't much. She lived in a nursing home for a while, and that ate up most of it. I have a feeling Mr. Moody paid her bills in the end. Richard is already paying for Rob's college tuition. I can't ask him for money for this too. I might have to use a little of my own money to fix up the house."

"Fix? I thought it only needed cleaning out." Vivien looked dubious. "Here. Have one of these." She reached behind her for a plate of cookies. "It's a recipe I'm testing for the baking book." Vivien took one and bit into it, dropping crumbs onto the pine table. "Hmm . . . could be chewier. I'll have to work on that." She pushed the plate in Caroline's direction. "So, what does Pete think?"

"I haven't told him yet."

Vivien's brows lifted. "Why not? He's advised you on everything else. Come on; have a cookie."

"Thanks." Caroline took one from the plate. "Things have gotten a little complicated with Pete."

Caroline was accustomed to telling Vivien everything. After Harry had died Vivien was the only one who seemed to know what she needed. She was always ready to listen, and yet she respected Caroline's need for privacy.

Also, Vivien had had no patience for Caroline's sister, Darcy. In Darcy's perfect world, husbands didn't die young or leave their wives with worthless shares of stock. Vivien had suggested that Caroline ignore Darcy's pleas for her to move home to Connecticut after Harry's death. Vivien had been right. Working on the cookbooks had helped her move forward, and having Pete to help her sort out Harry's affairs had been invaluable.

Vivien spoke more seriously. "I don't want to play guessing games, so you'd better define *complicated* right up front."

Caroline leaned back in her chair and told Vivien about the party and how she had slept with Pete. "I'm afraid this could be the start of something. He's been so good to me. He's not happy with Marjorie." She picked at a jagged cuticle on her thumb. "You must think I'm terrible."

Vivien sat quietly for a moment and then looked over at Caroline, her expression kind, reassuring. "You're human. These things happen." She held her hands around her mug and appeared to be thinking seriously about this turn that Caroline's life had taken.

"It's not right," Caroline said. She pressed her hands to her forehead and pushed back her hair. "I wish I could run away from this entire mess."

"Have you seen him since the party?"

Caroline shook her head. "He's phoned every day. He's left messages saying he wants to see me. I don't know what to tell him."

"Wait. This is perfect." Vivien set her mug down on the table. "Go to Maine. Take a few weeks away."

"What? Leave home?"

"Go up to Maine for a few weeks, even a month. It would do you good to get away."

"But the editing job, the vegetable cookbook?"

"Take it with you."

"To Maine?"

"Of course. Take your laptop. You can work anywhere. Plus, that way you'll be there to oversee the work on the house yourself."

"I'm just not sure."

"If you hire someone to manage the work in Maine it will take away from your profit when you sell the house."

"I see what you mean, but—"

"You just said you'd like to escape from everything."

"But Rob's coming home this weekend."

"So?"

"It's out of the question. I can't leave him this summer. He'll have his job at the tennis club and—"

"Caroline, he's nineteen. He can take care of himself for a few weeks. You do tend to coddle him. He'd probably like to have some time on his own."

"Oh, Viv. I can't do that. I'm worried about him. He never talks to me anymore."

"I know Rob. That's just his way. You're making too much of it. He doesn't need to be babied."

"Vivien, please. I can't leave him alone."

Vivien shrugged. "Well, think about it. East Hope," she said, seeming to look beyond Caroline at some distant place. "I like the sound of it."

The idea of escaping to Maine was tempting. Caroline thought of her visit to Lila's those many years before. She could picture the older lady, still pretty in her late seventies in a flowered shirtwaist dress, waving good-bye to her from the lawn. She remembered the freshness of the air and the house, crisp white against the blue sky. And the water, the sound of it, the smell of it filling every breath, the relentless movement of the ocean.

"I'd come and visit you," Vivien said.

"What?" Caroline's thoughts had turned to Rob. It was as if he were moving away from her, pulled out by a tide.

"If you went to Maine I'd come visit. Roger is up to his ears in a new project. You know how he gets. It would be easy to sneak away for a bit."

"Rob's coming home for the summer this weekend. I'm not going anywhere," Caroline said. She finished the last of her tea, knowing it was time to go home. She planned to stop at the grocery store to buy what she needed to make Rob's favorite dinner: lamb chops, asparagus, stuffed baked potatoes, and coffee ice cream with chocolate sauce for dessert. It had been Harry's favorite dinner too.

"You'd better call Pete," Vivien said. "The longer you wait, the harder—"

"I know." Caroline's stomach tightened. She started for the door. "Thanks for listening, Viv. You always make me feel better." She smiled at her friend and went out to her car. The sky was intensely blue that afternoon, and for a brief moment she thought again of Lila and the house in East Hope. Maine seemed very far away.

❦

Caroline came down to the kitchen and was surprised to find Rob already up. He had been home for a week, and though he'd frequently been out, meeting his old high school friends, she realized how lonely she had been without him. After months of living alone, she now found dishes lingering on the counter next to the sink, shoes on the floor by the TV in the den, wet towels in the hall bath, a steady thumping music coming from his room, the sounds of doors opening and closing, all part of having him home. With Rob back in the house it was as if her other life, her family life, had returned. This made her happy.

"You're up early," she said, and went to take a mug out for her coffee, which she had set to the timer the night before.

"Hey, Mom," he said softly. He was loading the blender with strawberries, his back to her. He turned and gave her a quick smile. He still had the loose-limbed puppyish gestures of a teenage boy, but his face had lost its former softness and taken on the more focused features of a young man. A large container of vanilla yogurt sat open on the counter beside him. He wore baggy shorts, putty colored, that hung on his thin frame. For a moment, from the tilt of his head and the angle of his spine, she thought Rob could have been Harry. She remembered Harry standing just this way in front of the stove when he made pancakes for them on the weekend.

The blender whirred loudly, like a rocket about to take off. Caroline poured her coffee and carried it to the table. The roar stopped. In the sudden silence she watched while Rob poured the soupy pink mixture into a glass. Just as it was about to overflow he righted the container and licked the rim.

"What time did you get in last night?" she asked.

"Mom. Come on." He frowned at her while pulling out his chair at the table.

"Okay. I know. No more curfew." Caroline took a sip of coffee, knowing it wasn't going to be easy to talk to him if she began like that.

She hadn't slept well, listening for Rob's car in the driveway, worrying about him and thinking about Pete, whom she'd finally spoken to the afternoon before. Fortunately, Rob had been at the tennis club when Pete had called from his office. As she expected, Pete had wanted to see her again. He had acted hurt when she said no, and his voice had cooled noticeably when she made her excuses, one of them being Rob.

Rob sipped his smoothie. What was he thinking about? Maybe his friends, his evening out, or maybe what it was like to be home again in the familiar kitchen, the sun hitting the table where it always had at this time of morning, though now there was no possibility of Harry coming in to join them or kiss them hurriedly on his way to the office.

"That looks good. Healthy too," she said.

"Yeah—it is." Rob wasn't interested in cooking, but he did like operating the gadgets she had accumulated: whipping up smoothies in the blender, cooking sandwiches on the panini press, and using the battery-operated wand to whip milk into foam for exotic coffee drinks.

"With skills like that you're going to make some girl very happy one day."

"Mom," he groaned. "You're so old-fashioned."

Caroline smiled. Rob had probably already made a girl or girls very happy. He had no girlfriend at the moment, at least no one he'd told her about, but she remembered some of the girls from college who had come home with him for Harry's service. Two of them had stayed at the house. "Just friends," he'd said at the time. Caroline had not forgotten their long shining hair, their concerned faces, the sound of their soft voices talking with Rob late into the night. She'd been relieved that he had this other world of friends, but also strangely sad. They seemed to be able to console him while she hadn't.

With his smoothie almost finished, Rob went to the cabinet to take out cereal. There the sun poured onto his hair, giving it the golden look he'd had when he was little, except that now his hair was coarser and less wavy than it used to be. Caroline had loved to kiss the top of his head when he was a little boy. She loved the smell of his hair, soft and cottony from sleep or matted and hot from play. Even now, when she caught him in a quick hug, he still smelled like that little boy, and despite the soaps and shampoo, there was that special warmth, the scent she'd always known, the scent of him.

He poured milk onto the cereal, pulling the drawer open for a spoon, and once again sat at the table. He seemed distracted, as if his mind were someplace else.

"Sweetie, are you okay?"

He nodded. "Yeah. I think I am. It's still so weird to come

home and not have Dad here." He rested his hand on her arm, smiling almost shyly. "How are you doing, Mom?"

"Better too. I'm glad it's summer. I'm ready for a change."

They sat quietly together. Rob pulled his hand back and resumed eating.

"I thought I heard you on the phone late last night," she said.

"Doug Hall called." Rob pushed aside his hair that had fallen across his forehead. He looked away, as if guilty of something. He had Harry's nose, straight and neat. His lower lip was full, more pronounced than the upper. "Sorry if it woke you. His uncle's got a camp out west. They run wilderness trips in the San Juan mountain range."

Doug was Rob's college roommate. Caroline had met him the day she took Rob to school, and one other time. It must have been parents' weekend.

"It turns out we got the jobs," he said.

"What are you talking about? What jobs?"

"Jim and I are going out to Colorado to work for Doug's uncle. Like I told you." He bent his head over his cereal bowl.

Jim was Rob's best friend and lived two streets over. They had known each other since the first grade. "You never told me anything about this." Caroline pushed her mug away. The coffee tasted too strong. "I don't remember discussing this. When did you tell me?"

"Come on, Ma. Remember at Granddad's? Over spring break."

Caroline thought back to the ten days they had spent with Richard, Harry's father. Harry had been an only child, and Richard was devastated by his son's death. Harry's mother had died only a few years before, and Caroline marveled at how Richard could survive so much loss. They had gone to see him in Florida, both for Christmas and also for Rob's vacation in March. Rob was close to his grandfather. Caroline had thought that time together would be good for both of them.

Rob looked up. "I know I told you." He looked betrayed—or angry because she didn't remember, or didn't believe him.

Caroline had a vague memory of some conversation about hiking in Colorado. Maybe Rob had mentioned Doug, but a job, a summer job? She was sure she would have remembered that. Then again, her brain had been muddled at the time. It had been only weeks earlier when she and Pete had begun to piece together the extent of Harry's financial losses.

The kitchen was growing warm. Caroline had delayed turning on the air-conditioning, hoping to keep the utility bills down. "I was looking forward to having you home this summer," she said. "I was hoping we could spend some time together. You've been away all year and—"

"I'm home for two more weeks. The camp's over in August." Rob got up from the table and carried his dishes to the sink. He turned back to her. "Mom, please understand. It's like I need to breathe. The sky is so open there. God, it's amazing. The camp's not far from where Dad and I went fishing when I turned sixteen."

Caroline felt her thoughts flutter about, as if birds were flying in her head. Everything she had looked forward to was disappearing before her eyes.

"But your job at the tennis club. Aren't you supposed to help with the youth clinics?"

"Mom, there are kids lined up to do that. I've already talked to the pro."

Caroline felt her throat tightening. She took a deep breath. "Remember I told you about Aunt Lila's house?"

"Yeah. You said you were going to sell it."

"Well, it needs some work. I was thinking of going up this summer to see to that and to clean it out. If you don't want to be here, we could both go up there."

"Mom, I want to earn money. You told me we have to be careful. I want to work at this camp. This way I'll have money for school in the fall."

"But it's expensive to fly out there."

"Granddad gave me money for the ticket for my birthday."

"But you'll be so far from home. Sweetie, you've had a rough year. I know how hard it is without Dad."

"Mom, please." He turned his back to her again, his arms braced against the sink. Rob sounded near tears. He shook his head.

Caroline went to him and placed her hands on his shoulders. "If it's what you really want . . ."

He turned. "I don't mean to desert you."

"It's fine, really."

He gave her a quick hug. "Thanks, Mom."

❦

Rob made his arrangements to leave. He dug out camping gear stored in the garage, stacked clothes on the floor of his room, purchased batteries and a new headlamp. He packed and repacked his duffel bag. It was as if he were a sailor getting ready to ship out to sea. He was leaving her and she could do nothing to stop it.

The day before Rob's departure Caroline awoke in the middle of the night. Her stomach felt off. She heard Rob's footsteps in the hall and saw that the light was on in Harry's study. She found him there, sitting in Harry's chair at the desk.

"Is anything wrong?" she asked.

"Remember how Dad used to get up early, way before us, to work?" He looked at her; his lower lip quivered. "Something makes me keep coming in here, like I might find him. Like the heart attack never happened. Some kind of sick joke." He turned away from her. "Sometimes I think I'm cracking up."

"You're not cracking up." Caroline went over and stood beside her son. She stroked his back. "It's a lot to get used to," she said. "It's going to take a while." She waited. He leaned forward, his arms resting on his knees, his face hidden from her in his hands. She couldn't tell if he was crying or not.

"You're sure you want to go?" she asked.

"Mom, don't." He got up, pulling away from her.

"Rob, please."

He turned and looked at her. His eyes had deep circles, as if he too had had sleepless nights. His hair sprang out from his head in uncombed clumps. He wore pajama bottoms that puddled around his feet and a ragged T-shirt, frayed at the neck. He looked a woebegone mixture of boy and man. "Good night, Ma." His face softened slightly. "I'm okay. All right?" He went to his room, his bare feet making no sound at all.

When Rob was a little boy he used to crawl into his parents' bed first thing every morning. Harry never lingered, but took off for his run as soon as it was light. Rob would snuggle up to Caroline's back.

"I'm breathing with you, Mama."

She would stay very still as Rob made funny little humming sounds. His breath was warm on her neck. She would start to hum along with him. No words, just the silly humming, a joke between them. After a few minutes she would say, "Okay, time to get up, cuddle bug." Harry, once back from his run, would be expecting coffee and his cereal with fruit, bananas in the winter, strawberries in late spring, blueberries in summer.

Those mornings were a long time ago. By tomorrow Rob would be gone. All spring Caroline had waited for these months with her son, a chance to be a family. Instead she had suffocating bills, a shrinking checking account, painful memories, and a man who wanted more than she was willing to give. She thought again of East Hope and tried to remember whether Aunt Lila had had lilacs in her garden.

4

The rest of the weekend with Mary Beth was strained. She stayed in bed nursing her cold while Will spent the remainder of Saturday and most of Sunday cleaning out the garage to have it ready to show to Realtors and potential buyers, but also to avoid spending time in the house with his wife.

Finally, on Sunday afternoon when Will came home after a particularly long run, Mary Beth laid out her schedule for the coming weeks. She was headed back to Los Angeles to meet with Drew and the others working on the project, and from there a trip to Tokyo to meet with their Japanese counterparts. She asked Will to arrange putting their furniture into storage and presented him with a list of the things that she wanted shipped to New York. "Come on, Will. It's not so bad. It's going to be a fresh start," she said, putting her arms around his neck. He kissed her and tried not to think about the life that they were leaving behind.

After her departure the days blurred together. Graduation came and went, but Will did not attend, knowing that Jennifer Whitely's father, a trustee, would march in the procession. During what would have been his tenth graduation ceremony at Habliston College, Will remained at home, cleaning out his office and packing boxes. He stayed inside all day, despite the great weather, feeling like a deviant or some kind of criminal.

The situation might have been different. If Mary Beth had

mustered some small amount of indignation, even if she had not been willing to help him fight the accusations, he would have walked in the ceremony with his colleagues, showing everyone that he would not be cowed by the bogus claims of one undergraduate. The more he thought about it, the more he began to brood. It was as if his wife had abandoned him.

Will's mood continued to darken each day as he readied the house for the move. Mary Beth had already taken the guest room bed and dresser to New York, along with a pair of love seats from the living room, some end tables, and an assortment of pictures when she bought the apartment at the beginning of the year. Will was used to the missing furniture, and the real estate agent told him not to be concerned, as it made the house appear larger. Indeed, the house sold its first day on the market.

As he worked, Will contemplated the state of his marriage. He knew all married couples settled eventually into a practical rhythm, that it was normal for the passion to fade, but the more he thought about his life with Mary Beth the harder time he had remembering any shared joy between them in the last few years.

Not only had they been living in different places, they no longer shared any important decisions. When Mary Beth had accepted the management job in New York without consulting him, she reminded Will that he had accepted the chairmanship of the English department without talking to her, either. She bought the apartment without him, and later decided it was his turn to commute. They were a couple, but they didn't work out their problems together. Had it always been like that?

He remembered how thrilled Mary Beth had been when he was offered the job at Habliston. That decision had seemed automatic. If he truly loved his wife, would he hesitate to follow her to New York now?

Late one afternoon he sat on the back steps and flipped through the latest issue of *Down East*. Tomorrow was trash day. He had been about to toss the issue in the recycling bin. Maine, he thought, and suddenly the idea of a trip there to celebrate their anniversary came back to him. A vacation together—would it maybe make a difference? He couldn't allow himself to give up.

Will thought of his parents, married nearly fifty years until his mother's death. His dad was not a quitter. His parents had seemed happy, but probably their marriage hadn't always been easy. Rough times in the hardware business had made money a worry. He knew his mother had longed to travel. She had come from a more affluent home and had spent her junior year of college in Paris. Will remembered arguments over his brother, Rusty, who was not a strong student and prone to falling in with a rough crowd in high school. His parents didn't always agree on how to handle their older son. Still, they had stuck by each other.

When Will had had his back problem in the tenth grade, his dad had told him not to give up. "Son, you can't play football like Rusty, but there are other sports." Following in his brother's footsteps, varsity quarterback, might have been impossible anyway, but Will had discovered running, a sport he enjoyed to this day. "Look on the bright side." "Don't give up." "Try harder." These were the maxims of his growing up.

He and Mary Beth had been so happy in Maine. The details of their honeymoon were sharp and real in his mind; he could still see it like a movie running in his head: mornings spent with Mary Beth, cuddled in bed, no hurry to get up, the thick fog that settled over them. He never forgot that place.

Mary Beth and Will had married over Labor Day weekend, a small family affair at Mary Beth's home in New Jersey. She and her mother had planned the entire wedding, and he had been happy to leave it to them. He said he'd take charge of the weeklong honeymoon, before he started his teaching job in Pennsylvania. When he told Mary Beth about his idea for Maine, he thought he saw the slightest flicker of disappointment in her face. She had been hinting for Bermuda or the Bahamas. She grew more enthusiastic when he described the cottage on the cove, lobster suppers, and cozy nights by the fire. They'd driven up the New England coast to the small home owned by his college roommate's family.

One morning three or four days into the trip, the fog that had stayed all week remained draped over them; the dampness seemed to seep through the walls. Will got up first and pulled on jeans and a flannel shirt.

"I'll go light the fire."

"Umm." Mary Beth didn't move. He pulled the covers up around her pale skin, loving the way her body almost disappeared into the white sheets and the contrast of her hair, a shock of darkness on the rumpled bed. She had a neat, well-proportioned figure, though her breasts were large for her small frame. Will had stared down at her. He could barely pull himself away.

The living room of the cottage was plain, almost austere. The owners of these old summer cottages were secure in the knowledge that they had far grander houses elsewhere; this simplicity was part of the message—the occupants had no need to show off to the world. The living room had a sensible clutter of mismatched furniture, two butterfly chairs, a wicker love seat that creaked when you sat, and a collection of wooden side chairs, two pulled up to a card table next to a shelf of jigsaw puzzles. Floor-to-ceiling shelves loaded with books gave the room a papery, library-like smell. The book covers were muted and looked like novels from the fifties or earlier. Will had finished reading the books he had brought with him and planned to take some time today to see what was there.

He knelt and made balls of newspaper from a stack on the floor, then layered three logs on top. He found matches on the mantel and the paper easily ignited. Watching to see if the logs would catch fire, he shivered and listened to the soft hiss of burning newsprint and was gratified a few minutes later by a cat's tail of smoke curling up the chimney.

Next he went to run a bath for Mary Beth. The only bathroom, a large square room at the top of the stairs, had no shower, only a claw-foot tub sitting under the window like a genial animal.

"The tub's ready," he called out. This had become their morning routine.

Mary Beth shuffled into the bathroom and Will pulled off her robe. "I can see my breath in here," she said. "Did you turn up the heat?"

He kissed her shoulder. "I got the fire going."

"Thanks," she said, now more awake. She smiled.

There were only two radiators on the first floor, designed to remove the damp rather than heat the house. Once they left, the pipes would be drained and the house closed up for the winter. "It'll be warmer by the time you get downstairs." Will sat on the floor opposite the tub, his back against the wall. The old-fashioned bathroom was Spartan. Besides the toilet, the tub, and a wide-lipped pedestal sink, there was a white-painted chest of drawers and two freestanding wooden towel racks. Mary Beth had said she'd seen ones like them for eighty dollars in an antique store. She lowered herself into the tub, her skin turning pink in the steaming water.

On their first morning in the cottage he had joined her in the bath. After a few minutes of them fumbling and splashing, the water had cooled quickly, and Will had had to get out and mop the floor. Knowing that there would be days and days of her, a lifetime of Mary Beth, he was content to watch her bathe; it was like having a good book that would never end, an infinite number of pages.

"What would you like to do today?" he asked.

"Well, as we can't see a thing, I guess it's going to be another day by the fire. You can work on your novel."

"I'll start writing when we get home," he said. "Why don't we go to Chauncey Point and walk on the pebble beach?"

"You don't think it's too cold?"

"I promise I'll keep you warm."

"You always do, Will." She blew him a kiss and then eased her head under the water, surfaced, and reached for the bottle of shampoo. Will closed the door after himself and went down to survey the day.

He didn't mind the fog. He didn't mind the feeling of being wrapped up, away from the rest of civilization, having Mary Beth all to himself. A delicious secrecy filled these days spent alone in this impermeable world. It was like dropping off the face of the earth into a mysterious land that was theirs alone.

During that week in Maine, Will imagined that his senses had become more acute. Everything inside the house took on the clarity of a Vermeer painting. He could practically feel the weight of the silence blanketing them. In the morning the acrid wetness of the chimney awakened his nostrils like a jab, and the warmth of Mary Beth's skin was like a drug. In the evenings when they came home from dinner, they sipped wine by the fire while he read aloud to her from a tattered copy of *Ethan Frome*. When the crackling flames dwindled to embers, they climbed the stairs, arm in arm, up to bed.

On the final day of their visit the sun came out. The water in the cove sparkled and bounced in jeweled radiance. Will scanned the horizon with amazement. They'd been living in paradise without knowing it. They sat on the lawn below the cottage and looked out over the harbor. The air had warmed up. A small lobster boat chugged its way out the neck of the harbor. Several sailboats had unfurled their sails in readiness for a day spent on the bay. Will squinted into the sun. The pristine blue water was punctuated with islands, mysterious and beckoning.

Mary Beth sipped her coffee. "God, it's gorgeous," she said.

Will draped his arm across her shoulder. They'd made love that morning and she had a lingering sweetness about her. She seemed as unspoiled as the landscape before them. "I'm so happy," he said.

"I love you, Will." She leaned into him. "Too bad the good weather came on the last day."

"Let's stay an extra day."

"Will . . ."

"We could drive home all in one day instead of two."

"Will, I don't want to be in the car for fourteen hours straight."

"I'll drive the whole way."

"I start my job on Monday. I have a lot to do to get ready." She reached up and put her finger to his lips. "You need to be at the college. It's not just me who has to get back."

He knew she was right. He took her finger in his mouth and bit it gently.

"Will." She pulled back and he moved closer, knocking her mug aside.

"I don't want this to end." He eased on top of her and kissed her lips. She tasted of coffee. "I'm the fog," he said. "I'm covering you, every last bit, every last place." He slid his hand under her sweater. He imagined the warm sun on his back reaching all the way through to her in one powerful ray.

"Let's never leave," he said, and rose up on his elbows. "Let's give it all up and stay here forever."

"You're crazy." She laughed.

He kissed her eyes. His lips filled one socket and then the next. "I'm the fog," he whispered again. "I'm everywhere."

Mary Beth softened beneath him. She returned his kiss, then gently pushed him away. "Come on. Let's enjoy today." She sat up and smoothed down her sweater. "Maybe one day we'll come back." She stood up and tried to pull him to his feet.

Will didn't want to get up. He wished that nothing would change: the sun, the sky, the water, and most of all, this moment with Mary Beth.

Now, ten years later, Will considered his idea for a trip. He flipped through the pages of the magazine, looking at the ads for inns, hotels, and B and Bs. He wanted something nice, a room overlooking the water for sure. Mary Beth was busy, but she had vacation days coming to her. Maybe early September, around the time of their anniversary.

At the very back of the magazine a photograph caught his eye. It was of a yellow clapboard building with black shutters and a wooden sign saying, TAUNTON'S USED BOOKS. Below, the caption said, *Summer manager wanted, free apartment, water views.*

The phone had started to ring inside the house. Maybe it was the lawyer to set the date for the walk-through. The house deal was moving quickly. Will turned back the page of the magazine and went inside.

It was Jack Mathews. Will fought an urge to hang up. His jaw clenched.

"How's it going, buddy?" Jack said with forced joviality.

"Have you hired my replacement yet?"

"Shit, Will," Jack said, his tone suddenly deflated. "You know this has been hell for me too. It's no picnic to lose the best English professor you've got, maybe one of the finest this college has ever seen."

"The best at Habliston. Now there's a compliment." Will had not returned Jack's earlier calls, voice messages expressing regret and explaining that he wanted to do what he could to help. Beyond being Will's boss, Jack was an old friend. Will knew that none of this was really Jack's fault.

"Sorry, Jack. You didn't deserve that." Embarrassed, Will tried to muster some goodwill. "Alice Field could teach American lit; she'd be really good. You could hire someone new for freshman comp. Plenty of adjunct English teachers out there," he added flatly.

"We're hiring no one. I need to get rid of another position too. Orders from above. No funds. *Nada.*"

"Lucky I had the run-in with the Whitely girl." Will hated the sarcasm in his voice. He couldn't stop himself. "Easy way to thin the staff."

"Jesus, Will." Jack let out his breath.

"Sorry. I'm feeling overwhelmed. On top of everything, Mary Beth's still gone." He sighed deeply and explained, "I'm doing all the packing. God, it's depressing as hell. It's like my life around here never counted. She wants me to move to New York right away."

"I've already written your recommendations. You should get

started on the job search. Full-time will be tough. You know the market."

"Mary Beth doesn't care if I teach. She thinks I'll be happy sitting in the apartment all summer writing my novel."

"You told me that commuting was getting to be a problem for her," Jack said. "You can start on the interviews and have some time together."

"Yeah, right. Except Mary Beth's hardly going to be there." Will explained that she had already taken a trip to Tokyo, and was working on a new project that required her presence in Los Angeles for most of the summer.

It felt good to talk about what had been festering inside him over the last few weeks. "What really burns me up is that we're giving up our whole lives here. Ten years, the house, our future. My career is over and she acts like it's of no consequence."

"Your career isn't over. I'm going to help you with the job. Alice is a huge fan of yours. She'll write you great recs, too."

"It's not just coming up with another job." Will no longer tried to hide his anger. "I don't want to sit sealed up in an apartment all summer while my executive wife supports me. Like I'm some kind of gigolo."

"You're a damn good teacher, Will," Jack said, changing the subject. "Don't forget that."

In the next few minutes Jack shared his own worries for the college. The financial picture was worse than ever. Even if the board voted to go coed, it might take years to rebuild the enrollment. Will listened to his friend, though his mind kept going back to images of Maine. He remembered the landscape: rocks, trees, water, sky. All so clean and elemental. He thought of the quality of the light, the ribbons of fog, nothing to interrupt the pure simplicity of the place.

"Don't worry," Jack said. "Things will work out with Mary Beth."

Mary Beth sparkled with energy when she came home to Habliston for the last time at the end of May. It was as if she had forgotten why Will was leaving the college, as if the move to New York had been part of their plans all along. The weather had warmed and the air had taken on a softness, a harbinger of summer. The trees had leafed out. The evenings were scented with freshly mowed lawns. The voices of children allowed to play outside after supper floated in from the sidewalks.

Their first spring in their house had been magical. One night Mary Beth had come home from work to find Will painting their bedroom. After his morning class he had rushed home to get started, wanting to surprise her. It was her favorite color, hydrangea blue. In her hurry to thank him she had rushed into his arms, spattering both of them with paint. "You're a dream, Will Harmon, an absolute dream," she had said. That summer he laid the stones for the patio, and she planted three hydrangeas to celebrate their third anniversary.

The hydrangeas had grown into large shrubs, but when they bloomed this July, new owners would be living in the house. Will had done everything on his wife's list. The papers were signed for the attorney so that the house settlement could take place without their presence the following month. The funds would be wired to their separate accounts. Mary Beth had always insisted that they divide everything equally. This was generous on her part, as most of the down payment on their home had come from her sales bonuses. The moving van was coming a few days later, and Will had arranged for a service to do the final housecleaning.

Since the kitchen utensils were packed, Will suggested going to dinner at Landini's, an Italian restaurant on the way out to Travers Lake. The college was closed for the summer, but the restaurant had never been popular with the academic community, and Will knew the chance of running into any of his colleagues would be slight. Jack had told no one about his resignation or what had caused it, but he doubted that Jennifer Whitely would keep it to herself. News traveled quickly in small academic worlds. They arrived at the restaurant at seven thirty. The sky was still light.

"The Japanese people are awfully nice, once you get used to all the bowing," Mary Beth said. "They're pretty formal, though, not at all like doing business in the U.S. Drew says Mr. Yoguschi thinks I do wonders with numbers. He was totally wowed by my first presentation."

"Are you ready to order?" Will asked. They had already requested drinks from their waitress, one of the regulars Will recognized. This was the restaurant that he had frequented when Mary Beth was away.

"Are you listening to me?" she asked.

"Of course I am."

Before he could reassure his wife further, the waitress appeared with their wine. She set two very full glasses of merlot on the table without spilling a drop and then lit the candle stuck into the Chianti bottle at the center of their table. "Romantic touch. Right?" Middle-aged, with a thick waist and black hair that looked too shiny to be natural, she pulled her order pad from her apron pocket. Her name tag said, DORIS. "Let me guess." She grinned at Will. "The steak platter, medium-rare, baked potato instead of fries, blue cheese on the salad?"

He grinned sheepishly and nodded.

"You must come here a lot," Mary Beth said.

"And for the lady?" She turned to Mary Beth, ignoring her remark, her pencil poised to write. The restaurant was busy that night. There were several tables of families. A chunky baby sat in a high chair at the table behind them. Will realized that he should have chosen a more romantic spot.

"I'll have the veal with lemon. For the salad, house dressing, but I'd like it on the side." Mary Beth looked at Will, eyebrows pitched a little higher, as if asking what sort of place he had brought her to. He imagined that Landini's was not as upscale as most of the restaurants in New York she had told him about.

"Thanks, Doris," Will said. He smiled at Mary Beth, thinking of his idea for the summer. He might have given up on the college, but he wasn't going to give up on her.

"Japan sounds great," he said. "I'm glad it's going so well."

"It's not easy," she said. "God, the jet lag. Still, it's worth the effort. Once this company is on board, well, there's no telling where we'll go. My stock options are going to be worth . . ." She looked down in her lap and picked up her BlackBerry on the banquette next to her. "Just a sec."

Will watched her face as she studied the message on the device. Who was trying to reach her on a Saturday night? Her mouth curled gently upward with the hint of a smile. She pressed a few buttons, put the device down, and tilted her head. Her face was flushed. She looked happy.

"Everything okay?" he asked.

"Just Drew. It's not important. I'll e-mail when we get back to the house."

If it's not important, Will thought, *why bother her now?* Didn't this guy know she had a husband, a life outside of work? He reached for his wine. He was getting sick of hearing Drew this, Drew that, and stories about all these other people he hadn't even met.

Doris arrived with their salads, and after offering grinds of pepper, as if it were an upscale place, she left them alone.

"June's going to be frantic, but I don't think July will be as bad," Mary Beth said while drizzling the smallest amount of dressing across her salad. "Some friends in our building in the city have a place out on Long Island. They wanted to know if we could come out for the Fourth. The entire weekend. It sounds like a gorgeous place, and—"

"I wanted to talk about the summer," Will said, glad to have this topic introduced. "This will be our tenth anniversary."

"Mmm," she said, her mouth full. She swallowed and picked up her glass. "You're right, darling." She reached across the table and gave his hand a squeeze. "Here's to us."

Will lifted his glass and took a quick sip. "I have an idea. Our honeymoon, remember?"

"Of course I remember. Maine. Gooseberry Cove." She grinned more fully, drank again, and put the glass down.

"I thought we could go back."

"This summer?"

"Yeah, to celebrate." An image of Mary Beth then, her hair longer, wearing a blue sweater she had worn, flashed in his mind. She was as lovely now as then.

"It's awfully far away."

"You're due several weeks' vacation. I thought that at the end of the summer you could come up. I've already found a great place."

Before Mary Beth could say anything else he told her about the ad in *Down East* and how he had called about Taunton's Used Books. He explained that the owner, an elderly man, had had a stroke and that his daughter hoped to find someone to run the bookstore for the summer. The building had an apartment upstairs. Not only would they have a free place to stay, but he might also make some money.

As he spoke Mary Beth looked more and more amazed. She had stopped eating her salad and leaned back against the seat of the banquette.

"I can't believe what you're saying." She shook her head slowly, and just as she was about to speak, the waitress appeared with their entrées. "Can I get you anything else?" she said, once the plates were lowered before them.

Mary Beth shook her head.

"I'll finally have time to write my novel," Will said. "I've always loved bookstores. I'll be running a business. You can come up on weekends and at the end of the summer, for our anniversary." He picked up his fork and knife and cut firmly into the steak.

"You're serious?" Her plate of veal cooled in front of her.

"Of course I am."

"You don't know the first thing about running a business," she said, her voice level, without enthusiasm.

"I worked in Dad's hardware store."

"If you wanted to work in a bookstore, there are bookstores all over New York."

"I know that. Geez, Mary Beth. This is about Maine. I'll have something to do this summer, and we can be together there. Remember our honeymoon? You loved it." Will's idea, to him so perfect, so filled with possibility, started to collapse like a sailboat caught on the ocean when the wind dropped and the sails luffed in a sudden calm.

"You want to do this because you're angry with me. Because I didn't want to get into your ridiculous mess at the college."

"That's over with," he said. "Jennifer's got her grade. I'm out of a job."

"And you're taking it out on me." She picked up her silverware and started to pick at her dinner.

"No. That's not it at all."

"Isn't it?"

"Don't you see? I just want us to go back to where we were happy." He put his fork down. "Besides, you're hardly going to be in New York. I thought that instead of just hanging around the apartment—"

"I see. It's all my fault. Here I'm working like a crazy person so my husband who feels sorry for himself can go hide away in Maine."

"I thought if we could just go back . . ."

Mary Beth pushed away her plate. The baby behind them began to cry. "That's exactly the problem. You always want to go back. I moved to New York for a future. You're stuck in the past. Habliston is over. You need to get going on the rest of your life."

"Please. I was thinking of us."

"Were you?"

Will could feel anger rising in him, coming up and taking him by the throat. He swallowed hard. "Why should I be in New York all summer? You're always telling me to write. Here's a great opportunity. Why does it matter if I go to Maine to do it for a few months? Christ, I want you to come."

She leaned forward toward Will and rested her hands on the table. Her nails were very red on the cloth. "So this means you're not coming to New York?"

"I need to do this, Mary Beth. I want you to come when you can. I know you're working hard for us, for our future. I'm thinking about that too."

"The point is, you agreed to move to New York. Now you're backing out."

He lowered his voice. "I just want the summer, one fucking summer." The family behind them got up to leave. Will waited. "You won't even know I'm gone. You're so busy with work, with what's-his-name. Drew? Drew, the big boss." Will felt uneasiness rise in him after saying the name. The memory of trying to reach Mary Beth in LA returned.

His last comment silenced her. He watched the mother carrying her baby walk toward the door. What would their lives be like if they'd had a child, a baby to hold them together? Mary Beth had wanted to wait to have a family. The years had slipped by. There was always another deadline, another sales quota she wanted to make. He had never pushed the matter. His life at the college was full, like a family of its own.

Mary Beth sat opposite him now, her mouth pressed in a straight line. She said nothing. Part of him wanted to take her in his arms and make them both forget all this unpleasantness. He wanted to erase the mistakes they had made, to begin all over again.

They finished their dinner in silence, the bustle and noise of a busy Saturday night all around them. While they waited for the bill she spoke at last.

"Fine. Go to Maine. See if you can figure out what you want."

"I want you," he said softly.

"Do you? I'm not so sure." She got up from the table and told him she'd meet him at the car.

❦

Three days later Will left Pennsylvania. He stopped once in New York to drop off two boxes of fragile china that Mary Beth had not wanted to put into storage. It was early afternoon and Mary Beth was at work. The doorman let him in. He barely glanced at the apartment that would soon be his home, but immediately left the city and drove north up I-95. He avoided the exits for Portland and veered left following the Maine Turnpike toward Augusta and points Down East. He stretched his mouth open and tried to ease the tension that had crept into his jaw. The events of the last month continued to surface in his mind as he drove farther and farther away from his old life. What had he set in motion? His back hurt. Shifting in his seat, he wondered what ached more, his back or his heart?

5

"You're sure you want to sell?" Hollis Moody asked. Caroline had arrived in the elderly lawyer's office in East Hope that morning after having spent the night at a bed-and-breakfast in Belfast. She had been a few minutes late, not having allowed quite enough time to navigate the winding country roads.

He had pulled up a chair for her before seating himself behind the desk. His shoulders were stooped, but his eyes, a watery blue behind thick tortoiseshell glasses, were watchful. Clearly Hollis Moody was a no-nonsense man, with his steel gray hair in a crew cut, faded seersucker suit, and navy blue rep tie, the kind of tie her father would have worn. He looked the part of a frugal, clearheaded New Englander, a man you could count on.

"My son and I live in Washington," Caroline said. "It's just the two of us." The familiar pang of longing clouded her mood. "We live too far away."

"I'm sorry about your husband." Mr. Moody shook his head. "You're too young to be left a widow."

There was nothing she could say to this. Today, for the first time in months, Caroline did feel young, certainly younger than Aunt Lila's lawyer. She felt better that morning. Her stomach had been a little off on the long drive, probably because of something she had eaten in the rest stop on the New Jersey Turnpike. It had been a hot, seemingly endless trip to Connecticut, where she'd spent the night with her mother, Margaret, Peg to her friends. Fortunately the visit was short, though her mother's worries had continued to resonate during the long drive through New England the following day. "Caroline, you shouldn't go off alone; you know nothing about fixing or selling a house, and you don't know a soul up there." The finale of every conversation: "Why don't you move back to Connecticut and live closer to me and Darcy?"

Ah, yes, she thought. The perfect sister, Darcy. The sleek blond chairwoman of everything. Her husband, Walter, an investment banker, had been Harry's friend. Caroline thought again of Darcy's wedding. In a sea of blue blazers on an August afternoon, Harry had been kind and attentive to Caroline. She had wondered whether Walter had put him up to it. Indeed, he'd probably given Harry the assignment. She imagined their conversation: "Take care of the little sister. The shy redheaded girl, a bit of a flake, the perennial bridesmaid—you know the type." Harry had surprised them all by falling in love and marrying her.

Caroline's doubts had started to dissipate when she reached the Maine Turnpike. As the temperature dropped she had felt her spirits lift. Vivien was right: It would do her good to get away. With Rob gone she had no reason to stay on in Washington. She'd managed to close up her house, arrange for a lawn service, and leave her forwarding address with the post office. She'd packed up her files as well as the vegetable recipes that Vivien wanted turned into a book. Everything she would need had fit into her aging Volvo wagon.

Now, across from Mr. Moody, she sat a little straighter and made an effort to pay attention.

"Lila put a new roof on a few years back, but the outside needs painting," Mr. Moody said. "Some of the sills may be rotten. You'll need a carpenter for that."

"Is there someone you could recommend?" Caroline asked, wondering what that might cost.

Hollis Moody paused and seemed to consider her question carefully. He didn't appear to be in any rush. Before explaining Lila's will, he'd told her that after years of practicing law in Boston he'd retired to Maine and opened an office here in East Hope, where he'd worked part-time ever since. He handled wills and estates, small commercial transactions, a few real estate closings, just enough to "keep the old brain in gear."

"Vern Simpson would be your man. He's familiar with old houses," he said, fumbling through the papers on the desk and retrieving a tattered leather address book. "I'll write down the number." He pulled a pencil from his desk drawer.

While he wrote, Caroline looked around his office. The heavy desk was covered with books and papers arranged in a kind of organized chaos along with a tiered basket, also brimming with papers. There was no sign of a computer, but three huge oak file cabinets with brass drawer pulls covered an entire wall. She sat in one of the two cracked red leather chairs that faced the desk. Everything in the room appeared to be as aged and sensible as Hollis Moody himself.

On the wall behind him hung a huge framed map—a nautical chart, really, of the entire peninsula. The landmass was punctuated by every type of body of water imaginable: bays, rivers, ponds, coves, harbors, and the arc of blue called Eggemoggin Reach. The coastline curved and wiggled in a million configurations, and tiny islands littered the vast open water like starbursts.

Mr. Moody tucked the phone number into the file for Caroline. "Vern's an old codger like me, but he knows what he's doing. Have him look at the furnace too. Lila had some trouble with it her last winter in the house. I'm afraid that after she got sick she let some things go. Old houses on the water can take a beating."

Caroline nodded. She worried that there might be other problems. She had only a little money left from her work on the cookbook. The balance in her checking account was sinking fast. She hoped it would be enough for the painting and repairs. Her plan was to use the money from the sale of Lila's house to keep her house in Washington for a few more years. "Mr. Moody, I'm so grateful for your help," she said.

"Nonsense. It's the least I can do for Lila. And call me Hollis, please."

"I'd be glad to," she said. Caroline was pleased to find him so helpful. "I understand that you and Lila were good friends," she said.

Hollis Moody turned toward the window as if to take in the view. His office was on the second floor of an old house on the main street of the village. It was a cool June day. A ray of sunshine shot across his weathered face. "I miss her greatly," he said. He rested his elbows on the arms of his chair. "There's a lot of history in that house." He had the hands of a very old man, a relief map of blue veins and bony knuckles.

"After Millie, my wife, died I used to stop by for a drink at Lila's most evenings on my way home. Millie and Lila were close friends. Sometimes I stayed for supper. She was quite a cook." He turned back to Caroline. His head had an almost imperceptible tremor. She could see that the memory of meals with Lila had cheered him. "She was a real lady, quite an amazing woman—but then, you know that," he added.

"She was so good to us years ago. My son, Rob, was a little boy when we visited. My husband wasn't able to take a vacation that summer—too much work, I guess. I hardly remember." What she did remember was the relief of escaping Harry's scrutiny as he watched her for signs of depression, and being able to turn all her attention to Rob, with his little face that blossomed so easily into smiles. "I wish I'd been able to come here more often," she said.

"The years do slip by, but no matter." He studied the backs of his hands. "You're here now, and that's what counts." He leaned back in his chair. "Lila told me you write restaurant reviews."

"I used to," she said. "When Rob was little I wrote a family dining-out column, child-friendly sorts of places." Caroline told Mr. Moody about her writing, her interest in cooking, and her plans for the vegetable book. "Once I get settled, I'd love to have you to dinner."

"No need for that. You'll be a busy gal with the painting and such. I hope you won't find too many problems." He lowered his head, then looked up, wrinkling his forehead more. His woolly eyebrows lifted. "I wouldn't mind stopping by for a gin and tonic on the porch, though, once the weather warms up."

"I'd like that," she said.

"Lila always added a sprig of mint, never limes. Mint patch is right by the back door."

"Gin and tonic with mint. Sounds delicious." She had the sense that there was more he could tell her about Lila and her house, though for now her only concerns were the rotting sills, an ancient furnace, and the much-needed painting. Would she be able to accomplish everything and put the house on the market by August? She wanted to be home in Washington for Rob when he returned from working at the camp.

"Nice view from the back porch." Mr. Moody rose and gathered his folder of papers and handed them to her, along with a ring of keys. "There's just one other thing." He seemed to be searching for words, and she waited, hoping there was no other problem with the house. "I've kept the clock going. Grandfather clock in the front hall, belonged to Lila's mother. If it's not wound regularly it will stop. I left the directions on the hall table. Thought it would be nice to keep it ticking awhile longer." Hollis seemed embarrassed by his obvious emotion.

"I'd be happy to keep it wound," Caroline said. "It will help me keep track of time. I'm not always good at that."

He looked relieved. "Call me, now, if there's anything I can do."

Caroline felt the weight of the keys in her hand. Part of her wished she could linger and hear more about Lila, but she was already worried about what might lie ahead. "Thanks, Hollis," she said. She turned to leave.

"It's quite a place," he said.

Caroline stopped and looked back. "Sorry?"

"The house. I think you're going to like living in Lila's house."

❦

Will stood for a moment taking in his new surroundings. He had just carried his own boxes of books from the car into the shop. He drew his hands to the small of his back and carefully made circles with his head, trying to loosen his neck muscles. Outside the front window the wooden sign was making a rhythmic squeak in the wind. He liked the name of the business, Taunton's Used Books. It had a spare New England sound. It was serious, but not too literary or, God forbid, cute.

Penny, Mr. Taunton's daughter, had shown him around the day before, the second Sunday in June. She was a stocky woman, quite a bit older than he was, wearing jeans and a sweatshirt.

"Sorry about the dust," she had said. "I work in Belfast. Between that, looking after Dad, the house . . . Just don't get over here much." She spoke with the clipped vowels of a Maine native, the *here* sounding like "heeya."

"When did your dad become ill?" Will asked.

"Had the stroke just before Christmas," she said. "We had hoped he'd be doing better by now. He's eighty-one. Wanted to have one more summer at the shop. He's just crazy about these books." She sighed deeply, as if weary from just thinking about her father's health. "My husband and I can't bear to sell this place as long as he's alive. Knowing it's here, that he might come back, gives Dad some kind of hope. Know what I mean?"

"Of course." Will glanced around him. "Don't worry; I can get this place cleaned up in no time."

"Dad didn't open until the Fourth of July. Not many folks around till then."

"I'm sure I can have the store ready by the holiday, if not sooner."

"You can open for business as soon as you like. Now, as for your pay." She lifted her shoulders and released them. "Like I told you on the phone, you get the apartment upstairs for free and any profits from the books. Afraid that's the best I can do."

"That will be fine," Will assured her. He had money in his savings account and knew he could make it on his own for a while. He was energized by the thought of reviving the bookstore. When Mary Beth came in late August he would have something to show for his efforts.

Penny took him upstairs and pointed out the linens and pots and pans, along with the rickety pie safe in the kitchen that held the dishes. While the apartment was plain, and also in need of a good cleaning, it would be comfortable, certainly all that he would need. The old-fashioned spareness had a humble quality that he liked. He eyed a large wing chair by the window that looked like a good place to read.

After Penny showed him the office and the ledger where her father used to record sales and expenditures, Will walked her to her car. He offered to come and see her father.

"It's tough for him to talk," she said. "Maybe later this summer." She had said good-bye and driven off, relieved, he had guessed, to have this business off her shoulders for the summer.

Will gathered confidence as he set to work in the store this first morning. The yellow clapboard building looked exactly as it had in the advertisement in *Down East*. The first floor was one large room with shelves along the walls and two banks of bookcases in the middle dividing the space into thirds. There was a small office in the back along with the stairwell leading to the basement and second floor. The apartment upstairs replicated the first floor, with a living room and open kitchen in the front.

The bedroom, directly above the office, held a double bed covered with a candlewick spread like the kind he remembered from his grandmother's house in Rhode Island. The bedroom window overlooked the field behind the building, where glimpses of water shone through the trees. The bathroom, remodeled in the sixties, had ugly peach-colored fixtures. A tattered shower curtain surrounded the tub. He would have to replace that before Mary Beth came.

He had finished cleaning the upstairs and unpacked his things. The next step was to tackle the shop itself. Dust was everywhere. Spiderwebs dangled from light fixtures, and dust balls blew about his feet when he opened the windows to let in some fresh air. Judging from the thickness of the dust, he guessed old Mr. Taunton had not cleaned for several summers. Will didn't mind the physical labor.

For the next several days he worked hard cleaning. He liked handling the books. Now and then bits of paper slipped from the pages: grocery receipts, ribbons, postcards. As he dusted and sorted, many of the books having apparently been set randomly on the shelves, he became more interested in the odd things that readers left behind in their books. One morning he found a pocket comb, the stub of a bus ticket, a recipe for "Mother's Johnnycakes," written in pencil on a sheet of oily paper.

There were letters too. Setting these aside with some of his other finds, he was struck by one written on faded blue stationery. The fine ornate script was almost impossible to read, as if the ink had blurred from having been left out in the rain. Only the first few lines were legible.

> *My dearest Ernestine, is there anything comparable to the power of one's first love? Truly, I have been swept away by the intensity of it, the sheer joy of knowing that I am capable of such feeling. Now I long only for your return to Boston.*

The rest of the lines were impossible to decipher.

Will read this last letter a second time and suddenly longed for Mary Beth, his first love. He'd been a "dweeb of the first order" in high school, according to his brother, Rusty, and his love life reflected it. College had been better, but the stars had never lined up for him. He had been flattered by the attentions of several young women, but when the relationships moved to more serious ground he found himself wanting out. They were like the soap bubbles of his childhood, glimmering and lovely for a while and then nothing at all.

Mary Beth was a student in the small discussion section that he led once a week in the spring of her senior year at the university. The course was on the birth of the English novel. Will was in his third year of graduate school and worked as a teaching assistant to cover his tuition. He felt an instant attraction to Mary Beth, as if there were a clear thread pulled taut between them. She was unlike any of the women he'd dated as an undergraduate, silly girls who thought of college as one big party. Mary Beth was smart, an economics major, and she was grateful to be getting a college education. She was not only hardworking and serious, but also beautiful.

At the end of the year she had lingered after class. It seemed that they both had plans for the future. She was starting business school in the fall. He intended to teach while writing his dissertation. He asked her out a few days before her graduation. It had been like diving into the ocean for the first time. He loved her energy and determination. She admired his ambition to become a college professor and was thrilled to be part of his academic world. They went out frequently that summer. His life changed.

Will put the forgotten love letter inside the old book for someone else to discover. The powerful message of those words written by someone long ago lingered inside him. He decided that he'd had enough of cleaning. Dust hung in the air. He put down his rags and decided to take a break. While cool, the day was sparkling. He pulled on a fleece jacket and set off on the path behind the store that led to the water.

Penny had told him that the property behind the bookstore had been given to a land trust so that it could never be developed. Will crossed the field and started along the path into the woods. The wind grew quiet in the protection of the trees, and the ground under him was soft and fragrant from years of decomposed pine needles. Small sticks and pinecones covered the forest floor along with mosses of all kinds, some soft and rounded, others rough and tufted in all shades of greens and gray. Miniature pines along with more fragile saplings managed to grow and thrive under the taller canopy of trees in this small slice of the world. This place felt primeval, untouched by modern time.

The path widened into a clearing, and the sparkling water lay before him. Will climbed across several large granite rocks and arrived at a pebble beach. He sat on a flat boulder and took in the view. Like a small boy he thought, *This is my beach, my rock, where I stake my claim and the adventure begins.* He lay back on the rock. The stone was warm from the sun and felt good on his spine. He closed his eyes.

Summer was usually the time of year when he'd start reading for the fall semester. The best part of teaching English was that it never got old. He liked to choose different books each year for his classes. Mary Beth used to compliment him on how fast he read. On warm evenings she would wander into his study, push aside the book in his lap, and insist he come outside. They would sit on the patio, gazing at the stars, and he would tell her about the novels he planned to teach. This summer he didn't need to prepare for the fall. It was like being unmoored.

Will sat up and blinked into the sun. Mary Beth. The sharp-edged memories of their final argument in Habliston had blurred. He wasn't stuck in the past, like she said. If she could just see him here now, beginning anew. In Maine he felt like a different person. Pressing his hands to his temples, he stared at the horizon. He'd planned to work on his novel that afternoon, but the day was too beautiful. It was the air, the light, the place. His body craved being part of it. He decided to take a run.

❦

Caroline set up her computer on the round table in Lila's living room and set to work. With the bookcases on either side of the front window, the beautifully proportioned mantel above the fireplace, and the ample light that flowed through the tall windows overlooking the back lawn, it was her favorite room in the house. The walls were painted a watery blue, and faded curtains, of the same chintz that covered the chairs and the long sofa that faced the fireplace, hung at the windows. On closer inspection she could see the pattern was of hydrangeas.

So far her only problems with the house appeared to be dust, accumulated clutter, and peeling paint. It was odd how she had so little memory of this house from her visit fifteen years before. Still, it was a long time ago, and that summer she was still in shock from Grace's death, coping with depression, all her senses deadened. On this visit Caroline was recovering from another loss, but now it was as if her senses were heightened, almost as if she'd awakened from a deep sleep to rediscover the world around her.

Caroline seemed particularly aware of her sense of smell. When she'd opened the door yesterday on her arrival, she noticed the stale scent of the house, in sharp contrast to the outdoor freshness of the day. Later she was assaulted by the damp mustiness of a linen closet when she reached in to find sheets for her bed, the faded perfume of some kind of talcum powder in Lila's bedroom; the smell of a cracked, yellowing bar of soap above the kitchen sink, floor wax, old clothing, furniture polish, moist plaster; the pinched scent of ashes in the fireplace, a hint of wood smoke, all the smells that suggested the layers of living, the closely guarded history of an old house.

Caroline liked working in this space, so different from the small nook off the kitchen where she had her writing desk in Chevy Chase. Though this room was large, it felt cozy. Everything about Lila's house was old-fashioned, even antique. The painting of the ship above the fireplace; the cream-colored jug on a side table; the threadbare Oriental rug in the front hall; the dining room furniture, a mismatched assortment all painted a pearly shade of gray; and the stacks of china in the butler's pantry—everything looked as if it had been lovingly chosen. Caroline half expected Aunt Lila to walk in the back door wearing an old cardigan against the wind, a bouquet of lilacs filling her arms. With the pleasant ticking of the clock, the house seemed to have a life of its own.

Caroline had spread her files across the table. Starting a new project was always a challenge, but knowing that she had to do this for the money and that she'd promised the first draft to Vivien by September spurred her on. Vern Simpson was coming tomorrow, and she hoped the noise of his work would not destroy her concentration. The clock in the hall struck eleven. She could taste the acid from her morning coffee and realized she hadn't eaten, so she went to the kitchen and toasted and buttered a slice of bread. She carried it to the back steps and sat outside in the sunshine.

Upon waking earlier that morning, Caroline had felt a sense of peace. Most days her first thoughts were of Harry—the shock of her loss. Today the sadness felt less intense. Being far from home and in such a beautiful spot definitely softened the pain. While she sat eating the toast, the sun warming her shoulders, she reflected on this place. Being here made her feel different. It was also a great relief to be away from Pete. That one emotionally charged night was fading from her memory.

The back steps of Lila's house were protected from the wind. Rounded pine-topped islands dotted the bay. Caroline counted seven. The sky was perfectly clear, and the islands looked enchanting in the sun-drenched water. She could picture Rob taking a kayak out to explore. His strong young arms would cut right through the sparkling water with the paddle. Caroline smiled. Rob was doing better too. She had phoned him at the camp shortly after her arrival in Maine to give him her telephone number. Hollis Moody had reactivated Lila's phone line, as cell phone coverage in East Hope was spotty. Rob told her all about the trip he was going to lead the next day. He barely drew a breath in his excitement, sounding like he used to when he came home from one of his trips out west with his father.

Harry, Richard, and Rob had started taking their "guys only" trips the summer Rob turned eight. Rob had done all the usual boy activities: soccer, baseball, years of tennis lessons. What he truly loved was time in the wilderness. Together the three males had fished, hiked, and taken river rafting trips. When Richard's arthritis had made it difficult for him to travel, Harry had continued the tradition with his son.

Caroline pulled her sweater more tightly around her and gazed at the view. These islands could appear near or far depending on the light. In the fog, they would disappear altogether.

She took another bite of toast. It was nutty and warm. The homemade bread came from a shop in the village. Caroline had been pleased to discover that a local woman brought in fresh baked goods two days a week. Her life now seemed to center so much on food, though meals during her childhood in Connecticut had been ordinary. She grew up eating roasts, chops, grilled steaks along with simple vegetables and always a starch. Her family never ate out except for an occasional meal at the country club, and that was considered a treat. For much of her life, eating had held little interest for her. In college, where the cafeteria food was truly awful, she splurged on pizza, deli sandwiches, and the Chinese takeout that kept her from starving. It was on her honeymoon in Paris with Harry that she discovered the delights of delicious meals.

They'd arrived in the French capital early in the morning after their flight. Numb and exhausted from lack of sleep, they wandered along the Left Bank before stopping at a neighborhood bistro for lunch. Caroline ordered roast chicken, fried potatoes, and salad. That first bite of chicken had tasted moist, flavorful, and different from any other chicken she had ever eaten. She marveled that something so simple could be so good. They had sipped a cool Alsatian white wine and fallen into a deep sleep that afternoon. When she awoke, she'd smiled at the pleasure of having Harry beside her, and thought about their next meal.

Harry, never one to enjoy lengthy trips to museums, had been happy to walk with her all over Paris, enjoying restaurants, bistros, and cafés of all types. Caroline came home from their trip eager to learn how to cook, and, though she didn't know it yet, also pregnant with Rob. In the hurried departure after their wedding, she had forgotten her birth control pills. When she told Harry, he told her not to worry; he would buy condoms. Caught up as she was in the food, wine, and passionate early days of their marriage, they had not been cautious enough. Harry, older and an only child, had been happy about starting a family. Caroline had barely gotten used to being a wife when she learned she was to become a mother.

During the queasy stretch of her pregnancy she forgot about the Parisian meals, and in the early years of Rob's life she couldn't seem to find the time for gourmet cooking. It was only later, after Grace, when Harry encouraged her to go out more, to get involved in something new, that she remembered her wish to learn more about cooking. She'd taken a class at the Cuisine Academy, and there she met Vivien.

Now, warmed by the Maine sun, Caroline finished her toast and walked across the lawn toward the water. The air was crisp. She turned up the collar of her sweater. The bay shimmered before her and the sun was high.

Vivien would be coming in a few weeks, and Caroline had not made much progress on the vegetable cookbook. Similar to the work for the soup book, her job included putting the recipes in order, editing the directions, and providing a few sentences of introduction for each recipe and the different sections of the book. This project appeared longer than the soup book.

Besides that daunting task, every closet in the house needed to be cleaned out. Also, the handle on the downstairs toilet was broken. She hoped that Vern would be able to fix it. The day was starting to slip away, so she turned and walked back to the house, resolved to get to work. A man in the distance jogged along the road with a funny loping stride. He had shaggy light hair and wore a ragged gray T-shirt and dark blue sweatpants. She paused for a moment, but by the time he drew closer she'd climbed the back steps, picked up her plate, and gone inside.

❦

Will drove to Hawley's Hardware on a gray afternoon. He'd come in earlier from his run and had tried to work on his manuscript. The adolescent boy in his novel, Jake, who longed to be on the basketball team in high school, had just been diagnosed with Scheuermann's disease, a spinal condition from too rapid growth. He had grown six inches in a year, and the front side of his spine was growing faster than the back, causing a curvature. The only remedy was a back brace. What good was all that newfound height when he had to wear the brace all day and was forbidden to play sports?

All of this had actually happened to Will when he was fourteen. The experience had been devastating to him at the time. Tending to shyness, not being part of the sports teams, and fearing ridicule from wearing a back brace, he had retreated to his world of books.

Will had been writing for several hours, but couldn't seem to get his bitter feelings of long ago into words: what it was like to fear becoming a monster, ridiculed and mocked by his peers. The computer monitor stared back at him. Why was it that with no classes to teach and plenty of time on his hands he found it impossible to write? He grabbed his car keys and a list from the kitchen counter.

Route 214 wound away from the water toward Route 1 and civilization beyond. Will had been in East Hope for three weeks, and the village was becoming more familiar. He passed Karen's Café, the East Hope post office, and the Congregational church, a beautifully proportioned white clapboard building. He stopped to get gas at the Quik Mart, where he bought the *Boston Globe* on Sundays as well as an occasional six-pack of beer. Then, driving around the next bend, he noticed that the Canberry Store had a new sign advertising "delicious cooking and wicked neat gifts." They were getting ready for the influx of summer people. More out-of-state license plates were coming through town, and already several customers had come into the bookstore and browsed. He'd sold a half dozen mystery novels to a carload of women who were on a trip antiquing up the coast, or "Down East," as he'd learned to say.

"Let me know if I can help you with anything." The man behind the counter at Hawley's Hardware wore a brown apron. A freshly sharpened pencil was perched behind his fleshy ear.

Will raised the pot of geraniums that he'd picked out from the display on the store's front porch. "Mind if I set this down here?"

"Not at all." The clerk, who appeared to be in his early sixties, wore a friendly expression, and looked like he was inclined to talk. Will knew the type. He could still recall the low din of male voices from his father's hardware store. The men who'd helped his father knew everything that went on in town and had the uncanny ability to picture how future events would unfold. He set the flowers down on the counter next to a display of key rings and pocket-size flashlights.

"You from away?" the clerk asked.

Will explained that he would be running Taunton's Used Books for the summer.

The clerk leaned on the counter. "A real shame about George. Can't talk, and Penny says he can't even read these days. Still, maybe he'll get better."

"I certainly hope so," Will said, picking up a basket. "I'll just look around," he added, and started down the first aisle to pick out lightbulbs. He also needed a washer for the faucet in the kitchen sink.

This store was laid out very much like his dad's old store, with the plumbing supplies set out on the back wall. Will used to help at the store after school, most often doing boring jobs: filling endless tiny boxes with screws and nails, putting on price stickers, dusting the shelves. Because of his back he wasn't able to do heavier jobs, like unloading the bags of mulch in spring or the loads of salt for icy walks in winter. Rusty did that. Still, his dad was proud of him, telling his buddies how Will had made the honor roll once again, how he'd gotten scholarship money for the university.

Walking down these crowded aisles of merchandise brought it all back. There weren't many small hardware stores left. Dad had sold out to a True Value chain, and the place had gone out of business two years later, when one of the mega home stores opened out on the highway.

Will added bug repellent to his basket. The front door squeaked open and banged shut. A woman with red hair entered the store and exchanged greetings with the clerk at the cash register. She wore loose khaki trousers and a heavy blue sweater and had the careless appearance of someone unaware of her own good looks. She spoke to the clerk, and a short while later they walked toward plumbing, where he pulled down a package of Teflon tape.

"First, unscrew the showerhead." He spoke slowly and patiently, as if convinced someone so feminine could barely grasp his directions. "Then wrap a piece of this—say, four or five inches long—tightly around the edge."

"You mean the showerhead itself or the part that comes out of the wall?" She had a calm, thoughtful voice. She didn't sound like she was from around East Hope either. Like him, she must be from "away."

In a few minutes Will joined her at the counter to pay.

"Oh, I forgot seeds," she said, and turned to Will. "You go ahead." In that brief glance he noticed that she had one blue eye and one green. It made him want to examine them again to check whether he'd seen correctly. "I'm looking for nasturtiums," she explained.

"We've got them." The clerk nodded, as if pleased he could oblige. "Seeds are in the other room, door on the left."

She walked to the back. Will unloaded onto the counter the lightbulbs from his basket, along with the bug repellent, the washers, more garbage bags, a plastic shower curtain, and some cleaning products. He caught a glimpse of the red hair at the far end of the aisle and thought again of her eyes.

"That'll be twenty-eight forty-two." The clerk raised his eyebrows at Will as if he too appreciated a good-looking woman. Will imagined he expected some kind of comment, a remark acknowledging their mutual interest. He hurriedly reached for his billfold.

6

Will had a chance to study those unusual eyes a few days later. It was the first truly warm day, and by the calendar it was now officially summer. Everyone in the village was talking about the July Fourth weekend and the influx of tourists it would surely bring. There were tubs of hot red geraniums placed along the main street, and the ubiquitous red, white, and blue bunting hanging above the windows of the town hall billowed in the breeze. Young people had begun to linger outside Berger's Ice Cream late in the afternoons and into evening.

Will had opened the shop ahead of schedule. Eager for more book buyers, he hoped the good weather would hold. He sat at his desk upstairs, keeping an ear open for customers. He'd mopped the floor of the shop that morning, and he'd planted his own red geraniums in a clay pot that he'd found in the basement. They were arranged on the large granite step by the front door.

He was forcing himself to keep to a morning schedule for writing, allowing himself to stop only for customers, but the work was not going well. He kept thinking that Jake was not the right name for this character. It was too close to *jock*.

Would adding a sex scene now give the story the oomph it needed? Of course, there had been no sex scene for him in the tenth grade. He tried to picture Jake making out with one of the hot young debaters. The awful memory of Jennifer Whitely began to slow his already lagging momentum.

"Anyone here?" The female voice below sounded familiar. He shoved back his chair and went to the stairs. When he reached the bottom he saw a woman standing tentatively by the door. It was the woman he'd seen last week at the hardware store.

"Yes. Hello." His words, tumbling out, surprised him, and he realized he hadn't spoken aloud all day.

"I wasn't sure if you were open," she said.

"Sorry. Forgot to put the flag out." He reached for the OPEN flag that stood neatly coiled behind the door. "You looking for anything in particular?"

She gazed around vaguely, as if trying to decide what she wanted. "No, I was out walking. They're painting my place. The fumes are terrible." She drew her hand to her nose as if still bothered by the pungent smell.

"You live near here?" Will studied her face. The unusual eyes. The red hair.

"Across the bay. You can see the house from here." She stepped over to the front window, raised her arm, and pointed. "It belonged to my husband's great-aunt. She died last year." Her trousers and cardigan sweater looked like the same ones she'd worn when he saw her at the hardware store, except now the sweater was unbuttoned. She wore a pink T-shirt underneath. Her hair was pulled back in a ponytail, but a fine haze of loose curls framed her face.

"The white house on the point?"

She nodded. Taller than Mary Beth but slight, this woman wasn't conventionally pretty, but rather old-fashioned looking, with a long, delicate nose. Her mouth was small, but full. In different clothes she could have been an Edith Wharton character, or maybe a gentle cousin in a Henry James novel.

"I run by there most mornings," he explained. "You've got terrific views of the islands." He was pleased that he knew her house.

"Oh, yes," she said. "You're the runner. I've seen you go by." She smiled. Her freckled skin made her look girlish, younger than she probably was.

"Not many runners around here," he said. He felt strangely embarrassed that he'd been observed.

"Not many people at all. They say after the Fourth it will get busy."

"You're new to the area?" he asked.

"I got here at the beginning of the month." She turned around, the light behind her. "I'm having work done on the house. I'm getting it ready to sell. What about you?"

"Well, I . . ." He hesitated, feeling foolish, still holding the flag. He wasn't sure what, if anything, of his story he wanted to tell: that he had lost his job, that he was feuding with his wife. "Excuse me a minute." He stepped out to the stoop, snapped open the flag, and set it in the holder beside the door.

She hadn't moved when he went back in. She said, "I'm assuming you're 'from away,' as they say around here."

"Yeah. I'm here for the summer. I'm running the business for Mr. Taunton. He's the owner. He's recovering from a stroke." Will touched the top of the counter. "It's taken a few weeks to clean it up." He raked his hair back off his face.

"It smells like a bookstore should," she said.

"I'll be getting more books throughout the season." Will had soon figured out that to make any money he would have to add to the stock. He wanted to add a shelf of new fiction too. The funds for this would have to come out of his own pocket. "Do you like to read?" What a stupid question. Why else would she have come into a bookstore?

"I'm interested in old cookbooks."

She didn't look like a cookbook sort. He would have thought her a buyer of gardening books (no nail polish, the old clothes), maybe poetry. He'd already had a few mystery readers. They always knew what they were looking for: the author who did the cat mysteries, the old-lady-detective genres, the series that took place in Venice. This woman seemed unhurried.

"I think I have some over here," he said. She followed him to the nonfiction. He got down awkwardly on his knees. He'd remembered shelving a few cookbooks below the art books. There were perhaps a dozen. "Yes. Right here." He pointed to the bottom shelf and straightened up. She squatted below him and studied the shelf.

"This looks interesting." She took a mustard-colored hardback into her hands and flipped through the pages.

Will wanted to linger near her, but stepped away, thinking she would prefer browsing on her own. "Take your time, and feel free to look around." He went back behind the counter near the door and tried to look as if he had something to do. From where he sat he could see the top of her bent head and the red hair. He remembered his idea to get a radio or small CD player to have in the store, something to fill the silence. He leafed through last Sunday's *Boston Globe*.

"I'll take this one." She handed him a book: *The Maine Farm Kitchen.*

"So, you like old recipes?" He looked at the flyleaf: *$2,* written in pencil. Will had decided not to change any of the prices already written in Mr. Taunton's books. Pricing was still something he was trying to figure out. So many things to consider: condition, rarity, popularity of subject.

"I've just discovered them. There's a whole shelf of old cookbooks left in the house." She reached into the pocket of her sweater and looked up at him. One eye had a greenish tinge, definitely a different color from the other. "I don't have any money with me," she said.

"That's okay. You can pay me later."

"Sorry. Silly of me. I guess I didn't think I'd need it."

"Please. It's not a problem." He handed her the book and a sales receipt. "I'll collect it one day when I run by."

"That's so nice of you." She accepted the book and leafed through it, as though still intrigued by what she'd seen earlier. Pale hands, narrow wrists, no wedding ring, he noticed. In fact, she wore no jewelry at all. Not even a watch. "Listen to this." She read,

" 'Jolly Boys, Spider Corn Bread, and Rocks.' That last one's a cookie recipe." She laughed.

"Sounds delicious."

"Wait. How about 'Apple Puffets'?"

"The names are certainly poetic," he said.

"I'm sorry." Her face grew serious again. "I'm taking up too much of your time." She closed the book.

"No. Not at all." He hoped he hadn't sounded unfriendly. "You know, people leave odd things behind in books. I found a recipe the other day. The paper was greasy. Like something had been spilled on it."

"Really?" She looked at him with interest. "Cookbooks reveal a lot." She tilted her head, then glanced at the clock above the door. It was a large-faced clock, like the ones he remembered from his elementary school classrooms. "I need to go. Vern—he's my carpenter—wanted to talk to me before he goes to the lumberyard at noon." She frowned, deepening a line between her eyebrows. "The list of repairs on my house seems to get longer every day."

"Stop by again," Will said. "I'll be on the lookout for more cookbooks."

"Thanks." She started for the door, then turned back. "I'm Caroline, by the way. Caroline Waverly."

"Like the town in Rhode Island." He felt like a jerk. "That's where I'm from." She appeared to be waiting for something more. It dawned on him. "Will Harmon."

"Glad to meet you, Will." She walked out the door. "I like your geraniums," she called back.

He waited a moment and went to the window. She carried the book under one arm and followed the road toward the harbor. He glanced at her house across the bay. It stood out clean and sharp in the summer sun.

❦

Caroline awoke certain that something was wrong. Exhausted from the physical labor of cleaning out another room, she'd fallen into a deep sleep before ten. Lila, a frugal New Englander, had carefully kept everything, and then grown too old to sort things out. Caroline had cleaned out two more closets that afternoon and had filled several huge garbage bags that Vern said he'd take to the dump. Fortunately, the work was satisfying. As she emptied cupboards and rearranged some of the china on the shelves, the house began to feel more her own.

It must be the middle of the night now. Her mouth was dry and the faintly queasy feeling had returned. The curtains by the open window were still. The wind had dropped. Perhaps it was the silence itself that had awakened her.

At home in Washington there was always a faint roar, the persistent hum of city life. At Lila's house she'd often go to sleep listening to the wind, sometimes the clanging of the sailboat masts in the harbor, even the faint sound of the waves on the other side of the point. The sounds depended on which way the wind was blowing. She didn't hear the familiar ticking of the front hall clock. Of course, she'd forgotten to wind it. She pictured Mr. Moody's gnarled hands and promised herself she would do it first thing in the morning.

A moment later something black whooshed across the room. *My God.* Had a bird flown in? All the screens had been taken down for painting and stacked against the house by the kitchen door. *Damn.* She didn't move. She heard it again, a quick movement sounding like the intake of breath. It must be a bat. Drawing the covers over her head, she felt her heart pound. Vern would have to get the screens back up tomorrow. At least the screens in her bedroom. Her legs trembled. She brought her clenched fists to her mouth, feeling totally alone.

Harry would have told her not to worry. He would have gone downstairs to get a broom, a tennis racket, something. Years ago, the first summer in their house in Chevy Chase, a bat had come down the chimney, soared through the living room, and landed on the armoire in the hall. Harry was as inexperienced as she was in regard to wild things, but he had bravely corralled the bat toward the front door and eventually it had flown out.

She remembered that incident vividly. Rob was just a toddler. Harry had teased her for cowering in the kitchen. They had laughed together when she had called him her hero. She could still recall the feeling of relief that Harry had been home. It must have been a Saturday or Sunday morning. She'd been pregnant with Grace and coping with morning sickness.

Morning sickness. Now, breathing heavily under the covers in the still night, she thought of it. The uneasy feeling of saliva rising onto her tongue and the unpleasant possibility of being sick. When had she started to feel that way? Could she be pregnant? By Pete? *Oh, my God.* She was too old. Her body grew rigid.

All those years after Grace she had never become pregnant again. Little Grace, born with a hole in her heart, a rare abnormality, discovered when it was too late. Then the months of depression. At first Harry had remained armored in silence and Caroline had said nothing. She didn't want to risk losing a baby again, go through that kind of loss. Neither spoke of it, and only their happiness with Rob made life bearable.

Eventually, when Caroline hadn't conceived, Harry suggested that they see a doctor. They were told that there was nothing physically wrong and to keep trying. By then Caroline had started writing the family restaurant reviews for the newspaper, was volunteering in Rob's school, and worked in her garden. Their lives had taken on a comfortable rhythm, and she thought that she had recovered from losing Grace. Caroline remembered when Harry had suggested adoption.

"We're just not meant to have another child," she'd argued.

"I've found out about an adoption agency," he'd said.

"I don't want to adopt." She'd been adamant. "I believe in fate. If we don't get pregnant, that's what's meant to be." Caroline had also worried that if they entered into the adoption process it would bring back memories of that terrible time after Grace died and trigger another depression. By then she was enjoying her work. Her life with Harry and Rob seemed complete.

Now, as she lay in the darkness, her thoughts raced. *Oh, God.* Could she be pregnant? Surely it was impossible. She forced herself to remember. She grew hot under the covers and began to perspire, but was too afraid to pull down the blanket for fear of the bat. Her periods had been erratic, late even. She couldn't remember the last one.

She had successfully put the memory of the night with Pete out of her mind. It had been six, maybe seven weeks ago. After that one tense phone conversation after the dinner party, his calls had stopped. When Rob had told her of his plan to go out west, she had nearly called Pete to seek comfort. It would have been so easy to open that door. Instead she had sent a note to his office telling him about the house in Maine and her plans for the summer in case anything came up having to do with Harry's estate. Now, curled up in this bed so far from home, Caroline grew hotter still. She felt as if she were suffocating.

She slowly lowered the covers from her face. Nothing moved. The bat must have flown out. She waited. Barely allowing herself to breathe, she counted again. How many weeks had it been? Sleep would be impossible now.

❦

Will rounded the bend and began the gradual climb toward the house on the point. It was the final week in June and the first hot day of the summer. He'd grown used to cool, misty mornings, and today he was too warm in the navy sweatpants he'd pulled on out of habit. He should have been wearing shorts. His T-shirt stuck to his back. He hadn't thought it ever got this hot in Maine.

He had spoken to Mary Beth on the phone last night. She was in New York, back from Japan. He told her about Taunton's, how he'd reorganized the shop, how he'd worked out a business plan, and how, by adding new titles, and by investing some of his own money, he could see making a profit. Her reaction had been cool and her tone unenthusiastic. When he suggested she fly to Bangor for the July Fourth weekend, her answer was no. She explained that she needed the time in the office to get caught up.

Sitting alone in the apartment above the bookstore, Will had begun to doubt the wisdom of leaving for the summer. Mary Beth had let him down, but was that enough of a reason to bail out for the summer? Maybe his leaving would drive them further apart. He had slept fitfully, restless in the first night without a breeze.

Now the stark whiteness of what he now knew to be Caroline's house shone like a beacon. He focused on that destination and not the gray strip of pavement beneath his feet. When he awoke early that day he'd remembered the grease-stained recipe he'd told her about, and decided to take it to her. It was in his back pocket.

Will had been running off and on since high school. He was good at it. It was the only sport he'd been allowed with his back problem. Running seemed to clear his head, though lately his thoughts had been stuck in the last miserable months in Habliston. As his feet pounded along the quiet roads around East Hope, the dreadful memories would flood back: the encounter with Jennifer Whitely, the meeting with Jack, his letter of resignation, having to give up the work that he loved. And Mary Beth, who had shown so little sympathy, who acted as if she couldn't have cared less.

Despite the heat and his fatigue from a bad night, he ran faster as he approached the hill. Within minutes his indignation turned back into doubt. Mary Beth had probably been right. A lawsuit would have cost a lot. They might have lost all their savings. And if his situation had been made public, it could have hurt his reputation, making it even more difficult to find another job. He probably should have moved to New York with Mary Beth right away and looked for whatever lousy adjunct position he could find. Their commuter marriage had been a mistake. He should have given up his job at Habliston long before the false accusation. In his heart he knew that he hadn't paid enough attention to their marriage.

There had been many good times with Mary Beth. In the early

fall they used to sit on the back steps of their house in Habliston and sip wine together. At that time of year it grew dark by six and there was a hint of cooler weather to come. Still, they clung to the last bits of summer, and he made her laugh with descriptions of nervous freshmen in his classes and the long-winded older faculty members who held forth at the meetings that marked the beginning of the semester. In those days she seemed to hang on his every word. Once her travel schedule picked up they had fewer talks. He missed moments like that, the intimate mixing of their voices in the dark.

Now, reaching the crest of the hill, he slowed to a walk, not wanting to appear at Caroline's door panting and in a full sweat. At least he had this summer in East Hope—the books, the quiet, a chance to think things over in this beautiful place. The sky was a brilliant blue and unmarred by clouds. Just before he reached the house, he stopped and twisted his back to the right and then left. If he stretched gently, his back muscles would stay loose and leave him alone. A red truck with Maine plates was parked on the gravel driveway. An older, dark gray station wagon was pulled up closer to the garage, a separate barnlike building away from the house.

Will walked to the front door and knocked. He felt the sting of a mosquito and slapped at his neck. Maine was famous for its black-fly season—more troublesome inland, he'd been told—but the mosquitoes had come out with the hotter weather. He raised the old brass knocker again and waited. After a few moments he left the steps and wandered along the side of the house. This side looked freshly painted. Squinting in the sunlight, he moved into the shadow and around the building toward the sound of voices.

Caroline and an old man were squatting and studying something under the porch.

"Hello, there," Will said.

Caroline stood and appeared surprised to see him. She wore a T-shirt, baggy shorts, and sneakers. Her legs were freckled. "Oh, hi. I didn't know anyone was here." She shaded her eyes and studied him. "I see you're out for your run." The older man beside her staggered to his feet and peered at Will through thick glasses that looked like they could use a good cleaning. "This is Vern Simpson." She nodded in the direction of the old man clutching a screwdriver. She introduced Will and explained, "Will is managing Taunton's Used Books this summer."

"That a fact? Good to meet ya," Vern said. "Hope the town of East Hope is treating you well." He put out his hand.

"Fine, thanks," Will replied automatically, and shook hands. Vern's grip was strong. Despite thinning white hair and a weathered face, Vern looked like the kind of man who, like the bark on a tree, grew thicker and tougher with time. Vern stood back to better size up Will and reached into his pocket for a tired-looking handkerchief. He proceeded to wipe his glasses, as if privy to Will's earlier thoughts.

"Vern is giving me more bad news," Caroline said. Maybe that explained her worried expression. She looked paler this morning, and her eyes had faint circles beneath them. "He very kindly doles out only as much as I can take at a time." She laughed gamely, trying to be a good sport.

"Porch he'ah," Vern said in his strong Maine twang, "completely rotted out." He poked the screwdriver into one of the posts. The sharp metal plunged into the wood without resistance, as if it were made of cardboard. "You'd be better off removing the whole thing and rebuilding from scratch."

"A whole new porch?" She looked close to tears. "What will that cost?"

Vern put his handkerchief away and pulled a small notebook and short pencil from his shirt pocket. "Maybe we can get away with just replacing the end supports. I'll take some measurements and talk to the guys at Bob's Lumber. Bobby's an old friend of mine. I'll get you a good price." He started around the porch.

"I'm sorry," Caroline said, and turned to Will. "I remember now. I owe you for the book."

"That's not why I came." He reached in his pocket. "I thought you might enjoy seeing this. I found it in one of the books."

"Oh, yes. The recipe." She took the yellowed sheet and bent to study the old-fashioned writing. " 'Mother's Johnnycakes.' " She smiled and looked relieved to put her mind on something else. Her hands were dirty, and smudges of mud edged her T-shirt. Wisps of hair clung to her neck in the humidity. She looked up at Will. "Please come in and have some lemonade."

"I don't want to bother you."

"It's no bother. I was going to stop anyway. I've been weeding. I'm trying to clear out under the lilacs by the barn." She called over to Vern, who was busy measuring the height of the porch supports. "Vern, a glass of lemonade?"

"Maybe later, thanks." He copied numbers onto his pad.

Will went with Caroline toward the house. "It looks like you have a lot of property."

"I'll say."

They went up the back steps and entered the hall that ran the depth of the house. He followed her to the kitchen. It was surprisingly cool. The ceiling was high and a breeze blew in off the water. Caroline bent and pushed the window open higher.

"Please sit down." She gestured toward a round pine table in the center of the room.

Will sat in one of the wicker chairs surrounding the table. The kitchen reminded him of his grandmother's house in Rhode Island. His parents had sold it after her death, and he remembered his mother complaining bitterly when the new owners tore it down and built an enormous tract mansion in its place.

"This is a neat old kitchen," he said. "Does that stove still work?" He looked toward the gas range that stood on legs.

"Surprisingly well," Caroline said.

On the wall behind him were shelves brimming with the cookbooks she had told him about. Caroline opened an antiquated-looking refrigerator and lifted out a glass pitcher. She set two glasses on the table and poured. "This is one of Lila's recipes. My husband's great-aunt who owned the house," she reminded him. "The green specks in it are mint."

"Thanks." Will lifted his glass, and the lemonade slipped down his throat like a magic elixir. "This is delicious."

"Vern and his nephew, Tim, can't seem to get enough of it."

"I can see why." He took another drink. "What's the secret?"

Caroline smiled, and her worried expression evaporated again. "You use something called ReaLemon juice. It comes in a bottle. You mix that with a sugar-and-water syrup. Lila wrote a note on the recipe that she serves it in a punch bowl for parties and adds blueberries on festive occasions."

She reached for a black loose-leaf notebook on the other side of the table. It looked like it held years and years of collected recipes. She leafed through the pages. Some of the recipes appeared to be written in a fragile-looking hand. Other pages were typewritten on the kind of onionskin paper that you didn't see much anymore. "I feel like Lila's with me sometimes," she said. "It's almost like she's leaning over my shoulder offering bits of wisdom as well as cooking advice."

"She certainly had a lot of cookbooks," he said.

"Some people read them like novels. I'm afraid I'm guilty of that." She closed the black binder gently and studied the humble scrap of paper he'd brought to her. "This looks good."

"I assume johnnycakes are like pancakes," he said.

"They're a cornmeal pancake. We think of them now as breakfast, but in the early days in New England they would be served with the midday meal or even supper. I think they were popular in Rhode Island. Isn't that where you're from?"

Will was glad she remembered, and told her about his grandmother's house and his childhood spent near the ocean. Caroline sipped her lemonade and listened. A swath of sun fell onto the cheerful red-and-white linoleum floor. She told him about the cookbook she was working on. Will felt an almost forgotten contentment come over him. She had said the house belonged to her husband's aunt. Where was her husband now? A clock in another room struck numerous bongs. He started to apologize for staying too long.

"Nonsense," she said. "I've enjoyed the interruption." She slipped the recipe he'd given her into the notebook and stood. "I'll get the money for the book. Then I'd better check on Vern. Tim went to buy more paint. This house seems to soak it up." Her frown returned. "Have some more lemonade. I'll be right back."

Caroline left him alone in the kitchen. Will liked the calm feeling of this house. He listened to the ticking of the clock from the hall, as steady and regular as a heartbeat.

That evening Caroline sat on the lawn in an Adirondack chair to watch the sunset. The paint on the chair, like everything else exposed to the Maine air, was peeling. She imagined dollar signs, the tally for more paint climbing still higher. Thank God for Vern. She'd explained her goal of doing all she could for the house within her limited budget. He'd quoted his mother's favorite verse:

Eat it up,
Wear it out,
Make it do,
Or go without.

With Vern, thrift would be the watchword.

It was nearly seven. The air had cooled. Tim had dragged the ladders back beside the garage after reinstalling the second-story screens. There would be no more bats in the night. She rested her head on the back of the chair. The day hadn't been that bad after all. She thought of Will Harmon arriving at her door with the recipe he'd found in a book. Why on earth had she invited him in? Was she that hungry for company? There was something endearing about him, with his mop of pale hair and disheveled appearance.

She could imagine him as a boy, his mother telling him that he needed to eat more, not to slouch, and to tuck in his shirt. He had kind eyes, deeply set, a soft hazel. There was a sensitivity about him. Though initially he had seemed shy, he had become more at ease with her as he shared memories of his childhood living near the ocean.

The sky went from a brilliant pink to a deeper violet, announcing the final moments of daylight. There was so much beauty here: the spare, clean lines of Lila's clapboard house, the gentle slope of the green lawn, the water, alive and ever changing from smooth to a wild chop, an array of blues, churning greens, the dramatic black in the dark of night. This part of the world was breathtaking. Rob would love it. Momentarily startled, she realized she hadn't thought of her son, who was usually so present in her mind, at all that day.

In the afternoon she had driven to the Super Drug, four towns away, and furtively purchased a pregnancy test like a fearful teenager. The box, neatly wrapped in cellophane, showed a young couple on it. The man had his arms around the woman, and she looked chastely down at a pink rose in her hand. The test was waiting for Caroline upstairs. The directions recommended using it first thing in the morning. She breathed in the stillness, the momentary peace. If only she could stop time. She rested her gaze on the bay and waited for the last glimmer of light. She drew her hand across her belly. It was taut and flat. And yet it might harbor life.

7

A few minutes before five, two women entered the bookstore, the creak of the screen door followed by a bang announcing their arrival. Will had been about to bring in his OPEN flag before locking up for the night. It was the last day of June. Business had begun to pick up. He was tired, having taken his usual run that morning and stayed busy with customers for most of the day. There had been no time to write.

"Glad to see that this place has reopened," said the taller of the two women. She had the weathered tan of someone who'd spent the winter in the sun. Older, though lean and fit, she might be a tennis player, he guessed.

"Do you carry new books?" the shorter woman asked. She, too, had a patrician voice, confirming his suspicion that these were some of the summer residents, returning for the season. They both looked dressed for a cocktail party, one in a silky T-shirt and pastel flowered slacks, and the other in a linen dress and wearing large gold earrings.

"All used for now," he explained. "I've ordered new titles. There's some fairly recent fiction over here." He directed them toward the center shelves. These women made him feel as if used books were undesirable, second-class. He thought of Rusty, who owned three car dealerships in West Palm Beach. The few used cars that he sold he referred to as "previously owned." Will was glad he'd decided to add new books to his inventory.

The women spoke in quiet voices, commenting on titles and authors as they wandered around the shop. Will returned behind his desk. He picked up the trade publication he'd been leafing through when they came in, though he kept half an eye on the women, trying to think of something else that might interest them. "If you like mysteries," he called over to them, "they're on the far wall."

The smaller woman gave him a brief glance of acknowledgment and shook her head to indicate that she did not. Eventually she came up to the counter carrying a paperback copy of *Anna Karenina*. She spoke to her friend, who joined her empty-handed. "We're doing this for our book group in September. Might as well get a cheap copy."

Will rang up the sale, wondering how this lady and her friends would "do" Tolstoy. He kept these thoughts to himself.

"You've heard of Holden Fox?" the tall tennis player asked.

"Of course, who hasn't?" her friend replied. "His last novel is still on the bestseller list."

"He's staying with the Morgans in August. I've heard they're giving a big party for him at the yacht club."

Will thought of the feeble beginning of the novel that awaited him upstairs. The more he worked on it, the less he warmed to the task. He had loved writing essays for academic publications. The job of researching, analyzing, and studying literary texts had been a pleasure. Writing a novel was entirely different. He put the paperback copy of Tolstoy in a bag and handed over the change.

"You're new here, aren't you?" the taller woman asked. Will had surmised from their conversation that she was the summer resident, the shorter woman her houseguest.

"I moved here from Pennsylvania," he answered, trying to remain polite while drawing an end to her questions.

"Philadelphia?" she asked.

Will shook his head. "I lived in Habliston, west of Philadelphia," he said.

"Where that little college is?" She put her wallet back inside her basket handbag and turned to her friend. "I think the Hartleys' daughter goes there."

Before this conversation went any further the houseguest unknowingly came to his rescue. "Shouldn't we be going, Marion?"

"You're right," she said. "Eddie and the girls are going to wonder where we are." Marion offered a friendly smile. "Have a fun evening," she said. The screen door banged behind them.

Fun, he thought. When was the last time he'd thought about having fun? All month he had thrown himself into setting up the store. He hadn't thought about fun in even the remotest connotation, though he had discovered certain pleasures: sitting on the front step of Taunton's Used Books after a good long run, his demons in momentary remission; a quiet stroll through the woods to his private beach to climb on his rock, his thinking place where the water lapped or crashed at his feet, depending on the weather; reading in his chair, the windows open, enjoying the generous smell of summer flavored with ocean air, pine woods, and freshly mowed fields.

There was also the satisfaction he took in running the store. He liked the regular routine, visiting with the customers and learning about the book collectors who came through the store on their travels up the coast. He enjoyed the simple pleasure of spending his day with books. Time seemed to slow to a summer pace.

The store was silent now. He pictured the two women joining friends, arriving at their party. The social part of his life had stopped. For him it would be another night alone. He thought of Mary Beth in New York and suddenly wanted to hear her voice. Maybe he could talk her into coming up for the long weekend. The last time they spoke she had agreed to come once in August and also for their anniversary in early September. That promised visit was a long time from now. Will brought in the flag, locked the door to the shop, and went up to the apartment. He poured a glass of wine, carried it to his chair, and dialed Mary Beth's home number.

A man answered. For a moment Will wondered if he had misdialed. "I'm calling for Mary Beth Harmon," he said.

"Just a minute."

Will heard voices in the background and the man who had answered saying, "M.B., it's for you." *Who the hell? M.B.?*

"Hello," she said, her voice pitched a level higher than usual.

"What's going on?"

"Will, it's you."

The voices in the background faded. He imagined her carrying the phone into the bedroom. He'd seen the apartment for all of twenty minutes and had trouble picturing it. He forced aside his irritation at finding her with friends and told her he'd been thinking of her, that he hoped she'd reconsider and come up for the Fourth.

"I told you I need to stay in the city," she said quickly. "I have to work."

"It doesn't sound like you're working. Who answered the phone?" His surprise was giving way to anger.

"Drew. He came east for some meetings. He's here with friends from the office. Taking us all out to dinner."

"That doesn't sound like work," he said.

"Don't sound so testy. We have to eat."

Will didn't know what to say. His hopes of having her here for the weekend disappeared.

"Remember," she said, "it was your decision to spend the summer up there—don't complain to me."

"I'm not complaining. I was hoping I could change your mind, that's all. I've been thinking. We need to talk."

Her voice softened. "I'll call you later. I promise." She hung up before he could reply.

Will remained in the chair by the window and finished his wine. He stayed inside all evening. He picked up the book he'd been reading, *We Took to the Woods* by Louise Dickinson Rich, a wonderful account of a woman who lived with her family in the

Maine wilderness in the 1940s, but after an hour or so he could no longer concentrate. After flipping through the stations on the small television in the bedroom, he tried reading again. Without cable, television reception was impossible. Mary Beth didn't call. At eleven he tried her again. The answering machine clicked on. The sound of an electronic recorded message made him furious. He slammed down the phone. He decided to go outside and get some air.

❦

Caroline began the first of July with her head above the white porcelain bowl of Aunt Lila's toilet. The off-and-on queasy feeling had become full-blown morning sickness. She reflected on the whole ironic series of events. Of course she was pregnant. The stick inside the box with the rose on the cover had left no doubt. Ludicrous, impossible, miraculous, and a plain fact.

She bent again to another wave of nausea. Within a few minutes she felt as if her stomach were inside out, and her forehead was covered with a cold sheen of perspiration. She opened the tap, waited for the water to become hot, and splashed the stream of warmth onto her face. It was just after five. The sky was lightening despite a damp fog curling in through the open windows. Caroline crawled back into bed and tried to relax into sleep.

She worked on breathing calmly, taking slow, even breaths, gathering her thoughts, willing herself to think clearly. She could solve this problem. All spring she had been solving problems: deciphering Harry's financial mess, working out some sort of budget on the little money that was left, sorting and disposing of Harry's effects, sending certain books and mementos on to old friends and family, and reaching out to Rob with phone calls, letters, and care packages. She had done all of this while editing the soup book for Vivien and keeping up with the regular business of life. Now, all by herself in Maine, she felt suddenly cold right through to her bones. She shifted onto her back, pulled the covers up under her chin, and looked at the ceiling.

Aunt Lila's room was the largest and on the southeast corner of the house. It was the sunniest room and caught the breeze off the water. Caroline had taken to sleeping in the very middle of the bed, and lying here, she tried to imagine Aunt Lila in her later years, alone in this same bed, and staring at this very ceiling with its feathery cracks like a miniature road map.

Perhaps Lila had had mornings like this, lying still in the quiet, waiting for the day to begin. Or lying alone in the long winter nights with the wind whipping against the house. Caroline wondered what her worries had been. Harry had not told her much about Lila, only that she had inherited the house from Francis, her much older husband.

Lila had been so kind to her the one summer that she had spent at the house in East Hope. It was the only time she had been able to talk about Grace's death. Caroline had been so consumed with her own loss that she had never thought to ask Lila about her life and what it was like living in this house. Caroline regretted that now.

When Grace was born with a defective heart, Caroline had read everything she could about children's heart problems, hoping to discover what had caused it. Could she have eaten better, taken more vitamins? Had she exercised too much or not been active enough? Was it an inherited problem? Could another child by her and Harry be born with the same ailment? If so, how likely was that? She knew that more could go wrong among older mothers—greater genetic risks, possible developmental problems, more of a chance of Down syndrome. Thinking of all this now made Caroline decide that from a physical standpoint alone, it would be a mistake to have this baby. She was under seven weeks pregnant, or was it eight? If she were to end the pregnancy, she would need to act quickly.

Caroline dozed. When she looked at the clock on her bedside table it was almost eight. Vern was due to arrive to finish the outside painting, and she remembered that she had invited Hollis for a drink that evening. She had planned to make a vegetable tart for the cookbook she was editing. The directions, still unclear, needed to be rewritten. The sun was trying to break through the fog, a familiar condition early in the day, and she had been told that there would be less fog in August, though she would probably be gone by then. Caroline pulled on her jeans. She had to tug to close them. Could they already be tight? She pulled on a white T-shirt, leaving it untucked, along with a beige cardigan that she had saved from Lila's things. The sweater was soft and comfortable, and Caroline found herself reaching for it more and more often these days. Her nicer clothes from Washington—linen pants, silk shirts, tailored blazers—stayed in her closet. She preferred her old khaki shorts, T-shirts, jeans, and, when it got cool, Lila's wool sweaters. It was amazing how few things she actually needed, living this quiet life.

She had tea, nibbled on some toast, which made her feel better, and started the new recipe. The vegetable tart required several cups of chopped spinach, along with basil and chives. After cracking eggs into a big ironstone bowl, she added a cup of cream and two cups of grated Gruyère cheese. Lila's kitchen did not have the usual modern kitchen gadgets that she was used to. There was no blender, no electric mixer, no juicer or food processor. If she were ever to stay on here and work seriously on food, she would have to bring some of her equipment up from Washington.

Lila had well-sharpened knives, in Caroline's mind the most essential tools for a good cook, and she loved the way time slowed as she diced and chopped on the big board next to the sink. She cut fresh basil into ribbons, and the sweet green smell conveyed the essence of a summer morning. Since coming to Maine and living in the simple old house, Caroline had discovered the many pleasures of doing things by hand. Without the noise of the machines, she could still hear the birds chirping at the feeder in the yard, the rustle of leaves when the wind picked up, and Vern's cheerful whistling as he went about his chores. She put down the knife, wiped her hands on a towel, and went out to the herb garden for the chives.

The sun was warm now. She kicked aside her shoes and felt the tickle of the soft grass beneath her feet. Lila had planted the herb garden just outside the back door in the shelter of the porch. On one side of the steps the mint had completely taken over. On the other side, three large clumps of chives with spiky purple blossoms stood at attention. Caroline cut some chives for the tart and picked a handful of the flowers to put in a vase for the table. The parsley that she had planted just after she arrived was thriving.

Carefully, setting her chives on the granite step, she knelt down to study the nasturtium seedlings poking up at the edge of the bed. The seedlings would not do well if they were spaced too close together. The heart-shaped leaves were a delicious sage color. She pinched a stem between two fingers and delicately lifted one out. The wee seedling came easily, still so new in the fog-moistened earth. The root was a bare sliver, a silken thread, nothing more. She pulled a second and then a third leaf, both crowding out the stronger plants adjacent to them. Caroline sat on the porch step and looked down at the tiny slips that would have become fully developed flowers if they had come up in a different spot of ground. They were so easy to pluck out and discard, mere specks wilting in her palm.

Pulling out the baby plants was the right thing to do. Like the decision not to have this baby. She already had a grown son. And, of course, she must consider Pete. The previous sleepless night she had been filled with images of telling him what had happened, of returning to Chevy Chase pregnant, resuming her old life at the garden club, the book club, as the pregnant widow carrying an illegitimate child. It was a ludicrous thought.

Then again, why couldn't she keep this baby? She could stay here in East Hope for the year. No one here really knew her; people in town kept to themselves. She could take the baby home next summer. The few friends she still saw in her neighborhood might wonder who the father was, but they would presume it had been some sort of brief love affair during her time away. Caroline didn't care what they thought anyway, except for Vivien. Vivien was coming the day after tomorrow, and it would be such a relief to tell someone, to try to make sense of what had happened, to come up with a plan.

Caroline lifted her palms, scattering the tiny bits of green, and wrapped her arms across her chest. What would it be like to hold a tiny baby again? A baby, a birth. Until now all she had thought about was death, trying to understand death, cope with death, live with death. A baby was all about life, new life.

She looked down at her bare feet. Rob's feet had once been delicate and small, the size of her thumb. When he was three his plump little feet, browned from the sun, had tottered around this same garden.

The loud jangle of Lila's old telephone in the kitchen interrupted her thoughts. She picked up the cut chives and hurried inside.

"Mom."

The sound of Rob's voice lifted her mood instantly; then it fell. "Sweetie, you're up early. Are you all right?"

"We just got off Jasper Peak. Cell phones are working again. Wanted to check in." His far-off voice came through in quick bursts. Caroline felt as if her body were being recharged just listening to him.

"Mom, it's amazing. This last trip we hiked eight days and saw no one. It's so great. And no rain at all. My group has really hung together. Sixty-pound packs, and nobody's complaining. And you should see the wildflowers. You'd love it."

"It sounds wonderful," she said. Thank God she had let him go. It was obvious that this time away—and on his own—was doing him good. The happiness rushing through her was all about the joy of children, having children as part of her life. She missed her son more than ever.

"I wanted to ask if it's okay to bring someone home," he said. "Before I leave for school."

"I guess so." She faltered. She wasn't sure she wanted another person around. "It's just that when you come home you'll only have a short time before classes begin."

"Is everything okay?" he asked. "You sound strange."

"I'm fine. Sure. Bring a friend. What's his name?"

"Her name's Melanie."

A girl. Caroline's stomach lurched. An unpleasant taste, metallic and bitter, came into her mouth. Why hadn't she thought he might have met someone? The program was coed. She shouldn't be surprised. "Of course. I'd love to meet her. Why don't you bring her to Maine? You'd love it up here."

"Mom, I want to see my friends in DC. Jim's going to have a big party. We might want to go down to Rehoboth, too. Besides, I thought you'd be home by August," he said, his voice mildly accusing.

"Everything is taking longer than I expected."

They talked a while longer, and Caroline promised she'd be home by the time he was. They would have so few days together before he went back to school. All the while, she tried to picture them at the house in Washington. Rob and Melanie, a couple, on one side of the table and Caroline with her secret on the other. Would it even be a secret by then? The idea of telling her nineteen-year-old son that she was . . . what? An unwed mother? She didn't think that would be the way to impress his girlfriend. How could she even imagine she could keep this baby?

❧

Caroline and Hollis sat on the screened porch. Vern had finished painting the outside of the house that afternoon. His next project was to replace the rotted part of the porch. She clinked glasses with Hollis before taking a sip. Her gin and tonic remained ginless, but a sprig of mint floated gamely on top, making it look like the real thing. She rested a hand on her belly, her pregnancy hidden to the casual observer.

"You live here, you have to love weather." Hollis Moody raised his glass. "Here's to Maine, the way life should be."

The green signs on the highway had touted that message when Caroline first arrived in the state. The way life should be. What would her life be like now?

"Yup," he continued, "it's the weather that makes Maine what it is, and it's not an easy place."

"The fog last week did get a little depressing," Caroline agreed.

"Fog's nothing nowadays, with GPS and all these other gizmos. Sailors used to get lost and trapped out there when the wind died. If that weren't bad enough, there were the storms. Devoured the fishermen, leaving the wives and children behind. It's made the people here strong. Know what I mean?"

Caroline agreed that Maine did seem to be a land of survivors. Even the old cookbooks offered clues to the resilient New Englanders. The growing season was short, and there were endless recipes using potatoes and root vegetables, crops that would grow in the hard climate and could be preserved to satisfy hunger when winter snows covered the rocky earth.

"Vern did a fine job with the painting." Hollis gestured with his glass and then sipped his drink.

"I'm pleased," she said. "He's about to do some work here on the porch. He thinks we can get away with just replacing a few of the supports." She gazed at the floorboards, which still needed paint, and the blue ceiling that made her think it was always a clear day. "I washed the old wicker this afternoon. It had been in the barn all winter. What a job."

"Have you met Vern's wife?"

"No. He talks about her a lot."

"Now, there's one Maine gal. They go fishing every year. The Rangeley Lakes. A few summers ago Dottie drove a bear right out of camp with only a mop." Hollis laughed so hard at the memory that he had to remove his glasses and dab at his eyes.

Caroline laughed with him. "I could never be that brave," she said, remembering her fear of the bat.

"I have a feeling you're braver than you let on." Hollis grew more serious and looked at the door leading inside the house. "Lila was brave too. Never went up against a bear, to my knowledge, but went up against certain folks. Worse, in a way."

"What do you mean?"

"The summer people would have nothing to do with her."

Caroline thought of the elegant old lady, a teacher at some private girls' school in Boston, Harry had told her. "But her husband, Francis, didn't he grow up coming to East Hope?" she asked. "I thought their house belonged to one of the old families who spent the summer here."

"All true," Hollis said. "Except for the fact that Lila and Francis never married."

"Never married? Harry never said anything."

"More than likely he never knew. All this happened before he was born. Families have their way of hushing things up. Francis was from one of the original old families that summered here for generations. This was during the depression years. He was a professor at Harvard. Lila taught at the Pine Hall school. She was twenty years his junior. They met and fell in love. Classic story, really. Both from fine old Boston families."

"So why didn't they marry?"

"Seems he was already married. His wife, Anna, was what they called an invalid. That's what they used to say. Truth is, she was mentally ill."

Caroline passed him the plate of cheese straws. "How very sad," she said.

"They married young. Anna had a series of miscarriages. She was a nervous sort, had a hard time coping." Hollis paused and chewed for a moment, brushing a few crumbs off his lap.

"When she lost a fourth baby," he continued, "she had some sort of breakdown. Her family insisted on putting her in an institution—not far from here, actually. Francis was beside himself and didn't want her to go. He thought her family wanted to keep him away from her."

Hollis stopped speaking and took a long sip of his drink. He glanced at his watch. "I'm going on too long."

"No. Please. Tell me what happened. I can't believe Harry never knew this. I'd wondered why they never had children. Now I understand."

"I'll keep it short." Hollis leaned back in his chair and craned his head around for a quick look at the water. "Francis was crushed. He lived the quiet life of a bachelor, going to see Anna in Maine whenever he could get away. My wife, Millie, knew the story better than I do, but eventually Anna sort of shut down. It might have been early Alzheimer's. She no longer recognized people. Terrible, really. In the meantime, Francis met Lila. They adored each other, but of course Francis wasn't free to marry. They saw each other in Boston, still leading separate lives, but after a while he started bringing her here to his house for the summers. This was before the war. You can imagine the scandal. The summer people would have nothing to do with them. They did have friends to visit. Some of their artist and writer friends came up.

"Francis died in the early fifties. Anna a few years later. He left his money to Anna for her care, but the house was for Lila. She loved East Hope. They had had all those happy summers. So after his death Lila gave up her teaching and moved up here for good. She became part of the winter community. Started the children's collection at the library, volunteered at all kinds of things through her church, entertained friends. Her own family managed to forget all those years when she 'lived in sin.' Funny about that. Lila never held a grudge. I think her one sister was your husband's grandmother. She died years ago. Not much offspring on either side of the family. I think your husband was the only great-nephew she ever had."

"What a sad love story."

"Not all the time. Lila didn't give a hoot for convention. She ignored the standards of the day. I guess she figured she had only one life, maybe only one chance at love."

"I'm so glad you told me."

"It's been a pleasure. But the sun's going down and I've got to be going."

"You're sure you can't stay for dinner?"

"It's my night for cards. Few old buddies. We get together every coupla weeks. I'll take a rain check, though."

Caroline gave Hollis a quick tour of the property, showing him all that Vern had accomplished, and then walked him to his car. Turning back to the house, she thought about Lila's story, all that had happened here, a secret of sorts right here in these rooms.

❦

Will did not take his usual run in the morning. It was a good day for business at Taunton's, a relief to be busy. Still fuming about Mary Beth, who hadn't called him back, he worked on putting her out of his mind. He had had a recent onslaught of customers, though not much money in the cash register to show for it. He was certain that would turn around soon. The summer people wanted books for the beach. When he'd called Penny Taunton to tell her about his plan to stock current titles, she had been enthusiastic. She had also told him that her dad was not doing well.

The weather had been strange all day, fog, drizzle, an hour of sun, and then more fog, as if the day couldn't make up its mind. By six that evening the sun came out, a golden syrup pouring across the lawn. After closing the store Will decided to take a run to the town beach.

Martha, the proprietor of Karen's Café, had told him about the town beach out on Route 219. "Just for the local residents," she had explained. "You gotta have your dump sticker on your windshield to park." The town of East Hope had no trash pickup. Some of the wealthier residents paid for private trash collection, but Will had acquired the town sticker to prove he lived in East Hope and was therefore authorized to use the dump. He dutifully cut all his boxes into two-foot lengths for recycling. All other garbage had to be dropped off in regulation-size black plastic bags. Will would never forget the precise instructions he was given the first time he brought his trash. An old man with a greasy baseball cap had chastised him for calling it a dump. "It's the transfer station," he snarled, "and don't you forget it." The memory still made him cringe.

This evening he pulled on his shorts and trail shoes, and, abandoning his usual running route, he took 219 and then the poorly marked turnoff to Hawthorne Beach. The rutted dirt road dipped down into the woods, and though dense, the forest floor was covered with ferns of all sizes. The taller ones bowed gently in the dappled light that filtered through the leaf canopy. Eventually he arrived at a parking area, also unpaved, where two cars were parked. He figured that the locals were home eating dinner—or supper, as most of them called their evening meal.

The beach road narrowed to a path with marshlands and a pond to the right and three weathered gray picnic tables up on a knoll to his left. Will followed the pathway to the end, stopped, wiped the hair back from his face, and allowed the wet salt air to cool his skin. He stared at the wide curve of beach before him. It was low tide, and the water lay far in the distance across the rippled hard sand where earlier the waves had molded the surface, each ridge as unique as a fingerprint. To his left the rough barnacle-covered rocks stood out wet and dark in the evening sun. A band of fog had sunk down along the opposite side of the beach.

A couple moved toward him from the water. They approached him without talking, and Will saw that they were dressed alike in baggy shorts, navy sweatshirts, and Teva sandals on their suntanned feet. The man wore a limp old-fashioned tennis hat, and the woman, hatless, had a sensible cap of steely gray hair. A large swaybacked Lab pranced between them, his face goofy with joy from their walk.

"Evening," the man said.

Will said hello to them and they exchanged a few friendly words, agreeing that the fog seemed to be lifting. The couple continued on to the parking area, and Will envied them the comfortable silence that seemed to knit them together. Tired from his run, he started to walk toward the fog, as if drawn toward an oasis at the far end of the beach. In addition to the ocean, a distant hum, he heard two foghorns, each a separate pitch that seemed to call out to the other in a mournful wail.

A few minutes later he saw a figure coming toward him out of the mist. Gradually he saw that it was a woman, her head bent and her arms drawn protectively across her chest. He rubbed his own arms, trying to bring warmth where the sweat had evaporated.

As she approached he saw her red hair. "Hello, there," he called out, having recognized Caroline Waverly.

She drew closer and her face came into focus. "Lovely beach, isn't it?" she said.

Will felt his mood lift at the sight of Caroline and he turned around and fell into step alongside her. "My first time here," he said. "I was about to turn back. No sense walking into the fog. Do you come here often?"

"I only just discovered it," she said. "My contractor, Vern, told me how to get here."

"How's the porch project?" he asked. His mind jumped back to the pleasant morning in Caroline's kitchen.

She told him about the work going on at her house, all the while her stride keeping up with his. Though she seemed a little subdued, her tone was pleasant. "It's taking so much longer than I ever thought." Caroline kept her gaze fixed on the water as they walked back to the beach entrance. Her face looked damp, and Will wondered briefly if she'd been crying or if it was only moist from the fog. He told her about his day at the store, hoping to amuse her with a few anecdotes. He described the two snooty ladies who had come in the previous evening, and how he had gotten the idea to order some new books. Before he knew it they had reached her car.

"Would you like a ride back?" she asked.

"Yeah, that'd be great," he said, pleased to have more time

with her. He opened the door to the passenger seat and watched as she removed a tan sweater, a notebook, and a pen from the seat, tossing them into the back. Her hair was curlier than he remembered and streaked with blond or maybe white. They drove in silence down the dirt road.

"Look there," Caroline said suddenly. She stopped the car and pointed into the woods. A mother deer and her baby stood watching them. The doe, in a proprietary gesture, nuzzled the ear of her fawn, barely two feet tall and flecked in white spots. A moment later they disappeared into the trees. As if caught in a trance, Caroline remained still, staring at the clearing where the animals had stood. Will could hear Caroline's breathing. A weighted silence fell between them.

"Are you okay?" he finally said.

"Sorry," she said. She removed her foot from the brake and continued to the main road. When they reached 219 Caroline picked up her speed and continued in the direction of Taunton's Used Books. Will couldn't think of what to say after seeing the deer. She seemed unreachable, their easy conversation no longer possible. It was as if the last remnants of the fog on the beach had worked their way into the car. A few minutes later they arrived at the store.

"Would you like to come in?" he said, surprised by his own invitation. "Maybe a drink?"

For a moment she looked young again, less preoccupied than she had walking by the water. "Thanks. That's nice of you, but I really need to get back."

"Sure," he said. He got out of the car and leaned down to the window. "Some other time maybe?" Will tried to keep the disappointment out of his voice.

"Of course." Caroline smiled briefly. Her face took on a distant expression again. "Some other time."

Will stepped away from the car as she drove away. What was he doing anyway? He was married. But he was lonely and the long weekend loomed. He thought of Mary Beth in New York. She was seeing friends. Why shouldn't he?

In their last few years in Habliston, when Mary Beth had been commuting from New York, they saw less of the friends they shared as a couple, other younger members of the faculty. When they first moved to the college they had gone to the monthly English department happy hours and had been part of an international supper club, a series of potluck dinners celebrating different world cuisines. In the months when Will was on his own he had remained close to Alice Field, from his department, and her husband. Also, Jack Mathews and his wife had invited him to dinner fairly often. He had enjoyed spending time with them.

It wouldn't be hard to make new friends now in East Hope. Martha and her husband from the café had asked him to join the small-business advisory committee. He was getting to know Edna Raymond, the town librarian, whom he'd met when he first came to town. Why couldn't he be friends with Caroline? They were both here for the summer. They were both "from away." He looked at the white house across the bay, what he thought of as her house now. Though it was not yet dark, the moon was full in the clear sky.

8

Vivien had taken her suitcase upstairs and changed into flowing linen trousers and a big cotton shirt, and now she stood looking about her in the dining room. "What a great place." Her voice filled the room. "Amazing views." After weeks alone, Caroline was unaccustomed to the sounds of another person moving about in Lila's house.

Caroline carried a second bowl of fish chowder in from the kitchen and set it down at her place. She had met Vivien's plane at the Bangor airport late that afternoon. There had been thunderstorms and the flight had been over an hour late. Fortunately she had made the chowder ahead of time except for adding the fish, which they'd picked up at the fish market on the way home from the airport. While the fish cooked she made a green salad and baked the cheddar biscuits, one of Lila's recipes. By the time dinner was ready the big clock in the hall had chimed eight.

"It's good to have you here," Caroline said as she pulled back her chair.

Vivien sat down before her own bowl of steaming soup and sniffed appreciatively. "This smells divine."

"I hope it's good." Caroline took a sip. "Thanks for bringing all the gourmet treats. It's hard to find good olive oil locally."

"You certainly have fresh fish." Vivien started into the hearty chowder. Caroline imagined Vivien's brain at work cataloging each ingredient. Caroline had always enjoyed having what they called "food chat" together, except that tonight it felt forced. Overtired from the hours in the car, she was unable to taste her own soup, though lately her sense of smell had been keen, another sign of pregnancy.

"Gorgeous little potatoes. Is this a new recipe?"

"It is." Caroline told Vivien about Lila's recipes and her collection of cookbooks. "One book is over a hundred years old."

"I can't imagine what you'd want to cook from that."

"You'd be surprised," Caroline said. "This recipe came from a book printed sometime during the Second World War. It talks about shortages and substitutes. It's fascinating to see which recipes still work and what you can do to update some of the dishes."

"Remakes of vintage recipes."

"Exactly." Caroline passed Vivien the basket of biscuits.

"Your kitchen here is vintage too." She broke open a biscuit. "Doesn't seem to hurt the finished product."

"I'm afraid my funds won't cover any remodeling."

"Whoever buys the house will probably rip it all out and start over."

Caroline set down her spoon. "You're right, though I kind of like it the way it is." She buttered a biscuit. The last of the sun had gone and the dining room fell into shadow. The summer solstice had passed and now the days were growing shorter. A wave of cooler Canadian air had blown in after the rainstorm. Vivien would experience some of the best of Maine weather.

"The wine's nice with this." Vivien raised her glass. "You're not drinking?" Caroline had poured sparkling water into her own glass. She still had not found the right moment to tell Vivien that she was pregnant.

"I'll have some later," Caroline said, and stirred her soup distractedly. "I decided to do the book by categories instead of by vegetable. It's easier to keep to a section on soups or salads rather than always trying to determine the predominant vegetable in a recipe. You know, do you put vichyssoise under potatoes or leeks?"

"Let's talk about work tomorrow." Vivien fixed her gaze on Caroline. "I really came here to see how you're doing."

"You can see for yourself that the house is wonderful." Caroline looked appreciatively at the dining room, sparely furnished, but elegant. "I'll be sad to give it up. This house makes Lila come alive for me. It's kind of like she's pulling me into her world."

"You can't afford to be sentimental," Vivien said quickly. "I'm sorry. That wasn't the best way to put it. Come on; have some wine." She pushed the bottle across the table. "It's no fun to drink alone."

"Rob called the other day. He was so happy and talkative," she said, hoping Vivien would forget about the wine. "They're out now on a three-week rafting trip. I'm missing him a lot more than he's missing me."

"Nineteen-year-old boys aren't supposed to be missing their mothers," Vivien said.

"He's bringing a girlfriend home in August."

"Do I detect a note of jealousy?"

"Of course not." She put her spoon down, almost too tired to eat.

Vivien looked at Caroline with the piercing gaze of someone wanting to get to the bottom of something. "Are you all right?"

"I'm a little tired. Besides writing, there's been so much to clean out and—"

"You know, you don't seem like yourself. I understand you're missing Rob. I mean, Harry is gone and now—"

"It's not just that," Caroline said.

Vivien sat back in her chair and waited.

Caroline wiped her mouth and put her napkin on the table. "I'm pregnant," she said.

Vivien stared across the table, her eyes widening in astonishment and then slowly darkening as they registered understanding. "Pete?"

Caroline nodded and looked away. The entire situation felt like some sort of sordid soap opera. This kind of thing didn't happen in her world.

"Oh, my poor girl." Vivien got up and came around the table and took Caroline by the shoulders. "Don't worry. We'll figure something out." She continued to pat Caroline on the back with her wide, competent hands.

Caroline felt a rush of relief. Every muscle in her body seemed to loosen away from her bones. Thank God for Vivien's visit.

"Come with me." Vivien took the bottle of wine from the table and filled a glass for Caroline. "This isn't going to hurt you. We've got to talk." Caroline followed her into the living room. "I thought it was just that once," Vivien said, handing her the glass of wine. "Why did you let yourself get involved with him?"

"It *was* only that one night. All those years when I couldn't get pregnant with Harry, and now this. It never crossed my mind. I loved Harry. Oh, God. How could this have happened?" She took a sip of the wine and collapsed onto the sofa. The wine tasted awful. She put it down and no longer held back her tears. "I'm forty-four years old, a widow, and running out of money."

Vivien sat beside her. "You're absolutely sure?"

Caroline nodded. "I did a home test a few days ago. You'll think I'm crazy. My body has been in such a state. I never even considered this. Ever since I've been in Maine I've had this heightened sense of smell." She pulled a tissue out of her pocket and blew her nose. "I'd been feeling slightly queasy, and then I remembered I hadn't had my period. You must think I'm an idiot."

"How far along?"

"Seven weeks." Caroline lost herself again to her tears. She held her head in her hands and cried like she hadn't since the morning she'd been told of Harry's heart attack. It was like an unstoppable force; she could hardly breathe.

Vivien went out of the room and returned with an entire box of tissues. She patted Caroline's back again. "Here. Wipe your face."

Caroline was relieved to be told what to do. She wiped her face and nose and eventually regained her composure. "I can't have this baby. It would upset everyone."

"I know. I know." Vivien handed her more tissues.

"I don't love Pete. He's been good to me. That's not enough." Her words came out in short bursts. "I don't want to break up his marriage. And Rob? My God. What would he think?" Her tears started to flow again. She leaned back and rolled her head from side to side on the sofa.

"I'll help you," Vivien said. "We'll call your doctor in Washington. It's not too late. You can fly home with me on Monday."

"I keep thinking of Grace. I can't go through that again." She leaned forward with her elbows on her knees and held her face in her hands.

Vivien patted Caroline's back again and smoothed the hair away from her face. Eventually Vivien was able to calm her, and they made their way back to the dining room. Vivien resumed eating her dinner and began to formulate the exact plan that would set all this to rights. It was as if Vivien had become her mother. Vivien was very much a take-charge kind of person. When they had first worked together it was Vivien who planned the projects and directed Caroline, advising her on how to go about her work. Later, as Caroline gained confidence, she made more decisions on her own, and Vivien's directives could verge on bossiness. Tonight Caroline did not have the heart to question or raise lingering doubts. The emotional turmoil of the past few days had taken its toll.

After dinner Vivien insisted on doing the dishes, and it was almost eleven when the kitchen was finally cleaned up. Caroline made a pot of herbal tea and sent Vivien to bed with a cup, along with a few of the choice cookbooks from Lila's shelves. "I'll be up in a minute," she said. "I'm all right. I promise." Caroline walked from room to room, lowering the windows and turning out the lights. She stopped in the hall. Lila's clock ticked along with its steady, reassuring sound. She took the key from the drawer in the hall table and carefully opened the face. The key slipped in easily. She turned it six small turns, according to Hollis Moody's instructions.

Once the clock was wound she opened the front door and stood briefly on the wide granite step. The front of the house faced the bay and the far-off ocean. The air was cool and the clean salt breeze soothed her skin. On her left a light on the other side of the bay shone brightly; maybe it came from Taunton's Used Books. Caroline wondered about the bookseller, Will Harmon. She'd been pleased to see him again yesterday when she'd emerged from the fog on Hawthorne Beach. He seemed like the kind of person who might step out on a night like this to savor the air and look at the stars.

Caroline shivered and drew her arms across her chest. When she was a little girl she used to go out into the backyard in Connecticut with her dad to watch the summer night sky. They would lie on the lawn, the grass cooling beneath her thin cotton nightgown while she listened to his descriptions of the constellations, her dad's voice a gentle rumble that often lulled her to sleep. Those childhood summers felt like a million years ago.

❦

That night Caroline had a difficult time falling asleep. She couldn't find a comfortable position and turned repeatedly from side to side. Vivien's presence and her knowledge of the pregnancy made it all the more real, and the magnitude of what lay ahead felt crushing. Eventually Caroline slept. During the night she awoke suddenly from a terrible dream, one so vivid, it was hard to believe it wasn't true.

As in most nightmares, it was difficult to see what was going on. She was trying to get to a baby. She kept reaching and reaching, trying to find the child. Now and then a faint pink softness, the gaze of a little face, pale hair, the curve of a cheek appeared only to disappear and remain out of sight. The need to get to this child drove her forward. There was no crying. The dream was eerily silent. As she lay in bed now fully awake, her arms were sore, as if she had actually been reaching in her sleep.

Grace had been born with multiple holes in her heart, though she weighed eight pounds and appeared to be quite perfect. Caroline would never forget the day following her birth. In the night the nurse had brought her the tightly swaddled bundle. Caroline had tried to nurse her daughter. The small pink mouth had grazed her hardened nipples, but Grace seemed to want to sleep. The nurse had reassured Caroline and said they would try again in a few hours. The next thing she remembered, Harry was looking down at her with tears on his face. Something was wrong. The baby had stopped breathing just before dawn.

❦

"I want to have this child, Vivien," Caroline said later the next morning. She stared out at the water. The weather couldn't have been more perfect. The air was fresh and summer sweet, and the water and sky were both the purest blue. She and Vivien had carried their mugs of coffee to the Adirondack chairs on the lawn. It was the Fourth of July, and Vern would not be coming to work on the house. They had the day to themselves. Vivien was leaving on Sunday and she had gotten up early and already booked a seat for Caroline on the same flight. Tired from her bad night, Caroline hadn't yet mustered up the energy to stop her.

"I know a termination is hard."

Caroline said nothing. She felt calm now, resolute. The sky was clear, cloudless. A gentle breeze ruffled the leaves of the lilac bushes by the garage.

"Having this baby would be a terrible mistake," Vivien continued. "There's the cost, your health—the baby's too."

Caroline put her mug on the arm of the chair and covered her ears with her hands. "I know, I know."

"Caroline, you agreed. You yourself said you can't go through with the pregnancy."

"Harry wanted more children. When it seemed I couldn't get

pregnant years ago, he wanted to adopt. He was an only child. He wanted a larger family."

"That was years ago. What does that have to do with your life now?"

"It was selfish of me. I was afraid of another depression, that a baby would remind me of Grace. I made a mistake. I see that now. Living here has been like starting over." Caroline looked over at Vivien, who was shaking her head. "I know that sounds hokey. I just want this child. I think I need to have this child."

"What about Pete? Have you thought about him?" Vivien put her mug down and waved one hand in the air. "Have you lost your mind? You plan to show up in Chevy Chase and waltz into the garden club, pregnant with Pete's child? And Marjorie? What about her?"

"I'll tell Pete," she said quietly, "though I don't want anything from him."

"Right." Vivien slapped her hands down on the arms of her chair. "Do you know what you're saying? This is so unlike you. Your lovely life is going to be chaos. Think of your family and how they would feel. And your friends—what they would say. Can you handle that?"

"You're my only real friend."

"You know what I mean."

Caroline drew her knees up and rested her feet at the edge of the chair. What Vivien said was true. She hated controversy. But it was too late. She wasn't sure how she had come to this choice, but as she'd said it, it seemed suddenly right. After days of confusion, it was as if her decision to have this baby was something she'd known all along.

Vivien softened her tone. "It's not only that. I want you to be able to move forward. Harry's death was dreadful, and then to have your money worries too . . . Please listen to me, Caroline."

Caroline looked at her knees.

"This baby is not Grace. You can't replace Grace." Vivien reached over and took Caroline's arm.

"It's not that," Caroline said sharply.

"Don't make me be the heavy."

"I know you're trying to help." She looked at her friend. "What you say is totally reasonable. But having this baby is something I want to do for me. It's not because I want to replace Grace."

But wasn't it? Caroline stared out at the water. The shimmering brilliance almost hurt her eyes.

"Come on," Vivien said. "You know you can't afford to raise a baby on your own. And what will Rob say? Have you thought about that? It's not fair to him to bring a baby into the world."

"You make him sound selfish."

"Caroline, he's nineteen. And the fact that you were with another man—his father's best friend, even—are you going to tell him that?"

"I'll explain it to him." Caroline remembered the last time Rob called from Colorado, so exuberant, his life back on track. Soon he'd be coming home to Washington with a girlfriend. Telling him would not be easy. She pressed her lips together.

"Or maybe that's it? Rob's growing up. You're going to be alone. That's understandable, but this is not the way to solve that problem."

"I'm not afraid of being alone." Caroline heard the defiance in her own voice.

"You're not thinking clearly." Vivien's eyebrows had drawn together, deepening the crease between her eyes. "Let's not talk about it anymore today," she said, and got to her feet. "Finish your coffee. I'm going inside to make the picnic lunch I promised, and after that you're going to drive us to Perkins Beach." She raised her arms. "No. Don't get up. You're on vacation today. Soon we'll be in Washington. I guarantee you'll feel differently when you get home."

Vivien marched back to the house and Caroline decided not to argue. Though Vivien could be hardheaded, she only had Caroline's best interests at heart. She would never forget how this kind and determined woman had taken her under her wing when they met years before at the Cuisine Academy. Vivien had said that Caroline had a gift for bringing all the wonders of cooking into words. Vivien had offered Caroline encouragement. Thanks to Vivien, she had discovered work that she loved.

No, Vivien was right. Why discuss it further? The day was lovely and she didn't want to spoil it. She watched a lobster boat cut through the light chop of the bay. Today the islands looked like clusters of mushroom caps. The breeze was picking up, and gulls swooped and dove across the sky.

❦

The perfect weather held on the morning of their departure. Vivien carried her suitcase to the car and waited for Caroline, who fumbled with her keys as she locked the back door. She locked the house only when going off the peninsula. No one locked their doors in East Hope, except perhaps at night.

"Where's your bag?" Vivien said.

"I'm not going to Washington," she said resolutely, and opened the door of her car.

"What?"

"Please get in."

"Caroline, you've got to come home."

Caroline almost said, *I am home, Vivien. I'm staying here and this is home.* Instead she said, "Please, Vivien. If we're going to make your flight we need to leave now."

"You said you'd come back to Washington. You agreed." Vivien paused, looked up to the sky, and took a breath as if to calm herself. "You'll be okay about it when you get home, when you return to your normal life."

"I'm having this baby," Caroline said. "I'm going to be a mother again. I'm not changing my mind."

"After everything I've said?"

"Please get in. We're going to be late."

"You've got to listen to me," Vivien insisted, remaining outside the car.

"But I have," Caroline said. "It's you that hasn't listened to me." Before she could stop herself the cruel words flew out: "How would you know what it's like, anyway? You've never had a baby. How would you know what it's like to have one die?"

Vivien looked as if she had been struck, her face blank with shock, but not yet registering the pain. A moment later a sheet of invisible armor dropped down around her. She showed no emotion. She got into the passenger seat and slammed the door shut. "Fine. Drive to the airport."

The ride to Bangor was awful. "Please," Caroline begged, "I didn't mean that. I've been so wrought up from everything. It was wrong of me to say that. You're the most understanding person I know."

Vivien kept her face angled to the window and acted deaf to Caroline's pleading. At the airport she got out of the car, took her suitcase, and, without a word, walked to the entrance without looking back.

❦

Will reached the top of the hill and slowed his pace. Caroline's house blazed white before his eyes. His morning runs usually brought him this way at first light. He hadn't seen Caroline since their meeting on the beach before the July Fourth weekend, and today he'd started his run later than usual, hoping to see her again. He was rewarded when he reached her drive. She was hanging sheets on the clothesline below the barn. Her hair was loose and fell to her shoulders.

He headed down the drive. "Need any help?" he called.

She turned and shaded her face with her hands. She was so tanned. It was as if all the freckles had blended together into one golden mass. "Hi," she called back.

Will's feet crunched on the gravel as he made his way to the clothesline. "How've you been?" he asked.

"Don't you love this weather?" She lifted her chin toward the sky.

"Really great."

She pulled her hair back in a self-conscious gesture and held it with one hand. Her fingers, while finely shaped, looked strong and capable. The sheets flapped behind her in the breeze. "Can you stop a minute?" She gestured toward the house.

"Thanks, but the store opens at ten. I'm late as it is."

Her face appeared softer, rounder than he remembered, like a ripe peach. She reached for a pillowcase that lay in a crinkled heap in her basket. He thought he saw a glimmer of disappointment shadow her face, and this gave him courage. "I wondered," he said, "have you ever been to Acadia?"

"The national park?"

"Yeah. On Monday I'm going to a town near there. Mr. Earl, an old friend of Mr. Taunton's, has died. The family is selling his house. Mr. Taunton's daughter, Penny, said I could go and take any of the books I want for the store. This guy had a huge library. I wondered if you'd like to come." He shifted his weight from foot to foot, the runner in him ready to move.

She paused and considered. "This coming Monday?"

Will should have known better than to ask her. He looked away. "I know you're busy, but I thought you could look and see if there were any cookbooks worth your while. I mean, you could have them." Will felt as if he were back in high school asking Missy Johnson out on their first date. It had taken him his entire junior year to get up the nerve.

"It's nice of you to think of me. It's just that—"

"I understand," he said abruptly. He felt her gaze on him. What was he thinking? Why would she want to go off with him for an entire day? Besides, Mary Beth was coming in August. Yet she was hardly pining for him. Days would go by before she returned his calls. Her few e-mails were brief.

"I could use a day away." She smiled, though her expression seemed tentative, as if she too were uncertain. "Monday will be good."

"How about I pick you up around nine?"

"Perfect," Caroline said. "Let me make a picnic lunch."

"That would be great. Thanks." He tilted his head and smiled. "Maybe you could make some of those cookies. Remember? The ones called Rocks."

"Rocks for dessert." At that she laughed lightly and snapped another pillowcase before pinning it to the line.

When Will started up the driveway he was sorry to have to leave. At the top of the drive he turned back. Caroline waved, then bent to pick up her basket.

9

Will stepped out of the shower when the phone rang. He pulled a towel around his waist and left wet footprints on the floor as he hurried to pick up. His first thought was that it might be Caroline calling to change her mind.

"I'm at LaGuardia," Mary Beth said.

"Hi," he said, feeling suddenly guilty that he had never considered that it might be her. "You're up early."

"I'm going back to LA. I'm sorry I haven't made it up to Maine yet."

"That's okay, really. You'll be here in August," he said. "Only a few more weeks."

"That's why I'm calling."

Will gripped the towel around his middle. His skin had dried and the cool air raised goose bumps on his arms.

"We're starting the final negotiations. I'll need to be in California for at least a month."

Another month. At least he wasn't waiting for her in the hot city. "I see," he said.

"Why don't you come out to see me?"

"California?"

"I can't take the time to travel back. You could come for a long weekend. Drew said the company would pay for your ticket."

"I'm afraid I can't."

"Why not?" She sounded surprised.

"Weekends are my busy time. I can't close the store."

"It's a free trip. We haven't been together in ages."

"I can't leave here," he said.

"Can't or won't?"

"I have another shipment of books arriving," he said. "They have to be unpacked and put out. It's the height of the season here."

"Get someone to cover for you. You don't even own that bookstore."

"You don't understand," he said, feeling the old anger once again. She didn't care that he had lost his teaching job, and she clearly thought his work at the bookstore was a waste as well.

"You're the one who doesn't understand. I'm asking you to come. I'm giving you the ticket, for God's sake," she said.

Will could hear the echoing boom of airport announcements in the background. She expected him to drop everything and become part of her world. He looked down at his bare feet.

"I get it," she said. "What you're saying is you don't care enough to make the effort to come."

"Mary Beth, wait. Please let me explain."

"Call me if you change your mind." She hung up. Will looked at the clock. It was eight thirty. He was due at Caroline's in half an hour. He went to the closet and pulled out a clean shirt, one that he'd actually ironed, a rare feat.

"We're in no rush," Will said. He closed his Jeep's passenger door and went around to the driver's side. The vehicle, dark green and well cared for, was the boxy old-fashioned style, not the new sleeker models with all the luxury options. He started the engine and Caroline fumbled for her seat belt, jerking it unevenly as she drew it around her middle.

She hadn't meant to be late. Vivien had called that morning while Caroline was eating breakfast. They hadn't spoken since Vivien's departure after the July Fourth weekend. Vivien had written a polite thank-you note for her visit, but had made no mention of the baby or the terrible argument on the morning she left. On the phone Caroline had answered Vivien's few questions about formatting the text for the vegetable cookbook. Vivien was all business, cool and efficient.

"Look, Vivien, I'm so sorry."

"Forget it. You've made up your mind."

"I think I'll have the manuscript ready sooner than September," Caroline said, hoping to please her, wishing she could break the ice.

"I've got to go. I have a call coming in." Vivien hung up.

Caroline sat by the phone feeling defeated and sorry for herself and then suddenly remembered Will's imminent arrival. She hurried to the shower. Her hair was still wet when Will's car pulled into the driveway.

Now, sitting next to him as he drove along the curving road toward Route 1, she felt distracted and regretted that she had agreed to spend the entire day with him. He had looked so lost that morning last week in her driveway. She had felt sorry for him and had hastily accepted his invitation. Today his thick hair was neatly combed into place. He seemed subdued, having yet to smile. Perhaps he was annoyed at having to wait for her, or maybe he had second thoughts about spending the day with her as well. She couldn't deny how attractive he looked wearing khaki trousers and a blue cotton shirt, the sleeves rolled to just below the elbows. His tanned forearms were covered with pale hair, making her think he must have been blond as a child. Caroline looked away, wishing she'd taken a little more care with her own appearance. She'd put on a soft flowered skirt that she had found when cleaning out Lila's closet, and she wore a tailored white shirt over this, having based her choices more on comfort than fashion. Her own clothes had begun to feel snug at the waist. But this was Maine, after all, and not a garden club luncheon. How long ago her other life now seemed.

The car eased onto the causeway, bringing them closer to Route 1.

"Amazing, isn't it?" he said.

"The water, you mean?" She looked off to the right.

"It's everywhere."

"What beautiful weather," she said unnecessarily. After the last patch of fog it had been perfect day after day. While hot in the daytime, it was never humid, and it always cooled off at night. So unlike Washington. In Caroline and Harry's first house there had been no air-conditioning. During the long summer nights she'd tried to lie still, sweating in the darkness.

"Yeah, it's a great day," he said. "I bet these roads are something else in the winter. You know, there are more unpaved roads in Maine than paved."

"You know a lot about Maine."

He glanced in her direction. "I just like odd bits of information. How about you? Have you come here forever?"

"Not at all." Caroline explained how she had inherited the house. "My husband came here when he was a boy. I've been only once before, years ago. My son was only three."

"You have a son?" He seemed surprised.

"Yes. He's nineteen."

Will was silent for a few minutes. They were behind a large fuel truck, and he needed to apply the brakes and slow the car as the road began to climb. The truck gave off great wafts of diesel fumes. Caroline closed her window and held her hand to her face, breathing in the lavender-scented cream she had put on just before running out the door. She wished she had brought a few crackers to munch on. Just when she thought she couldn't stand the smell another moment, the truck turned left down a gravel road.

"And your husband?" Will kept his eyes on the road.

"He died last November."

"Gosh—I'm sorry." Will waited at the intersection with Route 1 and watched the heavy oncoming traffic intently, trying to turn onto the roadway heading north. He gripped the wheel, craning his head from right to left. Finally, at an opening, he eased into the flow of cars. "How did it happen? Your husband?" His brows were drawn together in concern.

Caroline told Will about Harry's heart attack, but did not explain her financial worries and how she needed the money from the sale of Lila's house. Having to tell him about Harry's death stirred up all the memories, and she wished she were alone in Lila's airy living room, where, in solitude and quiet, it had become easier to forget those painful days. The table there was piled high with the old cookbooks. She'd been thinking more and more about what she could do with some of the recipes. The histories of nameless, forgotten women seemed to lurk within the yellowed pages. But she had agreed to spend the day with Will, and she had known this question might come up.

"My son is in Colorado this summer," she added. "It doesn't make sense for us to keep the house in Maine."

"You must have had your son at twelve." He smiled slightly and turned as if to gauge her reaction.

"Hardly," she said, secretly pleased that he thought her younger than she was. "I got pregnant on my honeymoon. I'm forty-four."

"Married at twenty-four? That was young."

"I suppose. I met Harry my senior year in college. He was working in New York then. We got married just before he took a new job in Washington." She folded her hands together in her lap, wishing again she'd said no to this day. Caroline bit her lip. Will was a nice man, quite attractive, she admitted to herself, though probably younger than she was. He was probably lonely too. She needed to banish any romantic notions right from the start. Her life was way too complicated. How could she enter into a relationship when she was pregnant from an adulterous one-night stand?

"I'm asking too many questions," he said.

"It's okay," she said quickly. She looked over at him. His eyes were a soft hazel. She liked their downward slant. He appeared to be thinking. "You were nice to suggest this." Her words sounded false to her. "I've been so busy working that I've hardly left East Hope all summer."

"Are the old cookbooks part of your work?"

"No," she said, and explained how the cookbook for World Life Books was more of an editing job and that it was the last one of a series. She was organizing a group of recipes for the book and writing the introductory texts.

"Do you have to cook every recipe?" Will's window was open and the air lifted his hair. The traffic had lessened and the road had climbed gently as the land became hillier. Wide-open fields of rock-scrabbled blueberry barrens bordered both sides of the road.

"That's done by freelancers, so I don't have to worry about it. I do make some dishes just to get a better feel for them." She looked back at the canvas bag in the backseat. "I've brought a few for you to sample on our picnic."

"I'm looking forward to that," he said. At the top of the next hill he turned right onto a side road.

"Have you always wanted to run a bookstore?" she asked.

"Exciting vocation, isn't it?" he joked. A moment later his mouth tightened. "How are you at reading maps?"

"Not great, but I'll try."

Will pulled the car to the side of the road and stopped. He reached behind her seat and pulled out the *Maine Atlas and Gazetteer*. Suddenly she felt his proximity, the kind of closeness unavoidable between two people in a car. He smelled of a botanical shampoo and freshly pressed cotton. She sat up straighter as he opened to a page and pointed. "I think we're here," he said, lowering the map to her lap. His fingers were long and tapered, the nails cut short and clean. Caroline forced herself to concentrate. He moved his finger across the page. If only she were younger, unencumbered.

"This is where we're heading." He handed her a sheet of paper tucked into the book. The lettering was in a neat print, sort of architectural, all uppercase letters in blue ink. "Here are the directions from Lincolnville."

He eased the car back onto the road and Caroline focused on the map. She didn't want to look stupid. They were expected at eleven, and because of her they were running a good twenty minutes late. Fortunately the instructions were clear and detailed. They made a left after the yellow farmhouse, went another three miles, and turned right after the bend in the road at the bank of mailboxes. Then a gray barn appeared on the right along with the drive they were looking for.

"We're here," he said. "You did it."

It seemed a good omen that they'd found the place without any problem. Will stopped the car in front of a large shingled Victorian house. He opened his door and stood stretching for a moment, as if trying to get a crick out of his back. She reached for her handbag and they walked together toward the front door.

❦

Ever since Caroline had gotten in the car that morning Will couldn't stop comparing her to Mary Beth. There were the obvious physical differences, but it was more than that. Mary Beth, so sharply defined in his mind, left nothing to his imagination. His wife was a person of contrasts: her dark hair against pale skin, her strong ideas, her enthusiasms, but also her somber moods and silences that would come over her when, despite her plans and hard work, things didn't go her way.

Still, despite those few uneasy moments, there had been times of unexpected happiness, the small things that caught him by surprise. Will had particularly loved early mornings in bed with Mary Beth. He liked to read over the texts he had planned for discussion in class each day. He would quietly open his book while she dozed beside him, always some part of her touching him: an ankle across his leg, a hand on his hip, her mouth on his shoulder, as if she needed to be assured even in sleep that he was there.

She had been so passionate then, so loving, but in the last years she had grown more distant. She had certainly forgotten him this summer. When he attempted to call her, more often than not she was in meetings, and when she was in California the time difference made her even more difficult to reach. This morning's phone call had done nothing to improve the situation. Her bitter words kept surfacing in his mind.

Caroline was still unclear to him, like a faded image in an old book that might disappear altogether. When she told him about her life and the death of her husband, she remained poised and calm. She seemed to be a private person, yet being with her gave him a pleasant feeling, making him want to know more.

Will never would have thought that a tumbledown farmhouse on a backcountry road could hold such a collection of books. The door was answered by a pained-looking woman in her fifties, Mr. Earl's niece, who had come up from Boston to empty the house.

"Take anything you want," she said. "Once you're gone I'm having the Salvation Army cart away whatever is left." And with heavy steps she had gone to the back of the house. From the clatter of dishes that rattled from that direction, Will presumed she was working in the dining room or kitchen.

Caroline was helpful. He asked her to look for any interesting novels or poetry and, of course, any cookbooks that would appeal to her. She surveyed the shelves, pushing aside the old encyclopedias and *Reader's Digest* collections, and pulled out the volumes that might be worthwhile. The room was a true library, with floor-to-ceiling shelves on three walls. The front windows had gold brocade curtains with threadbare linings that looked weighted with dust. Will pushed them back carefully in hopes of letting in more light. The sullen woman had not turned on any lamps, and he was hesitant to do so. Caroline worked diligently without bothering to make conversation. He discovered a first-edition John Steinbeck novel and several novels by Pearl S. Buck.

"Mrs. 'Arris Goes to Paris," she called out, after they had been sorting for a while. "I loved that book when I was little. It's about

a cleaning woman from London who goes to Paris to buy a Dior gown."

"It's yours," he said.

"Oh, no. I couldn't keep it."

"I insist. Your help is making this go much faster." He nodded toward the kitchen and whispered, "I have a feeling she's in a hurry to get rid of us."

Caroline smiled at him and set the book aside. She smoothed back a tendril of hair that had come loose from the large barrette at her neck. He thought again of how she looked like a woman of an earlier era. The dusty library, so dimly lit, gave her the soft, muted glow of a sepia-toned photograph. He still didn't have much sense of her, of what she was really like. Not knowing her, the uncertainty of what he was doing in her company added to the adventure.

After loading the car with boxes of books, they thanked the dreary woman and set off on the winding roads on Deer Isle to look for a picnic spot. They stopped once for gas and a restroom, and now it was nearly two o'clock. Caroline looked a little pale, and more wisps of hair had come loose from the barrette. He imagined reaching across to tuck a strand behind her ear. Would she flinch? Pull back? Or smile and meet his glance with her arresting eyes?

"Here's a good spot," she said, pointing to the right.

Will slowed the car and pulled off the road. Next to a grassy bank was a rocky beach along a stretch of water. Not the bay, but a cove offering a view of the larger bay beyond. He looked around and saw no house or sign of inhabitants. "Looks good to me." They got out of the car. The sun was hot, but a cool breeze came off the water. He fetched the canvas bag with their lunch from the backseat and followed her down the bank.

Caroline sat on a flat rock and Will lowered himself beside her. Before removing the food, she put on a large-brimmed cotton hat that had been tucked in an outside pocket of her bag.

"I know this looks terrible," she explained, "but I try to avoid the sun. I've already turned into one large freckle." She pulled the strap taut under her chin. The brim shaded her face. He tried to see which eye was the more blue one. He wanted to remember.

"You okay?" she asked.

"Sure. Just hungry. Sorry it got so late. I didn't know there'd be so many books to look through."

"I think there are some good ones. Certainly the first editions," she said, while taking a thermos from the bag. "The set of botanical books is amazing." She handed him a paper cup of cold soup. "It's a white gazpacho, one of the recipes I'm testing."

"Pretty fancy picnic food."

"I bet some of those books will be worth a lot." She poured a cup of soup for herself from the thermos. "How do you know what to charge?"

"Mostly I look at catalogs to see what similar books sell for. I'm still new at it." She seemed to be enjoying her soup. "I'm going to give Mr. Taunton half the proceeds of the sales. I don't think he had any idea what old Mr. Earl had in his collection."

"That's nice of you." She reached into the canvas bag again. "I have a feeling you're hungry for more than soup." She stopped and looked at him. "Oh, God, that sounded terrible." He could see a deep blush rising from her neck to her face. He grinned at her, and she laughed nervously while lifting a thick paper plate wrapped in foil and two plastic containers from the bag. Her hands trembled slightly as she served pieces of cold chicken, a tomato salad, and a bean salad flecked with bright pieces of corn. Everything was delicious. He noticed that Caroline ate as hungrily as he did.

"Unbelievable," he said when she opened a foil packet containing rich chocolate brownies. "I love brownies. I'm glad you forgot the Rocks!" She had unwittingly chosen his favorite dessert. He had always requested brownie sundaes for his birthday when he was a boy. He told Caroline about some of the dishes his mother used to make: the brownies, and peach cobblers during the summer. They compared lists of favorite desserts, favorite childhood meals. Caroline made him laugh describing the dried-up meat loaf and molded salads that her mother still made.

They sipped a mixture of iced tea and lemonade that wasn't too sweet. After they finished eating, Caroline put the containers back in the canvas bag and she stretched out flat on the rock, pulling the hat forward to cover her face. "Can your assistant book buyer have a small siesta?"

"You've more than earned it," he said, and watched as she kicked off her sandals and tucked her skirt around her legs. He extended his own legs alongside hers and leaned back on his elbows. Her feet were paler than her legs. He thought of Newland Archer, how any man from Edith Wharton's novels would be driven mad by the unexpected sight of a woman's naked foot. Seeing Caroline's bare feet, her freckled legs exposed to the sun, made him want to touch her, draw his hand along the smooth softness of her skin. He certainly couldn't pull the sun hat from her face and kiss her. *God.* He hardly knew her. He was also married, he reminded himself. He folded his sweater into a pillow and lowered himself entirely onto the rock, deciding to sleep for a while too. The warm rock felt good on his back. He savored the simple pleasure of this afternoon.

"Will?"

He felt a hand on his sleeve, a gentle pressure on his arm. He woke, momentarily disoriented, and wondered what time it was.

"Maybe we should get going?" She looked down at him.

He sat up and glanced at his watch. It was nearly four. "Sorry. I didn't mean to sleep so long."

Caroline had poured more of the iced tea mix from its thermos. His mouth was dry. He accepted the glass and drank. She was sitting cross-legged and watching him intently. The right eye was the blue one, he decided. The sun was losing its earlier heat. She put the thermos in the bag and they gathered their belongings and walked to the car.

&

It was after six when they reached Lila's house. Caroline left Will on the porch and came into the kitchen to pour him a glass of wine. He'd carried the box of old cookbooks and the *Mrs. 'Arris* book into the living room and left it on her worktable. She had offered to pay him for the books, but he looked almost hurt at the idea, insisting that she have them.

The trip home in the car had gone quickly. Will told her about giving up teaching in Pennsylvania, wanting to make a change and live near the water to write his novel. Was there something he wasn't telling her about leaving his job? He spoke of teaching with enthusiasm, of how lucky he had been to find employment at a small liberal arts college, given the abundance of English literature PhD candidates struggling to find work. It didn't make sense that he would leave that behind.

Caroline opened the antiquated refrigerator. The old-fashioned handle wobbled, and she hoped it would last as long as she lived there. She took out an unopened bottle of sauvignon blanc, left over from Vivien's visit, and carried it to the counter by the sink. She poured a glass for Will and a glass of sparkling water for herself. The wine was the same golden color as the dwindling evening sun. The smell of the wine no longer nauseated her, but she avoided drinking because of the baby. Her baby. For a good part of the day she had completely forgotten about her pregnancy.

Caroline put the glasses on a tray and poured some mixed nuts into a dish. It had been a lovely day. The drive, the dusty private library, their picnic on the little beach had been like taking a field trip from school. Or like playing hooky. It had been so pleasant dozing on the rock beside Will.

Beside Will. If only things were different. Caroline's life was now an endless list of if-onlys. If only she didn't need to sell this wonderful house, if only Harry hadn't lost almost all of their money; if only he had been truthful with her; if only he were alive. Caroline shivered, put a sweater over her shoulders, and carried the tray to the porch.

Will stood looking out at the water. "I can see Taunton's across the bay," he said.

"I'm almost directly across from you when I stand on the front steps." She set the tray down and handed him his glass. He had pulled on his sweater too, mussing his hair. He looked boyish again.

"I gather you're in Maine on your own?" She'd been meaning to ask this all day.

"Sorry?" He appeared not to have understood.

"I wondered," she said, feeling ill at ease again. "You live by yourself, so I wondered if you've ever been married. It's none of my business really, it's just—"

"No. It's a reasonable question," he said. His face drew in, accentuating the lines around his mouth. "I'm married." He seemed to be searching for some kind of explanation. He stared out at the water. "My wife lives in New York City. We had a sort of commuter marriage while I was teaching. I'm afraid it wasn't really working."

"I see," she said.

"She travels a lot for her job. This summer she's in LA most of the time. She wanted me to come to New York. I decided to come here. I guess we're sort of separated." He shook his head and stared down into his glass.

"That must be hard." Caroline couldn't think of what else to say. It explained why he sometimes had a faraway, pained expression.

Will slumped down into a chair. "We both have different ideas of what we want the future to look like," he said, and sipped his drink. "Hard to talk about."

"I didn't mean to pry. I can see it makes you unhappy." Caroline felt bad for Will. All his boyish exuberance seemed to evaporate. "So, tell me about your writing."

Will took another sip of wine and leaned back. "Oh, God. There's almost nothing to tell."

"You don't have enough time?" Turning to this topic only appeared to have worsened his mood.

"I wish it were that simple."

"Maybe you're not writing about the right thing. My friend Vivien always says that if you don't love what you're writing, you certainly shouldn't expect anyone else to want to read it."

They talked about writing, what he was trying to achieve, the importance of place, and how he wanted to capture his love of the water in the book. She asked him the kinds of questions that she hoped would be helpful. She told him how she wanted to do something with the old cookbooks, to find a way to make a story out of them. Will had a second glass of wine, and his face fell into shadow as the evening deepened. Their conversation gradually dwindled, and Will drew his hand to his chin. He rubbed it absently.

A moment later he spoke again. "Caroline, today was really great." He put his glass on the table next to him. "Look. I'd like to see you again. Forgive me. That doesn't sound right. I'd really like to be friends. I don't know many people around here." He leaned forward, his hands clasped. "Would you have dinner with me? Maybe Saturday?"

She shouldn't have been surprised. A chemistry had developed between them. Yet she couldn't let herself forget that she was pregnant. And he was married, at least for now. "Will." She stood and felt a fluttering in her chest, like an awkward schoolgirl. "Today was lovely. But you see . . ." She tried to think fast. All he was asking for was friendship, yet there was an undercurrent of something more that could only lead to further entanglements. He had no idea of what had happened with Pete, or how she still had to explain her decision to have the baby to Rob. So many problems loomed. It wouldn't be fair to involve Will. "I've been through a lot lately," she said.

"I know that. Your husband hasn't been gone for that long."

"It's not only that." She didn't want to hurt him, yet she knew some kind of attraction was there. She spoke more firmly. "It just isn't a good idea."

"Another time?"

"No. It really isn't possible."

His face took on a closed look. "I see."

Caroline knew he was disappointed. The lovely connection that they had built slowly throughout their day together had collapsed.

"Well, I'll be going then," he said.

"I'm sorry," she said. "It was a wonderful day."

"Yeah. It was nice," he said quickly, and walked to the screened door. He opened it and left without looking back, disappearing into the dusk. She heard the car start a moment later and the lonely sound of the engine diminishing in the distance.

10

On a hot afternoon early in August Caroline drove toward Washington, leaving Lila's house for her other life. Maine, New Hampshire, and Massachusetts slipped behind her, and after crossing into Connecticut, in less than two hours she would reach her mother's house, her childhood home.

She had stopped once at a rest stop on the Mass Pike to use the restroom and eat a piece of cold quiche while leaning against the side of her car. The iced coffee that she had bought earlier was helping to combat the drowsiness that plagued her every day after lunch, and she continued to sip it, though the ice had melted. Coffee had not tasted good to her since she had been pregnant. Maybe it wasn't good for her either, but staying awake on the highway took priority for the moment. Hour after hour she had listened to the radio, and after endless accounts of dire news, another car bombing in the Middle East, the drought in the Southwest, and a hurricane heading toward the Caribbean, she had turned the radio off, not bothering to look for a station with music. The world's problems only depressed her. At the moment all she wanted was silence.

With every passing mile her dread grew sharper. How would she tell her mother? What, if anything, would she tell Pete? Most especially, how would she tell Rob the truth? The truth. Caroline felt a lump forming in her throat and reached again for her coffee. A sense of shame, like an illness, seeped into every pore of her body.

She had decided to stay in Maine for the winter and have her baby in East Hope. By renting the house in Chevy Chase for the year starting this September, she would be able to pay her mortgage and have a little extra money to live on. She hoped she had calculated correctly. Rob could join her in Connecticut at her mother's house for Thanksgiving, and they could be together again in Maine for Christmas. By then she would be too pregnant to travel. She tried to imagine the holiday in East Hope with snow on the ground, the river and the bay shimmering in crystalline winter light, and a fire crackling in Lila's living room hearth. The important thing was having Rob with her, being a family.

The baby should come in early February. The exact due date was on her list of questions for her doctor, that and the many other worries that had been tormenting her. She had started taking some over-the-counter vitamins, and she knew that being almost three months pregnant, she should have seen an obstetrician by now. She was an older mother. Her last child had not survived because of a rare heart problem, though at the time the doctors had reassured them that it was extremely rare, and unlikely to occur again.

The traffic grew heavier near Hartford. Caroline eased over one lane and watched for the exit for I-91. She forced herself to concentrate on the road, but a mental door had opened and all of her negative thoughts came rushing in. She pictured the dark Maine evenings, being alone in a cold house with a tiny infant. She would have to get up at night, her bare feet on an icy floor, and make her way to a crying baby. And what if the baby got sick?

Caroline would never forget the first time Rob became seriously ill. It was winter, and he must have been at least two years old, because they were living in the house in Chevy Chase. Harry had called it their "grown-up" house. Caroline had been hesitant to give up their tiny brick row house a few miles away, worrying that this new house was too expensive. It had been an extremely cold winter, and they had not yet replaced the old boiler in the basement. Harry's business was building slowly and they didn't have the money.

Around four that winter afternoon, Rob, who had been fussy for several days, began to pull at his ears. His fever spiked, and Caroline drove her screaming baby through the dark streets and rush-hour traffic, in a panic to reach the pediatrician's office before it closed. Rob was diagnosed with a double ear infection. The doctor told her to monitor the baby's fever and to call immediately if it worsened. On the way home she managed to carry the heavy, crying baby in and out of the drugstore to buy the large bottle of antibiotics.

After she got home, Rob, still hysterical, gagged on his first dose and spewed the pink liquid all over her and his crib. Eventually she managed to get some medicine in him and soothed him to sleep. She had called Harry once in the midst of this, but he'd been with clients from out of town and needed to attend a dinner. When he got home after eleven he had found her standing by the crib.

Harry bent and stroked Rob's cheek. "He doesn't feel too warm."

She nodded. "I think the medicine is starting to work."

"I'm sorry I couldn't get home," he whispered. "Pete was away and I was the only one available." He drew his arm around her waist. "Come to bed, Caro. He's going to be fine."

They walked back to the bedroom and Caroline fell into bed, numb and exhausted from the hours of worry. A few moments later, as she was falling into sleep, she felt Harry draw close to her and kiss the nape of her neck. "I love you, Caro."

Now, driving in increasingly heavy traffic, Caroline realized how little she had thought of Harry recently. This made her sad. What she had done with Pete and the decision to have this baby had somehow erased her earlier life. There had been many happy times in their home in Chevy Chase: watching Rob take his first steps in their sunny kitchen, hiding Easter eggs in the garden, Harry walking Rob through the dark streets dressed up as a dragon, while she remained behind passing out Halloween candy. Harry had stayed home to see Rob off on his first day of kindergarten. Even when Harry worked longer and longer hours he always made time for them on the weekends.

Caroline wiped the tears off her face with the back of her hand. This situation was just insane. It was not too late. She could change her mind.

Caroline exited from I-91 to the Merritt Parkway on the final stretch home to her mother. One night there and then on to Washington. The road, covered by a heavy canopy of trees, wound southward toward New York. Eventually she passed Westport, Darien, and Stamford, all the familiar places of her childhood. The outside temperature registered eighty-seven degrees. Maine seemed very far away. She needed to pee and was anxious to arrive, though part of her dreaded this first stop. Summer was coming to an end; the season of back to school, back to work, back to real life would arrive soon. Her exit in Greenwich loomed on her right. She slowed and turned onto the ramp.

❧

A little after six that evening, Caroline carried a glass of iced tea to her mother's living room.

"You're tired, dear. Go relax," Peg had said. "I'll join you in a minute."

Caroline sat on the faded sofa that faced the fireplace. She pushed a pillow behind her back and shifted her weight to avoid the nudge of a spring beneath her. The arms of the club chair next to her were worn, and the seat bore the indentation of continual use, her mother's preferred chair. Each time Caroline came home to her childhood house in Connecticut, she was struck by how much smaller and older everything looked.

Her parents had lived most of their married lives in this Tudor-style stone house. It was situated on over an acre of land, and judging from the monster-sized houses on neighboring streets, this eminently forgettable modest house would one day be torn down to make room for something grander: a house with more bathrooms than bedrooms, a circular driveway, a gourmet kitchen with runways of granite countertops, and a three-car garage.

Caroline's father, an accountant with a modest firm in Connecticut, had made a nice living. Their family would have been considered well-off, even wealthy by many. Hers had been a comfortable life: bicycles, dancing lessons, piano, braces, a few family vacations (one out west, two to Florida), the annual week on a lake in New Hampshire, and college educations—all this had been provided. They belonged to a country club too. Her mother still played tennis there, as well as bridge several afternoons a week. She complained of the fees going up, despite the lower dues for widows, saying that the place was becoming too fancy for people on a fixed income like her.

Looking around this living room now, where the curtains hadn't been changed in thirty years, Caroline knew that her mother didn't have the means to help her financially. She was thankful that Harry's firm had agreed to cover Caroline's health insurance for another year. With her pay from the cookbook job, and by staying in Maine for the year and renting out her house, she would have just enough to manage. Harry's father paid for Rob's college, something he had asked to do even before Harry had died. This came as a huge relief to her now. Perhaps he had known something of his son's business worries.

The steady hum of the room air conditioner started to lull Caroline to sleep. Recently she had felt perfectly fine, except for sudden bouts of sleepiness, especially in the afternoon.

"Goodness. You are tired." Her mother sat in her expected place and set her drink, a small glass of bourbon and orange juice, on the table beside her.

Caroline straightened and sipped her iced tea.

"Darcy's on her way over," her mother said. "Walter has a dinner meeting, so Darcy said she'll eat with us."

This was not good news. Caroline wanted time alone with her mother, who would not easily understand or accept all the decisions she had made. Forty-something women, and certainly widows, did not become unwed mothers in this neat, predictable world. Her ever-perfect sister, Darcy, would be quick to point that out.

"I'd hoped we could be on the patio, but it's just too damned hot." Her mother rarely spoke so harshly. "We never had summers this bad when you were growing up." She frowned and reached for her glass.

Caroline's mother looked well for her age. All the years of playing tennis had kept her figure trim, though each time Caroline came home she noticed subtle changes. Tonight Peg seemed a bit less strong, less defined. It was as if she were fading and becoming slightly tattered, like her living room, gently worn, less and less of who she once was.

"Darcy said that she read—"

"Mom. There's something we need to talk about."

"Does it get this hot in Maine?"

"I've decided to stay there for the next year."

"In East Hope? But you said you were driving home." Her mother looked confused, and annoyed too. She didn't like deviating from any set plan.

"I'm driving home now, but I'm only staying for a few weeks. Rob will join me next weekend. After he leaves for school I'm going back to Aunt Lila's house."

"Isn't the place ready to sell?"

"Things have changed. I'm afraid Harry made some bad investments, and money is a real problem."

"Harry?" Her mother raised her eyebrows and looked doubtful. "Caroline, dear, there was never anyone so careful. I can't believe he'd ever do anything like that."

"Mom, I don't want to go into everything, but there was this one company—actually, there was one man who convinced Harry that a certain drug, a wonder drug, something to do with curing autoimmune disorders, would be a major breakthrough. I never really understood it."

The image of Sunil Gava popped into her head, that dark, handsome man whom they had entertained a few years before Harry had died. He had flown in from California, and after that one meeting Harry had taken many trips to Los Angeles. Sunil, whom she'd thought young to be involved in such an important business deal, had been charming. She remembered him wearing a black blazer and slim leather Italian shoes, making him look more European than what she'd assumed to be Californian, where she pictured a land of blond surfers and superfit outdoor types in jeans and flip-flops. He'd been especially attentive to her, complimenting her on dinner and sending her flowers the morning after the party.

"The market was so slow for several years," she tried to explain, "I think Harry thought this was his big break, a way of recouping some really bad investments."

"Harry had other investments too."

"Not in the end. He felt he needed to put all of our capital in Avistar."

"He put everything in one company?" she asked, her voice pitched high in amazement.

"Mother, I can't explain it. Harry was under a lot of pressure then. He wasn't really himself." In the beginning Harry had been so excited about Sunil's company and the promised drug. He'd explained to her about trial studies, FDA regulations, astonishing results in a Mexican clinic. He'd come back from the trips elated and couldn't stop talking about being so lucky that he'd discovered Sunil and had been allowed to be involved in the early stages of the venture.

"Can't you just sell the house in Maine and be done with it?" her mother said. She took another sip of what she called her nightly poison. Peg Russell was never one to ruminate over decisions. Everything about her was practical: gray hair cut short, hair color being too expensive and time-consuming, a no-iron beige skirt and bright blue knit polo shirt, the color of her eyes. Her tanned bare legs were speckled from years in the sun, and she wouldn't bother with stockings until the weather became cool in November.

"I'm going to wait and sell the house next summer," Caroline said. "There's another reason I plan to stay there. You may find this difficult to understand," she said. She took the paper napkin, cool and damp, from under her glass of tea and wiped her forehead. "I'm pregnant. I made a terrible mistake. Remember I told you about the dinner party I went to in May?"

"You're pregnant?" Peg stared at her daughter.

"I want to have this child. I know it seems crazy. I'm sure you think I'm making a terrible mistake, but I've thought a lot and—"

"Don't assume what I think, Caroline," Peg said abruptly. She set her drink on the coaster beside her, then looked carefully at her daughter. "It's because you lost Grace."

"It's more than that," she said.

"But that is why. You must have always wanted another child."

"Mom, her death was terrible. Harry and I got through it. We moved on. I just never got pregnant. Rob was more than enough. We were happy."

Peg seemed to consider this. "Goodness, it is quite astonishing, when you think of it."

"It is." Caroline had had that same thought over and over.

"It's just so much to take on. You'll be all by yourself."

"I won't be alone. I'll have my baby."

"That's hardly a reason to have a child. I mean, you could get a dog, for that matter. Certainly simpler."

"How can you say that? We're talking about a child, my family."

Her mother drew her hands together and held them close to her chest. "What about the father?" She spoke with remarkable calm.

"Mom, it was a mistake, a one-night fling. He means nothing

to me." She looked at the floor, once again ashamed of her situation. "I want to have this baby," she said defiantly. "It's a sort of second chance." Caroline leaned back on the sofa, limp with exhaustion.

"I can understand that." Her mother, still calm, reached for her bourbon, took a drink, and set the glass back on the end table. "You've lost so much. I'm amazed at how well you've coped." Caroline had expected a different reaction entirely, maybe disapproval, at least disappointment at her daughter's irresponsible behavior.

"You are?"

"First Grace. All those years without her. Not being able to have another."

"Oh, Mom." Caroline began to cry and drew one hand to her face.

"And then to lose Harry." Caroline's mother came over and sat beside her on the sofa. She stroked her hair and rested her arm around her shoulder. "You've had a terrible ordeal. I can see how a baby would seem like an incredible gift. But if you're determined to do this, you can't do it by yourself. You've got to come here."

"No, Mom."

"I can help you."

"I'm happy in Maine. I'll be fine there."

"You'll be so far from your family."

Caroline thought of having Lila's house to herself, the village all but empty once the summer residents left for their other homes, no one to watch what she was doing, no one to wonder why. The solitude and peace of that place flowed into her thoughts, so strong she could practically taste it. The combination of the land, even her small thriving herb garden, the water that caught her eye everywhere she turned, the air so clean and fresh, made her long to return. It dawned on her that she wished she were driving north tomorrow, back to East Hope, and not to Washington, the place she had long thought of as home. Lila's house had claimed her. She missed it. "It's okay. I'll be fine in Maine."

"Please, Caroline, just think about it."

"Maybe later. We'll see." Kindness shone in her mother's wrinkled face, but also worry, a shadow of doubt.

"There's another thing," her mother said. "If you're going through with this, you've got to be honest. You've got to tell Pete."

"How did you know it was Pete?" Caroline was shocked. She had never said he was the man at the party.

"You told me he and Marjorie had invited you to a dinner party. I may be getting old, but I'm not stupid." She tilted her head and raised her eyebrows. "You told me he's spent hours with you sorting out Harry's papers. He's always been fond of you. I can see how you two might have grown close." She smiled briefly before her expression grew more serious. "You've got to tell him. He has a right to know."

"Mother, there's nothing between us."

"That's beside the point. He's the father."

Caroline groaned. "You're right. I know."

"What about Marjorie?"

"She never has to know. It has nothing to do with her."

"Doesn't it? Though I guess that's Pete's responsibility." Her mother shot her a wry look. "You also have to tell Rob."

Caroline leaned forward. It was what she feared most.

Her mother took Caroline's hand and held it. "He's old enough to know. In another month or two he'll certainly know."

Caroline tried to speak, but couldn't. The tears were choking her.

"He's not going to understand at first. You shouldn't expect him to," her mother said. "He will in time. He loves you, Caroline."

"Oh, Mom."

"There, there." Her mother continued to hold her. "I'll help you. You seem to forget you're giving me another grandchild."

Caroline was grateful for her mother's touch. As a child she had often gone to her father for comfort—he'd been the more nurturing parent, a quiet man, always ready to stop and listen. Caroline heard a car on the gravel drive. "Don't tell Darcy yet."

"She's going to figure it out sometime."

"Just not yet. Rob should know first." She drew in another breath. "And, as you said, I have to talk to Pete."

"Where is everybody?" Darcy's voice could be heard from the kitchen. A door slammed. In that instant Caroline knew she could not stand to go through this pregnancy with Darcy close at hand, second-guessing everything.

"Go upstairs and wash your face." Caroline's mother stood, her efficient self once again. "We're in here, dear," she called back. She nodded toward the stairs. "It's all right. I'll get Darcy to help me serve dinner."

Somehow Caroline managed to survive the evening. Darcy, four years older than Caroline, and at least four inches taller, was everything that Caroline was not. She wore her perfectly straight blond hair shoulder length and pulled neatly under a headband. That night she wore cream linen pants and a white shirt that complemented her even tan. Darcy wore only beige and white in summer, and black and gray in winter. A few years ago she had sworn off color and given Caroline a stack of her luxurious cashmere sweaters, all in luscious bright shades. Darcy had gone to law school, married Walter, and, after two years working in a big New York firm, gave up her career to care for her two children, who were already on their way to becoming just like their parents.

Darcy passed the bowl of chicken salad to Caroline. "You're pretty quiet tonight," she said.

"Your sister's had a long drive," their mother said. She pushed a platter of tomato aspic across the table to Darcy.

"Mom, Caroline's not an invalid," she said while scooping a wobbly red mass onto her plate. "How's Rob liking his job at the camp?"

"He's having fun."

"I'm amazed you let him go."

"Why wouldn't I let him go?" Caroline asked, trying to mask her annoyance.

"You had a hard time when he left for college. You couldn't stop talking about how you missed him."

"Don't you miss your kids?"

"Caroline, what's your problem tonight?"

"Sorry, I didn't mean to snap."

Darcy shrugged and toyed with the food on her plate. She studied Caroline. "You're looking kind of pale. Are you feeling all right?"

"I'm fine," she insisted. She glanced at her mother.

"Tell Darcy about the old cookbooks you've been collecting," Peg said, an obvious ploy to change the tone of the conversation.

Caroline talked about the books and later asked Darcy about her own children. Darcy appeared more than happy to fill her in on the successful pursuits of her precious offspring. Peg never served dessert during the week, and after dinner they drank weak decaffeinated coffee in the kitchen while loading the dishwasher. As soon as they were finished Caroline pleaded exhaustion and went up to bed.

The next morning Caroline's mother hugged her again and said she wished Caroline would reconsider having the baby in East Hope. Caroline didn't commit to any specific plan other than to say that she would be in Connecticut for Thanksgiving with Rob. She loaded the car and set off for Washington. Already the thermometer beside her mother's back door registered ninety-one degrees.

❦

August in Washington was the worst month of the year. Weeks of hot, humid weather squeezed the life out of everything. The leaves curled in listless discontent; planters of impatiens, though watered at daybreak, hung limp from the effort to stay alive; even geraniums, the hardiest of flowers, became dust-clogged and anemic. Waves of heat rose from the asphalt, and the buildings baked in the relentless sun. The heat persisted well into the night. The sky, bleached white and cloudless, locked the polluted air in like a prison.

Caroline arrived in Chevy Chase in the middle of just such an afternoon. She'd had a terrible time staying awake on the last part of her trip along the Baltimore-Washington Parkway, but as she maneuvered through the four lanes of traffic on the beltway, her adrenaline kicked in. She pulled into her driveway and got out of the car. The Volvo's air conditioner was not the strongest, and her skirt remained stuck to the back of her legs. She pulled it away and stared at her house. Fortunately, the lawn had been mowed, but clumps of weeds had shot up in the shrubbery on either side of the door. Maybe it was the oppressive heat, all the hours in the car, the strain of her situation, but standing here now looking at her front door, Caroline felt terribly old. A dense weight seemed to settle on her shoulders, and she worried that she might not be able to move.

Stop it, she told herself. *Get inside. Rob arrives this weekend.* Rob and Melanie, his girlfriend. She pulled her keys from her pocket and unlocked the door. It was swollen from the humidity, and she had to shove it hard with her knee to make it budge. After a final push it gave way. A pile of mail littered the hall floor. The mail was no longer being forwarded in August. A sea of catalogs, flyers, and bills lay at her feet. She bent down, gathered an armful, and carried it to the dining room table. After scooping up the rest of the mail, she lowered the thermostat that had been left at eighty degrees to ward off the humidity, and went to the kitchen for a glass of water. The silent, stale house seemed strangely alien to her.

She drank thirstily and filled the glass a second time. Somewhat revived, she went out to her car, eager to unpack and get ready for Rob, but while coming in from the garage, she noticed an envelope on the floor that had slipped partly under the chest by the door. It looked like an official letter, not junk mail, something from Century Mortgage, addressed to her.

❦

At nine thirty the next morning Caroline sat perched on the edge of the leather sofa in Pete's office and shivered. The air-conditioning made her think of a meat locker. She wore a pale green linen shift, and her bare arms were covered with goose bumps. Despite the chilly air, her palms had started to sweat. She needed to pee, but Pete's assistant, someone new whom she'd never met, had been annoyed with her when she had shown up first thing that morning without an appointment. The new assistant had claimed Pete was in a meeting, and that she would have to wait. Caroline didn't want to be in the ladies' room when he returned.

"You've come back," Pete said. He walked behind his desk and sat. In a dark suit and brilliant white shirt, he looked cool and immaculate. "I couldn't believe you'd take off for Maine without even talking to me."

"I'm sorry," she began. "I'm not sure I understand this." She put the letter on his desk and went back to the sofa, grateful for the space between them.

He read the letter and documents. He drew his brows together, then shrugged and let the papers fall to the desk. "It's a balloon payment."

"I owe a hundred and fifty thousand dollars on November first?"

"It appears that Harry took out a second mortgage when the Avistar deal started to look bad." His voice no longer sounded angry. "This isn't good, Red."

"Oh, God," she said, lowering her head. She thought she'd caught everything. How had this slipped through? "I don't remember signing anything. We owned the house jointly, and Harry would—"

"Did you always know what you were signing?" Pete asked. "Tax forms? Proxies?"

"Not always," she whispered. She couldn't look at him.

"You signed it." Pete shoved the papers to her across the desk. "Your signature is right here."

She picked up the sheets and tried to read through a blur of tears. She drew in a gulp of air and forced her eyes to focus. "I guess I did." What had Harry said to her? She had no recollection. Was it one morning as he was dashing out the door? "Here, Caro, sign this. Yeah, this is a different company. We'll get a better rate." A hurried signature—why ask questions? Harry took care of all the money. He would know best.

"I'm going to have to sell the house," she said.

"I'm afraid that's the only solution," Pete said, his voice kinder. He came over and sat beside her on the sofa and handed her his handkerchief.

Caroline drew the white cloth across her eyes and under her nose.

"You're cold." Pete stroked the skin of her forearm. His touch was gentle and slow. "I've missed you this summer. I know what happened between us was sudden. But, Red, it did happen." His touch grew firmer.

"It was a mistake," she said, sliding away.

He didn't try to touch her again, but cocked his head and watched her, as if trying to understand something. "What's the matter, Red? I can help you with the house. It's a seller's market. You won't have any trouble." He reached for her chin and turned her face toward his. "Look at me." Pete's eyes had softened, and his lips remained parted as if he were about to speak. He drew his hand along her cheek to her neck.

Caroline stood as if stung. "Don't touch me anymore." She started to cry again.

Pete looked up at her. "Caroline, I don't want to hurt you. You've suffered enough. We do need to talk about what happened."

"Nothing happened." She blinked back her tears and blew her nose. "Or it shouldn't have happened."

"Don't say that." He stood.

His face had lost the harsh expression of when he'd first come in. She noticed the fine lines around his eyes, his dark brows lifted in expectation. The thought of telling him about the baby was unbearable. This was controversy enough.

He turned away from her and held his hands together as if trying to figure out how to proceed. It wasn't like him to be at a loss for words. The office fell silent except for the sound of the air-conditioning system that roared relentlessly. "I admire what you're doing—taking charge, going to Maine," he said. "I haven't stopped thinking about you—about us."

"No," she said. "Don't say that."

"Red, I was glad to help you with Harry's estate. He was my best friend, but I realized that even though it was a terrible time for you, it gave me a chance to really know you. Last winter I felt I was getting close to you."

"Please," Caroline said. "Pete, I don't have those kind of feelings for you."

"But it's the truth." He moved toward her.

That word again. Caroline remembered her mother and what she had said. "There's something you have to know." She raised her hand. "You've got to hear this." By now she no longer felt cold. She would never have the courage if she waited. "I'm pregnant. You're the father."

He stared for a moment, his features blank of all expression. A moment later he shook his head as if this were the last thing on earth he had ever expected to hear. He went to the sofa and sat like a man who'd been wounded, unable to support his own weight.

"That one night?"

She nodded.

Pete bent his head into his palms. "Jesus, Red," he said. He blew out through his teeth and leaned back.

Caroline picked up her handbag. She hugged her arms across her chest. The memory of their night together came back. Feelings of regret and sorrow flooded through her. It was too late. The welling of sadness in her throat didn't matter. "I can't talk about it now," she said. Her voice grew stronger. "I'm going back to Maine soon. No one around here will know it's yours."

"You're keeping the baby?" He stared at her, looking suddenly older, his eyes deep within their sockets.

"I don't want anything from you. I'm doing this for me. This is something I want."

Pete remained silent. She imagined him thinking of their night together. Or was he thinking of Marjorie? Their marriage? Perhaps he was thinking of Harry, his friend? Three red lights on his telephone blinked, and then a fourth came to life. She moved toward the door. He started to get up. "No," she said. She motioned for him to stay where he was and said quietly, "I want nothing from you." She put her hand on the door handle; it was icy cold.

"Caroline," he said, "please don't say that."

"I want nothing from you," she said again, "but I felt you should know." She opened the door to leave, and quickly tried to draw her face into some form of composure. His assistant was typing rapidly on her computer. The shiny pink nails flew across the keys.

"Red," she heard him call after her before the door clicked shut.

11

Caroline sat with Rob and Melanie at the wrought-iron table on the patio in the garden. They had arrived together and had been with her in Chevy Chase for a week. It was now the weekend. There had been a thunderstorm in the late afternoon, and water still dripped from the gutter by the back door. The evening was unexpectedly cooler. When Melanie had offered to set the table for dinner, Caroline suggested that they eat outside to take advantage of the pleasant evening. The earth, wet from the heavy rain, smelled fertile. Long days of heat coupled with a good amount of rain that summer had made the garden especially lush, junglelike in its fullness.

"We need to go soon, Mom." Rob sat across the table from Caroline. It was dark in the garden, but the glow of the kitchen lights illuminated Rob's face. He looked tanned and healthy. Caroline thought he had grown taller over the summer.

"Have some more tomatoes," Caroline said, lifting the platter. She had bought them this morning at the farmers' market, along with fresh corn on the cob.

Rob reached across the table, and Caroline noted how his forearms were muscled and strong-looking, the arms of a man, no longer those of a boy.

He passed the plate to Melanie. "It's getting late," he said, giving Melanie a look that seemed meant for her alone.

"Your mom made a peach tart for dessert," Melanie said. She

sat with her back to the house, her face in shadow. Despite the darkness, Caroline knew her expression would be willing and kind, the corners of her wide eyes lifted in concern. She had been a quiet and ideal guest, moving easily into their lives; she was as fluid as the sound of her name. A lovely young woman almost as tall as Rob, with silky light brown hair, Melanie could not be faulted. And yet, because of Melanie's presence, Caroline's time with Rob was not the same. With no chance of their being alone together, Caroline's joy in being with Rob was in some way diluted.

"Can we have dessert later, Mom? Jim needs a ride to the party."

Melanie and Rob had been late coming back from tennis, and it had taken a long time for the charcoal to get hot enough to grill. The chicken had been delicious, and worth the wait, but now they were in a hurry. "Of course," Caroline said, determined to keep any disappointment from her voice. "I'll leave the tart on the counter."

A few minutes later they carried their dishes into the kitchen. Melanie began to load the dishwasher.

"I'll do these," Caroline said. "You two go on."

"Thanks, Mom." Rob bent and kissed her cheek. "Great dinner." He smelled of shampoo and he wore jeans and a pressed shirt. His browned feet slapped lightly in well-worn flip-flops. Taking Melanie by the hand, he started down the hall to the front of the house.

Melanie looked back at Caroline, lifted her shoulders, and offered a smile of apology. "I guess we're off then," she said. She turned to Rob, but called back, "Thanks for dinner. See you in the morning."

Caroline heard Melanie's light steps as she went upstairs to get something for the evening—her handbag or maybe a sweater. Melanie was staying in the guest room directly above the kitchen. Her duffel bag, partly unpacked, lay open on the luggage rack by the window, and other clothes were strewn across the loosely made-up bed. Despite the separate rooms, Caroline was certain that they were lovers—from the small gestures, a touch here and there, the knowing way they looked at each other. A sexual energy glowed between them like an aura.

One night she had come into the small den off the living room where they kept the television. Rob and Melanie had rented a movie. They had all been to a neighborhood barbecue earlier, and Caroline, tired from several hours of standing and visiting with the neighbors, had been eager to go to bed. She went into the den to say good night. Rob and Melanie sat together on the sofa, as closely side by side as if they were sewn together like two rag dolls, leg to leg, hip to hip, and arm against arm. Rob's hand rested on Melanie's thigh as if it belonged there. They both got to their feet, and Rob gave Caroline a perfunctory hug before sitting beside Melanie once again.

Caroline had retreated awkwardly, wishing she hadn't gone in to say good night. Once, years ago, when she came home from college, her mother told her not to bother Darcy and Walter, who were alone in the living room. "You don't want to be *de trop*." The words had stung at the time, and Caroline realized that despite the pleasant days she was having with Rob and Melanie, it was really she who was *de trop*.

Caroline put the leftover chicken and tomatoes into the fridge and covered the bowl of couscous. Rob might help himself to more when he got back from the party. That and the peach tart. It glistened under an apricot glaze on the counter. She thought she might have a piece herself after she finished the dishes, and sit once more in the garden. A few minutes later she heard the front door bang closed and the sound of her car going down the driveway. They were gone. She doubted they would even think of her now that they'd left the house. They were off in their own world: college friends, parties, time by themselves, a place where she didn't exist.

Once the dishes were done, Caroline turned out the lights and stood by the sink looking out at the garden. Grace's lilac bush stood illuminated by the moon. No longer hungry, Caroline decided against cutting into the peach tart. She thought for a moment of the Maine sky. There, she would see not only the moon, but also the glittering of stars. The city lights in Washington obscured the stars here.

And Will. What would he be doing now? Again, Caroline was filled with regret, remembering how she had sent him on his way after their day together in July. He had only wanted to be friends. She pictured the slant of his eyes and imagined the feel of his hair soft against her hands. A familiar surge of loneliness welled in her.

The doorbell rang, a jarring interruption in the silent house. Had Rob and Melanie forgotten something? But they had a key and would not ring the bell. Caroline looked out the living room window, across the lawn, and to the street. A black BMW was parked at the curb. She stopped. The bell rang a second time, longer and more insistent. She went to the door.

"Are you by yourself?" Pete asked.

Speechless, she stood at the open door. It had been a week since she had told him about the baby.

"We have to talk, Caroline," he said. "I took a chance. Thought that Rob might be out with his friends." Pete had deep circles under his eyes. He wore a polo shirt, untucked, and faded khaki shorts. Caroline found herself staring at his bare legs. "May I come in?"

She nodded and stood aside. He walked past her to the living room, and she thought it amazing how the casual clothes—sloppy, almost, something he would have thrown on after a day at the office—made him seem smaller, more vulnerable. She resisted the urge to reach out for a casual hug. Having been intimate that once, not so long ago, precluded their habitual greeting.

"Marjorie?" Her voice felt weak. She swallowed.

"Nantucket. I'm going to join her this weekend. The kids are already there."

"I see," she said. "Would you like something to drink?" That instant she wished she could have a stiff drink herself, something to dull her senses.

He shook his head. "Where's Rob?"

"He and his girlfriend left for a party. Please," she said, and gestured toward the sofa.

He went to sit down, and Caroline could feel the tension of that May night coming back—the memory of his hands on her skin, the sense of letting go of everything, of feeling desired after months alone. Being in this room again with Pete jolted her to the realization that the baby was indeed his, not some magical whisper of life, not hers alone, but a small being fathered by this man. Pete. She sat in the wing chair across from him. Of course he would come to talk to her. She had to stay strong. Having him in her living room only reminded her of how vulnerable she once was.

"I'm rarely taken by surprise," he said. "My God, Red."

"I'm sorry to have shocked you. I never imagined this could happen. Harry and I had given up on ever having more children." She felt like a schoolgirl trying to make up excuses for not doing her homework. "It was wrong for us to have . . . I mean, I didn't think—"

"I've thought about you all summer."

"Pete—"

"Wait. Hear me out." He sounded again like the businessman he was. Tough. In control. "The last few days I kept thinking of what you were doing. How you decided to have this child. It makes no sense. You know that. I know that. The money, of course. But Rob? I don't think he's going to take it very well. What kid would?"

"I'm going to tell him."

"Of course you are. You're being so strong. I'm still trying to get a handle on all this."

"First I have to tell him about the house. Why we have to sell."

"That's nothing compared to your having a baby. I'm worried for you, Red."

Caroline sat rigid and listened. The room was dark. In her panic at seeing him again she hadn't bothered to turn on a lamp. It was odd, really. Here they were again in her living room in the dark. Her hands had tightened into fists.

His voice grew soft. "You're being incredibly brave. I've hardly slept for thinking about you. It's like there's a side to you I've never known. I'm truly amazed at what you're doing."

She stared at him. "You are?"

"But you've got to let me help." He stood and turned on the lamp next to her. He reached into his pocket and took out a folded piece of paper. "It will take time to arrange for more, but here's twenty thousand." He handed her what she could now see was a check.

"I don't want your help," Caroline said, not taking the check. She got up and walked to the hall. "I told you I don't expect anything. . . ."

"I know you don't expect anything," he said, following her. "I want to give it to you. You need it. I know that better than anyone."

"You're wrong." Suddenly it became easier to talk. "I'm putting this house on the market. I'm going to stay in Maine for a year. I've got it all figured out. I don't need your money." Caroline suddenly felt stronger. "I've learned a lot in Maine. I want to support myself and be independent. I need to do this on my own."

He stared at her, then shook his head. "I think you're taking on more than you can handle." He stepped toward her.

Caroline crossed her arms over her chest and leaned against the banister. Less than an hour before, Rob's carefree footsteps had echoed in the hallway. "I know you want to help. I appreciate what you're doing, but it would be simpler if we just ended this now."

"End it? How can you say that? This is only the beginning. We're talking about my child too. How do you think I feel? It's more than just the responsibility."

Pete drew his hand through his hair, cut shorter than she remembered. He appeared to be earnest, as if he really cared. "You can't just leave town, go to Maine, and start over." He placed his hand on the banister, moving closer to her. "I think you're fooling yourself. It's not that simple."

"Please," she whispered. It would be so easy to give in to him, to have him hold her. He was kind. He seemed to want her in spite of everything. Yet, she didn't want to be taken care of anymore. She pictured the house in Maine, lifted her chin, and met his gaze. "I'm going back to East Hope."

"Is that really what you want?"

She nodded her head to indicate yes. All she wanted now was to be left in peace.

"I don't know." His voice cracked as if he might break down. He took a deep breath. "I can't stop you from going to Maine. But I won't forget that this is my child. At least take the money." He offered the check again.

"No." She kept her arms tucked around her.

"You can always change your mind." He shoved the check back into his pocket and moved toward the door. He paused and spoke again. "I care for you, Red. I'm part of this too. Don't forget that." He pulled open the door and went out.

She crossed to the window and watched as he got into his car. The night was clear and dry, like a Maine summer night. Her baby was also Pete's child. That connection weighed on her like a stone around her neck. Caroline looked again at the night sky and felt the coldness of the moon.

❧

The next morning Caroline met Vivien for coffee at the Coffee Break, a nearby café. They had not seen each other since Caroline had taken her to the airport in Maine. When she had called about delivering the finished manuscript for the cookbook, Vivien had suggested meeting at the café because she had painters working at home and her entire home office was boxed up in her living room. Vivien didn't usually have the time to meet with her writers. Caroline knew she was seeing her now more as an old friend.

"It looks great." Vivien leafed through the manuscript pages. "I've got a good person lined up to do the illustrations," she said. "Her work is charming. I think you'll like it." They were both nursing large cups of café au lait and had opted to sit inside the restaurant and avoid the surge of rush-hour traffic booming noisily along Connecticut Avenue.

Caroline was relieved to have finished the project and glad Vivien had taken the time to see her. "I wanted to have it done in time to bring it to you in person."

"So," Vivien said, "ahead of schedule." She looked the same as ever, but she remained cool and professional. "I'm impressed."

Caroline gathered her courage and looked Vivien in the eye. "I feel terrible about the argument we had." Caroline still regretted accusing Vivien of not understanding her wanting to keep her baby. Vivien might not be a mother, but she was a daughter; she had a loving husband. She understood the intractable power of human bonds. Accusing Vivien of not understanding the yearning that possessed Caroline that summer had been unfair. "I'm so sorry, Vivien."

"How are you getting on?"

"I saw my doctor earlier this week. She gave me hell, of course, for not coming in sooner." Caroline smiled at Vivien and thought she saw a glimmer of understanding. "Everything looks fine. I'm set to switch to a doctor in Maine. I'm due in early February."

"A winter baby." She smiled.

"Having a baby is a different business now. A lot's happened in nineteen years." She told Vivien about the series of tests she would need to have, but how it had been a relief to learn that her situation was not all that unusual, being pregnant at forty-four. "I'm not the dinosaur I thought I'd be," she added.

"How has Rob taken the news?"

"He's had his girlfriend visiting all week."

"You haven't told him?"

"There hasn't been a good time. They sleep all morning and

are out the rest of the day. I also haven't told him that I'm going to sell our house." Caroline quickly explained about the balloon payment and her plan to put the house on the market.

"But he knows about Harry's losses?"

"Some of it. I told him that money was tight."

Vivien leaned forward and rested her elbows on either side of her cup. "Caroline, you've always hated confrontation. I know you." Her voice was kind. She was acting like a friend once again. "You mustn't put it off. He's leaving soon for college. He has to be told."

"I know," she said. "I just dread telling him."

"Caroline," Vivien said, heaving a sigh. "First, we need some of those really great brioches. What are we thinking by only drinking coffee in this place?" Like her old self, Vivien bustled off to the counter to buy the wonderful egg-rich rolls for which the Coffee Break was known. When she returned, Caroline told her all that had been happening since her return home: Pete's visit and his unexpected kindness, his willingness to help.

"I don't want Pete to be part of this," Caroline said. "I know he's not happy with Marjorie. Still, I don't want to be responsible for what might happen. I don't love him. We're old friends. He's fond of me. Nothing more."

"It sounds like he's more than just fond."

"He seems to think that we grew close working together on Harry's estate."

"Did you?"

"He's just carried away by all that's happened. That's why it's better that I go away."

"I can't believe we're talking about your life," Vivien said. She wiped her buttery fingers on her napkin. "But we are, and we've got to get you through this." She no longer seemed angry with Caroline and began to offer advice. "Rob won't want to live in Maine. When he's home from college he'll want to be near his friends. Why don't you rent a small house here?"

"Under Marjorie's nose?" Caroline pushed her plate away. "What would everyone think? You know they'd figure it out. Arthur and Julia were at that dinner. Remember?"

"What Rob thinks should be your first concern."

"Of course he's my concern."

"Then tell him. He may have an opinion about what you should do. You need to treat him like a grown-up."

Caroline listened and agreed. How could she not? "Vivien. There's something else I wanted to talk about. I have an idea for a cookbook. My own, this time. Remember what I told you about Lila's old cookbooks? There are some amazing recipes with wonderful old-fashioned names. I'd like to do something with them. Maybe a vintage collection, a sort of retro look at New England or even Maine cookery."

Caroline could see she had caught Vivien's interest. "It would be a sort of cultural history," she went on. "Maybe including photographs of old farm kitchens or the landscape itself? Remember the great farm stands we saw when you visited?"

"I'm not sure World Life would be the right publisher," Vivien said. "They usually stick to instructional series." She finished the last of her brioche. "It's an idea, though. A different slant. Why don't you work on a proposal? You'll need to find an agent first. I have a few contacts in New York."

"I'd be grateful for any ideas."

"Don't get too excited. The cookbook market is pretty saturated. Still, this is a little different. There's a strong trend back to the 'real' food of our grandmothers going on. Your idea might fit. The right photography could add a lot too."

Besides the pleasure of searching for old recipes, Caroline had the niggling hope that she might be able to make some real money if she could produce a book. More than that, working would take her mind off her problems. If she could just get through the next few weeks.

❧

"Why didn't you say anything before?" Rob pushed back from the table. They were eating an early dinner in the kitchen. He had taken Melanie to the airport that morning and had spent the rest of the day running errands and packing. Jim was picking him up in the morning and they were driving together back to college.

"Sweetie, Melanie was here and I didn't want to upset you." Caroline had explained to Rob about the balloon payment and her plan for the house.

"You're telling me the night before I leave for school that we have to sell our house?"

"Of course it's upsetting."

"I thought selling the house in Maine would be enough."

"I'm afraid not. We need the money from this house because of the balloon payment. Eventually I'll sell the house in Maine too. We'll be able to buy something smaller here."

"I don't want another house." He stood up, knocking back his chair. "I want to be here. This is where Dad lived. Don't you care about that?"

"Of course I care."

"You should have told me sooner."

Pain and confusion filled his voice. He had lost his father and now he was losing the place he'd grown up in. In all fairness, certainly she could understand his feelings.

"This is just temporary. For a while Maine will be our home."

"It's not my home," he said. "Give me a break, Mom."

"I'm so sorry, Rob. There's another reason I want to—"

"Fine. Okay. Sell the house. See if I give a shit." He stalked out of the kitchen and called back, "I'm going out."

Caroline was in bed trying to read when he returned. All she could think about was how to tell him she was pregnant. A myriad of explanations swirled in her head. It was just after ten. He stopped in her room.

"I'm sorry I blew up, Mom."

"It's okay, sweetie. I was wrong not to have told you sooner."

"I know it's hard for you too." He bent and kissed her cheek.

"I'll put everything in storage," she said. "Once we have another place it won't be so bad."

"Let's not talk about it now, okay?" He walked toward her door. "Did Melanie call the house?"

"No. No one called." She swallowed. "Rob, there's something more—"

"I've got a lot on my mind right now. Good night, Mom." He stepped into the hall, seeming not to hear. She heard him retreat to his room, his door closing.

Again, she'd lost her nerve. Pete was wrong. She wasn't brave at all.

❦

By the end of the following week Caroline had accomplished almost everything she wanted. The Tuesday after Labor Day the house would officially be on the market. Sara Josephs, her Realtor, had put the shiny FOR SALE sign in the garage in readiness. Sara had also suggested that Caroline have a professional crew do a major cleanup of the garden. The real estate market in this neighborhood of Chevy Chase was especially strong, and the attractive landscape was one of the selling points.

Room by room, Caroline had cleaned and organized, packing away personal mementos, clearing out closets, uncluttering countertops, doing her best to make the house look fresh and appealing. Several boxes of cookbooks and photographs were already packed and in her car, ready to go to Maine.

Rob had been at school for a week. He seemed a little preoccupied, but at least he had returned her phone calls to let her know that he was okay. Getting the house ready was much easier with him away. She knew he didn't want to talk any more about giving up their home. When she called to ask if it was okay to throw out a box of old soccer trophies that were on a shelf in the basement he answered brusquely, "I don't care. Do whatever you want. I don't want to hear about it." His way of coping was to distance himself from her, and for now she would have to accept it. Her way of coping was to keep her mind on one task at a time.

On the day of her departure she awoke just before dawn. Instinctively she ran her hands across her belly. It was there: a gentle roundness filling the cavity between her hip bones. The pregnancy was real. Instead of feeling anxious or uncertain, today she felt calm and resolute. She got out of bed thinking she might as well get started.

This time she wanted to drive to Maine without stopping for the night, and doing the thirteen hours straight was not going to be easy. Still, it was easier than seeing her mother again and having to admit that she hadn't told Rob the truth. She had told herself she would talk to Rob after he had had a few weeks to get settled into school.

Still in her nightgown, she walked through the silent house. In the early hour each room was bathed in a bluish haze. From time to time she paused, straightening a lamp shade, plumping a cushion, tossing away an old magazine. Everything was neat and impersonal, ready for the intruding eyes of potential buyers. She went into Harry's office. What Rob had said was true. Even with many of the personal items packed and put away, something of Harry seemed to linger there. When the house was sold that would be lost too. Forever.

She walked behind the desk and sat in his chair, a wooden Windsor style. They'd found it together in an antique shop in Pennsylvania. Caroline had made a bargello needlework cushion for the seat. Her mother had shown her how to do the stitches, and she had worked on it during her pregnancy with Grace. That had been a time of waiting. Waiting for Rob to get up from his nap, waiting for Harry to get home for dinner, waiting for Grace. She had never done needlework after that.

Sitting here now in silence, she tried to remember the sound of Harry's voice. How quickly everything was starting to fade. Like the cushion she sat on. She stood and walked to the doorway and looked back at the empty chair.

She and Harry had had an argument in this room almost exactly a year before. Rob was at the beach with his best friends, the final week before they all left for college. Harry had been on the phone the entire evening talking to the people in California. His voice had been tense and angry. She had heard the name Sunil, quick bits of conversation, swear words amid other harsh language. Later, when Harry appeared to be off the phone, Caroline went in. With his elbows on his desk and his head cradled in his hands, he looked like a man weeping or possibly praying.

"What's wrong?" she asked.

Startled, he looked at her blankly, as if for a brief moment he didn't even recognize her. Then he shook his head and looked at his watch. "I've got to go in to work."

"The office? Now?" She watched him stand and gather up the papers strewn across the desk. "It's late. Certainly it can wait until morning."

"I have to go to California tomorrow."

"But we're taking Rob to college this weekend. Will you be back by then?"

"I doubt it." He put the papers and heavy folders into his briefcase. "I'll know more in a few days."

"I was planning a special dinner for him." Caroline sat in the upholstered chair next to the bookshelves. "I don't want to take him to school by myself and then come home to an empty house." Caroline had felt a sinking sensation. Her only child was leaving. "It's going to be so hard to have him gone."

At this, Harry had paused and stared at her. His expression had softened a little. He stopped gathering his things. "You know, life can be tough, Caro. Pretty damn tough." He looked at his watch. "Don't wait up for me." From the set of his jaw she had known there was nothing she could say. She never heard him come in that night.

Rob had returned from the beach two days later. Harry was still in California and didn't make it home in time to take him to school. She had been angry and resentful that Harry had let business interfere with Rob's departure.

When Harry had returned from California, Caroline had acted cool toward him. He had seemed tense, and when she finally had asked if everything was okay at work, he told her not to worry. September was busy. Some days they hardly saw each other. Those first weeks without Rob at home reminded her of the time after Grace died. Harry kept to himself and seemed to grow more remote. He put in longer and longer hours at the office. Caroline, sometimes angry, sometimes worried, said nothing. It was easier to maintain harmony than seek the truth.

A ray of sunshine shone across the now-empty polished desk. It must have been that night when Harry found out that the entire deal with Avistar was a sham, that there was no breakthrough drug, and that his chance for a huge win had instead become a devastating loss. Caroline turned away. She should have tried harder. She should have tried to get at the truth last summer.

She also should have told Rob about the baby before he left for school. What would he think if he knew she was carrying Pete's child? Could he ever forgive her? In her heart she knew that his learning about her pregnancy might drive him away from her. Once again she felt her belly, the truth hidden beneath her nightgown.

12

"Yoo-hoo." Penny Taunton stepped into the shop, her yellow hooded slicker dripping with rain. It was the last week in August, a Tuesday, the day Taunton's was usually closed. It had rained all night. Will stood up from behind the counter, where he was unpacking a box of books that he had brought back from a house sale the week before.

"Good to see you," he said. "Nasty day out there."

"Nothing but a bit of weatha'," Penny said in her crisp native vowels.

"Here, let me," Will said, taking her wet jacket. He shook it over the mat and hung it on the coatrack behind the door. She wore shapeless blue jeans, a turtleneck, and a sweatshirt.

"Glad I caught you in. Thought you might be out book hunting again."

"It can get addictive." He grinned. He had been pleased with this recent purchase and decided to use his day off to add the titles to his computerized inventory and to get them on the shelves. August had proven to be a busy month. The current titles that he stocked were selling briskly.

"The place looks real good," Penny said.

"Thanks. How's your dad?" he asked.

"That's why I came to see you."

Will could see from her expression that she didn't have good news. "Not any better then?" he asked.

Penny's mouth pulled in and she seemed to blink back tears, but her voice was strong. "He understands he can't come back. If anything, he's weaker still."

"Sorry to hear that."

"You've done a fine job here. Dad wants you to stay on. Hold the fort down till the end of October, if you can."

"I'm not sure, Penny. My wife expects me in New York soon." Did she? Will was beginning to have his doubts. Her supposed August visit still hadn't happened. They hadn't talked since he'd refused to go see her in California. Their time away from each other was taking on a permanent feel.

"You could make it real part-time. After Labor Day Dad kept the shop open only Thursday to Sunday. There'd be time for you to travel."

"I'd like to help you," he said, knowing that the time had come for him to make plans for the future. "Can I fix you a cup of coffee?" They had been standing by the door. He gestured to the pot he'd set up behind the counter. He offered it to his early morning customers. He had a few regulars stopping by. Besides serving free coffee, Will kept a stash of dog biscuits on hand and a water dish on the porch to welcome pets. On Fridays he set out wine and chips from four to six. Edna, from the library, called it Wine and Read, instead of Wine and Cheese. It proved to be a popular event.

"Coffee'd be nice." Penny followed him behind the counter and sat in the chair next to his desk. Will filled cups for both of them and sat in what had always been her father's chair, a smooth, old-fashioned wooden one that spun from the base and slid easily across the floor on casters.

"Dad gave me the okay to sell the place. He wanted me to ask if you'd be interested."

Will shook his head. "Penny, I—"

"Just think about it. We'd give you a good price. The building's not much, but the land's real nice."

"It's a great place." He looked over her shoulder out the rain-streaked window to the field below. It was beautiful property, and the land behind it along the shoreline could never be developed.

"You could fix up the building. Maybe add on, if you wanted more space."

"Thanks, Penny." His heart beat faster. "I will think about it."

They chatted a few more minutes and shared local news. Penny reported on who was staying on for the winter, about the snowbirds who fled to Florida.

"Oh, almost forgot." She had started to put her rain jacket on and paused. "Edna, down at the library, wanted to know if you'd be interested in volunteering in the tutoring program after school. We thought that since you used to teach English you might be willing to help out."

"I'm not sure how much longer I'll be here."

"It's not remedial," she continued. "It's to help some of our young folks. There's some here who are really talented, but we don't have money in the budget for those advanced classes—you know, the AP and such."

Will agreed to talk to Edna and said he'd try to keep the shop going as long as possible after Labor Day.

"I hope you'll consider taking it on. If you bought, you'd be doing us a favor." She buttoned her slicker and looked once more around the bookstore. "I hear good things about you in the village." She gave him an angular grin. "That's saying something. Tough crowd to please."

"I like living here, Penny. I'm tempted by your offer."

"Have a good think. I'll be talking to you again."

Will walked with her to the door and out onto the granite step.

"Seems to have let up," she said, leaving off the hood of her jacket. She reached out her hand. "Ahuh. Gonna be a nice day after all."

The rain had stopped and bits of blue shot between the clouds. Will went inside. Slowly over the weeks, as he had spent more and more time working at Taunton's, he had almost come to think of the place as his. He hadn't needed to set up a computerized accounting system; he certainly didn't need to keep adding to the inventory, but he had enjoyed doing it. His innovations were successful. The sun now flooded through the front windows. Penny was right. It was going to be a beautiful day.

When he had finished flattening some cardboard boxes for recycling, he decided to go for a run, one of his favorite ways to think. He put on his running clothes and stepped outside. As he started to lock the door he heard the phone. Thinking it might be Penny again, he went back in, catching it on the final ring.

It was Mary Beth. "I've been missing you," she said.

This took him by surprise. He assumed she was still angry at him for refusing to make the trip to California.

"I don't know what to say," he said. "It's been so long."

"Too long," she said. "If it's okay, I'd like to come up this weekend." It was as if their last heated exchange had been entirely forgotten.

"In time for our anniversary?"

"Is that all right?"

"Sure." He cleared his throat, still wary. This change in tactic was a shock. She sounded different—not apologetic but kind. Maybe things had changed. What would she think of East Hope? Perhaps if she saw this place she would understand why he was drawn to it.

Mary Beth said she'd e-mail him her flight information, and he offered to pick her up in Bangor. She said she preferred to rent a car, and he agreed to send directions. She explained she couldn't talk longer and they both said good-bye.

Oddly, Mary Beth had sounded a little nervous, even shy with him. It had been almost three months since they'd been together. She had missed him. He couldn't quite believe that this was happening after all the nights alone. Yes, he had missed her too. He was sure of it.

He looked around the store. All was in order. With a little part-time help, he could run it from New York and check in periodically during the summers. His thoughts galloped ahead. It might be possible to renovate the building, add a few rooms, make it livable for two, maybe a family one day. It could be their escape from the city. Maybe it could work. For the first time all summer he allowed himself to dream, to look ahead at the possibilities. No matter what he decided about the store, he felt obligated to stay on until October and finish out the season for the Taunton family.

Will stepped outside again and started off on his old route through the village, around the bay, and up the hill in the direction of Caroline's house. There hadn't been lights on over there for quite some time.

Summer was drawing to an end in East Hope. While the official beginning of autumn was a few weeks away, all the predictable signs were there. Some of the maples had started to turn color, a few preliminary branches of reds and yellows. The orange daylilies that had adorned the roadsides all summer were disappearing.

A weedy purple flowering plant had emerged in the field behind the store. And the field itself had turned from green to gold. The air in East Hope now had a definite bite, as if to remind Will to pay attention, as if a notice had been posted informing him that the hard Maine winter lay just ahead.

What Will loved most these days was the change in the water. On sunny days the ocean was so deeply, richly, intensely blue it almost hurt his eyes. The clarity of the light delineated everything with sharp precision. Will had good vision, but it was as if he'd been given glasses that made everything more distinct, more vivid. Caroline's house, now within view at the crest of the hill, was a crisp white, like a freshly laundered shirt. He wondered where she had gone. He figured he would see a FOR SALE sign soon.

His mother used to talk about the change of light. "Look how you can see the houses more clearly on the point," he remembered her saying one afternoon years before, as they looked out on Narragansett Bay. She had been removing the dead blooms in her flower garden and had stopped to stare out at the water in the distance. He had gone to ask her something, something long forgotten and unimportant. What was important to him now was knowing that she too had appreciated the light.

Will's parents had been honest, hardworking, loyal, like many of the people Will was beginning to know in East Hope. His mother and father had rarely been apart, even dying within months of each other. For his mother it had been cancer, for his father congestive heart failure. Each time, he had gone home and made arrangements for the funeral and taken charge of all the details. Rusty had been grateful for that. His father's old friends at the hardware store had told him that his dad would have been proud of the way he'd come home and helped out.

His parents would have liked East Hope. He could imagine them doing errands in the village, stopping in for coffee at Karen's Café the way he did, buying the paper there. Martha and Steve, the owners, treated Will like a friend. They talked about the crowds, the weather, and then the lack of crowds, the cooler weather. His parents would have fit in here. Like he did, he thought, pleased with this realization.

Will passed Caroline's house and looked across the water at Taunton's. The view was great. He stopped to catch his breath. His heart pounded in his chest. Mary Beth would be here on the weekend. She wanted to see him. New York might not be so bad, if he knew they had this place as a possible escape. Will resumed his run, following the road through the village.

❧

Several afternoons later Will stepped outside Taunton's to bring in his flag. The weather had remained clear, though unusually cool for the final days of August. He decided to close the store early and walk down to his beach. Mary Beth was arriving on Saturday. He hoped the good weather would hold. He grabbed a fleece jacket and turned to lock the door.

"Hello," a female voice called out.

Will turned and saw Caroline. He hadn't heard anyone approach. A momentary delight quickly clouded to confusion when he remembered their last meeting, the book trip to Acadia in July. She had made it clear that she didn't want to be friends when she had turned down his invitation to dinner. That hardly mattered now. Things had changed with Mary Beth.

"You're closing up?" she asked. There was something woebegone in her manner, but her gaze was steady, one eye blue, the other decidedly green. It made him pause and consider whether her face was in some way out of balance.

"I'm closing a little earlier now. Not as many people coming through." He stepped down to her level and turned back quickly. "If there's something you want I'll—"

"No. I was just out walking. I drove back from Washington yesterday. God. More than thirteen hours." She drew one hand to her neck and rubbed. "I'm not sure I'll ever recover." She wore a brown corduroy jacket that didn't suit her. Her neck appeared very white and too thin.

"I was going to walk down to my beach." He glanced up at the sky. "It's getting dark early."

"May I come along? I remember your telling me how you discovered it when you first moved here." She fell into step beside him.

He could hardly tell her not to come. "I haven't seen your lights for a while. I thought maybe you were gone for good."

"I'm back now." Caroline didn't explain further, but thrust her hands into the pockets of her coat and followed him along the narrow path through the field behind the store. The tall grass, heavy and golden, brushed against their legs. They reached the woods. For a while neither of them spoke. The damp forest floor smelled of pine, pungent and pleasantly sharp. The gray-green mosses stood out against the dark earth.

Will had almost forgotten she was behind him. She walked soundlessly. "We're nearly there," he said over his shoulder.

A few minutes later they emerged onto the pebble beach at the neck of the bay. It was small, twenty or thirty yards wide, cradled in between two large rock formations. The water, crystal clear and smooth like a lake, lapped gently at the shore. Will led Caroline to a flat rock where they could sit and look out across the bay and to the ocean beyond.

"This is a hidden treasure," she said, and sat down with one leg outstretched and the other bent. "My God, the light." She leaned forward, hugging her knee.

"Nice, isn't it?" He sat beside her and began to feel more at ease.

"First time I've been warm today."

"You haven't turned the heat on?"

"Vern's coming tomorrow to help me with the boiler."

He adjusted his position on the rock, moving slightly away from her. Her hair, in the sunlight, was not only red but streaked with gold, lighter than he remembered. She wore it pulled back in a barrette. One loose piece blew across her cheek. Again he thought of her old-fashioned demeanor. She was like a woman in a Winslow Homer painting, a simple New England woman, her thoughts impenetrable, her eyes fixed on the sapphire ocean in the distance. He tried to think of something else to say. Why, for God's sake, had she presented herself at the store? The last time she as much as told him to get lost. The memory of her bare freckled legs when they had their picnic shot into his mind.

"Do you miss not going back to school?" She turned toward him and shielded her eyes against the sun. "Teaching, I mean."

He shrugged. "I might do some tutoring." He shifted his position on the rock. "There's an after-school program at the library. Edna is looking for volunteers. She's been so helpful to me all summer. I told her I'd work with one of the students."

"What about your own writing?"

"I realized I enjoy research more, and writing essays."

"I see."

"I've given up on the novel. It was really my wife's idea. I guess because I read them all the time and taught literature, she thought I could write one."

"How is she?"

"My wife?"

"You told me you were separated."

"We have been." He didn't want to explain any more. How could he explain what he didn't understand himself? "The summer's gone quickly," he said, "and the store has kept me plenty busy."

"I'm glad to hear that."

The beach pebbles made a gentle rolling sound that became more noticeable as they were pulled out with the tide. Will fingered the stones beside him, all worn smooth from the endless movement of water. "George Taunton isn't doing well," he said. "It's sad. The family has decided to sell the place."

"So you'd have to leave?" She appeared concerned as she asked.

"I've been thinking about buying it. It would be a good seasonal business."

"I can see you doing that."

"You can?" He smiled at her.

She nodded. Then her face grew serious again. She bit her lower lip. "Will?"

"Yes?"

"There's something I have to tell you."

She looked directly at him, and the openness of her expression made him turn away, as if her gaze could in some way hurt him, the way if you stared at the sun too long it could blind you. He focused on the horizon.

"I'm going to have a baby."

For a while he sat completely still and tried to comprehend this amazing statement. He turned back to her. "But I thought—"

"It's not my husband's child. Last spring—"

"You don't have to tell me any of this," he interrupted. Why was this news making him angry? He could feel himself clenching his teeth. The rock under him felt hard, and the sun was almost gone from their piece of beach. He zipped his jacket to the neck.

"Please listen. I want to tell you the truth. It's why I felt awkward about seeing you again after our trip to Acadia in July. Going out to dinner and all that. Oh, God. This is crazy. I loved that day. It was such an escape. For a while, anyway, I totally forgot what I'd done." She shifted her position on the rock. "It happened in May. There was a dinner party, hosted by my husband's partner and his wife. Things sort of fell apart at the end of the evening. We had lots of wine. There was this bizarre thunderstorm. He drove me home."

"Caroline, you don't need to tell me this."

"I'm sorry. Please." She reached over and touched him lightly on the sleeve. Just as suddenly, she withdrew her hand. "I was lonely. Confused about so many things. We slept together. It was a terrible mistake. Now you know what happened. At first I didn't know what to do. Having a baby at this time in my life doesn't make any sense. I mean, picture it." Here her tone of voice shifted. "Grieving widow, pillar of the community, member of the garden club, mother of a nineteen-year-old son." More quietly she said, "Money has also been a problem. I can't really afford another child. Anyway, I've always been responsible, done what was expected of me. For a while I just couldn't make up my mind what to do about the baby. Then I knew." She pushed strands of her hair behind her ear. "I couldn't decide to end the pregnancy, and by not deciding, I had of course made the decision." She drew her other knee up and slowly rubbed her temples with her fingers. "You see, I lost a baby. A daughter. Fifteen years ago. I don't want to lose another child."

Her entire body looked sad, her eyes empty of color, her lips pale and pressed together, her shoulders sloped. Seeing her like this made him feel oddly protective of her.

"I needed to tell you," she said. "I don't want you to think that

I didn't like you. My life is so complicated. I didn't want to drag you into all that."

"I see." From the corner of his eye he watched her awkwardly push forward onto her feet and press one hand into the rock as she stood. He got up as well. After this declaration, it was as if some layer of herself had been peeled away, worn smooth like the pebbles. "When?" He looked quickly at her belly, but could see no noticeable swelling under her coat.

"Not until February."

The sky was slowly darkening, and Will's energy drained out of him like the last vestiges of the sunlight. "What will you do?" he asked.

"Stay here. For now anyway." She stood beside him, looking out at the water. Soon the rich blue would become a nighttime black. An awkward silence grew between them. She shrugged and forced a smile. "I have one idea, actually. I think I mentioned the old New England recipes I've discovered. Who knows, maybe some kind of book."

"A book?" He couldn't imagine who would be interested in a book of old recipes.

"Remember I told you about the books in Lila's house? Some of them might be worth something."

"I'd be happy to look at them if you decide you want to sell any," he said, glad to move to this safer topic. Larger waves had begun to slap into the rocks. "Maybe we'd better go back."

Caroline nodded and walked with Will along the path through the darkening woods. They entered a clearing under the tall pines. Just as the path narrowed and turned sharply to the left, her foot caught the edge of a root and she pitched forward. Will reached out to break her fall and instinctively moved to take her in his arms to keep her from hitting her head on a nearby branch. She staggered briefly and leaned into him, her hair touching his face.

"Are you okay?" He quickly withdrew his arms. She stepped away, having regained her balance.

"I'm fine." She brushed distractedly at her sleeve.

Her hair had been unexpectedly soft. "It's hard to see in these woods after sunset," he said.

"I'll be more careful." A few minutes later the path opened and they crossed the field behind the store. When she reached the building she made a hurried apology. "I hope we can still be friends."

"Of course," he said, still pondering all that she had told him.

"Good friends, then." She cocked her head and smiled, the smile he remembered her giving him the afternoon of their picnic. She turned away and started down the road toward the village.

❦

That night after supper Will sat in his chair reading. After an hour or so he set his book on the table beside him. The book was one he'd found in the box from last week's house sale, a yellowed paperback copy of *Summer,* a lesser-known novel by Edith Wharton. In Wharton's story a young woman's sexual awakening drew her into an affair with a young man of a higher social standing who would never marry her. The young girl became pregnant. At the end of the novel she accepted marriage to a cold, older man, her legal guardian, the price she paid for her summer of passion. Was this Caroline's story? A moment of passion with her husband's friend? He glanced at the book on the table next to him and stretched out his legs, feeling restless.

It was only eight thirty. Too early to crawl into his solitary bed. He got up and grabbed his jacket and car keys. A beer out at Crosby's was better than another evening alone.

❦

"Kind of fitting, isn't it?" Mary Beth said.

"Fitting?" Will asked. He dipped a second lobster claw into the dish of melted butter. She had arrived late that afternoon bearing a bag of lobsters, a loaf of French bread, and two bottles of white wine. Fortunately Will had a pot large enough to boil the creatures, still alive and kicking. He had planned to take Mary

Beth out, but having food to prepare had given them both something to do and had made their first encounter easier. Instead of kissing or not kissing, they had carried bags, handled the food, opened wine. He showed her around the store. She had been admiring, even respectful, asking questions about the business.

Indeed, to Will's surprise, Mary Beth's arrival had gone smoothly. Sitting with her in his living room, feasting on lobsters, was like being on a first date. She had set the table by the window using his cloth dish towels as napkins. An empty wine bottle holding a candle flickered and dripped heavy globules of wax.

They both seemed mindful of wanting the evening to go smoothly. The unhappy period of their marriage had been in Habliston. That was where it had all unraveled. So far neither of them had spoken of that time, as if they'd agreed to skip over a bad chapter in a book.

"Fitting," she said again. "It's fitting to be back in Maine where it all began. I remember our honeymoon like it was yesterday." Her wineglass was blurred with smudges from her buttery fingers. "Three more days and it will have been ten years."

"A lot's happened since then," he said.

Mary Beth wiped her fingers and lifted her glass. She sipped. "Maybe some of it had to happen. I think we can learn from it."

"You're sounding like the teacher now."

"Being apart for so long has been hard." She turned to the window. The reflection of a half-moon glittered on the bay.

Will couldn't help wondering how it had been hard for her. Had it been hard traveling business-class to Japan, being the rising star of her company team, out for dinner with Drew and her office friends? He thought of his own confused state: missing her, not missing her, thinking he could live without her, that it might be possible to give it all up and stay in East Hope. He shook his head, suddenly uneasy.

She turned back and met his gaze. Her hair was longer now. Shiny and thick, it almost reached her shoulders. She wore the strand of pearls that he had given her for their fifth anniversary. Will had forgotten how lovely she was. He knew now that he had missed her. Yet something in him was telling him to be cautious.

Her expression grew more serious. "If we want to be married we have to be together." She reached over and took his hand. "You have to come home, Will."

He nodded, feeling the pressure of her fingers. New York would never be home, and yet he knew she was right.

She withdrew her hand and picked up her glass. "Let's drink to us. Ten years. A new beginning."

He lifted his glass.

"You agree then?"

"Yes. I want us to be together."

The rest of the room had darkened around them, drawing them into a pool of light. Everything in the apartment felt different now. Having her with him seemed to have charged the air with feminine energy. The place looked different too. Her handbag sat on the chair by the top of the stairs, and she had tossed her jacket, a coat almost too soft to be made of real leather, on the end of the sofa along with a red-and-black silk scarf that smelled of a new perfume. She'd brought a large pot of yellow mums and placed them on the end of the kitchen counter. Only her overnight bag, on the floor by the bedroom door, but not in the bedroom, indicated the tentative nature of her presence.

He needed to tell Mary Beth about staying on in East Hope and helping out until Columbus Day, and that he had the chance to buy the place. He finally decided he didn't want to let Penny down by closing the bookstore early. Also, with his own investment of time and money, it made more sense to keep Taunton's open until the end of the season. Eventually, he would explain this to Mary Beth. Being with her didn't feel quite real yet. Better to proceed slowly. They would have the whole week. So much could happen.

"You're very quiet," she said.

"I'm amazed," he said. "I can't quite believe you're here."

"Did you miss me, Will?"

"I did," he said, sensing that the mood was shifting. He couldn't think what to say. So that was it? Where had all the anger gone? What was to come? He was glad for the wine. It numbed his ability to think.

Mary Beth got up from her place and came over to stand behind his chair. She placed her hands on his shoulders and bent down, leaning her cheek against his. "You look good, Will." He recognized the familiar softness of her skin. "I think we need to start celebrating our anniversary." She started to massage his shoulders and then, gently, the long tendons of his neck. It had always been her signal, a private prelude to her wanting to make love.

"I don't know, Mary Beth."

"What don't you know?" she whispered by his ear.

"There's still a lot to talk about."

"We'll talk later." Her hands came around and unbuttoned the top of his shirt.

Will closed his eyes. How easy it was now not to think. He took her hand and led her to the bedroom.

❦

The next morning a few fragile rays of sunlight streamed across the foot of the bed just after dawn. Mary Beth drew her arm over Will, bringing one hand up against his heart.

"Are you awake?" he asked.

"Umm," she said, pressing up against him.

"Mr. Taunton's not well. The family—"

"Later, darling," she said. Her breathing deepened. They were once again enveloped in the final moments of quiet before the start of the day.

13

Caroline sat on the front steps of Taunton's Used Books and waited. Since her return to Maine she had thrown herself into her new cookbook project. She hadn't seen or spoken to anyone since she'd walked with Will down to his little beach the week before. Work kept her mind off her worries, though part of her longed for company. Here, protected from the wind, she felt the sun almost making her hot. Another mild day in a stretch of glorious weather—the first week of September, but almost like summer. She was surprised that Will was not there, as it was almost noon and time to open the shop. His car was in the drive, and another one was parked close beside it. If this was a customer's car, it seemed strange that the building was locked.

She had brought Will a copy of Lila's oldest cookbook. It looked valuable, though she had no intention of selling it. He might be able to tell her something about it, maybe something she could use in her book proposal.

Or was bringing him the book just an excuse? Despite the awkwardness of their conversation on the beach and having to tell him that she was pregnant, it had been pleasant to see him again. Pleasant. She smiled to herself. Who was she fooling? She couldn't deny being drawn to this serious bookseller who had some kind of story to tell. Why had he separated from his wife? There had to be something that brought him to this far corner of the country. Why would a teacher give up his job for this out-of-the-way place? Her mind kept going over the possibilities. She wished she knew more about him. The cookbook project would keep her busy. Still, it would be nice to have him for a friend.

Caroline stretched out her legs and leaned back against the shop door. She was glad he knew the truth. She hadn't forgotten how she had hurt his feelings when she sent him home after their day together in July. It had been on her conscience, and she'd wanted to make amends. He was the only one in East Hope who knew, though there was certainly no reason to keep it a secret. Besides, soon the odd bits of loose clothing she had found in Lila's closet would not be large enough to hide her emerging belly. She planned to tell Vern and Hollis Moody too.

And, of course, Rob. But when? She was ashamed to have lost her courage and not told him the truth when they were together in Washington. They had talked a few times on the phone since then. He had said nothing more about giving up their home, just that classes had started and were okay. When she asked about Melanie, he told her they were having problems.

"What do you mean?" she had asked.

"I don't want to talk about it." His voice had changed, taking on a cool edge, the stay-out-of-it tone he used when she intruded too much into his world.

Once he knew about the baby, Caroline feared he might retreat, withdrawing more into himself, as he had after Harry's death. Maybe she could get him to come to Maine for a weekend. If he were here it might be easier. At the right moment she would suggest it. East Hope might make him feel better too. With his love of the outdoors, he couldn't help but fall in love with the place.

Caroline decided to wait a few more minutes before resuming her walk around the bay. The sun now fell upon her ear, a lovely sensation. She remembered her grandmother, Ruth, saying that the feeling of sun in your ear had to be one of life's greatest luxuries. Caroline smiled and closed her eyes.

Today was a perfect day for a walk. Dr. Carney, the obstetrician she had seen in Ellsworth, had recommended a good long walk every day, and Caroline had been pleased with this advice, as her body seemed to crave air and movement. Her doctor, an outdoorsy-looking woman close to Caroline's own age, whose office came equipped with all the latest monitors and the newest technology, seemed to offer plenty of solid old-fashioned advice: get plenty of rest, exercise, and eat a healthful diet. She had even recommended an organic-foods market and suggested that Caroline be mindful of everything she ate.

Most important of all, Dr. Carney had assuaged Caroline's fears by saying that she was not too old to have a healthy baby, and furthermore, Grace's condition had been a rare abnormality, extremely unlikely to occur in another child. Caroline's second sonogram had been fine. In any case, Dr. Carney would monitor Caroline's pregnancy closely, and if there were any unusual symptoms she would send her to a specialist in Bangor. Caroline felt in capable hands, and she instinctively liked this woman who seemed inclined not to worry.

Last week, staggering out of her car after more than thirteen hours on the road, she had almost cried with joy to be back inside Lila's house. The simple square rooms, the comfortable old furniture, the paintings on the walls, all looked familiar to her now. The silent house had a calming effect. After putting her suitcase down at the foot of the stairs, she had gone first into the hall to wind the clock, which had stopped during her absence. She picked up the key that lay in the Chinese porcelain dish on the hall table, opened the case, and, after gently moving the hands into place, she gave it the six neat turns that Hollis had taught her. In an instant the warm even ticking, like a pulse, brought life back into the house. Once upstairs, Caroline had stood at her bedroom window and looked out at the bay. The moon illuminated the dark expanse of water.

Now, on the steps of Taunton's, Caroline became aware of voices coming from the side of the building. She must have fallen asleep. She stood up, quickly wiping the corner of her mouth as Will and a young woman came around the corner. Caroline blinked into the sun.

"Hi," Will said.

Caroline wasn't sure if his face registered annoyance or surprise, but he quickly introduced the woman beside him. His words were hurried, and Caroline caught only a few. But most definitely he had said, "my wife."

Caroline shook the hand offered to her, cool and smooth, and tried not to stare at Will's wife. Her dark hair fell to her shoulders, and she wore a rich red lipstick that matched the color of the turtleneck sweater that brushed against her chin. Her leather jacket was buttoned against the wind, and she quickly put her hands back into her pockets and stepped closer to Will.

Caroline handed Will the book. "I was hoping you might be able to tell me something about this. I'm not sure the publishing house still exists. I'm working on my book proposal." She felt ridiculous next to this fashionable woman and remembered she hadn't put on any makeup that morning.

"I'll see what I can find out." He fumbled for his keys. "Would you like to come in?" The dark-haired woman, Mary something, looked displeased at his invitation.

"No. I'm afraid I don't have time." Caroline turned up the collar of her jacket. She shifted her weight from one foot to the other. "I'll come back another day," she said, and started down the drive. "Nice to meet you," she called back, but the woman, Will's wife, had already stepped inside.

&

"So, who's the redhead?"

Will eased Mary Beth's coat from her shoulders. She turned and lifted both hands to his face, smoothing his brows. "I think she likes you."

"Mary Beth." He shook his head, pulled away, and carried her coat to the hooks by the door.

She cocked her head and smiled. "Someone you know well?"

"Hardly. Come on. Let's go up and I'll make some soup." Mary Beth was leaving later that afternoon. She had extended her visit, and they had been together over a week. Will couldn't deny that the sex had been great, like a second honeymoon, like getting to know her all over again. Each day it had become easier to be with her. She told him about her job, the apartment in New York, her friends. He showed her the town and they ate dinner in some of the nicer restaurants that remained open into the fall. The days when he was busy at the store, she went down to the beach on her own, and one day she went by herself to Belfast.

As her departure grew nearer they firmed up their plans. Mary Beth was pleased to hear that Will had contacted Jack Mathews about recommendations. Will had explained that he missed teaching. He would interview for jobs when he got to New York. Knowing this, Mary Beth had accepted his wish to work at Taunton's until after Columbus Day.

"I guess a few more weeks won't matter," she had said on their walk back from the beach. "Still, I can't see that you'll have much to do this late in the season."

"There's quite a bit of paperwork in closing the books for the year. There won't be many customers. I told the librarian that I'd help out for a bit in their tutoring program."

"Working with the students?"

Will nodded. "I owe Edna a favor. She's sent a lot of books my way."

"What if they knew about Habliston?"

"What's that supposed to mean? You say it like I'm some kind of sex offender."

"I didn't mean anything. You know schools are so careful. They have to do background checks in New York."

"This isn't New York," Will said testily.

"Don't be a grump." She had leaned into Will, giving him a teasing nudge, as if trying to improve his mood and reassure him that all would be well when he got to New York. She assured him that he would love her building, a prewar, on a side street with plenty of trees. They both seemed to remain careful with each other, tenuously offering compromises, their footing still a little unsure. He still hadn't told her that Taunton's was for sale. Then they had rounded the corner and found Caroline standing on the front steps of the store.

"Why is she bringing you cookbooks?" Mary Beth asked now, following him up the stairs into the apartment. She settled into his chair by the window while he poured a can of soup into a pan.

"She edits cookbooks. Now she's working on one of her own."

"I see." She interlaced her fingers and leaned back in his chair. "How's your writing, by the way? You haven't said anything about your novel."

"There's nothing to say."

"You haven't been writing?"

"Mary Beth, I discovered that I'm a reader, not a writer."

"But you've always liked to write."

"Sure. Articles for journals. Fiction is different. I know that now."

"Maybe you'll change your mind when you get to New York." She got up and went to the refrigerator. "Let's have some of this cheese. Are there any more crackers?"

Will didn't answer, but reached for the box of crackers from the cupboard. He carried them to the table with one bowl of soup. Mary Beth followed with the other bowl and the cheese that she had arranged on a platter.

"This morning was lovely," she said. They had spent several hours on his little beach.

"All this could be ours," he said, gesturing toward the view outside.

She pushed the plate of cheese in his direction. "What do you mean?" They sat at the table by the window, as had become their habit.

"Penny's dad is never going to be well enough to run it. She asked me if I would consider buying it."

Mary Beth pushed abruptly back from the table. "You promised me you're coming to New York."

"I am. This would be for vacations. I've given it a lot of thought. It could be a seasonal business. I could get some part-time help. We could spend summers up here."

"Aren't you forgetting about my job?"

"In the beginning we could come on weekends. I'd still live in New York and could come up now and then to check on it. We could have days off here. You said yourself that you love Maine."

"That doesn't mean I want to live here."

"It would be a great investment." He explained that the field behind the building, as well as the woods beyond that led down to the water, could never be developed. Though the store faced the road, there was room to expand the building on either side.

"How long have you been thinking about this?" Mary Beth pulled her chair in again. She looked wary.

"Penny asked me a few weeks ago. I can't stop thinking about it. This place has always felt so right."

"Why did you wait until now to say anything?"

"I guess I wanted to know where we stood." Will was aware that they had made too many decisions separately, one of the problems in their marriage.

"I thought we'd decided on our plans." Her eyes hardened. "Has this time together meant nothing to you? You said you wanted to be together."

"I do. You know I do. It's just that this seems like such an amazing opportunity. I really love it here. I was hoping you would too."

"A visit is one thing."

"Please consider it. If only as an investment."

Mary Beth picked up her spoon and started to eat her soup. "It's not only the money. We need to build a life together. That means living together."

"I know that." He thought of their nights in this apartment, the warmth of her in his arms. "I'm just asking you to think about it," he said.

"We'll talk about it when you come to New York. You might feel differently when you get away from here. Don't forget there's a whole other world out there."

Will looked out at the water. A large cloud covered the sun, and the bay had turned a steely gray. "It feels good to be with you again," he said. And it had been good having her in East Hope. He leaned back in his chair and gazed across the water. Caroline's house stood out, a bright white. He turned back to Mary Beth. "Do you ever see us with children?" He watched her face, wanting the truth. He wasn't sure he could imagine it himself.

She reached for his hand and he let her take it, but her face betrayed nothing. "That's something we should talk about too."

❦

Caroline accepted Dr. Carney's hand and the gentle pull up from the examining table. She smoothed the sheet across her lap and waited while the doctor studied her chart. She had to come to the obstetrician for her September appointment.

"I'd like to see you gain a little more weight. Now that you're past the queasy stage you probably will." Caroline nodded, but then wrinkled her brow. "Blood pressure's a little elevated. I wouldn't worry about it. You're probably a bit tense from driving here. The fog's been bad all day."

"I haven't felt the baby move yet." Caroline was almost afraid to say this.

"Eighteen weeks? Hmm. You will soon. Everything is normal. Heartbeat is just fine."

"You're sure?"

"You're into your second trimester. The biggest hurdles are behind you." Dr. Carney patted Caroline on the arm. "Listen, get dressed and get on your way. The only thing you need to worry about is getting home before dark in this kind of weather. I'll see you next month."

Caroline dressed as quickly as possible and went to the outer office to make her appointment. The receptionist was talking on the phone while communicating by hand signal to the woman ahead of her, pointing at one date and then the next, and finally she wrote out a date on the reminder card. The patient took the card and stepped aside.

"Yes, yes. I understand. I'll remind the doctor," the receptionist said, still speaking into the receiver, and then placed the phone on her desk. "Be just a moment," she told Caroline, and disappeared down the corridor to the examining rooms. Caroline fished her calendar out of her handbag so as to be ready to write down the date for her next visit. The waiting room had emptied, and she could see that it was quickly growing dark. She waited, but the receptionist didn't return. She tried to focus on her womb, wishing again that she would feel the baby move.

"Sorry, dear." The receptionist came back and picked up her pencil. "She'll want to see you in another month. What time of day works best for you?"

By the time Caroline got to the parking lot it was four thirty and rapidly growing dark. The fog was not too heavy here in town, but she worried about what she would find when she turned off the main road and started toward the water. She settled herself in the front seat, relieved to be in her sturdy old Volvo. In her handbag was a list of ingredients for two recipes that she had been wanting to try. One was for cookies for a care package she planned to send to Rob. However, instead of stopping at the grocery store, as she had intended, she decided to skip all of her errands in order to make it home before dark.

As soon as she turned off Route 1 on the road to East Hope, the fog thickened, as she had expected. At first it moved around her in sickening swirls, and then it magically lifted for a few minutes, giving her a better view of the road. Gradually it grew denser, and

Caroline turned on her lights. Instead of making it easier to drive, the light made it harder. She was being sucked down into a sea of clouds. The sensation was one of floating, not pleasantly, with a fear of the abyss. It was almost like drowning in some kind of deep silence. Twenty feet of visibility, at most, lay ahead. When she made the turn onto Salt Marsh Road, the painted lines on the roadway disappeared altogether.

She had six miles to go, six miles of winding road, including a narrow causeway dividing the tidal marshes and the mouth of the Hope River. Caroline gripped the steering wheel and leaned in toward the windshield. She wanted to pull over, but at this point she couldn't tell whether there was any shoulder. Slowing the car to a crawl, she bit her lip and prayed. *Please,* she thought, *please.* What was she to do? Stop in the road? Hollis had told her that the fog could come in and settle for days at a time. She couldn't wait it out. Besides, it had grown colder, and the big cardigan sweater that had seemed cozy earlier that afternoon would never be warm enough to get her through the night. She was too nervous to look at the gas gauge, not wanting to take her eyes off the nightmarish scene ahead. Would a tank of gas keep a car running with the heater on all night?

Suddenly she was aware of lights behind her. She didn't dare increase her speed, but she knew she had to pull over to let this person pass. She put on her blinker, held her breath, and eased the car slowly over to the right. With relief she heard the crunch of gravel and drew to a stop. She was thankful she had not driven into the marsh. The car behind her passed and stopped just ahead of her. The driver appeared to be getting out, and the figure of a man emerged from the cloud. With shaking hands, she lowered her window.

Will rested his hand on her door and looked in. "I thought I recognized your car. Are you okay?"

"Oh, thank God it's you," she said, greatly relieved to see his familiar face. "This is awful. You must think I'm crazy, but it's like her bag for her keys. "I could put together some dinner." She forgot for a moment that he might need to hurry home to his wife.

"Thanks—but I should probably keep going. I don't think this is going to let up for a while. I'd better get around the harbor while the road is still passable."

"Of course," she said. The back door yielded to her push and she flipped on the lights. "Thanks again, Will." She stepped inside and let out a small cry.

Will spun around. "You sure you're okay?" He hurried up the steps and followed Caroline into the hall.

She stood very still, a hand on her belly. "Wait." She looked down and then up at him. "I felt the baby. Oh, my. It's just a flutter, but yes, I'm sure."

"Is that good?" His forehead wrinkled and his expression grew worried.

"Yes," she said. "Very good."

"It can already move?" He glanced at her belly and drew his eyebrows together in concern.

Caroline bobbed her head up and down, smiling foolishly, her hand across her abdomen.

"You're truly okay?"

"Truly, Will."

"I'll be off then." He looked at her as if he didn't quite believe her, then backed down the steps before turning to go to his car. Caroline stood at the door and gave a final wave as the green Jeep eased out into the night.

❦

The following week Will showed up for his first tutoring session at the East Hope Library. He had become a good friend of Edna, the head librarian, who had called him on numerous occasions when patrons brought in boxes of books that they no longer wanted. The East Hope Library, a square stone building in the center of the village, had limited shelf space, and Edna and Mr. Taunton had exchanged extra books over the years. She had been happy to continue this arrangement with Will. She liked talking about literature with Will and had stopped in at the bookstore numerous times over the summer.

"Penny said you'd help us out for a while," she said. "These poor teachers are so overworked. It's usually the troublemakers who take up all their time." Edna had short graying hair and wore old-fashioned-looking blouses with cardigan sweaters.

Will had already gone to the high school to fill out the forms necessary to become a volunteer and had met with the guidance counselor, a frazzled-looking woman called Janet Wiseman. She had explained that he would be working with a senior girl, Crystal Thomas, who needed help with writing.

"Edna said you used to be a teacher," Janet had said, sizing him up with dark eyes set deeply in a doughy face.

"Yes. I taught at a small women's college in Pennsylvania."

"Where was that?"

Will told her that the school was west of Philadelphia, but that he gave up teaching to follow a lifelong dream to live on the water, that he'd always loved bookstores, and that he'd found Taunton's Used Books in an ad in *Down East,* thus not responding completely to her question.

"As you can imagine, we need more volunteers in our schools." She had seemed to be sizing him up and looked cautious, as if his story weren't believable. "I must say, it's surprising to have someone like you show up."

After a few more cursory questions she had sent him on his way. The unpleasant business at Habliston stirred in his mind, but it seemed a long time ago.

Sunlight streamed through the tall windows onto the one wooden table in the main reading room. Edna's desk was set in front of the side window and was filled with pots of geraniums hungry for the last of the day's light. This library, like every library he had ever known, had the warm, weighty smell of books, and reminded him again of his childhood library and the Saturday-morning trips there with his mother. He and Rusty picked out two books every week.

Edna directed Will to the reference room, where his student was waiting. He found her hunched over a notebook, drawing, her hair hiding most of her face.

"You must be Crystal," he said.

She put down her pencil and looked up. "Hi," she said, and tucked her hair behind her ears. She pushed back her chair as if to rise.

"Please don't get up," he said, and sat quickly in the chair opposite her. "I'm Will Harmon. Miss Raymond said you could use some help with your writing."

Crystal was pale, with hair the color of harvested wheat. She wore a cream-colored T-shirt, and, Will guessed, faded jeans, though he couldn't see from where he sat. A navy jacket lay crumpled on the table beside her.

"I need to do an essay," she said. "It's for a scholarship. Ms. Wiseman says I've got a good chance at it." Her eyes, a deep blue, surged with life. "I've got to win this."

"Ms. Wiseman says you've had high honors every year."

She looked away as if embarrassed by this fact.

"Do you like to read?"

"I love to." Some color started to warm her face.

"What do you like reading?"

Crystal told him that her favorite book was *Jane Eyre* and that this past summer she had read *Middlemarch,* all 680 pages.

"If you're reading books like that, you're not going to have any problems," he said.

"Yeah, right. But reading English stuff doesn't help me write about Maine." Crystal explained, "I have to write about a pivotal event that shaped my life growing up here."

Will groaned inwardly. He'd like to see some of the judges tackle a topic like that.

"Probably the hardest part of an essay," he said, "is before you even start to put words down on paper. It's the thinking part, coming up with the ideas. After that it's simply a matter of ordering the ideas, clarifying them, and putting in specific examples."

"You make it sound easy."

"It's not exactly easy, but I bet you'll like the work once you get started."

She leaned back and sighed. Her blue eyes darkened and appeared to challenge him. "It's getting started that's my problem. And it's got to be at least a thousand words." She picked up the pencil and began doodling in her notebook.

"Look at it this way: Just your being here and asking for help is already a start."

Crystal gave Will a level gaze, as if to tell him not to kid around. This was a chance at college. Without the scholarship she'd be right here in East Hope commuting to the community college and working part-time, a much longer and more tedious road.

"I'm serious." He pointed across at her notebook. "You're just sketching—doodling, right?"

She nodded and stopped moving the pencil.

"Before you write, you've got to have some ideas. The best way to sort out ideas is by writing them down."

Crystal looked at Will more intently. "What's that supposed to mean?" Her doubting expression returned.

"Don't start with sentences. Let's just sketch with words."

Will launched into a series of questions, asking Crystal who were the important people in her life, how she knew them, what she did with them, how she felt about them. He encouraged her to jot down only words, phrases, in no certain order. After a while he told her to keep jotting, doodling with the words. They agreed to meet again the following day after school.

When Will returned to Taunton's late that afternoon, it was almost dark. He hurried up the stairs to the apartment. He wanted to find some good examples of essays for Crystal to study, nothing too literary or erudite, just good, accessible writing. Helping her think through and construct an essay was going to be a challenge, but he had a good feeling about it. It was a feeling he'd been missing.

Lights were on at Caroline's house across the bay. He thought of her all alone in that big house with a baby coming. Talk about a challenge.

The light on his answering machine blinked. He pressed the replay button and Penny Taunton's voice filled the room. "Give a call, Will. Dad's had an offer from a developer over at Bangor. He wants to buy the property, tear down the store, and build some fancy new house. We'd rather have you buy and keep the business. We need an answer right away."

14

Several weeks later, on a perfectly clear night, Will drove to Caroline's house. The village of East Hope was quiet, with only a few cars parked on the street. Most of the residents had already eaten supper, and the aqueous blue light of televisions glowed steadily from windows along the way. People had started to prepare for Halloween. The neighboring yards and porches were already decorated with pumpkins and corn husks.

Will was oblivious to the decorations marking the upcoming holiday. He and Mary Beth had had a terrible argument. Their peaceful reunion at the beginning of September was long forgotten. After Penny's message, Will had tried to reach Mary Beth. He found out that she was on a business trip in Phoenix, and by the time he had tracked her down on her cell phone he had already put a bid in on Taunton's to meet Penny's deadline.

"You did this without telling me?"

"I tried to reach you in time."

"Not hard enough."

"Mary Beth, you can't believe how reasonable this place is. I couldn't let it go. Besides, some guy was going to tear the building down. Penny and her dad didn't want to sell to him."

"That's charitable of you."

She was furious. He knew she had a right to be. "Mary Beth, you're a businesswoman. We can't lose on this."

"Are you still coming to New York?"

"Of course. Nothing's changed."

"You said you'd be here after Columbus Day."

"Buying the place has tied me up. It will take a few more weeks. Definitely by Thanksgiving."

"I'm starting to wonder, Will." Her voice had taken on a lifeless quality.

Will had started to wonder too. He couldn't get Mary Beth out of his head. After her angry reaction, all of the arrangements for buying Taunton's made him feel uneasy, instead of filling him with happy anticipation. He couldn't bear to let go of this piece of East Hope, yet his decision had become another stumbling block in their marriage. He tried to convince himself that once he got to New York he and Mary Beth could smooth things out.

Caroline had called Will to invite him to dinner, as a thank-you, she explained, for rescuing her in the fog. He had looked forward to this evening all week. Along with his doubts about Mary Beth, an unexpected loneliness had come over him. The days were growing shorter and the dark came early this far east. He found the evenings especially difficult. The darkness itself fostered an inward brooding.

There were very few customers at Taunton's these days, and of course no one to talk to at the end of the day, no one to connect with or share even the most mundane thoughts. He wasn't going to give up on his marriage. Ten years was a long time.

In preparation for dinner with Caroline, Will had showered again. He put on pressed khakis, a clean shirt, and, instead of a sweater, he reached for a favorite tweed sport coat. He couldn't remember the last time he had worn it, but knew it must have been in the spring back at Habliston. Putting it on made him think of his old life, when he had stood in front of a roomful of students, maybe with his hands buried in the pockets, as he encouraged discussions of Wharton or James. This fall he had had no reason to wear the jacket, but it was Saturday night, an appropriate occasion, he thought.

Will picked up the book he was taking to Caroline as a house present, *Miss Annie's Tea Time Treats,* a funny little volume with a cracked binding that he thought whimsical and something she might like for her recipe collection. He had found it in a box of books that he had purchased at a tag sale over Labor Day weekend. Then, taking his coat from the hook by the door, he saw that the silk scarf Mary Beth had left behind had fallen on the floor. He picked it up and brought it to his nose. The scent of her perfume had faded. Not wanting to be late, he replaced the scarf on the hook, making a mental note to take it to her when he went to the city for Thanksgiving.

❦

It was an odd assemblage gathered around the dinner table that October night, all brought together because of their connection to Lila's house: Caroline, more than five months pregnant, and the current owner; Vern Simpson, the contractor and carpenter who had rebuilt the porch, fixed the rotting windowsills, and coddled the old furnace back to life; his wife, Dottie, who had helped Lila with parties many years before when Lila and Francis were entertaining friends from Boston; Hollis Moody, Lila's lawyer and friend, who had obviously taken a shine to its new inhabitant; and, sitting to his right, Will, who had run by the house all summer, watching its progress and keeping an eye out for the redheaded new owner.

Yet it would be years before the white clapboard building would be known as anything other than Lila's house, much the way Taunton's would remain Taunton's even if Will decided to change the name. The collective memory in East Hope was long.

Everyone seemed to be enjoying themselves that evening.

"I thought I'd make it a party," Caroline had explained when she helped Will out of his coat. He had assumed that they were going to spend the evening by themselves, but he had acted pleased to meet Hollis Moody, whom he had encountered numerous times in the village, and happy to see Vern again and to meet Dottie.

After drinks by the fire in the living room, they had taken their seats at the round table in the dining room. Caroline had filled a bowl with greens, wild grasses, and bittersweet and placed it in the center of the table surrounded by four brass candlesticks. This pleasing natural arrangement reminded Will of the bouquets that his mother used to make.

"This is just the kind of meal that Lila would have prepared," Hollis said, looking distinguished in a blue wool blazer and red bow tie.

"I'll take that as a compliment, then," said Caroline.

"Indeed you should," Dottie said. "Lila loved parties." Dottie had a halo of gray hair, and while Vern's wrinkled face had a weathered appearance, Dottie's lined skin looked soft and powdery. She wore a red turtleneck with a gray wool jumper. Though certainly as old as Vern, she stood very straight and appeared to be a vigorous woman, unlikely to give in to a frail old age.

"Lila's cabin-fever suppers were famous," Dottie continued. "Usually, about late March, after what seemed like the hundredth blizzard, during some wretched storm or other, she'd start calling all her friends, insisting that they bundle up and come on over for a cabin-fever supper. The grown-ups and the children. My goodness, it was fun."

"Dottie, dear, these folks don't need to hear about all that." Vern's voice was teasing. He wore dark gray trousers and a corduroy jacket, and his hair looked wetted down and recently combed. Dottie had probably had a say in his grooming for the evening.

"Sure we do," Will assured her. Dottie had regaled Will with stories about the local history of East Hope while they had their drinks, pleased to have a new audience. She had not met Will before, not being a book person, she'd said, but a woman who enjoyed handiwork in the evenings, such as quilting or a bit of knitting if the light wasn't too bad.

"Vern's told me you're a wonderful cook," Caroline said, smiling at Dottie.

"He always appreciates a hot dinner. I do my best." She glanced lovingly at her husband. "But this, now, is something special."

"I'm glad you like it. I've been working with some old versions of New England boiled dinners."

"The boiled dinners I remember can't hold a candle to this," Hollis said, helping himself to more from the earthenware dish that Caroline had brought to the table.

"I've been studying the old recipes in Lila's books."

Will added his own praise and served himself a second portion. He thought that Caroline looked happier this evening. Her cheeks were pink and she wore a loosely fitting green dress. It was made of some kind of soft material, and her belly protruded in an obvious way, as if now that her secret was out, she could relax and show the world her changing shape. Now and again he'd thought about the man she'd been with, the fact that she'd had a love affair. He'd even found himself fantasizing and wishing that he'd been the one she had turned to in her loneliness and grief. Then, with embarrassment, he would remember Mary Beth.

He tried to picture his wife seated with him at this table, but couldn't. They never had small dinner parties; when they had entertained it was always a big cocktail party or buffet supper. Mary Beth had started hiring caterers once her income grew larger. "You might as well have lots of people if you're going to go to the trouble," she'd said. Was it a character flaw to prefer smaller gatherings?

"Your Harry certainly loved Lila's cooking," Dottie said, looking at Caroline. "She viewed it her summer duty to put some meat on that child's bones. Remember, Vern?"

"Sure do," Vern said. "Harry was a skinny kid. Strong, though. Those summers when he was still in high school, he had no trouble sailing those bigger boats."

"He practically lived down at the East Hope Yacht Club when he worked there," Hollis said. "The girls used to flock around him. Harry'd go back to Boston at the end of the summer, and those gals would mope about for weeks."

"I'm going to check on the dessert in the oven." Caroline stood. "Will, would you mind pouring everyone some more wine?"

"I'd be glad to," he said, meeting her gaze. The wine had started to loosen all of their tongues, and Will could see that these memories of Harry's visits in the old days had upset Caroline.

The others hadn't seemed to notice. Earlier, the Simpsons and Hollis Moody had talked openly about Caroline's pregnancy, and she had told them she had been feeling so much more energetic recently, better than she had felt in a long time. No one present that evening mentioned the obvious absence of a father.

After Will poured the wine he began to clear the plates, telling everyone to stay seated and that Caroline would not want her guests to follow him into the kitchen.

"You okay?" he said when they were alone. He piled the plates onto the kitchen table.

She nodded, but stood very still next to the oven, pot holders gripped in each hand. She drew in her breath and opened the oven. "You like apple crumble?" Her eyes glistened, either from the oven's heat or the approach of tears.

Will went to her and placed his hand on her shoulder. He couldn't deny the protective urge that came over him in her presence. He had felt the same way when he saw the panic on her face when he found her beside the road in the fog. "It'll be okay," he said, and quickly withdrew his hand. "This smells great."

Caroline spread five plates onto the counter, and while she spooned out servings of the apple crumble, Will stood beside her adding scoops of vanilla ice cream. They could hear the others talking in the dining room. The conversation was about Harry again. Something about racing the Comets, and how amazing it was that Rob, Harry's own son, was older now than Harry had been then.

"Makes you wonder what he'd think now, her having some other man's baby," Dottie said, unaware her voice could carry to the kitchen.

Caroline dropped the serving spoon. Will picked it up and carried it to the sink. Caroline didn't move.

"What I'm wondering is why the father hasn't shown up," Vern said. "What kind of man gets a nice lady like that pregnant and leaves her to fend for herself?"

"I don't think that's any concern of ours," Hollis said.

Will took another spoon from the counter. "I'll finish this," he whispered. "Do you want to go upstairs for a minute?" It pained him to see her stricken expression. In the meantime Hollis had turned the conversation to the University of Maine's ice hockey team. Vern and Dottie's grandson played for Orono.

"It's okay. Really," she said. "If you'd just carry out the plates, I'll be there in a few minutes."

When Caroline joined them in the dining room there was much praise for the crumble and how the cranberries were an excellent addition to the apples. The topic of Harry was dropped.

Later, after finishing his coffee by the fire, Hollis announced it was past his bedtime. "Can't remember when I've had such a lively evening," he said, and Vern and Dottie agreed that it was getting late, and it was time for them to retire too. Will helped Caroline retrieve their coats from the hall closet.

"Please don't leave too," she said softly.

He was glad to hear her say it. The thought of returning to his lonely apartment above the store was growing steadily more unappealing. "Would you like me to put more logs on the fire?" he asked.

Caroline nodded and returned to the living room to help her guests with their coats.

"Now, once that baby comes, I hope you'll let me help," Dottie said.

"She's the expert," Vern said. "After our three kids and the eight grandkids, there's not a trick she doesn't know."

"I'll certainly take you up on that," Caroline said. "After nineteen years, I'm a little out of practice."

"Once a mother, always a mother," Vern said, "but Dottie here won't want to miss out."

"Look forward to meeting that son of yours too," Hollis said.

"He'll be here for Christmas," Caroline said. Will thought her expression had saddened at the mention of her son. She must miss him. He followed her to the back steps and waved along with her as the cars left the driveway. The night was cold. She shivered in the doorway. They went back inside.

&

Caroline settled into the chair closest to the fire. She watched while Will crumbled a wad of paper and forced it under the last smoldering log. The fire sent forth a hearty flame and Will added two more logs. He moved awkwardly, with a boyish uncertainty, as if aware that he was being observed.

"Thanks for staying," she said. "I didn't want to be alone just yet."

"It was a great dinner," he said. "They all really enjoyed it. I know I did." He looked at his hands as if to check for soot from the fire and then settled into the chair across from hers.

For a moment neither of them said anything. The fire crackled in the grate and the clock ticked in the hall.

Will cleared his throat. "That must have been hard—hearing them talk about your husband."

"That's a Harry I never knew." She stared into the flames. "I should have anticipated that they would wonder about the baby's father."

"They care about you, Caroline. I'm sure they're not concerned about who the father is or why you're here for the winter."

"Do you ever get lonely?" she asked. "I mean, I know your wife doesn't live with you, and I wondered. I'm sorry. I shouldn't be asking. . . ."

"No. It's okay. I remember that I told you I'm separated. You must have wondered what was going on when Mary Beth showed up."

He let out a sigh and said nothing for a moment. "I lost my job in Pennsylvania because of a terrible misunderstanding. I hated giving it up. Everything I worked for was over in a matter of weeks. It really threw me. Mary Beth wanted me to move to New York right away. That's where her office is. She'd been commuting to Pennsylvania for several years. It was my turn to live there. This summer she had to be on the West Coast for work. I wanted to come here. Part of the problem is that I hate the city. When I first got to East Hope, it was like a huge relief. I instantly loved the place: the old buildings, the land, the water everywhere you look."

He paused and stretched out his legs. "The job market in New York is going to be tough. Coming here was a way of avoiding the whole thing." Will turned to face her. "I have been lonely. Mary Beth kept saying that she'd come and then she'd put it off. I didn't know where our marriage stood. Then she came. But you know that. You met her."

"She's lovely."

"Yeah, she is. It felt good to be with her, except something had changed. I keep asking myself if I still love her."

Caroline kept her eyes fixed on Will. She was glad to finally get a glimpse of what was going on inside him. She'd known there was some story. She was glad he felt comfortable enough to tell her.

"The thing is—we used to be so happy. Ten years."

His eyes in the firelight appeared more deeply set. He held his hands steepled together under his chin, seemingly deep in thought.

"What will you do?" she asked.

"I'm going to go live with her in New York at Thanksgiving."

"I see."

"Mary Beth wants us to try again."

"You mean try being married?" She pictured the sophisticated dark-haired woman who had stood by him in front of the store.

"It sounds stupid, I know," Will said. "You're either married or you're not."

"Would you like more coffee?" She leaned forward to get up. "Or maybe another glass of wine?" She remained perched uncertainly at the edge of her chair.

"No, please. I don't want anything else. I'm probably telling you more than you want to know."

"Of course not," she said, easing back into the chair. "It helps to talk. I must admit I don't get many opportunities to talk much myself these days. I've even thought about getting a cat or dog just to have some company. But that doesn't make sense with the baby coming."

"It's so strange." Will leaned forward and rested his elbows on his knees. His face looked a little gaunt to her. Too much running and not enough eating, she thought. "When Mary Beth came to see me last month, I didn't know how I'd feel seeing her again. I love it here. Taunton's has been really good for me. I've learned so much. I'm also tutoring a very bright girl at the high school. It makes me realize how much I've missed teaching. Mary Beth seemed to understand. She said she loved it here too."

"That's good then."

"It was fine until I told her I bought the place."

"You bought it? Will, that's wonderful."

"I haven't told anyone yet. I wanted to wait until the financing came through. It looks like everything's set. The settlement is in a couple of weeks."

Caroline felt her spirits lift for the first time that evening. Will would be here now. Except not in the winter. She felt a draft on her neck and thought briefly of turning up the heat.

"Mary Beth doesn't think it's wonderful. Even when I explained it would just be for summers, that I'd get part-time help. Now that I've done it, I worry I may have made a terrible mistake."

"I'm sorry," she said.

"I'm the one who's sorry. Here I am, rambling on about my deteriorating marriage. This is nothing compared with all that you've been through. Please forgive me." He got up and poked at the fire, stirring up the flames. The larger of the two logs broke into two pieces. He pushed them deeper into the hearth.

"I don't mind at all. Marriage is a complicated thing. I was married twice as long as you, yet there were things about Harry I never knew."

"I don't want to make you unhappy." Will sat again. The sweet earnestness in his manner made her feel she could tell him anything.

"You're not. I don't mind talking about Harry. I was married fairly young, a common scenario really: swept off my feet by an older man. Harry was a classmate of my sister Darcy's husband. Darcy is the beautiful one in my family, smart too, and I couldn't believe that any friend of theirs would be interested in me. I was working at a magazine in New York, living with three roommates, barely able to make ends meet. He proposed when he accepted a job with the firm in Washington."

Will appeared to want to hear more. "For a long time," she said, "everything was perfect. We had Rob, bought our big house, and Harry threw himself into building his career. Then we lost Grace. She died the day after she was born. It was like a light went out. It took me a long time to get over that. Working on the cookbooks and writing the food columns helped. Harry became more absorbed in his work too. I think it gradually became an obsession. When the stock market was down for so long, he made some terrible decisions."

Caroline leaned forward, resting her hands on her knees. "I made awful mistakes too." She closed her eyes.

One winter night the year after Grace's death, Harry had come home late from work. She had built a fire in the living room, and after he'd looked in on Rob, she brought his dinner on a tray by the fire. Harry had started to eat distractedly, pushing his food absently with his fork. It had been a new recipe for a beef bourguignonne that had taken all afternoon to cook. She had let Rob paint at the kitchen table to keep him occupied. Cleaning up the huge mess he made had taken a lot out of her.

"Do you like this recipe?" she had said.

"I've had a rough day, Caro," he replied.

"Mine hasn't been easy either." She had spoken harshly, annoyed that he wasn't appreciating her efforts. Angry that he'd been late from work once again.

"I lost a major client today. One of my biggest portfolios. They're taking their business to Anchorage Trust."

"Losing a client. Is that all you ever think about? Losing a daughter is a whole lot worse than that."

Harry's face had gone ashen. He stood and set the tray on the table next to him. "You think you're the only one who remembers? I wake up every day wishing for my little girl. Still, I have to keep doing my job, trying to make a living. Believe me, Caroline, you don't have a monopoly on grief." He had stalked out of the room.

The clock in the hall ticked loudly. She opened her eyes, almost surprised to find Will in the room with her.

"I'm sorry, Caroline." She felt Will's hand on her shoulder. "You shouldn't have to explain all this. Now I'm afraid I've ruined your evening."

"No, honestly. It's not your fault." Stupidly, she began to cry. He must think her truly pathetic—in tears at the side of the road and now this. "I must be crazy. I wake up every day and try to convince myself that this baby will change everything." She stood and walked in front of the fireplace. The flames had died out. A steady heat rose from the coals.

"But you have your son," he said, and, stepping behind her, he tentatively placed his hands on her arms, as if afraid that touching her might upset her further.

Caroline lowered her head and brought her hands to her face.

"He doesn't know." She wept openly.

"You haven't told him about the baby?"

She was too upset to speak.

Will drew his arms around her more firmly, as if to support her, to hold her together. She felt the warmth of his grasp above her belly and below her breasts, at her very center. "But you will tell him," he said, "and if having a child makes you happy, surely he'll understand that and . . ." His voice trailed off, as if finding words to console her was too much to manage.

He continued to hold her while she cried, rocking her lightly like a boat on the waves. She felt his breath in her hair and then his lips on her neck as he kissed her gently there. She took her hands and covered his, still above her belly. Then she froze. The memory of Pete and his kiss, there, on her neck like this . . .

Caroline pulled out of his grasp. "Please, no."

Will stepped back. "I'm sorry. I wasn't thinking. I shouldn't have—"

"You should go."

Will looked dazed, as if struggling to wake from a dream. She walked with him to the back door and handed him his coat. He didn't put it on, but fumbled with the door, pulling it open wide. A gust of wind blew into the hall. "I'm sorry," he said again.

She looked up into his eyes and, before she could stop herself, reached out and took his hand once more. "Thank you for being here." She squeezed his hand firmly and let go. "It's fine. Truly."

Will was gone. Caroline went back to the fire and watched the final embers flicker in the dark. He had put his arms around her. She couldn't think. Could life become any more complicated than this?

❦

"Yeah?" Rob's voice was clouded with sleep. Yet it was eight thirty in the morning, and Caroline knew that his first class began at nine.

"Sweetie, it's Mom." There was a pause, and Caroline pictured Rob in wrinkled sheets dragging himself up to a sitting position. She tried to contain her excitement. Now, two days after the party, she'd learned from her Realtor that a couple returning from a diplomatic assignment abroad had offered to buy the house in Chevy Chase. The contract came in five thousand dollars under the asking price, but there were no contingencies. They were offering cash, and they wanted to settle immediately so they could start redecorating and have the house ready for their children, who would be starting school after the new year.

"Is anything wrong?" Rob asked.

She told him the good news. "I'm going in a few weeks to meet with the lawyers and see to having our things go to storage."

"So?" He sounded annoyed.

"Shall I buy you a ticket? I'd love you to come home the first weekend in November. Our last time in the house."

"Look," he said, "I don't want to think about this now. Do whatever. I don't care anymore."

"Rob, I need to talk to you about something important. It can't wait." Caroline remembered Will's arms around her. He had given her courage.

"Mom, I have a midterm in twenty minutes. I gotta go."

"Can't you come that weekend?"

"I've got papers due and—"

"You can bring your books. I've missed you."

"Look, I'll see you at Gram's at Thanksgiving." He sounded stressed. "I can't change my plans now."

"I wouldn't ask you to if it weren't important."

"Fine. Okay. Don't send a ticket. I'll borrow a car. I'd rather drive."

Caroline agreed, and he uttered a hurried, automatic "Love you, Ma," before hanging up.

She sat quietly, savoring her relief. It was set in motion now. She would finally tell Rob the truth. At that moment she felt a few fierce kicks from the small person inside her and a tightness in her chest. Her blood pressure had probably gone up. She sat for a minute on the chair next to the phone and tried to slow her breathing. Listening to the hall clock, she breathed in for four ticks and then out for four more. The baby's kicks subsided. She grabbed her coat from the back hall and went out to her car.

❦

There were no other cars in the parking lot of Hawthorne Beach. Caroline slammed her door shut and set off along the sand. The air stung with cold and her eyes watered in the wind. She drew her scarf more tightly around her neck. The ends snapped against her jacket. She remembered her one encounter with Will on this beach. She thought again of his arms around her, the way he held her by the fire. She had wanted that kiss. She should be thinking of Harry. East Hope had been his place.

Today the sky was filled with fat, blowing clouds pummeling against one another as far as she could see. Rob had probably toddled along this beach that summer long ago. He would have picked up shells and bits of driftwood, his small head bent to study the contents of his bucket. Such an easygoing boy. Always happy to play on his own, but well liked by other children. He would dig happily in the sand and in no time he'd have a posse of helpers joining in his play. It was no different in high school. He had started the Outing Club. His wilderness trips were popular with all his friends.

All of that was behind them. *Look, Rob. I'm going to have a baby. It's nothing I planned. It happened; that's all. I want you to be grown-up and accept that this is something I need now.* She walked faster. What did it matter what she needed? Children didn't consider that their parents might have needs too. *Such insanity,* she thought. *You bring a baby into the world. You feel an overwhelming, passionate attachment to a child, and that child grows to an adult, makes his own life, and leaves.*

Caroline's boots slogged along in the wet sand. Eventually, short of breath, she stopped and stared out at the ocean. The waves crashed onto the beach at a distance. Low tide. Next week at this time she'd be back in Washington, back in the house where all her old memories were still alive. The wind whipped at her ears. She should have put on a hat.

She turned to walk back to her car. There was still no one on the beach, and she thought again of Will, and pushed aside the half hope that he would appear. Just before she reached the parking lot she looked back at the water once more. Caroline brought her hands up to cover her ears and momentarily muffled the roar of the waves.

15

As Caroline moved through the house in Chevy Chase, sorting clothes, packing boxes, adding to the growing piles in the garage, the memories of all the years in this house tumbled unchecked into her mind, unstoppable. The corner in the living room where they put up the Christmas tree each year, the dining room where they had had so many happy family celebrations, the kitchen table where Harry had helped Rob with school projects—the flour-salt-and-water relief map of the state of Maryland, Harry wishing it had been someplace easier, one of the square states with straight lines.

Now it was November and the leaves of the old maples around the house had fallen. The trees, planted before the days of air-conditioning, shaded the house in summer, but by November the sun shone brightly through the windows. Caroline had always loved the way the fall sunlight poured into her house. Once the heat of summer passed, the sky became a more crisp blue, though not quite as vivid as the sky in Maine. She thought of Will, how he had put his arms around her. *Stop,* she told herself. It was wrong to think of him, especially today, the first anniversary of Harry's death.

Harry had died on a beautiful day like this. Caroline looked out at her garden and thought of the hours she had spent there. Building a garden was a way of controlling nature, creating order, making your imprint upon the earth. Yet so much was out of your control. The lilac, planted by her father in memory of Grace, was testament to that.

The house closing was at the end of the week. Packing up the house was a huge job. Every muscle in Caroline's body hurt, and she ached in ways she had not thought possible. Her huge belly felt like lead. A lawn crew was coming to rake the yard one final time. The leaves would be swept away, the furniture put into storage, in the same way that her life with her family in this house would be totally erased, nothing left but the memories. For a long time to come, Caroline would be able to close her eyes and picture this garden. What would she remember of Harry?

And Rob? By selling this house she was erasing his memories too. How much of this house, the things in it, the times they shared here as a family, would he be able to recall? Would he live in a house like this one day, look out at a yard, and remember soccer games with Jim, sitting around with his friends eating pizza, his father helping him with homework? Being in their old house was bringing back all the memories of both the good times and the bad.

Caroline turned away from the window and rested for a moment in the chair in her bedroom. She was thankful Rob would be here soon and she could finally tell him everything. Each time she spoke to him by phone after he went back to school, she had always found an excuse to hold back: He had been rushed, overtired, busy with midterms; or other times he had been especially happy: a good grade on a paper, Melanie coming to see him unexpectedly, being accepted into a seminar with a favorite professor. She realized now that what would have been merely an unhappy and difficult discussion had ballooned with the passage of time.

She got up and looked at a box of mementos on the bed that she had set aside for Rob. She studied the framed photograph of Rob and Harry on a rafting trip in Montana, taken the summer Rob was twelve. Rob leaned into his father, whose arm draped around his young son's skinny shoulders. Compared to Rob, grinning at his side, Harry looked more serious, as if he were already aware that this young boy was on the cusp of becoming an independent young man. Harry had lived for those wilderness trips with his son.

Caroline put Harry's favorite fleece jacket in the box. She had found it while cleaning out the front hall closet. She also added the small clock that Harry always kept on his dresser. Harry once told Rob, six or seven at the time, that the frame of the clock was covered in pigskin. "You mean the skin of a pig?" Rob had asked, cocking his head in wonder. The clock had belonged to Harry's grandfather. Earlier she had put away Harry's gold cuff links, and the pocket watch that had belonged to his great-grandfather, planning to give them to Rob on his twenty-first birthday.

She looked again at the fishing vest that she had placed on top of the box. Harry's fishing equipment was in the garage, packed and ready to go to East Hope in her car. The fishing vest was so like Harry, sensible and well made of a durable beige cotton fabric, softened from use. It was practical; each pocket and strap served a purpose. Every time Harry came home from a fishing trip, he carefully removed everything from the pockets and then folded it neatly and put it on the shelf to await the next trip. How could such a thoughtful, sensible man make such a dreadful decision with their investments? She shoved down the top of the box.

The phone rang. She drew in her breath, startled. Very few people knew she was in town. Pete had called periodically to check on her and still kept insisting that he wanted to help her financially. He was going to be on the West Coast during the time she would be in Washington. Vivien was coming to help with some final packing in the morning. Another ring. She picked up.

"You okay, Mom?"

Rob's voice lifted her spirits immediately. "Oh, sweetie, I've been thinking of you," she said.

"You called me, Mom. This day last year." Rob's voice broke.

"It's not easy, is it?" Caroline was filled with guilt. It was she who should be checking on him. "It's been a hard day so far," she said, looking at the box of Harry's things.

"Yeah," Rob said.

"Are you okay, honey?" He said nothing. She tried to think clearly, feeling a creeping sense of dread. Maybe she should tell him now. Certainly not now. Better in person, as she had planned.

"Remember the day you called?" he asked.

She nodded. Tears flowed freely down her cheeks.

"I almost missed the call," he said. "I was leaving for a test." She could hear him crying softly on the phone. "You told me Dad had a heart attack. And it was serious."

Caroline nodded, unable to speak.

"You never said he was dead. But I knew."

That morning, a year ago, Pete had called her from the office. He told her he would take her to the hospital to be with Harry and that he would drive up to Pennsylvania to get Rob from college. She had forgotten how Pete had helped. Pete had been the one to tell Rob that his father had died.

"You're so good to call," she said.

"It's okay, Mom. I just wanted to talk. Sorry I've been so shitty about selling the house."

"I'm sad to leave it too." Caroline stood and looked down at the garden. The wind had picked up and the leaves blew up and around Grace's bench. She swallowed and hated herself once again for not having the courage to tell him the truth.

"I'll see you Friday," he said.

Her dread sharpened. "You'll be okay, then?"

"I love you, Mom."

&

Vivien arrived the next morning. "It may be a little rough at first," she said. "When you explain, I'm sure he'll understand."

Caroline sealed another box of china with brown sticky tape. She had opted to pack as much as she could herself to keep down the cost of the move. She placed another wine goblet on the stack of beige paper in front of her, brought up one side of paper, then the other, and smoothly rolled the glass to the end of the sheet before adding it to an empty carton.

"He's so important to me. He's lost his dad. I don't want him to think he's lost me." Caroline drew her hand across and then under her belly. The baby had been moving and kicking vigorously for the past few days. She was anxious to get through this move. Dr. Carney was not keen on her driving all the way to Washington and back again.

"Just tell him that."

"I will, though sometimes the simplest things are the hardest."

Vivien reached for an empty box. "Oh, I have some news that might cheer you up."

"About my cookbook idea?"

"I've got the name of an agent who might be interested. She specializes in cookbooks. She'd like to see your proposal."

"That's really good news."

Vivien put the packing box aside and rummaged in her handbag. "Here's her name and contact information." She handed Caroline a sheet of paper. "You might want to include a sample chapter with some recipes too."

"But that's wonderful. I can't believe it. Vivien, you're such a good friend."

"Don't get excited yet. If she likes your proposal and decides to represent you, she still has to sell it to a publishing company."

"I'll work on it as soon as I get to Maine." She hoped she could do a good job. Not only did she want to get an advance for the project, she needed the work, something to keep her busy in the long months ahead.

"You're a fine writer," Vivien reassured her friend, as if privy to her thoughts. "You can do this. I know you can." Vivien picked up a flat carton. "Let me give you a hand with this."

They worked together, stopping only for a quick lunch.

Before Vivien left at the end of the afternoon, Caroline asked her to help her carry Grace's bench from the garden to her car. Caroline had decided it was the one thing she didn't want to put into storage. The bench would fit perfectly alongside Lila's house by the herb garden. It would be a lovely place to sit, protected there from the wind.

"Let's each take an end," Vivien said.

Caroline's hair blew into her face as she lifted. The teak bench was heavy and clumps of dirt stuck to each foot. They carried it awkwardly to the car. When Caroline glanced back at the tangle of plants, a few still green and not yet felled by the early frosts, she started to cry. The bench could go with her but the lilac, Grace's lilac, had to stay.

"It's okay, old friend," Vivien said, setting down her end. "Come on now. Have a good cry. That's just what you need."

❦

Will put down Crystal's essay. They had been meeting twice a week at the library and this was the second draft he'd seen. It was four thirty and already dark. Rain was supposed to move in that night. Maybe it would even snow.

"So what do you think?" Crystal's steady gaze never left his face.

"It's coming along well," Will said. He gave her an encouraging smile. "You're almost there."

"But not totally?" She twirled a few strands of hair between her fingers.

"Remember I told you that the real writing is in the rewriting."

"Like, every time I see you." She rolled her eyes in a joking way.

After a rough junior year, life as a senior seemed to be going better for Crystal. Her mother was recovering from surgery and she appeared to be in remission from her cancer. Will had done nothing special for Crystal except to listen, and take the time to help her organize her thoughts. He told her that a pivotal event she was supposed to write about didn't have to be some huge or highly dramatic moment. Sometimes small encounters had the power to alter the course of your life. For him, seeing the ad for Taunton's in *Down East* had been the insignificant thing that seemed to be affecting everything in his own life, especially now.

"Do you still make the fairy forts in the woods?" he asked.

"You won't tell anyone?" She raised her thin shoulders slightly.

He shook his head no. "One day you'll have to show me how you do it."

Crystal's essay had been about the times her mother had taken her into the woods behind their house in the summer and sat her down on the ground, soft and fragrant with pine, to make miniature villages out of sticks, pebbles, moss, and the other natural materials that they found on their walks. They began by constructing little dollhouses for the fairies. Fairy forts, they called them, tiny log cabins of twigs with moss-covered roofs.

As Crystal grew older, their creations grew more elaborate. Crystal and her mother made tiny paths, pretend villages, a church steeple with acorn caps, a store made from birch bark, and a school surrounded by a wall of tiny pebbles. An inverted clamshell filled with water served as a pond. Crystal's mother, who studied art as a young girl, had spent a summer on Monhegan Island, where building fairy houses in the woods was a tradition.

For Crystal, the project didn't end in the woods. Once home, she wrote stories about the imaginary little people that populated that world. She explained in her essay that this was what made her want to become a writer.

Become a writer, Will thought. In his mind, Crystal *was* a writer, and Will felt happy that he had been able to help her in this small way. "We'll go over it one more time next week," he said. "Be sure every sentence, every word is working, there for a reason. I suggest you read it out loud."

It was five o'clock and their time was up. They gathered their books and coats, and he followed her outside. A light icy rain had begun to fall.

"Do you need a lift home?" he asked. His car and Edna's were the only ones in the parking lot.

Crystal lifted her face to the sky. "Could you? It's pretty gross out. I live out on Bartlett Road. It's the turn after Karen's Café." She shifted her books in her arms, her shoulders hunched in the cold. "You're sure you don't mind?"

"Not at all."

Crystal followed him to his car and got in. The road was wet and potentially slippery, so Will took it slowly, periodically testing the brakes.

"Mr. Harmon?"

Will glanced at her; she looked waiflike, wet pieces of hair on her face. Crystal wasn't dressed warmly enough. No hat or gloves and it was November.

"I was wondering if you'd be willing to read some other stuff? Stories, I mean."

"Sure, anytime," he said.

"It's right here." She pointed to a small cape set back from the road. "Just leave me by the mailbox," she said.

Will pulled the car to a stop and Crystal got out. He watched her walk up the dirt drive, relieved to see lights on in several rooms and smoke rising from the chimney. He backed out of the drive and turned his car toward Taunton's.

Caroline's house was dark. He reduced his speed as if to linger, as if a light might go on at any moment, signifying that she was home. Maybe she had gone to see her son, to tell him about her baby. He remembered holding her the night of the dinner party. The scent of her hair, floral with a touch of wood smoke from the fire, soft against his cheek, kept coming back to him, as did the feeling of her hands on his.

Why was he going to New York? Was it the simple New England stick-to-itiveness that had been drummed into him since childhood, or the longing for an enduring marriage like the one his parents had? Could he recapture what he once had with Mary Beth?

The range of Will's feelings toward his wife was troubling. On the one hand he knew he was guilty: He hadn't gone to see her in California, he'd insisted on this summer in Maine; he'd gone ahead and bought Taunton's with the knowledge that she wouldn't approve. But she was at fault too, he persuaded himself. She was constructing a whole new life for them in New York, as if he would happily comply with the future she envisioned. He thought again of their week together, the final days of summer that he had spent with her. They had reconnected, strengthening the slender threads of tenderness and affection between them. Or had that time been a sort of fantasy, like Crystal's make-believe fairy world, a fleeting construction that would not stand the test of time?

After ten the next evening Rob came in through the door to his old house in Chevy Chase.

"I'm in here," Caroline called out. She sat on the sofa in the living room in front of the fire. Her knees were drawn up to her chest. She had draped a blanket across her legs.

Rob put down his bags in the hall, a backpack and a black computer bag that used to be Harry's. His hair was longer and shaggy. He came over to his mother, bent, and kissed her cheek before collapsing in one of the upholstered chairs next to the sofa.

"I'm so glad you're home," she said. "Do you want some dinner? I could heat something up."

"I ate on the way. Thanks."

Caroline's heart felt heavy in her chest. "There's something I have to explain." She had lit only one lamp. The room was in shadow. He could probably see nothing yet. "This has been a terrible year for you," she went on. "You miss Dad, and I know it's been rough for you to give up our house and—"

"Mom, you don't have to say all that again."

"It's been hard for me too."

"I know that, Mom."

"Something happened that I never could have imagined. I had to make a very difficult decision."

"What do you mean?"

"In a way, it's an amazing blessing."

"What are you talking about?"

She heard the impatience in his voice. "Rob, this is so hard to explain." She drew in a large breath and let it go. "I'm going to have a baby."

He said nothing. Caroline felt as if the air had been sucked out of the room.

"You're what?"

"Yes. You see . . ." She stretched out her legs, her belly now clearly visible.

"But . . . Dad?" His voice came out barely a whisper.

Caroline couldn't seem to get her mouth to speak.

"Shit," he said. "So you've got some boyfriend?" His voice cracked like a fourteen-year-old's. "That didn't take you very long."

"Rob, let me tell you what happened."

"You'd better tell me," he said. "How could you?" He looked shocked. His mouth hung open.

"I don't have a boyfriend," she said. "You know how hard this winter was, and you know how Dad lost almost all of our money. I spent months trying to work things out. Pete was so kind. He explained what had gone wrong and he . . ." The months and months of planned explanations swirled in her head. She had to get this right. "Last May I went to a dinner party. It was that strange warm weekend, and Pete and Marjorie had me to dinner and . . ." *Wait.* She didn't want to bring Pete into this.

"Mom, get to the point."

"I hated being there. I really didn't want to go out. I had too much to drink and when I came home . . . Pete drove me home. I was at a low ebb, and that and the wine . . ." She couldn't go on. She had already said too much. For a while Rob said nothing. His expression was at first confused, then clouded with disbelief.

"You mean Pete Spencer?" Rob asked.

"Let me explain."

"Uncle Pete?" he shouted at her. "Dad's best friend? You're lying."

"I know it was terrible of me. It wasn't his fault. We didn't think."

He brought his hands to his head. "You waited until now to tell me about this?"

"Please." Caroline started to get up.

"Don't come near me."

This was going far worse than she'd ever imagined. She sat very still. "I wanted to tell you this summer. But Melanie was there, and you were so upset about giving up our house."

"Mom," he said, his voice choking on a sob.

"Please don't be upset."

"You don't think I should be upset when you've been screwing the guy who I thought was Dad's best friend?" His words flew at her like bullets.

"Stop saying that. It was one night, one mistake." Her voice was pleading.

"Have you totally forgotten Dad?"

"Of course not. I would never forget your father."

"Yeah, right," he said with disgust.

"It shouldn't have happened, but it did. When I found out I was pregnant I was shocked and scared, but after a while I realized that I want this baby very much." Caroline pulled a tissue from her pocket and wiped her face and nose. "You see, I—"

" 'I, I, I.' How do you think this makes *me* feel? Do you have any idea?"

"Rob, please."

"First my dad dies; then my mom goes and screws his best friend. Then she lies about it. Then she decides to have his baby. Maybe you never loved Dad. Maybe that was a lie too. If you loved Dad, none of this would have ever happened."

"Never say that."

"Dad worked a lot. But it was for us, Mom. He loved us. How could you forget that?"

"I haven't. It's just—"

"Just what? You remember him one day and start screwing Uncle Pete the next?"

"Stop it. You can't say that." Caroline was suddenly angry. She had wanted to protect Rob, to spare him some of her pain, but now she was exhausted from trying to smooth things over, from carrying this burden alone. "There are things you don't understand." Caroline paused and wiped her eyes with the back of one hand. "It's hard to talk about. I think you'll see in time . . ."

He rose to leave the room.

"Rob," she said, "don't walk away from me."

"I'm out of here. You're disgusting. I can't stay here."

"Where are you going?"

"Back to school."

"At this hour? No. We need to talk."

"There's nothing more to say."

"When you come to Gram's house for Thanksgiving—"

"Gram knows?"

"Yes. Gram understands why I want to do this."

"I'm not coming," he said defiantly.

"Gram expects you and—"

"I'm not coming, Mom."

"Don't say that."

"You don't have any right to tell me what to do."

"I'm your mother. I expect you to be on that train."

"You don't act like a mother."

"Rob." Caroline tried to sound forceful.

"You've forgotten my dad." His words were measured and harsh. Rob was right: For a few hours she had forgotten Harry. There was no going back.

"Rob—" she said again.

"Tell Gram I'm sorry."

"Please, for me . . ."

Rob stalked out of the room. She heard him take his belongings from the hall, go out the front door, and slam it behind him. Her son knew the truth. He was gone.

16

"Mom has some sort of half-baked idea that having this baby is going to be good for you." Darcy looked up from the cutting board. She was dicing celery for the stuffing, cutting the long green shafts into evenly sized nuggets. Afternoon sun poured into their mother's kitchen in Connecticut.

When their parents had remodeled in the 1970s, they kept the knotty pine cupboards with black iron hinges, but added olive green Formica countertops to match the stove and refrigerator. Caroline remembered washing lettuce at the kitchen sink, and Darcy racing in before they sat down to dinner, always too late to be of any help. They used to argue as to whose turn it was to clear the table or whose turn it was to actually do the dishes.

"Did you hear what I said?"

Darcy's voice brought Caroline back to the present. She stood by the stove waiting for the pan of cranberries to come to a boil, shifting from one foot to the other, aware of the weight of her belly. "Did Mom buy lemons?" Caroline asked. She had only been half listening to her sister, preoccupied by Rob's threat not to come for Thanksgiving. "I want to add some grated rind to the sauce after it thickens."

"If it makes you happy to have a baby, that's fine with me," Darcy said, more kindly. "But you haven't said anything about Rob. This has to be hard on him."

"He's not very happy about a lot of things." Caroline left the stove and rummaged in the produce drawer of the refrigerator, pulling out a dried-up-looking orange as well as a lemon. She carried the fruit to the counter and stirred the cranberries that were now beginning to pop. It was Wednesday afternoon. She had tried to reach Rob several times since he had stormed out of the house in Chevy Chase. He had never called back, despite her repeated messages. Now she could only hope that as Thanksgiving grew closer his anger might have lessened and he would still come to Connecticut. Before he knew about the baby he had agreed to come to his grandmother's house for the holiday after stopping one night in New York for a party. Once they were together she wanted to tell him more about Grace. In his angry departure he hadn't given her the chance to fully explain her decision.

Caroline and Darcy were alone together for the first time that day. Their mother had gone to the grocery store to buy nutmeg for the apple pie. The three of them had been working in the kitchen since morning, and once the cranberry sauce was finished, Caroline planned to escape for a rest.

"Mom said she's going to Maine for Christmas and staying on to help you with the baby."

"Is there some problem with that?" Caroline sounded irritable and instantly regretted it. "You'll have your kids home and Walter and his family."

Darcy resumed chopping more vigorously. "Mom's not getting any younger, and now, thanks to you, she has to traipse off to some godforsaken place to spend the winter." Darcy's face was flushed, but as usual she looked perfectly in control in a gray cashmere sweater the same shade as her pants. Caroline felt like an elephant in her maternity jeans and the large plaid shirt that covered the turtleneck that had grown tight across her breasts.

"It's not a godforsaken place. You're only going to upset Mom if you keep saying that."

"Mom's not as strong as she used to be. You haven't been around enough to see that."

"I'm grateful you're close by. You do a lot."

"Traveling isn't easy for her anymore." She dumped the celery into the bowl of cubed bread.

"I know that. If I could travel then I would. I want to give Rob more of a family Christmas."

Darcy emptied a bag of pecans into the stuffing and tossed the mixture with two wooden spoons. Caroline would have used her hands, but she said nothing. She grated the lemon into the dark red mixture in the pan and stirred. The fresh tang of the lemon would temper the sweetened cranberries.

"You amaze me," Darcy said.

"What's that supposed to mean?" Caroline wiped up the spatters around the stove.

"The long Maine winter, living all by yourself, having a baby, no husband . . ."

"Please don't keep going on about it."

"Girls!" They hadn't heard their mother come in. "I don't want to hear any more arguing." She set one bag on the kitchen table along with a bakery box tied in white string. "Luckily, I remembered the rolls. Now we won't need to go out again today."

Caroline's thoughts had turned to Lila. She'd lived alone winter after long winter. She had defied convention in her day too.

"What time is Rob's train, dear?" her mother asked.

Caroline put the sponge back beside the sink. "I think he's coming out from New York tomorrow afternoon," she said quietly.

"Why is he spending tonight in New York?" Darcy asked.

"There's a party he wants to go to." Caroline poured the cranberry sauce into a serving bowl.

"You spoil that boy," Darcy said.

"Letting him go to a party? You call that spoiling him?"

"Girls, let's just enjoy this time together."

"You're right, Mom," Darcy said.

Caroline stretched plastic wrap across the top of the bowl. Steam clouded the fragrant red mixture. "Actually, there's a chance he won't even come."

"What do you mean?" Peg asked.

"I didn't tell him about the baby until two weeks ago, when he came home before the move. He was furious. He said he didn't want to see me and wouldn't come for Thanksgiving."

"Why didn't you say anything?" Darcy asked.

"I thought you told him about the baby last summer," Peg said.

"I never told him. He was only home for a few weeks, and his girlfriend was there the whole time. He would have been upset no matter when I told him."

"Though now it's much more real." Darcy shot a quick look at Caroline's belly.

"I'm still hoping he'll come," Caroline said. She went to the kitchen table, sat, and covered her face with her hands.

"I hope so too," Peg said.

"What train was he supposed to take?" Darcy asked.

"Before all this happened he had planned to be on the one-o'clock."

"I'm sorry," Darcy said.

"I'm going to go lie down," Caroline said.

"Of course," her mother agreed. "You've been on your feet all morning."

"I'm fine, Mom. I'm just a little tired." Caroline stood and carried the cranberry sauce to the fridge. Turning to her mother, she bent and kissed her papery cheek. Darcy was right: Her mother seemed to have aged more lately, crossing the line from older to old woman.

❦

"Will, you're not listening."

Will looked up, startled. It was Thanksgiving afternoon, and he and Mary Beth were at L'Espoir, a French restaurant not far from her apartment. "I'm sorry," he said, and looked down again at the narrow lavender-colored menu. "We should probably have the turkey. I mean, it is Thanksgiving," he said as he continued to look over the menu, trying to find something in keeping with the American feast day.

Mary Beth sat opposite him on a velvet banquette wearing a gray sweater with a fur collar. She had cut her hair since her visit to Maine. The front pieces swept across her forehead, but the back was shorter than he had ever seen it.

"Why would they serve fig sauce with turkey?" he asked.

"You're grumpy because we're eating out."

"Sorry," he said again. "The butternut-squash-and-chestnut soup sounds good. I think I'll start with that." He doubted that the pilgrims ate squash soup accompanied with chipotle cream.

Last night, when he finally got to the city after driving for ten hours, he couldn't seem to shake the gloom that had come over him. He thought about the friends he'd left behind in Maine, his work at the store, tutoring at the library, and Caroline. He hadn't even said good-bye. Though, what could he say? He'd made the decision to remake his life in New York with Mary Beth. Almost immediately, hoping to settle the rift between them, he apologized to Mary Beth again for buying Taunton's without consulting her.

"I'm willing to put that behind us," she'd said. "We'll view it as an investment."

"An investment?"

"I believe those were your words. Once you've found a job, you can arrange to rent it."

"Yeah, I guess. . . ."

"Darling, you're here. We're going to forget all that."

She had pulled him into her arms again.

Instead of going out for dinner, Mary Beth had ordered in from a Brazilian restaurant and made him a mojito. She was obviously trying to do her part too, and told him a funny story about a neighbor, who, wearing only his boxer shorts, had had to hunt for his cat that had escaped in the service stairwell. The poor man ended up having to climb eight flights before finding his pet, which had wandered into another apartment where the back door had been left ajar. Will knew Mary Beth was doing her best to coax him into a better mood and to make him happy in New York.

She had played a Brazilian CD, poured him a second drink, and then a third. After that they had made love. As in Maine, the physical part of their relationship worked fine.

Will had awoken on this Thanksgiving morning with a predictable headache. He had not minded initially when Mary Beth had told him that they would have dinner at a restaurant. Her tiny kitchen would have been a difficult place to roast a turkey. He only wished it had been a restaurant with a more traditional Thanksgiving menu. The gray-and-lavender color scheme of L'Espoir and the contrived French menu did nothing to inspire thoughts of an autumnal celebration of thanks.

The waiter came and took their order and served the bottle of champagne that Mary Beth said would go well with turkey.

"Here's to us," she said, lifting her glass.

"Cheers," Will said, and sipped. "Delicious. Anything will taste good with this." He smiled across at her, determined to be cheerful. The restaurant was quiet, soothing.

"Remember how you used to read to me?" she asked.

He nodded. The memory rose in him from some far-off place. They had been two different people then.

"It was so lovely," she said. "I'd come back frazzled from being on the road, totally numb from all the sales calls. You'd make a fire; I'd pour the wine." She smiled at him. Her lips had a gleam from her lipstick or the champagne.

"I used to read from what I was teaching at the time," he said. "Remember *Mrs. Dalloway*?"

"I do." She laughed. "Your voice used to lull me to sleep. Maybe you'll read to me again. It would be something to look forward to after a hard day at the office."

"I've started to look," he said. "There aren't a lot of jobs where I could teach books like that."

"Will, you're going to get a good job. You've got to think positively."

He thought of her motivational sales meetings, the psychobabble of techniques that she insisted could move a person to the top of the corporate ladder. That would never fly in academia. He passed her the basket of rolls after taking one himself. He had a raw feeling in his stomach.

Mary Beth put her glass on the table and leaned toward Will. "You asked me to think about children," she said.

Will pulled himself up straighter. "You mean our having children?"

"Of course. You brought it up. Remember? In Maine?"

Maine. Taunton's, the fading yellow clapboard building. His life in East Hope seemed very far away. "I've started to think about it," he said, knowing that this question was still unresolved in his own heart. "I know we're not getting any younger and . . ." He reached for his champagne glass, not knowing where to go from here.

In Maine, when he and Mary Beth had made love, it made their marriage once again seem real, as if they could go forward. Yet could this woman opposite him, so calmly sipping champagne, be the mother of his children, their children? Sexy and sophisticated, Mary Beth was as beautiful now as she was when she had shown up in the undergraduate seminar on Henry James. The professor who was supposed to have taught the class had become ill, and Will, his doctorate completed except for the thesis, had been brought in to teach at the last minute. He had been attracted to her immediately, but had waited until after graduation before asking her out.

The waiter returned and set down two enormous flat bowls. The small amount of ocher-colored soup sported a slash of pink, like the drip from a paint can, and a thin sprinkling of chives.

"I do want children," she said when they were alone again.

"That's good," he said. "I guess I always assumed we'd have

kids one day." At that moment a vision of Caroline flickered in his mind, the last time he saw her, the night of her dinner party when she was flushed from cooking, her rounded belly prominent in the soft green dress, her eyes glowing in the firelight. He couldn't forget the moment at the end of the evening when he had bent and kissed her neck. What had come over him? Caroline had pulled away, justifiably, but there had been a second, maybe two, when she had placed her hands over his. At times he thought he had imagined it, but she had responded; she had covered his hands with hers.

"Still, we need to take it one step at a time," Mary Beth said.

"What do you mean?"

"Do you want to have this discussion or not?" Tension had crept into her voice.

"Forgive me," he said, and put his spoon down and reached across the table for her hand. "I think our night in Rio wore me out."

Mary Beth smiled. She gave his hand a squeeze and resumed eating her soup. "This next year is going to be a tough one," she said, lowering her spoon to the bowl. "Not exactly tough, but challenging."

Will tried to listen to what she was saying while his soup cooled in front of him.

"We're looking into acquiring a German company. Drew wants to pull me from marketing and have me work full-time in mergers and acquisitions. It's a management position." It seemed that Drew was now in the New York office. Hearing his name yet again rankled. She continued, explaining how eventually this new position would still mean some travel, and the learning curve would be steep. She'd be the youngest person in the group, the only woman too. Will was impressed with all that Mary Beth had achieved.

"It sounds like you'll still be working pretty hard."

"I'm afraid so. But Drew said it won't mean long hours forever."

"So when exactly will you be free to have a baby?" He heard how this sounded, like a challenge.

"You don't have to get testy."

"I'm not." He swallowed and tried to be more positive. "I just want to know when your job might allow for some time off."

"You don't have to have time off," she said quickly. "Where have you been, Will? Working women have babies all the time."

"I know that." He felt them both being sucked into that dark realm of adversity, she tense, he prickly, a place where compromise was impossible. He had to pull them out. "But you do have to stay in one place for a while. You know, go to the doctor, have a hospital."

"Of course," she said.

"All I'm saying is that when you're traveling or working long hours, it might not be the best time."

"I'm only talking another year or so. After that my schedule should ease up."

"I see."

"We don't need to rush into a family."

"No," he added. "I suppose not." The waiter reappeared and set down the plates of turkey, anemic slices drizzled with the purplish fig sauce.

Maybe what Mary Beth said made sense. It was going to take time to get things back to where they were. Once he found a job in New York, he could hire someone to manage Taunton's. Perhaps he could eventually convince her to spend part of their summers in East Hope.

East Hope. Will missed it, but at the same time he also missed what he and Mary Beth once had. He longed for that huge wave of happiness that had carried them along when they first met and buoyed them up in the early years of their marriage.

Mary Beth started to talk about the party she was hosting in his honor the next evening to introduce him to her friends in New York. Besides many of her usual colleagues from work, she had invited some top people from the company. "I can't believe it," she said. "Hugh Longman, the head of the North American division, is coming." Will nodded. "His new wife is a major deal lawyer, or so I've heard, at Millwood and Austin."

Will raised his eyebrows in appreciation and reached again for the basket of rolls. After finishing his turkey with fig sauce, he was still hungry. This restaurant was all wrong for a Thanksgiving dinner, but at least he was here with Mary Beth. He hoped he could make his life with her right.

❦

When Rob was little Caroline had always loved the end of the day. After organizing the adult dinner, she would sit with Rob while he ate his supper. She might have half a glass of wine while Rob pushed around his vegetables, ate his chicken fingers, or spooned mashed potatoes into his mouth. For the most part he was a good eater, and she sometimes served him bits of what she and Harry would eat later on: mushroom tortellini, wild rice with raisins, or butternut squash soufflé with sherry.

"Now, tell me about your day," she would say, as if he were an adult coming home from work.

"Owen had to go to the nurse."

"He did?" She put on a worried face.

"He flew up on the playground," Rob said, meaning *threw*.

"I see," she said, knowing that Rob's friend Owen suffered frequently from stomach bugs and other illnesses. "Poor Owen," she would add.

After Rob's bath Caroline would take him onto her lap and read to him. They each chose one book, their bedtime ritual. By the end of the second story Rob's eyes would grow heavy and he fell asleep easily.

"Night-night, little one," she always said, sitting at his side and stroking his soft forehead.

"Night, Mama."

"I love you, Rob."

He would reach up and stroke her cheek. "I love you more."

Then Caroline would laugh and say, "Oh, no. I love you more," giving him his good-night kiss.

When she turned out the light his small voice would carry across the darkness: "Mama, I love you more than you love me, ever and ever." After shutting his door, she would smile to herself, knowing that he would say the same thing the very next night.

❧

Rob's train from New York, or what she hoped was Rob's train, was due any minute. Caroline stood by her car and squinted into the sun. The trains were on a reduced holiday schedule and the platform was empty. There were a few cars in the parking lot, probably others waiting for family members coming out from the city. She pushed her hands deeper into pockets; her coat barely buttoned around her growing belly.

A grime-encrusted commuter train pulled into the station. The few passengers disembarking walked to the parking lot and awaiting cars. Caroline watched for Rob. After a few minutes everyone had gone. She stood alone by the car and, shielding her eyes from the sun, looked again in each direction. He had not come.

She got back into her car. What had she expected? Rob would not forgive her. She couldn't force him to come home for Thanksgiving. He was nineteen. In a few months he'd be twenty, and he was already lost to her. She leaned forward, resting her head on the steering wheel. So what if she'd sold the house, cleared the mortgage payments, leaving what she hoped was enough money to get through the winter? Rob didn't want to see her. She had failed as a mother. The wind picked up. A few dry leaves blew across the vacant parking lot. A moment later the baby kicked hard, a swift jab up high, near her heart.

❧

The pungent smell of ripe cheese in the East Side Fromagerie assaulted Will's nostrils, and the handbag of the woman behind him continued to poke him in the back despite his effort to nudge forward in line. It was four in the afternoon on the Friday after Thanksgiving, and he was running the final errands for Mary Beth's cocktail party. It seemed as if everyone in New York was also on the street, all pushing along the sidewalks at a frenzied pace in the coming darkness.

Will clutched his numbered ticket. A shopping bag with four more bottles of wine banged against his legs. Mary Beth was worried that the two cases of wine delivered that morning would not be enough, and she had asked him to pick up four more bottles of white wine. He had a feeling he had bought the wrong kind. She had wanted a pinot grigio, but he couldn't remember the vineyard she had requested. After a few glasses no one would care what they were drinking anyway, as long as it was the right color, he reasoned.

"Forty-seven," a male voice bellowed from the far end of the counter. Will looked at his number. He would be next. The long open cases and shelves behind offered more cheeses than he had ever seen in one place in his entire life. Mary Beth had instructed him to select a goat cheese, a blue, two other soft, and two hard cheeses. Will studied the array before him. There had to be twenty kinds of goat cheese alone.

The handbag behind him poked him again, and when he turned to glower at the offending owner he caught sight of a woman entering the shop, removing her hat, and shaking out a tangle of red hair, the same shade as Caroline's hair, a light red filtered with strands of gold. When she turned in his direction to reach for a number, he saw that it was not Caroline. This woman had a broad face and dark eyes. Will felt strangely let down.

"Forty-eight?" A young woman with spiked maroon hair called out from behind the counter.

Will tried to raise his arm without jostling the woman next to him. "Yes, here," he said, and nodded toward the cheeses before him. "First, I need a goat cheese."

"Foreign or domestic?" she snapped.

"I don't really care. It's for a wine and cheese party and—"

"So you want a log? Herb covered? Black pepper or wood ash?"

Will could hear the impatience in the clerk's voice. "That one looks fine." He pointed at a green-speckled one. The girl picked it up with a sheer sheet of paper and wrapped it artfully on the ledge of the counter.

"And what else?"

She had a lisp or maybe something in her mouth. He tried not to stare at the row of concentric rings running along one ear or the silver stud perched in the flare of her nostril, but then caught sight of the glint of metal at the tip of her tongue. "Brie." He looked away. "A large piece."

"What percentage milk fat?"

This was not going to be easy. "I don't know. What's average?"

"Look, sir, nothing here is *average* cheese." She glared at him. "There's thirty people waiting their turn."

The tongue stud wiggled in front of him. He tried a different tactic. "What would you suggest?" he asked, deciding it would do no good to lose his temper. At this point he didn't care what he purchased. He simply wanted to get out of the crowded stores and away from people. She reached down in the case before him and lifted out a prepackaged piece of Brie with the nonaverage price of $16.98 written above a bar code.

Will recalled the Brie-and-ham sandwiches that he and Mary Beth had eaten on a picnic early in their courtship. They had frequent dates the summer after Mary Beth's graduation. Will was writing his doctoral thesis and she was working in an office before starting business school that fall. They'd seen several movies together, been to dinner a few times, and one hot August afternoon they went on a picnic at an arboretum near the university. The Brie oozed out the sides of the sandwiches with each bite. He didn't remember if they had wine, but they went back to her apartment to escape the heat, and made love for the first time. He would never forget the creamy feel of her skin and the happiness that filled him as he dozed, pressed against her as the uneven roar of the air conditioner droned into the evening.

"And what else?" The owner of the annoying handbag had moved to the other end of the store, and somehow Will manage to select four more cheeses along with the boxes of crackers that were to supplement the French bread he and Mary Beth had bought when they went out for breakfast that morning. He handed over his credit card at the cash register and winced at the $137 total, enough to feed a family in East Hope for a week.

His final stop was the dry cleaner's, just around the corner from Mary Beth's apartment. *Wait,* he caught himself thinking. *My apartment. This will become my apartment and the place I'm going to live.* This thought added to his growing unease.

❧

That evening Mary Beth looked beautiful in a slinky red dress. She kissed Will just as the bell rang announcing the first guests, and then blew playfully into the whorl of his ear. "You're going to have fun, Will. You are." She slipped out of his grasp and headed to the door. The caterer handed him a glass of wine.

The apartment held the spring scent of flowers from the large arrangement that had been delivered that afternoon. The caterer and her helper, both in tuxedos, had come soon after, bearing trays of hors d'oeuvres that would be heated and passed. Mary Beth had praised Will on his selection of cheeses and she had arranged them on platters and set them on the dining table at the far end of the living room.

Within minutes the apartment filled with guests, and Will tried to relax and enjoy himself. The hum of conversation filled the apartment. Mary Beth introduced him to the Babcocks, an older couple who lived on the floor just above. They were a pleasant pair who loved going to concerts and visiting museums. They told Will not to miss the van Gogh drawings at the Met.

Later in the evening he met Hugh Longman, the chief operating officer at Mary Beth's company, who actually turned out to be a nice guy. Hugh explained that his wife was in Florida visiting her elderly mother and couldn't be at the party, but they both loved Maine. Hugh liked to fish, and he and his wife sailed as often as they could. Will enjoyed hearing about their travels in Maine.

When Mary Beth smiled at them from across the room, Hugh leaned in closer, as if to share a confidence. "Mary Beth is really something," he said. "Drew convinced us to put her on the fast track."

That name again. Will was about to reply when they were interrupted by a distinguished man in a navy blazer with a crest on the pocket.

"Clive Martin," he said, thrusting out a ruddy hand. "Mary Beth says you're quite the writer. I know your wife from the co-op board."

Will had no idea that Mary Beth was on the co-op board of the building. What else would he be learning about her life in New York?

"Written anything I might have read?" Clive's voice seemed to boom across the room. Hugh stepped away.

"I've only been published in academic journals," Will explained. "Not the kind of thing you'd pick up at a local bookstore." Clive seemed to be waiting for something more, as if it were Will's job to keep the conversation rolling.

"I tried writing a novel once," he said, "but I'd rather teach literature than write it." He told Clive about Taunton's and his interest in old books. Clive's attention waned.

The caterer stepped between them with a tray of hot mushroom tarts. Both men reached for them, as if glad to find a way to break the conversation. Will drank the last of his wine, planning to excuse himself and move on.

"Great party," Clive said. A flake of pastry hung on his lower lip.

Will nodded and looked down into his empty glass.

Clive smiled toward Mary Beth and lifted his hand as if in salute. A few guests were already starting to leave the party. She appeared to be deep in conversation with a broad-shouldered man. Will had not noticed him earlier. They had not been introduced.

Just then Clive turned toward the server, who was passing a tray with more wine. As Will exchanged his own glass for a new one, he saw the broad-shouldered man reach over and lift a strand of Mary Beth's hair and tuck it behind her ear. That familiar gesture happened so quickly that Will wondered, when he took his new drink and looked back again, if it had happened at all. Mary Beth, looking flushed, then turned to say good-bye to a young woman from her office. The man who had touched his wife's hair was helping another guest with her coat.

Will felt a pounding in his ears. The roar of the cocktail conversation buzzed around him. He was suddenly cold, as if a fog were moving in, damp and heavy, blocking the warmth of the sun. He took a gulp of wine.

"Mr. Harmon?" A voice at his elbow jarred him. The female server stood beside him. "Mr. Harmon, your wife said there is another case of wine, but we can't find it anywhere."

He tried to make sense of what she was saying. "Oh, yes, wine." He excused himself from Clive and started toward the kitchen to look for the wine when he noticed Mary Beth's assistant, who had come to the party with her boyfriend. They had been among the first guests Will had met. She was on the periphery of a large group who appeared to have had lots to drink. They were all laughing louder than normal. He tried to remember her name.

"Mr. Harmon?" The server was motioning toward the kitchen.

"Excuse me," Will said to the young assistant. "It's Sheila, right?"

Sheila stepped away from the crowd and smiled up at Will. "Yeah. Super party."

"I wondered . . ." Will tried to act only mildly interested. "I don't think I've met the guy standing next to Mary Beth."

Sheila looked across the room. She was a tiny woman. Despite wearing very high heels, she had to crane her neck to see whom Will was talking about. She looked back at him and leaned closer. "Didn't Mary Beth tell you?" She giggled. "That's Drew Kramer. Just moved here from the LA office." Sheila raised her eyebrows. "After the deal he did in Asia, they say there's no stopping him." Sheila stopped speaking and appeared suddenly flustered. "I assumed Mary Beth told you about him."

"Yes. Yes, she did. I just didn't know if he was going to be here tonight." The server was at his side again. "Thanks, Sheila. I'll introduce myself in a minute."

Will went into the kitchen and directed the server to the back door. Will had left the extra wine in the service hall, as there had been no room in the tiny kitchen. After he had seen to this, he tried to work his way back to Mary Beth. The Babcocks stopped him to speak to him about a gallery opening the next night and asked if he and Mary Beth would like to be their guests. Will, who hardly heard them, stammered that their plans were still up in the air. By the time he reached Mary Beth, Drew was gone.

His wife hooked her arm through his. "Clive and some friends from the building have a table at Romanos and they want us to join them after the party."

Clive, standing by her side, said, "We'll celebrate your return to New York."

Will could only think about what he had seen between Mary Beth and Drew. He mumbled something about being tired and wanting to stay in after the party.

Mary Beth spoke quickly. "Nonsense. Will, you sound like some cranky old salt from Maine." She pushed her hair back from her face. "We'll join you in a little while, Clive." She kissed him on both cheeks. "Be a darling and save us two seats."

17

Will sat slumped on Mary Beth's sofa. She was in the kitchen talking to the caterers. He heard the clattering of glasses, the sound of the service elevator, and finally the banging of the back door. She came into the living room and went to the mirror by the front door. She opened the drawer of the narrow console table below it and took out a lipstick. He caught her eye briefly in the glass as she leaned close to the mirror to apply color to her mouth. Once again he pictured the way Drew had lifted her hair and tucked it so easily behind her ear in that knowing way; the ease and familiarity of the gesture, somehow more intimate than a kiss, had pierced him.

"What are you staring at?" she asked.

"You never introduced me to Drew," he said flatly.

"What's that supposed to mean? Come on. We need to go. Clive's holding the table."

"Are you having an affair with him?" Will's question seemed to fill the room, the sound of his few words ricocheting off the walls and the black expanse of windows like an interminable echo. Then silence.

"Oh, Will," Mary Beth said. She didn't look at him, but reached into the same little drawer for her keys. She turned to face him. "Drew came late. He wasn't here long. You were talking to Clive on the other side of the room." She opened the closet and pulled out her coat. "We really have to go."

Will's chest felt tight. He didn't move. "You haven't answered my question."

She sighed and threw her coat onto a chair. "There's nothing to talk about. We're very good friends. I see him every day at the office. That's it."

Will crossed his arms across his chest. He stared at the floor. He thought that if he looked at her he would lose control. *Calm,* he thought. *I must stay calm.* "Something's going on," he said. "I'm not a fool. I saw how he touched you." The image flared again. He pictured Drew touching more than her hair—her throat, her back, her breasts. There had been those other times: Mary Beth going out to dinner with Drew and their office friends, Drew picking up the phone in her apartment, Drew giving her the nickname M.B. He had been a fool not to confront her before. Or had some part of him wanted it to happen, giving him an excuse to end their marriage?

"Okay, fine." She went to her handbag and pulled out her cell phone. "I'm calling Clive."

Will leaned forward and rested his elbows on his knees. He flexed his hands and waited. She spoke quietly. He paid no attention to whatever excuses she made.

She sat at the edge of the chair opposite him. "Okay. Maybe there's something. I don't know." She paused. "Some kind of connection. Drew and I get along well. We understand each other." She pushed the hair from her face.

"So you are," he snapped.

"Nothing has happened." Her voice softened. "You have to believe me. This entire summer was like being caught up in a whirlwind. The work, the travel. It was a real high."

He groaned and leaned back.

"Wait. Despite everything going on, I still kept missing you." She stood up and looked down at him. "I thought about the way you'd disappear for hours into your books, the way you walked around the house reading, the way you talked about your students, your diligence, our old life in Habliston." She began to pace in a measured way, as if to calmly recall all the good parts of their married lives. "I missed how we used to talk late into the night, the way you rubbed my feet, fixed me soup. You were good for me, Will. We balance each other." She sat again, seeming hopeful that her words had reached him.

Nothing felt in balance to Will now. He shook his head. The noise of the city filtered up from the many floors below. "This doesn't feel right."

"Oh, please," she said, sounding impatient, exasperated. "I don't want to talk about Drew. We need to talk about us. But it's going to take some effort on your part, too."

"Is that what I am? An effort?"

"You know what I mean. You've got to stop moping about Habliston and get on with it. Running off to Maine and pretending to start up some bucolic life in the middle of nowhere isn't going to hack it."

"It's not nowhere, and people there have full lives too."

"You know what I mean."

"I have tried," he said. "You had a good time in East Hope. You seemed to be happy there. I was happy. It was like when we were on our honeymoon." As he said these words, a terrible sadness caught in his throat. It was the past he was talking about.

"It's not working anymore, is it?" She started to cry.

Will stood. He almost went over to her to take her in his arms, to try to fix it. He rejected the impulse. He thought again of Drew. Was she telling the truth? Did it even matter?

"I guess we want different things," he said. His emotions waffled. At one time he had thought it would be liberating to say these words, to be free of it all, to admit the end of their life together. Instead he was sickened by sadness. He was on the edge of tears. He pressed his clenched fist to his mouth and tried to hold his feelings back.

Will got up from the sofa, feeling the old familiar pinch in his lower back. His childhood back problem flared up under stress.

"Will, I wanted this to work," she said.

"I want to believe you." He shook his head.

"I'm sorry," she said, her voice thick with tears.

The noise of the city, the steady rumble of cars, a distant siren, filled the room.

Will had not anticipated how difficult this conversation would be. "I loved you very much," he said. "You were everything to me." He forced himself to meet her eyes. "Your life will never be mine. I'm sorry." He said nothing more and went into the bedroom to pack his things. He had to get out of New York. He only hoped that the pain would lessen once he returned to East Hope.

❦

Caroline sat by the fire with Hollis in her living room in East Hope. They had just finished eating dinner. She had prepared a recipe for a beef stew with root vegetables, a recipe she planned to include in her proposal for the cookbook. Hollis had been delighted with the invitation to test the recipe, and she had been glad for the company. She was thankful to have the work to keep her mind off Rob. The book project was all she had now, that and waiting for the baby.

"That was a fine dinner," Hollis said.

"What did you think of the vegetables?" she asked.

"I would almost call them sweet," he said. "I'd put it in your book for sure." He extended his legs and drew his hands across his belly, a man content after a good meal. He wore a sweater under his sport jacket. Winter was upon them. Hollis looked older. His craggy face was drawn.

"Sounds like an endorsement to me," she said. She too was glad to sit by the fire. The dishes could wait. Still tired from her trip, she knew that fatigue was normal at this stage in her pregnancy. Her drive from Connecticut to Maine had been long and depressing. This time, crossing the bridge at Portsmouth, New Hampshire, had felt very different. The water below had looked black and cold. The ocean had been a gray blur on her right, not at all like the sunny day last June, when, crossing into Maine, she had felt lighthearted and hopeful.

"I want to show you something," she said to Hollis. She went to the mantel and picked up a letter that she had found caught in the back of a desk drawer earlier that afternoon. Finding the letter had made her feel sad all day, her heart heavy like the gray sky.

Hollis took the envelope, which had probably been cream-colored originally, but was now dingy with age. He removed the letter. It appeared to have been crumpled up at one time, such were the wrinkles and creases. He remained bent in concentration as he read.

"Doesn't surprise me," he finally said.

The letter had been to Francis requesting his resignation from the East Hope Yacht Club. Caroline had imagined Lila finding it. Or had Francis read it, crumpled it into a ball, and thrown it in the trash, only to have Lila discover it and save it by hiding it in her desk?

"It makes me so sad," Caroline said. "They wanted him out of the club because Lila was spending the summer in his house?"

"Life wasn't fair then. It's not now either." Hollis placed the letter back into the envelope and gazed into the flames. "Lila seemed to put it behind her. She was strong."

Hollis looked lost in thought. Maybe he was missing Millie. He too was going home to an empty house to spend the rest of the evening alone. He stirred. "I like hearing the old clock," he said. "It's as if Lila is with us in the house."

Caroline agreed. "Can I get you more coffee?" she asked.

"Time for me to hit the road," he said. "Will your son be coming up for Christmas?"

Caroline told him that Rob was coming, as well as her mother. She wouldn't allow herself to think of him not coming. She promised Hollis another tasting evening soon and showed him to the door.

She filled the sink with soap and hot water. In her first house in

Washington there had been no dishwasher either. Most nights after dinner she and Harry had lingered at the kitchen table and played a game of backgammon.

"What do you mean, you're doubling me?" she had shrieked, and given him an indignant shrug. Harry had a way of quietly maneuvering the board, luck often on his side.

"If you kiss me," he'd said with a laugh, "I'll let you off the hook."

"No sexual favors allowed." And she would flash him what she hoped was an alluring look. The stakes were high: The loser had to do the dishes.

As she lowered the dishes into the suds this evening, she was the loser again. The sound of Harry's laughter was but a faint echo in her mind.

She went to the phone to try Rob. No answer again. She had moved her computer to the kitchen, where it was less drafty than the living room. The Internet connection was slow tonight. She composed another e-mail message, telling him first about her work on the recipes, then her dinner with Hollis, whom she hoped he would meet soon, and finally ending with a plea to give her his vacation dates so she could arrange for a plane ticket for Christmas. She pressed send, imagining her words flying off to him through the void.

Before climbing the stairs to bed she stopped in the living room. From the front window her eyes traveled across the dark sweep of lawn in the moonless night to the bay beyond. A light shone from Taunton's. Hadn't Will gone to New York to be with his wife?

❧

The first December morning in East Hope dawned bright and clear. All the leaves had fallen from the trees, but the landscape didn't yet have the hard-edged look that came from the long months of frozen ground and the relentless beating of sharp winds. The chill air tingled in Will's nostrils when he went out to start the car, and the seat was stiff with cold against his back. He waited a moment for the engine to warm. Three large gulls screamed and dove in the sky, all brilliant white against the vivid blue. The days were growing shorter and this precious sunlight felt like a gift. It became dark now by four in the afternoon.

Will worked hard at staying busy, and now that he was the owner of Taunton's he continued to tackle the mind-numbing task of entering the stock (title, author, publisher, date, condition of book, and price) into the computer, a good way of keeping his mind from dwelling on the wreckage of his marriage. He tackled this job early in the day over his first cup of coffee, when it was still dark. He didn't like to take his run until it became light. With winter moving in, his days of running on clear roads were numbered.

Today he'd just finished entering two shelves of books into his database when Caroline called. She had asked him for a ride to the obstetrician's.

"Not an emergency, is it?" he'd asked.

"I'm sure I'm fine. I saw the doctor yesterday, but I had a little problem. It's probably nothing, but she wants to see me just in case. She didn't want me to drive on my own."

Will agreed to come right over. He thought about her going into labor. Certainly she would have sounded more alarmed if there were a chance of that.

Now, in his car, the heat slowly began to eke out the vents. Will slipped off his gloves and blew on his hands to warm them before placing them on the cold steering wheel. He put the car in gear and started along the edge of the bay through the village and out toward the point to Caroline's house. He thought about the night of her dinner party. This morning it had felt so good to hear her voice. He was glad she felt she could turn to him. Maybe those awkward moments at the end of that evening could be forgotten.

Will glanced at the water from the car window. The surface rippled in a steady chop. He liked this colder weather. There were fewer people in the village, and the town seemed to be stripped bare to its essence. The few fishing boats moored in the harbor now were the big trawlers that could weather the rougher winter seas. The pleasure boats and sailing craft used during the summer had been pulled out of the water. He had discovered a yard filled with them a few miles away, sitting clumsily on the land, all wrapped in tarps and tied securely, looking like bears hibernating for the winter.

When Will pulled into her driveway Caroline came out the back door promptly, ready to go. By the time he opened his door to help her she was already getting into the front seat. Her hair was pulled severely into a ponytail low on her neck, and though she was bundled into a voluminous wool coat, he could see that she was now a very pregnant woman. In spite of her serious expression, there was a loveliness about her, almost a gravitas, like a woman in her prime.

"Sorry to keep pulling the damsel-in-distress routine," she said, referring to the time she had needed to follow his car home in the fog.

Will restarted the engine and turned the car around to get back on the road. "I'm glad you called," he said.

"I didn't want to bother you. I tried Hollis," she explained, "but I think he went down to Portland to visit his daughter. Vern's truck is in the shop, and Dottie is babysitting for her grandchildren in Port Clyde."

Will looked over at her. Caroline's face was tense; a frown line that he hadn't seen before pinched the pale skin above her nose. The summer freckles that made her look younger had faded. He could feel that protective urge rising in him again. All she'd been through. Will remembered her telling him how her last baby had died, and that was why she'd decided to have this child. What if she were to lose this one? What if it were premature? Would the hospital in Ellsworth be able to manage? At least she had her son.

"How was your Thanksgiving?" he asked, feeling the need to make conversation. He had seen her lights. Maybe he should have called her before now.

Caroline's face was colorless, like the landscape. Even her red hair looked faded. They had reached the main highway and Will made the turn. No other cars in sight.

She finally broke the silence. "The worst of my life." She kept her gaze fixed straight ahead.

"You were with your mother?" he asked gently. "In Connecticut?"

"Yes. My sister and her husband were there too. They live nearby. Their children didn't come home this year. My nephew is in London for the year, and my niece stayed in California."

"What about your son?" He remembered how she had wept when she told him that she hadn't had the courage to tell her son about her pregnancy.

"He never came. I told him about the baby when I went to Washington to close on the house. It was worse than I expected." Her lower lip quivered. She let out a sigh, as if she had been holding her breath for a while. "I never thought he'd take it so hard. He was so angry, and he went back to school before I had enough time to explain."

"I'm sorry." Will accelerated, wanting to get her to the doctor's office as quickly as possible. The road climbed and across the open fields lay the ocean, stunningly beautiful, a vast expanse that sparkled a sapphire blue. "Boys are tough at that age." Will couldn't think what to tell her, what sort of anecdote from his own youth would compare to this.

"I keep going over and over it. I made all these excuses as to why I didn't tell him sooner. I suppose at the heart of it I didn't want him to think badly of me. I was so afraid of losing his love." At this her voice broke. "He hasn't talked to me since."

Will reached across the seat and touched her arm. "He'll come around. I'm sure he'll understand once he thinks about it."

Caroline wiped at her tears. She opened her handbag and took out a tissue, then turned to him. "I thought you had planned to stay in New York. I was glad to see your lights the other night."

She smiled, a forced smile, the determined smile of someone who didn't want to allow herself to fall apart.

"I left Mary Beth. Our marriage is over," he said.

"Oh, Will." Her face softened with concern. "I'm so sorry. I had no idea. . . ."

"It's okay. We're both better off now."

"Your wife was lovely. When I met her this fall you seemed so happy."

Will looked at her briefly, seeing one blue eye and the other, so green, still wet with tears. He returned his attention to the road. "I think we were both hopeful then," he said. "We wanted to make it work. Ten years is a long time. I mean, it's a long time to just give up on."

Caroline nodded. Will found himself wanting to tell her more. His sorrow had lessened, as if telling her about Mary Beth had helped to reduce a burden that he still carried. They came into Ellsworth and she directed him to the doctor's office.

They arrived at a rambling clapboard Victorian house that had been converted into medical offices. Several clumps of rhododendron bushes skirted the foundation, and the leaves, though green, were curled against the cold. Will helped Caroline out of the car and went with her into the waiting room on the first floor. The nurse, after checking her appointment book, directed Caroline back immediately. Will picked up a tattered magazine, ready to wait. Two very pregnant women sat opposite him, deep in conversation about the foods that were upsetting their stomachs.

Will tried to relax as he flipped a few pages of the magazine *Car Mechanics World,* something left behind by a father in waiting. Perhaps Rusty would have been happy with that. Rusty had called only last week, inviting Will for Christmas. Will had told him that he and Mary Beth were separated. He'd given Rusty a few lame excuses as to why he couldn't come. The thought of the glaring Florida sun, and his ever-successful brother, was more than he thought he could bear. It also pained him to think about the warmth and joy of Rusty's family life, something that still eluded him. Still, he liked spending time with his nephews, three wildly energetic boys, all under ten, and their mother, Jenna, a relaxed, easygoing woman who was a wonderful cook. Maybe declining the invitation had been a mistake.

The other patients eventually disappeared into examining rooms. Will sat in the waiting room by himself for what seemed a very long time. Just as he was about to get up and ask about Caroline he heard the door open.

"Not to worry." A heavyset nurse in blue pants and a flowered smock smiled down at him. "Your wife is going to be fine. Nothing to worry about. Take her out for a nice lunch. It will do you both good."

Will stood and started to explain, but the nurse had hurried back behind the door. He thought of Mary Beth, and how if he had stayed in New York, one day he might have been waiting for a child of his own. They would have shared the months of anticipation, purchased baby furniture, talked about names. They might have become a family, that whole new entity that turned you into someone altogether new. Some days it was hard to convince himself that he had done the right thing. This was a hard time of year to be alone.

❦

When they came to the causeway leading to East Hope, the water appeared to bounce in the sunlight and lapped up against the wet black rocks on both sides of the road. This time Caroline felt safe. The car was warm and she rested against the seat, knowing that her baby was fine. Dr. Carney had reassured her that the spotting that had terrified her at the beginning of the day was normal and had been brought on by the pelvic exam the day before.

Will spoke. "How about we stop for some chowder at Karen's Café?"

"Sure." Caroline smiled. "That's a great idea."

The trip home had passed quickly. He had told her about closing the bookstore for the winter, his tutoring at the library, his plans to find a job. Though he looked more cheerful telling her of these plans, he could probably use some company too—or was she trying to convince herself of this?

They took a table by the window. The small restaurant was warm, steamy from the heat of the stove.

Martha came to take their order. "I hear you're going to stick it out with us all winter," she said, speaking to Will. "Gets pretty quiet around here. Hope you won't find it dull." She flipped open her order pad. "What was that college where you used to teach?"

"Habliston, Pennsylvania," he said. "It's a small town too. Martha, do you know Caroline Waverly?"

"Sure do," Martha said. "Heard you did a nice job fixing up Lila's place."

"Thanks," Caroline said. "I'm staying for the winter too."

"You'll find that friends come in handy," Martha said, looking over her glasses in a knowing way. "What'll it be?"

Will and Caroline both ordered bowls of chowder.

"Why did you leave your job at the college?" Caroline asked after Martha left to put their order in.

Will hesitated at first and looked around at the tables near them as if afraid of being overheard. Seemingly satisfied that no one was near, he told her what had happened.

"How terrible for you," she said, trying to imagine the kind of student who would contrive such a story, a lie that cost Will his job. Caroline had no doubt that Will would never take advantage of a student. He was attractive, charming in a self-effacing way, and not the kind of guy you'd ever picture moving in on a young woman, she was certain.

"Mary Beth was convinced it was useless to argue," he said, "lawsuits costing a fortune and everything."

"You must have felt trapped," Caroline said.

"I was angry, and the thought of being stuck in New York with Mary Beth away all summer made me all the more determined to do something else. Like I told you, I saw the ad for Taunton's and here I am." He shrugged and smiled.

Martha arrived with the bowls of chowder. They both ate hungrily, and Caroline thought it amazing how a day that had started so badly had really improved.

❦

"Looks like you have a visitor," Will said, turning into her driveway. It was almost three. They had lingered at the café.

"I'm not expecting anyone." An unfamiliar car was parked next to her own.

Will pulled in behind it, and a man got out.

"I can't believe it," she said, feeling the warmth of the past few hours draining away.

Will turned off the ignition and looked over at Caroline. "You okay?"

"No. Yes. Yes, I'm fine," she said, almost under her breath.

Pete Spencer, wearing a formal topcoat with the collar turned up against the wind, lifted his hand and waved vigorously. "Thanks for driving me, Will." She fumbled for the door handle.

"Do you know this guy?" Will looked out at Pete. "Do you want me to stay?"

"Yes. I mean, I know him. And no. There's no need to stay." Caroline pushed open her door and glanced quickly back at Will. A shot of cold air flooded the car. "Please. I need to go."

Will's expression became wary, his eyebrows lifting in concern. "You're sure?"

Caroline nodded. Pete was approaching Will's car. She slammed the door behind her and hurried to meet him.

He bent down and kissed her cheek. How long had he been waiting, and why hadn't he called to say that he was coming? She heard Will slowly backing out of the driveway as she and Pete walked toward the house, then the sound of the Jeep growing fainter down the road. Pete stood close beside her as she unlocked the back door.

18

Pete seemed a complete stranger to her. To say that he was from away was an understatement. Caroline had nearly forgotten the velvety Southern accent that he had never lost. In his polished city clothes, an expensively cut sport coat and wool pants, he looked out of place seated in one of Lila's wicker chairs at the kitchen table. Caroline thought of Rob's wooden shape box that he had played with as a toddler; it had solid, colorful wooden pieces: a circle, a square, a rectangle, a star, each one slipping through the one correct hole in the lid. There was no hole in Lila's house that was meant for Pete.

"I wish you'd told me you were coming," Caroline said. She stirred a pot of bean soup that she was heating for his lunch. Knowing that he had waited for her all the while she and Will had been enjoying their chowder in the village made her feel guilty.

Pete laughed uncertainly. "And have you try to talk me out of coming?" He sipped from the glass of red wine that she had poured for him. He set the glass down and ran his hand across the old table, as if uncertain where he was.

"How did you find me?" Caroline asked. His presence made her wary; he might be capable of putting a crack in her fragile existence. As the baby's father, he must have some rights. Could he force her to go back to Washington? He was a powerful man.

"Your mother told me that you were in East Hope," he said. "The town isn't very big."

Caroline reached for a pottery bowl and sliced bread from a loaf on the counter. Her hands shook. For a while he watched her and said nothing. If it weren't for the ticking of the hall clock, the silence would have been complete. She had forgotten how handsome he was, how assured. Memories of her other life floated back—that comfortable existence, a time of ease when her life had been so calm, so worry-free, like a story that read, "Once upon a time there lived a woman whose life was quite perfect."

From the fridge she took a platter of cheese along with a bottle of sparkling water. She ladled the steaming soup into a bowl and set it down in front of him. His eyes followed her every gesture. His physical presence seemed to overtake the room. Her own movements felt slower, as if bogged down from the weight of the baby inside her, his baby too.

"Why are you here?" She tried to keep her voice strong and calm.

"You make a beautiful mother," he said.

She shook her head. "I don't want to hear that." Steam rose from the hot soup in front of him. "I thought we had an understanding," she said, sitting down across from him.

"You never did like small talk." He smiled and took a spoonful of soup. "This is great. You can always count on a foodie for a good meal—even at the last minute."

"Please," she said. "This isn't easy for me."

Pete set his spoon down on his plate. "For me either." He looked serious. Last summer's tan had faded, and his dark hair was graying slightly at the temples, noticeable in the unforgiving winter light. Yet there appeared to be something kind about his eyes. He didn't look as if his every comment would be laden with innuendo, some ulterior motive just beneath the surface. "I wanted to tell you a few things in person," he said.

"I see," she said, hoping he was not here with some greater bad news.

"After you left I thought about a lot of things." He stirred his soup distractedly. "I admire how you left your old life behind and started over."

Caroline looked away from him. "I made certain choices because I had to."

"But that's it. I started to think, Why not me?" He ripped off a hunk of bread and helped himself to a piece of cheese.

"Pete, really I . . ." Caroline couldn't think what to say. She was amazed that he was considering this, that he might follow her example. Pete leaving town? He was a fixture in Chevy Chase, with his big fancy house, his cool, unflappable wife. Suddenly she felt chilled. Did he want to come here?

"Red," he said, using her old nickname, "let me finish." He put the bread down, leaned his elbows on the table, and clasped his hands. "I've left Marjorie. You know I haven't had a relationship with her for years."

Caroline took a deep breath. "I never wanted to break apart your marriage."

"It was broken long before us."

"No," she said, losing patience, "there is no 'us.' I think you'd better leave." His declaration early in the summer that he had thought of her, even wanted to be involved with her, overwhelmed her again. He had offered to help her but, wisely or not, she had rejected the idea.

"Wait. You've got to hear me out." More color came to his face. "I remember when I first knew you and Harry, those early years in Washington. What I'll never forget is the way Harry looked at you. He was blinded by love. You used to look at him that way too. Marjorie and I never had that. Never." He stopped speaking and stared across the table at her. The creases around his eyes made him look weary.

"I'm so sorry," she said. Had she and Harry really been like that? How had she let herself forget?

"You've always been good to me, Red. Even if you'd let me share your life, it would never be like that. I know you. It's not there." He pushed back from the table and sighed. "You'd never look at me the way you used to look at Harry."

Caroline glanced away. "I'm sorry," she said again. It seemed now as if everybody's lives were falling apart.

Pete pulled back to the table, picked up his spoon, and concentrated on eating the bean soup. A few moments later he spoke again. "I went to California this fall. That's where I was when you came back to Washington for your house closing."

She nodded, remembering she'd been relieved not to have to see him then.

"An old friend from business school has taken over a small brokerage firm in San Francisco. I've been helping him, and he wants to have me come out as a partner."

Caroline tried to focus while Pete filled her in on his plans. "All the way across the country," she said, realizing that he would indeed be far away.

"It's a little risky, actually, but I'm loving it. I'm on the way there now."

"I see." She had never considered this possibility. Some part of her had counted on his being in Washington, ready to advise her. It was as if a bridge were being closed off. Here she had been worrying about his forcing her to come back home, while he had every intention of going farther away than ever. To her surprise, she felt a wave of regret.

Pete finished his soup and rested the spoon on his plate. "Last summer you asked me not to"—he paused—"intervene." He looked at her belly and put a hand out toward her, resting it tentatively on the table. "I'll respect your wishes. I promise. But I want you to know that I'll always be there for you. Whatever happens. I know you don't want me in your baby's life, not now anyway. But there may come a day . . ." His voice faltered. "There may be a time when he or she will want a father, will want to know who their father is." Caroline saw his expression dim.

"Yes," she said. "I've thought about that, but I didn't want to force us into some kind of family. It wouldn't be fair to any of us."

Pete nodded. Again, just the ticking of the clock. Caroline thought of Rob. She was forcing her son into a new family, a family he never chose to have, and because of this he refused to come home. This entire life that she was trying to construct now seemed like a terrible joke. A mother with her son and a baby, bonding together, was nothing but a romantic notion—worse, a sham. She reached now for Pete's hand.

A memory of her kitchen table in Chevy Chase—quick, like a snapshot—flashed before her: Harry seated next to her, Rob a little boy in a booster chair, platters of food before them. Suppertime, a winter evening, Harry's tie loosened, Rob's bib spattered with spills, the smell of roast chicken, the clanging of the hall radiator. Almost as quickly as she pictured that scene it vanished, spinning out of her vision as if in outer space, beyond the reach of gravity.

Pete gripped her hand firmly, then cleared his throat. His eyes met hers. "Caroline, I want you to promise that you'll stay in contact with me. I won't bother you or the child. Besides, I wasn't the greatest dad." He leaned toward her. The old wicker chair squeaked under his weight. "Always working, not there for my kids as much as I should have been."

"You mustn't say that," she said. "You always did your best." She reached out and placed her other hand on top of his, wanting somehow to comfort him.

They sat quietly for a few minutes. The enormity of what was ahead seemed to impose a shared weight upon them. Pete squeezed her hands briefly, got up, and fetched the briefcase that he had brought in earlier from the car. "Here's where I'll be." He placed a sheet of paper with an address and a series of phone numbers on the table in front of her. "You'll let me know about the birth?"

"I will." She stood and turned to face him, still overwhelmed and not knowing what to say. She now understood the expression *change of heart*. "I want to thank you for this." Her voice faltered. "For everything, for understanding."

He smiled at her. "You know I care about you."

Caroline believed him. She met his gaze and swallowed back tears. "I just wish Rob could understand."

"Does he know everything?"

"He does now. I don't think he'll ever forgive me." She drew her hands to her belly.

"I'll call him. I owe him that." He stood straighter.

"You will?"

"Of course. We need to give him time. He'll come to understand."

Pete placed his hands on her shoulders. "I have a flight out of Bangor early this evening, so I'll be on my way." He held her shoulders intently, as if trying to reassure her, as if to support her and keep her in one piece. "Whenever you want me, please call. Promise?"

Caroline couldn't speak. She nodded, not wanting him to leave. They shared a history.

He touched her cheek and looked at her as if he didn't want to forget this moment.

"Wait," she said. She reached for his right hand and placed it on her belly, large and taut. "It's moving." He said nothing for a moment. His hand was warm and firm. She felt his face close to hers and then his lips in her hair.

"My God," he whispered. "It's always a miracle." He withdrew his hand, but lingered close to her, as if needing time to gather himself. Then he stepped away, took his coat and briefcase, and went out the back door. The sun had gone under a bank of clouds. The child kicked again and then stopped.

"So, what do you think?" Crystal watched Will's face. She twirled a strand of her pale hair between her fingers. Some days she looked like a child, gawky and uncertain, still a girl, and on others Will caught glimpses of the young woman she would become, confident and ready to tackle the world, the bigger world beyond East Hope.

"You nailed it," Will said, tapping the pages on the table in front of him. "You've really got it right." She had brought him the final draft of her essay. It was good, really good.

"Right enough to get the money?"

"If it were me, you'd get the award today," Will said. "I don't know how these things work, but it's a fine essay regardless of what it's for. The writing is wonderful. So clear. Crystal clear," he joked.

"You're bad, Mr. Harmon." She shook her head and gave him the slightly crooked smile that she had shown him more and more often that fall.

They talked awhile longer. Crystal's English teacher had asked Will to help Crystal with some creative writing that was not included in the regular curriculum. He asked her how the short story she was working on was coming. She told him she would spend more time on it now that her essay was done. It was after five, and Will knew that Edna would be waiting to close the library. They put on their coats and headed to the front of the building. Edna was deep in conversation with Janet Wiseman, the guidance counselor, who was standing next to her at the front desk. Will wondered briefly if Janet would assign him more students. Until he found a teaching job, he would have plenty of time for tutoring. Will and Crystal passed the desk and headed to the front door. He zipped his jacket and tightened his grip on his briefcase.

"My dad's here," she said, looking through the glass pane.

A brown pickup truck idled in front of the building. Crystal turned back to Will. "I'll bring you my story next week," she said, her eyes bright with excitement. The successful essay seemed to spur her on; she was ready to tackle further challenges.

"Great," Will said. He reached to push open the door for her as she stopped and turned back.

"Mr. Harmon, thanks for all the help on the essay." She smiled up at him, her gaze earnest and steady. "I never could have done it without you." She put one arm around him and leaned into him, offering a fast hug.

"You're welcome." He stepped away from her and awkwardly reached again for the door. As he pushed it open he heard Janet Wiseman's voice behind them.

"Could I see you a moment, Crystal?"

She turned to go back and Will stepped outside. He waved to Crystal's father and walked to his car. Crystal's burst of affection had surprised him. A moment later he worried briefly that Edna or the guidance counselor might have seen and gotten the wrong idea.

There was no wind that evening, but the air was seriously cold. He was glad he'd ordered a cord of wood from a friend of Vern's. He'd started using the wood stove to help heat his apartment above the store. How had old Mr. Taunton managed in the drafty old building? When the wind came up the windows rattled, as if the building might not be able to withstand another winter. Will started his car and headed toward the village.

The streets were quiet. He stopped for gas at the Quik Mart and bought a six-pack of beer. Karen's Café was open, but rather than stay there and eat early, he picked up a quart of chowder to heat up later. He felt the need to get home.

Driving through the darkness, he couldn't shake the image of the man waiting for Caroline in her driveway a few days before. The guy had been good-looking in a rich, smooth way in that fancy coat. City clothes, Will thought, reminding him of Drew and Mary Beth. The man was certainly nobody local. His kissing Caroline with such authority had irritated him. When he had pulled out of her driveway Will had looked in his rearview mirror and seen the guy put his arm around her as they walked into the house. Observing that familiarity with her had bothered him.

Will thought with some certainty that the dark-haired man must be the father of Caroline's baby. Yet what was it to him? He had no claim on Caroline. She shared a past with someone else.

Will arrived home and unlocked the front door of Taunton's. The familiar smell of books greeted him, but instead of lingering in the shop to do a little work, he decided to go up to the apartment. He turned on the lights. The sky was now fully dark. It was going to be a starless night. The young woman working behind the counter in the café had been talking about snow. She told him they usually got one good blizzard before Christmas. It might be soon.

He set the container of soup on the kitchen counter. The red light of his answering machine blinked. He pressed the play button. Crystal's voice, choked with tears, made him stop short. "You can't tutor me anymore," she said. "Ms. Wiseman's really angry too." Then a pause. "My dad says don't call here." The automated voice clicked on: "There are no more messages. All messages have been played back." Will collapsed into his reading chair and lowered his head into his hands.

❦

Caroline thought of Pete's visit again a few days later. How odd that a man who had stirred up her life in such a dramatic way—one night of unexpected lovemaking, with the unintended consequences—was really gone from her life. A kind of calm fell over her in knowing for certain that there was no going back, but it was unsettling too. Such a strange turn of events. She pulled herself up against the pillows and looked out the window. It was still dark.

It didn't get light until almost eight thirty in the morning. In the north and so far east, the Maine days were extremely short. She had had a bad night, sleeping fitfully when she slept at all. Leg cramps had awakened her throughout the night. Lila's bed, always such a pleasure at the end of each day, now seemed hard and lumpy to her, and it was becoming more and more difficult to find a comfortable position for sleep.

Caroline dressed and went down to the kitchen. She turned on the radio to get the weather. The sky was a leaden gray, the air damp. People in the village had been talking about snow. She had purchased a bag of some snow-melting material at the hardware store and stocked up on groceries the day before. Still, Lila's house was cozy. Vern had put up the storm windows while she had been away at Thanksgiving. Caroline felt snug and safe from the weather. Vern's nephew, Tim, was going to plow for her, and Vern said that for a little extra he would also be willing to shovel a path from the house to the garage. Dottie called every few days to check on her.

She had finished her book proposal, but found that the outline itself was proving more difficult. Even though she didn't need to flesh it out in great detail, she had to have a good idea of what each chapter would cover. Her goal was to submit it to the agent Vivien had recommended by the end of January so she could put her mind on the baby's arrival in February.

Besides working on the book, she had turned her attention to cleaning the house and getting ready for the baby. She'd stopped at a children's store in Ellsworth after a doctor's appointment and purchased most of the essentials for a newborn. She'd washed the clothes and placed them in a drawer in her bedroom. The bassinet she'd found in a used-furniture store was in need of a coat of paint. After scrubbing it down outside, she'd set it on newspapers to dry in the living room. That chore still awaited her.

The dining room table was piled high with cookbooks, some from Lila's collection, some that Caroline had brought with her from Washington, and a selection that Will had given her from his shopping trips. The little book of teatime treats, his thoughtful gift to her the night of her dinner party, topped one pile. She hadn't spoken to Will since the trip to the doctor's office, the day Pete arrived unannounced at her door.

She needed to call Will. Indeed, she *wanted* to call him—but each time she picked up the phone, once even after starting to dial, she would stop. It was true he was getting a divorce, but he was younger, had no children. What on earth would he want with her in his life? A pregnant woman with an alienated nineteen-year-old son? And yet her mind kept going back to their lovely afternoon last summer, when his very presence made her forget her worries. Sometimes just glancing across the bay at the yellow clapboard building where he lived made her feel better. He, like her, had chosen East Hope over another life. They shared that common bond. But that was all. She was ridiculous to expect anything more.

Caroline chastised herself. She had no business thinking about Will like some kind of lovesick schoolgirl. Her work now was to produce a healthy baby, sell this house in this faraway, forgotten piece of the world, and win Rob back so that they could resume their old life. Was that even possible? Right now she needed to get all the books in order and back on the shelves. She set aside the little book from Will and carried a pile of books below it over to the shelves in the living room. As she pushed aside a few volumes to make space, a book fell out onto the floor: *Travels and Tastes of India* by Laura Alcott. Caroline decided to take a break and took it to the kitchen to read while she had a cup of tea. Lila had traveled a great deal when she was a teacher in Cambridge. Maybe she had hoped to go to India one day.

After filling the kettle for water and setting it on the stove to boil, Caroline turned the musty-smelling pages. It was mostly a travel log, with a few recipes interspersed among the essays. She flipped a few more pages and a letter slid out of the book and into her lap. She drew in her breath, shocked to see Harry's writing, the small neat script that she knew so well, a letter to his aunt Lila. Suddenly it felt as if he had just walked into the room. For a few moments she held the envelope in her fingers, caught in a trance. Seeing Harry's writing here in Maine made it seem that this past year had never happened.

She remembered finding the letter to Francis asking him to resign from the yacht club. Now this one, another ghost from the past. With shaking hands, she opened the flap and took out the pages of heavy cream paper. The letter was dated April nineteenth, fifteen years ago, the spring that Grace had died. She read. At first it appeared to be a thank-you note, a response to Lila's condolence letter. In the second paragraph Harry asked Lila if Caroline and Rob could come for a visit to Maine that summer. He told Lila that he would not be able to join them, but that Caroline was suffering greatly and needed a change.

> *This has been tough on all of us. I'm trying to hide my feelings from Caroline. I've got to be strong for her, but sometimes I feel I'm going to burst from the pain.*
>
> *I'll never forget my great summers in East Hope. You once told me that East Hope was a special place, that it made everyone feel better. Maybe if she could come to you she'd feel better too.*
>
> *Love,*
> *Harry*

Caroline sat totally still, staring at Harry's words. The teakettle whistled sharply, startling her. She staggered to her feet, lifted the kettle off the burner, and slammed it aside. "Blinded by love," Pete had said. What a fool she was. She was blinded by stupidity not to have seen it. The years after Grace died she had been so self-absorbed, so caught up in her own sorrow that she had ignored Harry's suffering. Later Rob had always been her priority.

She took the letter to the kitchen table, and, smoothing it, she ran her fingers over his words. If only they could have shared their pain. If she had encouraged Harry to open up to her more, would their lives following Grace's death have been different? Her entire body began to tremble. She couldn't stop shaking, and a sharp pain pinched into her lower back. *Oh, God, please not now.* It was too soon for the baby. She moaned in despair.

Was this why Harry had thrown himself into his work, distancing himself from her, afraid that her suffering would make his own all the worse? Caroline had so many questions now. Now, when it was too late. The fragile years when they had tiptoed around each other, each of them hiding their pain, trying to go on, if not for each other, then for Rob.

And Rob? All those years of putting her energy into being a mother, more a mother than a wife—but for all that, she had failed Rob too.

Caroline leaned forward, pressing her hands to her temples. So unselfish, Harry had thought only of her. He had wanted her to have that summer in Maine, hoping that it would be a place where she could heal. In the strange way of the world, Harry was giving all this to her again, as Lila had left her house to him and, through him, to her.

Caroline folded the letter, and, moving slowly, she carried it to the small table in the hall next to Lila's clock and tucked it under the Chinese porcelain bowl that held the key to the clock. Then she walked to the front of the house and looked out across the bay. The bleak winter view of the water offered no comfort.

❦

Will sat outside the guidance office at Benjamin Franklin High School, the central school for the surrounding villages and towns. Crystal's message had come on Wednesday night, but he had been unable to reach Ms. Wiseman until school opened first thing on Thursday morning. She had told him that he'd best come in to the school to talk about what had happened. Friday morning was the earliest she could see him.

Thursday had been torture for him. Obviously the guidance counselor thought that Crystal's hug was out of line. More than anything he needed to protect Crystal. He was determined to straighten out what was clearly a misunderstanding.

This morning the students were at a weekly assembly, and the hallway, lined with gray metal lockers, was silent. Will shifted his position on the hard wooden bench and wished he'd brought a book to read, not that he'd be able to concentrate. He stared out the high windows above the lockers. The sky was pewter gray. Snow was predicted for later that afternoon.

Finally he heard the burst of applause and, a moment later, the roar of students being released into the halls. A crowd of denim legs, sweatshirts, and beat-up book bags scattered in all directions.

"Mr. Harmon?"

"Yes." Will stood.

"I'm Gordon Perry, principal of Benjamin Franklin." The principal didn't offer his hand. He was a slight man with an erect posture that made him seem taller than he probably was. His graying hair was slicked neatly in place. "Ms. Wiseman should be joining us shortly. We're meeting in my office."

Will, feeling like a truant, followed Perry around a corner, down another hall, and into his office. Why was the principal being brought into this? They took their respective seats, Perry behind the large oak desk, a relic of the 1950s, and Will on the other side.

"We seem to have a bit of a problem," the principal said.

Uneasy with that inclusive beginning, Will didn't want anything to do with the sallow pinched-looking man seated across from him. "I think more is being made of this than is necessary," he said. "I called Ms. Wiseman so that I could come in and explain."

Two flags flanked the principal's desk, the U.S. flag behind him on the right, and the state of Maine's on the left. There were no books in sight. A map of Maine hung on the wall to Will's right, and this caught his attention briefly. Out of habit he sought out the location of East Hope on the ragged coastline.

Perry picked up a perfectly sharpened pencil from the leather cup on his blotter and furrowed his brow as he looked down at his notes. Will waited. A door opened behind him and Janet Wiseman came in.

"Let's begin, shall we?" Mr. Perry put down his pencil and folded his hands on top of the papers in front of him.

"Sorry to keep you waiting," Ms. Wiseman said, and pulled up a chair.

"I understand that you've been tutoring Crystal Thomas," Mr. Perry said.

"Yes," Will said. "I've been working with her twice a week. Since September."

"With English?" Mr. Perry's level gray eyes bored into Will.

"Yes," he said. "I've been helping her with her essay for the state scholarship. She's done a fine job. I hope she gets the award."

"Crystal seems to have grown very fond of you."

"Look, Mr. Perry, I called the school asking to see Ms. Wiseman and—"

"Ms. Wiseman told me that she saw Miss Thomas hugging you on Wednesday in the East Hope Library," Mr. Perry said, tapping the papers with his pen.

"It was nothing," Will said. "Crystal didn't mean anything. She was excited about finishing her essay. She thanked me and in her enthusiasm—"

"It is our job—our responsibility—to protect our students," Ms. Wiseman said.

"I understand that," Will said. "Crystal didn't mean to do anything wrong. I certainly would never encourage anything of the kind."

"Edna said that you gave her rides home from the library."

"Only once—when the weather was bad and her dad couldn't pick her up." The memory of having to defend himself from Jennifer Whitely's accusation rushed to his mind. He should have known better than to put himself in this position. "Mr. Perry, I want to straighten this out right now." Will felt a pulsing in his temples. He was not going to let his past ruin everything for him here in East Hope.

"Mr. Harmon." Janet Wiseman spoke firmly. "I've made some inquiries. I called Habliston College and was told that you left employment there because of problems with a student. The woman I spoke to thought it had been a case of sexual harassment."

"Who told you that?"

"I'm not sure. I never got her name. The receptionist, I guess." Ms. Wiseman averted her gaze.

"You should have spoken to someone in authority. In the first place, I have nothing to hide. Yes, I used to teach at Habliston College and yes, a student there—"

"Mr. Harmon, we are speaking about sexual harassment, inappropriate behavior with a student." The word *sexual* seemed to slither out of Mr. Perry's mouth, and under his stern gaze, Will thought he detected in Perry a glimmer of satisfaction, that the principal was pleased to have this explosive information and the power to use it against him.

"I was accused of sexual harassment by a student, but no charges were ever brought. And that, Mr. Perry"—Will could hear the anger in his own voice and he didn't care—"is all that happened. I decided to leave Habliston for other personal reasons. The student was the daughter of a trustee of the college. She was lying. My only mistake was in not staying to clear my name."

"Mr. Harmon, it's not up to me to decide whether what happened at Habliston was true or not," Mr. Perry said.

"You should have been forthcoming earlier," Ms. Wiseman said, her tone more placating. "You've done a good job working with Crystal. I read her essay. It's excellent."

"I don't want Crystal to get into any kind of trouble," Will said. He thought again of her tear-choked message.

"Perhaps I got the wrong impression," Ms. Wiseman said. "I'll talk to Crystal and her family. You have to understand that our primary concern is for our students, and we have to be extremely cautious."

Mr. Perry spoke again. "All the same, in view of what's happened you will no longer be welcome to participate in our tutoring program. We don't want to take that risk."

"Sitting in a public library across the table from a student is a risk?" Will asked, barely containing his fury. He looked to Ms. Wiseman, who appeared to have come around to his side. "That's ridiculous. I'm a teacher, Mr. Perry. That's what I'm good at, and that is all I'm interested in doing."

Will stood and placed his hands on the edge of the desk. He looked down at the principal and then at Ms. Wiseman. "I probably should have told you about Habliston earlier," he said. "I'm sorry about that. I didn't think it would ever matter. I'm going to call the dean of the college. I hope when you hear from him you will reconsider."

"You do what you want to do," Mr. Perry said. "I'm responsible for these students, and I don't want you in this program."

"Maybe," Janet Wiseman said, "once we hear from the college—"

"The matter is closed," Mr. Perry said. "Don't attempt to contact the Thomas family either."

Will put on his coat and stormed out of the office. When he reached the parking lot, a few flecks of snow were already starting to fall.

19

The morning after Caroline discovered Harry's letter, all of East Hope was buried in a white world. It had snowed steadily since the previous afternoon, and the wind continued to blow hard. Drifts were growing deep against the side of the house. The house felt cool to her, and she realized that the furnace had not clicked on since she had come downstairs that morning. She called Vern and he promised to get over to take a look within the next few hours.

Her body felt like one large, dull ache, as if Harry's words had soaked into her very muscles. Regret permeated her every thought. Harry had always loved her. She had been the one who had forgotten how she had loved him. She had closed herself off from Harry, allowing an invisible barrier to remain between them. She cried most of the night. When she awoke, nothing had changed. The house was cold.

Her mother was driving up next week to arrive in East Hope before Christmas. By then the roads would be cleared. At least this storm had come at a convenient time. Caroline began her grocery list for Christmas, first making a list of the staples she would need for baking. Her mother loved her recipe for rum cake, and Rob would want shortbread with orange zest, his favorite. That is, if he came. She thought of the unanswered e-mails. At this point she could not expect him to come; all she could do was hope.

Caroline went to the cupboard to see if she needed vanilla and stopped at the window to look out at the snow. They rarely had big snowstorms in Chevy Chase. She pressed her face to the glass, feeling the pinch of cold against her forehead. One winter day when Rob was only six, maybe seven, over a foot of snow had covered the city, surprising everyone.

Harry had brought his childhood sled down from the attic. He'd carefully sanded and oiled the rust-tinged runners, and the three of them, attired in layers of sweaters and jackets, had walked to a neighborhood golf course, where a huge hill behind the clubhouse was quickly filling with children.

During the course of the morning, parents gathered outside to watch the children knife through the deep snow, creating faster and faster descents to the bottom. Caroline could still remember the riotous colors of winter hats and mittens, rosy-cheeked children, along with shouts, laughter, and runny noses. Harry had shown Rob how to position himself on the sled, advising him to keep his head down, and how to use his hands to steer, and then gave his son the running push that launched him down the hill. Rob had loved having Harry beside him, beseeching his dad on every descent to push the sled off faster and faster.

They had been a family then, possessing that precious invisible bond. Had they come home after sledding for hot chocolate or soup for lunch? Rob loved split pea, unusual for a child. The discovery of Harry's letter forced her to look back. Grace had died several years before, yet that morning surely they had been happy.

Caroline moved away from the window and put the kettle on for a cup of tea. When the water boiled she poured it, then wrapped her hands around the steaming mug and went to the living room to sit in the patch of sun in the increasingly chilly house. She covered herself with a soft woolen throw that she carried from room to room over the course of the morning. Her baby, now so large, and moving less, pushed gently into her ribs. She felt her worries fade. That small gesture from the mysterious creature within her was the one thing she could look forward to now.

It was almost noon when the telephone rang, breaking into

Caroline's thoughts and the cold silence of the house. She hurried to the kitchen to pick it up.

"Mom's not coming." Darcy's voice came as a surprise. Caroline had thought it might be Vern calling about the furnace.

"What do you mean?" She clutched the phone and sat at the table.

"She fell on the ice walking to her car."

"Is she all right?"

"Her hip is broken," Darcy said, her tone matter-of-fact. "At her age it's serious. We're at the hospital now."

Caroline listened to Darcy's account of her mother's fall. How could this have happened? Peg, her darkly tanned legs nimble on the tennis courts summer after summer, had become fragile and old.

"I'll come home then," Caroline said. "Mom's going to need help. And it's Christmas."

"You shouldn't travel now. Your being here would only worry Mom more."

"But I won't have any family here."

"Rob's coming to you, isn't he?"

"I don't know. He still won't talk to me." Caroline hated saying this out loud, as if by her uttering her deepest fears, they would all come true.

"He'll come around," Darcy said.

Caroline heard the doubt in her sister's voice. More than anything she wanted to have Rob with her in Maine. Somehow, she thought, if he could just be with her in East Hope, away from everything, they could find a way to start over. She was growing more and more frustrated and impatient with him. She had sent him information on flights along with the train and bus schedules from Philadelphia to Portland, but he still hadn't called or told her his plans. Her initial sadness when he didn't show up at Thanksgiving was giving way to anger. It was time for him to stop being upset.

Caroline promised to call her mother once she was home from the hospital. She hung up the phone and went to look at the thermostat. It registered sixty-one degrees. Where was Vern? Had he forgotten about her too? She pulled her cardigan across her belly. And now her mother wasn't coming. God—this baby. What the hell was she doing? Having this baby was making everything impossible. She had been such a fool.

❦

The snow had stopped completely when Vern banged on the back door a few hours later. Caroline greeted him with relief. She had been dreading the possibility of having to go through the night without heat.

"First I'll have a look at the boiler down in the cellar," he said. He stomped the snow off his boots, his face red with cold, and headed to the basement. Caroline heard him tapping on pipes and after a few moments he reappeared.

"Can't see anything wrong yet. Let me take a look at the thermostat." Caroline followed him into the hall. The clock bonged two o'clock, and despite a weak wash of sun now coming through the windows, the house felt as cold as the inside of the refrigerator.

"Ayuh. Here's your problem."

"The thermostat?"

"Gummed up, looks like." Vern had removed the casing from the wall, and he blew heartily into the workings before pushing a small lever. Caroline heard the boom of the boiler in the basement below them. "This'll do for now, but I'm going to get you another one."

"Vern, you're an angel."

"Don't know if Dottie would agree with that." He grinned at her. "How 'bout I stop by in the morning?"

"Wonderful," Caroline said. The radiators were sputtering back to life.

"Speaking of Dottie," Vern said as he put the casing back on the old thermostat, "she asked me to invite you and your family to the house for Christmas dinner."

Caroline explained that her mother wouldn't be coming because of her hip, and Vern quickly said that she and Rob would be more than welcome. "Dottie won't take no for an answer." Caroline, grateful for his kindness, thanked him and saw him to the back door.

As the house warmed she felt her mood improve. She could manage without her mother. She would give Rob a good Christmas. Of course he would come. They needed time together, that was all. Last summer Melanie had made it hard for Caroline to connect with her son. Here in East Hope they would have hours by the fire to talk. They could rent videos and watch some of the old movies they used to enjoy.

She decided to spend the afternoon baking shortbread cookies. Her body warmed from the work of incorporating the butter and sugar, and by the time she had mixed in the flour the kitchen had heated up too. She rolled the dough out on a big wooden board and reached for an old-fashioned cutter in the shape of a heart. The first few stuck to the board and broke when she lifted them to the cookie sheet. Broken hearts, she thought. She pulled the dough back together, kneaded it once more, and rolled again. This time she cut the shapes and lifted them without difficulty.

Rob would like Vern and Dottie, and she wanted to introduce her son to Hollis and Will. She would invite them all for another dinner, maybe a Sunday lunch after Christmas. She wanted Rob to meet her friends and to see that she had a life in Maine. Indeed, her small world here was sustaining her.

She put a second tray of shortbread in the oven. After setting the timer she walked through the dining room and into the hall. The sun shone on the snow. The world outside dazzled in its whiteness. The bay was a deep blue. The pleasure of thinking of Will and inviting him again for a meal brought back the memory of his kiss. What would have happened if she hadn't pushed him away? Many weeks later, that evening by the fire seemed more like something imagined, a dream she tried to summon forth upon waking. It was easier to remember their more recent meeting, when Will had taken her to see Dr. Carney, her worry on the trip to Ellsworth, and the ride home, when being with Will had made her feel safe, less alone.

Why not call him? Maybe he would be in East Hope for Christmas too. After five rings his answering machine picked up.

"Hello," she said, trying to sound assured. "I'm going to make the German Jam Bars recipe from the book of teatime treats. Maybe you'd like to come for a tasting? It's Caroline," she added, feeling silly. "Give a call when you have a moment."

After hanging up she went back to her baking. She would send some of the jam bars to her mother too, along with the rum pound cake.

The rest of the afternoon passed quickly, with smells of butter and sugar baking and filling the kitchen. The book she'd been reading about pregnancy spoke of the final burst of energy, the nesting instinct that often clicked in toward the end of a pregnancy. Tired, but pleased with her accomplishment, Caroline crawled into bed before nine. The night was still and the sky filled with stars; the moon, half-full, was bright. She was just dozing off when the phone on the bedside table startled her awake.

"Caroline. Richard here."

Harry's father. He had been so kind when she called to tell him about having the baby. After Rob had reacted so terribly to the news, Caroline knew that she had to tell her father-in-law everything. The conversation had not been easy. He had been quiet at first, but then understanding. He remembered when she had lost Grace, and he had told her that at his age you learned not to judge.

"Richard, it's good to hear your voice," she said, fighting off a sense of worry. She fumbled to light the lamp, but couldn't find the switch.

"I'm not sure you're going to like what I have to say."

"Is something wrong?" She pushed up onto her elbow.

"Just had a call from Rob."

"Is he okay?" She felt a surge of adrenaline and was now fully alert.

"Hasn't he been in touch?" Richard asked.

"No. He hasn't. He's been pretty upset with me."

"I gathered that." She heard him clearing his throat. "He asked to come here for Christmas."

Caroline didn't move. At first she couldn't speak. Another phone call with more bad news. "But I need him with me. I need him to come home."

"He said Maine wasn't home and that it would upset him to see you."

What could she say to that?

"I know this is tough," Richard said. "I'll try to make him understand. I can always put him on a plane from here. He's in the middle of exams right now and not thinking clearly."

"I wish everything could be the way it used to be."

"I know," he said, as if trying to soothe her.

"I've done so many things wrong." At this point she could no longer speak. She fell back onto her pillows.

"What matters, Caroline, is that you're trying to make things right."

She shook her head. Rob was all she had of Harry, all that was left of their life together. Alone in the dark house, far away in Maine, she felt her future seemed impossible.

Richard asked again when the baby was due. She told him early in February, and a few minutes later he said good night, promising to stay in touch.

Moonlight flooded the bedroom. Her heart felt tight in her chest. She struggled to sit and, placing her feet on the floor, she cradled her hands under her enormous belly and walked to the window at the front of the house. The lawn sloped in a silvery blanket down toward the bay, cold in the moonlight. Caroline searched for Will's lights across the water. It was still early, not even ten, but his place was dark. She remembered her foolish message. He probably had plans to go away for the holidays. Maybe, she thought, he had gone back to his wife.

Caroline shivered. That night she felt the weight of winter. The floor was icy on her bare feet. She lumbered slowly back to bed and pulled the sheet, now cold, and blankets up to her chin. Hot tears streaked her face. The baby's feet moved, pressing into her ribs as if to remind her that she was not alone. Instead, that small jolt made her loneliness all the more acute. How she longed to be held, to be comforted, to have arms around her as she sought the temporary solace of sleep.

❧

"Will, why don't you move down here?" Rusty asked. Two years older, Will's brother was a shorter, more solidly built version of himself. They sat together in the lanai, the screened-in room at the back of Rusty's house in West Palm Beach.

Will shook his head. He had just told Rusty that he and Mary Beth were getting a divorce and he planned to stay in Maine and run Taunton's.

"Let's have a nightcap." Rusty stood. "Come on, it's Christmas Eve."

"Sure, why not?" Will stretched his legs. The novel sensation of moist tropical air made him feel good. This was the perfect place to unwind and relax. Rusty's wife, Jenna, was upstairs reading to their three boys. She had insisted that Will and Rusty should have some time together after dinner. The day had been filled with errands, a few hours at a public park tossing around a baseball, a noisy spaghetti dinner, the boys' favorite meal.

"I mean, seriously, how can you make any money selling old books?"

"You can't," Will said. He laughed. "Well, maybe a little. I've sort of gotten hooked on it, though."

Rusty handed Will a snifter of cognac and, after pouring one for himself, sat again, swirling the contents of his glass. Will leaned back and cradled the back of his head with his hands. Though Will hadn't been there for long, he could already see how his brother had made a good life for himself: big house, fancy cars, but most important, he had a great family.

"Okay, okay. So you like this business," Rusty said. "Run it in the summer and come on down here for the rest of the year. The boys would love to have Uncle Will at their beck and call."

"Thanks." Will took a swallow of his drink. "I need to earn a living, and I'm looking for a teaching job near me up there."

"Tons of colleges around here. It might be easier to find a job here."

"You're probably right. Crazy as it seems, I want to be there. I'm going to make it work. There's something about the place itself that draws me. It's partly the water, the land. I'm not going to give up."

Will told Rusty about Crystal, tutoring, and his mistake in not telling the school about Habliston. "Jack Mathews is going to write to the school. I think I've got the guidance counselor on my side, but the principal is a little dictator. This time I'm going to stick up for myself, like I should have in Habliston."

"Do you wish now that you'd stayed in Pennsylvania?"

"I should have stayed to clear my name, or at least tried. Maybe it all happened for a reason. I don't miss the place now. I guess there was more wrong there with Mary Beth than I let myself believe." Will looked out into the night. The moon shone down across the lawn, the same moon that shone tonight over the bay in East Hope. Will rubbed his forearms, which were bare to the night air. So strange not to feel cold.

After a pause Will spoke again. "There's also a woman." It was easy saying these things in the dark.

"In Maine?" Rusty asked.

"Yeah."

"Is it serious?"

"I can't really answer that yet."

"Here's to your future," Rusty said, lifting his glass.

"To the future," Will said. He sipped his drink. The cognac slipped smoothly down his throat. Will closed his eyes and thought of Caroline. Maybe one day there would be more of a story to tell his brother.

Christmas dinner at Vern and Dottie's helped fill what would have otherwise been a long and lonely day for Caroline. The small cape was filled with family of all ages, but as soon as she had stepped inside, she realized that this lively family celebration was uniquely theirs, and try as they might to include her, she would never be a part of their world.

A large fir tree with blinking colored lights filled the bay window in the living room. Two of the grandchildren were busy with a game on the computer, and Vern's son and brother were caught up watching a Boston Bruins hockey game on the TV in the den.

Vern seemed pleased with the wool vest that Caroline had brought him, and Dottie was visibly touched by the quilted tote bag that Caroline had bought that fall at a craft fair in Belfast. Dottie said it would be perfect for her knitting, and she presented Caroline with a hand-knit yellow baby blanket bordered with ducks. She was delighted by this lovely gift, which must have taken Dottie many long evenings to complete.

When the flurry of gift giving subsided, Dottie and her daughter-in-law went off to put the finishing touches on dinner, and Marsha, Vern's nephew's wife, pulled Caroline aside to talk about babies. To Caroline, Marsha, skinny in tight blue jeans and a pink mohair sweater, didn't look much older than Rob, yet she was the mother of a three-month-old baby, Victoria, who slept blissfully in her bassinet next to the sofa.

"She's beautiful," Caroline said.

"An easy baby too," Marsha said, "or so I've been told. She's our first."

Indeed, little Victoria slept through the noise from the television, Dottie calling out for Vern to come and carve the turkey, and the thumping sound coming from the computer game on a table in the corner, along with periodic outbursts from the two grandchildren as to whose turn it was. Caroline wondered briefly whether Marsha had been given the assignment to convey all the joys of caring for a newborn, sharing tidbits of wisdom with her, as if Caroline had never been a mother. Marsha told her that nursing wasn't all that it was cracked up to be, where to go for the cheapest disposable diapers, and how her girlfriends had given her a glider, much better than a rocking chair, as a shower gift.

Caroline, after hearing a long account of Victoria's sleep schedule, was relieved when it was time to go in to dinner. It struck her that she was the only one there not part of a pair—all couples, two sets of children, and the lovely balance of Vern at one end of the table and Dottie at the other. Though they were seated far apart, Caroline noticed the ease with which they exchanged understanding glances, a happy complicity, surrounded by the members of their family. All were kind, but Caroline couldn't help feeling like the odd man out, the extra guest at the table.

"Wonderful sweet potatoes," Dottie said, and lifted Caroline's casserole to pass once again.

"Caroline writes cookbooks," Vern announced. "Pretty fancy stuff."

"You mean for bookstores?" Marsha's husband looked up from his plate piled high.

Caroline told them about the vegetable book she had edited recently, and that she was working on a proposal for a new book based on vintage New England recipes.

"Kids nowadays don't eat enough vegetables," Vern's brother said, and asked his wife to pass the gravy.

In the next few minutes the talk turned back to the upcoming football play-offs and, eventually, back to ice hockey. Caroline was glad to no longer be the center of attention. Along with the sweet potato soufflé that she had brought as her contribution, they ate turkey, stuffing, mashed potatoes, a green bean casserole, and creamed onions. Caroline took only small portions of each dish, as her baby was giving her heartburn after even the smallest meals. Still, she drizzled Dottie's lush velvety gravy over everything, knowing that later she might have to pay the price for this indulgence. The meal seemed to go on a long time. It had begun to get dark.

"Haven't seen your friend Will lately," Vern said to her.

Caroline straightened in her chair. "He must be away," she said. "I haven't seen any lights over there for a while." She wondered again if Will was back with his wife.

"Said he was closing Taunton's for the winter," Vern said. "Not many tourists passing through this time of year."

Charlie, Vern's brother, an older, frailer version of Vern, said, "That bookstore fella? Martha, down at the café, said he went to Florida."

"Funny," Dottie said, "I wouldn't have thought him one of the snowbirds."

"I thought he was sticking around this winter," Vern said.

Caroline pushed back her chair. Her stomach felt queasy. She never should have eaten the gravy. The others started to rise from the table to clear plates. The next game was about to start.

"Now, now," Dottie said. "You know I can't have everyone in the kitchen at once. Besides, there's dessert coming."

"Please, I'd really like to help," Caroline said. Why hadn't Will told her he was going away? He had said nothing about Florida when they had lunch at Karen's Café. He had really opened up to her that day, or had she imagined that? He probably never heard her stupid message.

"I'm going to help Dottie," Marsha said. "Caroline, you need to stay off your feet. Believe me, in another month you're never going to sit down." She gave Caroline a knowing glance.

"I really don't mind," Caroline said.

"Here," said Marsha, handing to Caroline in one swift gesture little Victoria, who had been sleeping in her arms. "Why don't you go rock her in the living room for a bit. I'd love her to sleep a little longer. Besides, I know Dottie's kitchen. You can practice up for your baby."

Vern's daughter told her two children to clear the table. Her kids, who earlier had been vying for time on the computer, had been passing an electronic game back and forth under the table. "We want to help Grandpa with his puzzle," her son said, looking to his sister for support. Vern collected jigsaw puzzles, and an array of pieces of the new one, a painting of an antique schooner, had been spread out on a card table in the living room.

"You'll clear the table first," their mother reprimanded gently. "I'm going to help set out the pies."

"Please, Grandpa?" begged the older granddaughter.

"After dessert, kids," Vern said, reaching over to tug at her ponytail in an affectionate gesture.

Caroline rose and walked carefully into the living room with Marsha's baby in her arms. She lowered herself into the rocking chair next to the Christmas tree, moving slowly so as to not wake her. Victoria had a miniature sweet face and downy fuzz on her head that stood straight up, giving her an astonished appearance, though her eyes remained tightly closed. She was tiny in every way, nose, hands, fingers, perfectly formed nails, yet she was a person, her very own person, reminding Caroline that soon another such person would be in her arms.

She cradled this baby as best she could. Her own baby, in the gigantic form of her belly, was very much in the way, already filling her lap. This child felt strange to her, awkwardly perched in her arms. She worried that the urge to love and nurture that had gushed forth twice before in her life would remain atrophied within her.

She was glad to have a few moments alone, and longed for the moment she could politely make her departure. The blinking Christmas lights reflecting in the big picture window behind the tree partly masked the dark night outside. Not a star in the sky. Victoria's head wiggled against Caroline's arm and the baby began to fuss, small noises of displeasure, as if she suddenly realized that Caroline's arms were not her own mother's.

❦

Before going upstairs on Christmas night, Caroline went into the hall. Even over the rattling of the windows and the roar of the wind, she could tell immediately that the clock had stopped. She reached for the key in the Chinese bowl. Harry's letter to Lila was still tucked underneath. She had hoped to show it to Rob.

She opened the face of the clock and inserted the key. Gently she turned it to the right, but after half a turn the key wouldn't move, as if blocked. She withdrew the key and inserted it once again. Nothing. It remained stuck in the same place. The hall remained silent. There was nothing she could do tonight.

When she was halfway up the stairs the phone rang. She tried to hurry. Her huge belly made it impossible to rush. In the bedroom she picked up just before the answering machine kicked in.

"Hey, Mom."

"Rob." Weeks of anguish came out in a moan. "Are you okay? You're with Granddad?"

"He said he called you."

So much to say, but she remained speechless. "Merry Christmas," she said. "I'm so glad you called."

"I'm coming to see you. Granddad will get me a ticket."

"When?" Her heart was beating fast.

"Early February. I'll e-mail you the flight."

"Sweetie, I'm so glad you decided to come."

"Pete called me."

"He did?" What could he have said? Something that worked. "There's so much I need to tell you," she said. "You'll love it here." Now she couldn't stop herself. All her hopes and wishes came out in a torrent. "We'll be a family again. We can make plans."

"What do you mean?"

"You know. We'll buy another house in Chevy Chase after I sell this one. It will be like it used to be."

"That's over."

"What do you mean?"

"It will never be like it used to be." His voice was not angry, just incredibly sad.

After he hung up she sat very still at the edge of her bed. How wise he was. How foolish she had been. Nothing would ever be the same.

20

Caroline awoke to a quiet house on January tenth. Less than a month to go. She had been up to use the bathroom several times in the night. Her baby was pressing on her bladder, typical in the final weeks of a pregnancy, something else that she had forgotten from her earlier experiences. She rolled onto her back, pulled the covers up over the mound that was her child, and turned her head toward the windows.

So far the day appeared to be sunless. Hollis was right when he'd told her at the beginning of the summer that living in Maine was always about the weather. There had been three snowfalls already, and winter had barely begun. How had the early settlers survived? The tip of her nose was cold. The silent house seemed to be waiting too. Not for much longer. Soon a baby's cries would fill the rooms. Caroline closed her eyes and focused on what it would be like to hold an infant, that helpless sweet warmth curled in her arms once again.

When Rob was born, moments after the delivery the nurse had placed the bundled baby on her chest. In that instant Caroline went from being one kind of person to being another. The intensity of that mother love was like the power of gravity, timeless and intractable. Harry had looked down at them, tears on his face, as if she had performed a miracle.

How different she might feel now if she were carrying Harry's baby, if Harry were still alive, if having another child could have erased the sorrow they'd carried with them for so many years. She swallowed hard. She thought of Rob's call, his voice remote and far away. Still, he would be coming soon. As promised, he had e-mailed his travel plans, his visit coinciding with her due date. She was sure that Richard had something to do with arranging that. The heat clicked on.

❦

"What's the news from the northland?" Vivien's voice boomed across the line.

Caroline turned off the radio. She had been listening for the weather. They were expecting a storm. Vivien had been calling Caroline several times a week lately, attempting to bolster her spirits. Their conversations had been of some comfort. Caroline enjoyed hearing news of her old friends in Washington, and during the holidays she had valued these talks on the phone more than ever.

"The outline's almost done. I'm going to send it off later today." She glanced at the window. "More snow on the way too."

"I'm glad to hear you're nearly finished. Mapping it out is tough."

"I don't know what I would have done to keep busy otherwise. Let's just say it's no longer gardening season."

"Work's good for all of us." She laughed. Caroline pictured Vivien in her cluttered kitchen, the two sticks protruding from her topknotted hair, manuscript pages on the table spattered with whatever she was writing about. "How's your social life?"

Caroline had told Vivien about her Christmas with Dottie and Vern. She had also been pleasantly surprised when Hollis called and had taken her out for a New Year's Day brunch. "You need to start dating younger men," Vivien joked.

"Let's just say I'm living a quiet life these days. Rob will be here soon."

As if on cue Caroline's belly seized up, tightening. Another one of the preliminary contractions.

"You still there?"

Caroline nodded, unable to speak.

Vivien explained that she'd come up to see her after the baby was born and Rob had gone back to school. "I don't know the first thing about babies, but I'll be on duty in the kitchen. There's nothing you can't manage when you're well fed."

"I'm nervous, Vivien."

"About the birth?"

"That. And having Rob here." Her heart felt yanked in every direction. She should be happy about this baby. But the thought of Rob hanging around the house with his anger, his sullen moods, his silences would certainly put a damper on any joy.

"Caroline, hold on. You're having this baby. This is the life you wanted. Remember? And you want him to be part of it."

"I know," she said quietly. But that didn't make it any easier.

After Vivien hung up Caroline stood at the kitchen sink and stared out at the snow-covered garden. It was hard to believe that there was life buried under the cold ground. Vivien was right: She had chosen her life. Working on her book proposal had been a satisfying way to spend her time. If the agent agreed to take on her project, and if an editor agreed to buy her cookbook, maybe she could earn some money. With that and the sale of Aunt Lila's house, it might be possible to go back to Chevy Chase to re-create the life they once had. Though maybe Rob was right when he said their old life was over.

Will returned to East Hope in the third week of January to the blinking light of his answering machine, bright red as if with holiday cheer. Caroline had called him. She had thought of him. Indeed, she had baked cookies for him. He went to the window and could see the lights from her house. His visit with Rusty and his family had been a pleasure, the warm weather an indulgence.

Following his visit to Florida, he had stopped in Pennsylvania to visit Jack and his wife in Habliston. The financial situation at the college had become serious, and Jack had wanted to get Will's take on possible ideas for further trimming the department. Will was flattered that Jack sought his counsel, and touched that his opinion was important to his old boss. He had stayed nearly a week and had enjoyed reconnecting with a few old friends. In the end he was ready to return to Maine, which he thought of as home. The sharp cold that greeted him when he got off the plane felt good, clean and bracing, like an awakening.

He returned Caroline's call immediately. When the line was busy, he decided not to call again, but to go and visit the next morning. As he puttered around getting the apartment in order and thinking about the new year, he realized that the pain from his failed marriage had lessened. Mary Beth's visit to East Hope felt more like a dream; it might never have happened.

After a hurried breakfast, Will made a quick stop in the village before heading toward Caroline's house. His steps were almost soundless in the chill air as he hiked along Old Harbor Road. There had been a huge snowfall in the night. He shivered, then smiled, enjoying the sensation of peace filling him up like a new warmth. The snow was light, making it easy to walk through, though in places the drifts reached almost three feet high. It was still snowing, but less hard.

At the Canberry Store in the village Will bought some supplies for Caroline. After rounding the bay, today a deep sapphire, he followed the road, or what he could make out as the road, up to her house. The plows had not yet reached this side of town.

In the brilliant morning sunlight her house appeared simple, spare, yet welcoming. The hot Florida sunshine seemed a million miles away, another world entirely. Will leaned his head back and opened his mouth, trying to catch a lingering snowflake on his tongue. He had missed the quiet remoteness of this place. He eased his backpack off his shoulder, made his way up the walkway, and knocked at the back door.

❦

"No baby yet, I see." Will smiled at Caroline.

"How did you get here?" she asked, blinking into the light. "They haven't plowed." She looked over Will's shoulder at the white world. The baby was due in two more weeks, and that was all she could think about. She was nervous about getting to the hospital on the snowy roads. Her mind seemed to have burrowed into a place that allowed no other thought, as if it were hibernating from the rest of her life. She stared at Will, dazed, then wondered if her happiness at seeing him showed.

"I've never seen so much snow," he said. "They've plowed in the village. The trucks should be out this way soon." His eyes crinkled up in the bright sunlight. "I walked over, wanted to be sure you were okay."

Having an unexpected visitor was exciting. It must have been like this in earlier days, when it was impossible to make plans ahead by phone. "Please come in," she said hurriedly. The cold streamed in around him, and she remembered her dismay when she'd learned that Will had left East Hope without telling her. Hurt that he had not said good-bye, she had almost convinced herself that he had left town for good.

He brushed the snow off his coat, pulled the navy watch cap from his head, and kicked his boots against the threshold, knocking loose clods of snow before stepping into the back hall. "I brought you a few things. Just some oranges, bread, and milk." He unzipped his bag and set the food on the counter. "I'd be happy to get you anything else this afternoon."

Caroline wanted to reach out and touch his face. His teeth looked very white against his tanned skin. She pushed those thoughts aside.

"You're so good to me," she said. The pure delight and surprise at seeing him again made her almost light-headed. "Why don't you take off your boots? I'll make us some tea. Or maybe you'd like coffee?" Caroline remembered her phone call to him just before Christmas and her message offering home-baked cookies. That disappointment was melting away as quickly as the clots of snow turning into damp spots on her rug.

"Coffee would be great, thanks." He bent down and unlaced his boots. He looked young to her now in his stocking feet, rumpled pants, and turtleneck sweater. His thick hair was mussed from being under the hat. He smelled of the outdoors, wood smoke, and wet wool. She asked him to have a seat at the table while she made the coffee, deciding to use her French press. She put a tea bag in a cup for herself.

"I haven't seen your lights for a while," she said.

"I've been in Florida." He sat in one of the wicker chairs, making it creak. "Sort of a last-minute decision. I went to my brother Rusty's for Christmas. He and his wife have three boys. Between throwing baseballs, constructing galactic LEGO villages, and playing electronic games I hardly had time to think. It was great to be with a family."

Caroline, who had been pouring hot water into the carafe, put down the kettle. The handle was too hot for her hand. She fumbled for a pot holder and completed the task, then made her tea. A huge swath of sun fell across the tablecloth. The snowy landscape sparkled in all directions. "Where in Florida?" she asked, thinking again of Rob.

"West Palm." He shrugged. "Weather was great. After that I spent some time with my former boss and his wife in Pennsylvania. He's going through a tough time, and it was good to see my old friends. But I missed this." He seemed about to say something more, met her gaze briefly, and then looked out the window instead.

"I never thought that winter could be so beautiful," she said. The wind had dropped completely. Now, with Will in the kitchen sitting at her table, the silence felt peaceful and good. She poured his coffee. She swirled her tea bag in the steaming water.

"There's something I've wanted to ask you," Will said. He sat up a little straighter, as if trying to gather his courage. "After we came back from lunch the day we went to Ellsworth, there was a man here." He paused. "I wondered if everything was okay."

"I should have called to thank you." She paused. "I should have explained."

"You didn't need to thank me." Will's brows drew in, causing his forehead to wrinkle. "You seemed a bit distraught when you saw him."

"It was Pete Spencer. The baby's father."

Will said nothing. He lifted his mug, but the coffee was steaming hot. He set it down without drinking.

"It was a shock to see him here." Caroline leaned forward, resting her arms on the table closer to Will. "He's changed a lot."

"Now he wants to be a father?" Will said sharply.

"He came to say good-bye. He's moved to San Francisco, and we've agreed to stay in touch." She lifted the tea bag out of her cup. "There will be a time when the child will want to know him." She tried to put on a brave face. Lately the reality of having Pete so far away felt very real. Other than the medical help, there would be no one with her if something was wrong when she gave birth. She had no future with Pete, yet he was the father. Harry had been with Caroline for Rob's birth, and also for Grace's. Giving birth that first time had been the start of a family.

Rob had spoken the truth on Christmas night: That family no longer existed. Since his call she had thought more and more about the transitory nature of a family. Children grew up, people died, marriages broke apart. Hadn't families always been about change? The hard part was adapting to the flux, the unstoppable flow, that was the essence of family life, so much like the river and the bay outside her windows, ever changing with the weather, the seasons, the moon.

"He won't be here for the birth?" Will said, not looking at her.

"No," she said. "I didn't know how hard it would be to do this on my own." The moment of happiness that she had experienced when Will appeared at her door evaporated. "I want this baby. It's just not easy." Her mouth quivered. Caroline pushed away her tea and looked down at her belly. The weeks of trying to be strong weighed heavily on her. Now here she was ruining her chance to connect with Will. What had started as a simple conversation was getting stirred up and confused, like a sauce curdling on the stove.

"I wish you'd told me you were going to Florida," she said. "I had hoped to have you here sometime over Christmas." She thought again of their lunch together. After the meal he had walked her to the car and had held her arm closely. Or was he only trying to keep her from falling on the ice? Maybe in her loneliness she was looking for something that wasn't there. She glanced out the window.

Will set his mug on the table and slumped back in his chair. "I thought of calling you," he said. He shifted his weight and the wicker chair creaked beneath him again. "I kept thinking of that guy coming to your house. I figured he was the father. There was that." The sun fell across his face, which was more lined than she remembered. He bit his lower lip, as if unsure of what else to add. A moment later he asked, "Did your son come for Christmas?"

"He refused." She said this dully. "He spent Christmas with Harry's father."

His voice softened. "I'm sorry to hear that."

"Vern and Dottie had me for Christmas dinner."

"That was nice of—"

"It was terrible." Her eyes welled up with tears. "What I mean is, they were lovely to have me. But it wasn't my family." Caroline didn't bother to keep the bitterness from her voice. "I've never been so lonely in my life."

"You've been on your own all this time."

"Yes. But I still miss my son."

Will appeared to consider this. "Maybe he needed to be with his grandfather right now," he said. "You know, his dad's father."

"You're right. They're very close. Still . . . I guess I'm selfish." She brushed her tears with the back of her hands. "This was my first Christmas without Rob. It was hard."

She cradled her belly with her arms and wished Will would understand. If this baby would only come. She took a deep breath. "I've made such a mess of everything. I'm old and I'm having a baby. My son will barely speak to me. I feel so alone. Do you know what that's like?" There, she had said it. She was sick of being brave, sick of the mess that she had created for herself, sick with regret. She turned away from him. Tears rolled down her face.

Will pulled back and grew quiet. "You're right. There's a lot I don't know." He let out a sigh and placed his hands on the table, his fists clenched. He spoke more forcefully. "Caroline, look at me."

She choked on a sob.

"Please," he said.

Slowly she turned her head. His eyes looked a deeper color than they ever had.

"I do know what it's like to be lonely," he said. He opened his hands, palms up, before her. "And I want to understand. I thought of you a lot when I was in Florida."

Caroline got up from the table.

"Please," he said again, and stood.

She turned her back to him and bent her head, holding her belly as if it might drop. She felt Will's hands on her shoulders.

"I want to help." He spoke gently. "I don't know how. Please don't push me away."

She cried harder. She brought her hands to her face. "Oh, God," she said. "That's what I did to Harry." Her shoulders rounded as if to protect herself from a physical blow. "I couldn't face him after Grace died. Harry was devastated." Between sobs, her voice halting, Caroline told Will about finding Harry's letter to Lila. "Harry was as hurt as I was. I selfishly ignored that he was suffering too."

"You mustn't blame yourself."

"But I do. All Harry did was work. In the past few years, things went badly for him at the firm. I'm sure the fact that I didn't want to know about any of it made him all the more desperate, frantic to prove something." Caroline explained the financial mess that her husband had left behind.

Will put his arms around her, finding her hands and placing his on top. She felt the strength in his arms, the warmth of his breath on her neck.

"You came to East Hope," he said. "You found a way to go on." He held her firmly and rocked her gently. "Having this baby is brave. I kept thinking of that while I was away."

"I'm so alone."

He didn't release his embrace, and slowly, like rays of sun on the snow, the warmth of his body radiated into hers. "I'm here now." He continued to hold her.

His words sank in slowly. She wanted this moment to last. The sun streamed in around them. Though the greater part of winter was ahead, the solstice had passed; the days would grow longer. "Remember when you came to dinner this fall?" she asked.

"Umm," he said, not releasing her from his grasp.

"You started to kiss me. I wish now that I hadn't stopped you." She turned to him. Her face was streaked with tears. Why not tell him this? She had told him everything else. Her large belly kept him at a distance.

He shook his head, smiled, and, leaning into her, took her face in his hands. He kissed her lips, slowly and gently this time, nothing like the confusing moment that long-ago night by the fire. He took her hands. "I worried that I'd overstepped my bounds the last time," he said.

She shook her head. "You didn't."

"Is it okay now?"

"It's a little awkward." She placed her hands on her belly. "It won't always be like this." She looked down and gave a nervous laugh.

They sat again at the table. For a moment neither said anything. Caroline smoothed her hair back. "I'm really a mess," she said.

"You're never a mess." He smiled. "And you're not old."

"You're not much of a liar," she joked, and suddenly the atmosphere lightened. Caroline convinced Will to stay for a bowl of soup. A new, sweet intimacy hung between them. He set the table and carried their plates to the table, as if he were used to being in the kitchen, as if he had performed this task numerous times.

They talked more easily. She told him about sending the cookbook proposal to the agent in New York. He told her that he had an interview the following week at the university in Orono. She was sympathetic when he told her about Crystal Thomas and agreed that he was right to fight back and clear up the misunderstanding about what had happened at Habliston College.

Later on, he insisted on picking Rob up at the airport the following week. He told her that little by little things would get better with her son. And slowly that lovely sense of hope, as ephemeral as the warmth of that first spring day when you could once again smell the earth, filled her heart. The possibility of happiness was real to her. Will was right: Things could change. Tonight, she thought, the sky would be clear and a full moon would shine on the snow.

❦

"So, are you my mom's new boyfriend?" Rob asked sullenly after Will introduced himself in the baggage claim of the Bangor airport.

Will chose to ignore this comment and instead told him to grab his bag. "My car's this way." Will led Rob through the terminal to the short-term parking lot. Rob's flight had been three hours late. It had been snowing on and off all day. Will was relieved when the plane had finally landed, knowing how eager Caroline was to have him arrive home safely.

Will had recognized Rob immediately. He was fair, almost as tall as Will, with that loose-limbed walk of youth. His eyes, though blue, were replicas of his mother's. As they walked to the car Will called Caroline to let her know that they would be on their way soon.

Will opened the back of his Jeep. "Go ahead and put your bag in there," he said. "The roads are a mess. It might take a couple of hours to get to East Hope."

"Thanks, Mr. Harmon," Rob said coolly.

"Call me Will."

Rob said nothing and heaved his duffel bag into the back of the car, slamming the tailgate. He wore a light jacket over a cotton shirt and sweater, not the kind of clothing for a snowstorm in Maine.

Will drove out of the parking garage into the dark night. The sky had a steely heaviness, as if weighted with more snow to come. The roads had been plowed, but they were still covered with several inches of hard-packed snow. Rob slumped down in the other seat and stared out his window. He remained silent, asking no questions about his mother.

Rob had lost his dad, Will thought. That was a terrible thing. Still, he was a young man with many privileges, a mother who adored him. He was getting a fine education, and he had a whole life ahead of him. Plenty to be thankful for.

They stopped at a light before turning onto the main road. Will sensed that this young man was hurt and confused. The frayed cuffs of Rob's shirt stuck out below the sleeves of his sweater; his nails were bitten to the quick. Will suddenly remembered what his own dad used to say when Rusty had gotten into some kind of trouble, usually another speeding ticket. "What that boy needs is a swift kick in the pants, knock some sense into him." That was not the answer.

The heater began to warm the car, and Will slipped his gloves off and gripped the wheel more tightly. He had enough to think about now. The driving was treacherous. The wind had picked up and snow whirled in every direction. He switched on his high beams, but that did nothing more than further illuminate the snow. Will turned the heat to defrost and reduced his speed, keeping his eyes fixed on the road. Rob had eased farther down in his seat, leaning against the door. His eyes were shut; he was asleep or feigning sleep. That was fine with Will. The thought of making conversation with this unhappy young man for several hours appealed to him not at all.

When they reached the coast road, Will was lucky to get behind the plow. For a while the giant monsterlike machine with flashing lights and a roaring engine escorted them through the weather.

When the plow turned off, Will reduced his speed to a crawl. He thought back to the foggy night in the fall when Caroline had lost her nerve beside the road. He relaxed a little, the way he often did when he thought of her. It was strange how she had worked herself into his life. Since he'd been back in Maine he'd gone to see her every day. Will found himself drawn to her, wanting to be near her, like wanting to sit closer to a fire in the hearth.

At last they reached the final stretch on the causeway, Caroline's house only a few miles farther on. The roads were better here. There was less snow this close to the ocean. Rob began to stir. He opened his eyes and straightened in his seat.

"Sorry. Didn't mean to sleep," he said.

"You haven't missed anything. The snow's not as bad now."

Rob craned his neck to the front. "Is it like this all the time?" The wipers beat steadily. Large, wet flakes of snow continued to fall.

"This is the worst night we've had."

Rob seemed to remember why he was here, and his face took on a moody pout.

"We'll be there soon," Will said. He glanced quickly over at Rob. "Your mom is eager to see you."

Rob looked out the side window, angling his back to Will. He didn't respond. He seemed to stew in an angry silence.

After hesitating for a moment Will spoke. "I know this has been a rough year for you."

"What do you care?" Rob crossed his arms and threw Will a defiant look. "You don't know anything about me."

"Only that your mother loves you. She's been miserable about what's happened between you." Will slowed the car. They were climbing the hill to Lila's house. Caroline's house, he thought.

"I don't have to talk about that with you," Rob said.

"No, you don't."

Finally Will turned into the driveway. Light glowed from all the windows. He parked as close as he could to the house and turned off the engine. Rob reached for his door handle.

"Rob, wait."

"What?" he said tightly.

"I know it was hard to lose your father," Will said. "You're the only one your mother has. She needs to hear that you love her and that you support her having this baby."

"You have no right to tell me that."

"Maybe I don't, but I know your mother."

21

The headlights of Will's car flooded the driveway. Caroline looked at her watch. It was nearly ten o'clock. She waited by the back door, peering out into the darkness. A moment later Rob and Will entered, enveloped in a cloud of cold air.

"Sweetie, you're here." Caroline threw her arms around Rob. After the short walk from the car his hair was damp from snow. She stepped back and brushed a few flakes from his jacket.

"Hi, Mom," he said quietly. He backed away from Caroline and slipped off his shoes, leaving them on the rug in the back hall.

Will remained by the door. "I'd better keep going." He glanced quickly at Rob. "It's snowing pretty hard again."

"I was worried about you on these roads. Really, I can't thank you enough." She looked at Rob.

He stared down at the floor. "Yeah, thanks for picking me up," he said flatly. She could feel the tension between them and wondered what they had talked about in the car. The journey to East Hope on this February night had been a long one.

Caroline went to Will and reached for his hand. "Thank you," she said again. She felt the warmth of his grip, but let go quickly.

"Call me for anything," Will said. Then he was gone.

❦

"You probably don't remember this house," she said. "You were only three the summer we were here." She watched as Rob pulled off his jacket. His shirttail hung beneath the edge of his sweater. He wore wrinkled cotton pants that looked too big for him. The way he moved, hanging his coat on a hook, his narrow shoulders, his fine hands, made her think of Harry when she first knew him. Rob looked more and more like his father. He was Harry all over again.

Rob followed his mother into the kitchen. He looked tired and ill at ease.

"I've made a pot of chili," she said, aware of the speed of her words, not wanting her nervousness to show. "And some corn bread. The kind you like. Remember the one with cheese?"

Rob looked dazed and uneasy. He appeared to be picking at a hangnail on his thumb. "I'm not really hungry, Mom." He bit at the nail.

"You need to eat something." She didn't want to force him. Here he was in her kitchen at last, the place where she thought of him so often. She had imagined this homecoming almost too many times. "Maybe just a little?"

"Yeah. Okay." He went to the table and pulled back a chair. After sitting, he folded his arms on the table and rested his head, like children at school when told to put their heads down on their desks. His light hair was streaked from the Florida sun.

She went to the stove and ladled the chili into a bowl. Her hands shook. Some of the red sauce dribbled onto the stove. She cut a piece of corn bread and placed it on a small plate and carried these to the table.

"Here you are."

Rob leaned back to make room for his dinner.

Caroline retreated to the counter, where she had put her cup of herbal tea earlier. Rob picked up his spoon and leaned over his bowl with his elbows on the table.

"Wait," she said. "I forgot the grated cheese in the fridge."

"It's fine like this." He began to eat, still not looking at her, as if afraid of seeing her very pregnant belly.

She placed her tea opposite him and sat down. She took a sip. It had cooled completely.

"Do you remember anything from that summer?"

Rob shook his head and continued to eat. She could see that he liked the chili, judging from the speed with which he ate, or else he wanted to finish quickly to get to bed.

"You were very little," she said. "Dad loved it here."

Rob finished eating. His spoon clattered down onto his plate. "I don't want to talk about Dad."

"Rob, please."

He pushed back in his chair. "I'm here, aren't I? I'm going to bed."

"Wait. You can't stalk out." She raised her voice. "You're grown-up and you need to hear this."

He said nothing, but remained seated.

"I love you very much. That will never change." She took a deep breath, suddenly calmer. She had said what mattered most. "On Christmas night you said that our life as a family was over. I didn't want to believe that. Still, I made the decision to have this baby. It's what I want. You don't have to approve. But it doesn't mean that I don't love you. Our life in Chevy Chase is over; you're right. Our lives will never be the same, but I will always be your mother."

Finally he looked up. His face looked tight, drawn in, as if he were working to keep his composure. "Why would you have his baby?" He looked like he might cry. "You've got me. You already have a child. Why would you have another? One that's not even Dad's?" His voice broke and he leaned his elbows on the table, rubbing the heels of his hands into his eyes.

"You knew I lost a baby, your sister, Grace."

Rob drew his hands across his chest and jutted his chin out, his lower lip coming to meet the upper in a fierce line.

"After Dad died, all those memories came back," she said. "There had been so much death. Deciding to have this baby was like having a second chance."

"Fine, Mom." His voice grew hard. "Pete told me all that. Okay, have your baby. Now just let me live my own life."

"You mean everything to me," Caroline said, finding the words coming to her more and more easily. These were words she should have spoken months ago. "I was wrong to think I could just move here, a million miles from everything, and that that would be enough. It takes more than moving to a new place to start over." She placed her hand on his sleeve, slowly fingering the texture of his sweater.

Rob sat very still. Caroline hoped he was beginning to come around. "Sweetie, you're young, and you're strong. This past year has been very hard, but you're making your way. It's like when you're rock climbing. You find one foothold, then a handhold, then the next. We each have to find a way to move on. I hope your knowing how much I love you will make it a little easier. That's all I can do." She breathed out and the tension in her back eased away.

She stood and picked up his dishes to carry them to the sink.

"I'm going up to bed," he said hoarsely, and started to rise.

"Wait," she said. "Take this." Caroline reached into her pocket and handed him Harry's letter, which she had read and reread so many times. She placed her hands on her son's shoulders and watched as he studied the envelope. "I found it in one of Aunt Lila's books. It's to her from Dad. He wrote it after Grace died."

Caroline took off her apron and put it on the back of her chair. Rob sat still, his eyes on the page of his father's letter. "I'm going upstairs," she said. "Your room is at the very end of the hall. I'll see you in the morning." She bent and kissed Rob's cheek.

❦

The next day the world sparkled a brilliant white. The bay was calm, deeply blue, and almost as smooth as a lake. Caroline awoke to the sun pouring into the bedroom. She looked at the clock. After nine. She never slept that late. She pulled the covers to her chin and placed her hands around her belly. The image of the doe and her fawn that she had seen in the woods by the town beach last summer came to mind. Where were the deer now? How did they survive these long Maine winters? How long did a mother deer look after her young? Was there a certain age, a season, a particular moment when a young deer separated from the mother? The animal world was governed by instinct and the forces of nature, so much simpler than the world of human hearts.

She got up and pulled on her robe. The smell of bacon made her realize she was very hungry, and she could hear sounds coming from the kitchen. Could Rob be up already? Holding the banister, she made her way downstairs. The treads creaked with her weight. There, at the stove, Rob was turning a piece of bacon. Butter sizzled on the griddle next to it.

"Good morning," she said.

He turned around and spoke quickly. "Hey, Mom."

"Are you all right?" she asked.

"Pretty hungry," he said, and almost shyly turned back to the stove. "How many pancakes can you eat?" he asked over his shoulder.

"A lot," she said. "I'll pour the juice." The sight of Rob at the stove cooking breakfast the way Harry used to touched her deeply. She went to the refrigerator and stared inside, trying to remember what she was looking for. She took a deep breath and picked up the carton of juice.

"I didn't know you could make pancakes," she said carefully, not wanting to ruin this moment, so unexpected, so fragile. Here he was, kindly making breakfast when she had feared more accusatory looks, more sulking. Dared she hope for forgiveness?

"Not as good as Dad's," he said, his voice a bit shaky, "but not bad, either." He appeared to concentrate on his task, carefully easing the spatula under the edge of the cooking batter.

Caroline set the table. She moved slowly, trying to ignore the persistent ache in her back. Rob continued to pour out batter, and the pile of pancakes grew on a plate near the stove. She found some maple syrup in the pantry cupboard. The house was quiet but for the sounds of cooking, the opening and closing of drawers, the tinkling of dishes and silverware.

Rob carried the platter of pancakes to the table. The tightness in his face that had been there the night before was gone. Still, she wished he would smile.

Caroline served herself and passed the plate to Rob. "Thanks, sweetie. These look wonderful." She smeared her pancakes with butter and poured on a generous amount of syrup.

He helped himself, set the plate down, and kept his eyes on his breakfast.

Caroline swallowed and wiped her mouth. "You doing okay?" she said tentatively. "I mean, did Dad's letter . . . ?"

"Please, Mom." His face crumpled. He shook his head and brought his hands to his face. His body shook. "I don't want to talk about it."

"Oh, Rob, my sweet boy, I'm so sorry I've made you unhappy."

"Mom, it's not you." He let out a sob, almost a moan, from someplace deep within him. His body curved forward, as if he'd been punched.

Caroline reached out for him, but her hand remained in the air. She was too frightened to touch him. She didn't want to upset him more. Her own body ached deeply, the old sadness flowing out of her heart. It had never left her. She brought her hand back and lowered her head. She had said all she could say.

Rob slowly seemed to pull himself back together. He spoke softly. "I'm okay about the baby." He picked up his napkin and wiped his face. "Really. I am." He looked at her squarely. His mouth softened. She thought she detected a tenderness in his gaze that wasn't there before. "Pete explained everything. He apologized. He said he hated making it hard between us." Rob let out a deep sigh. "I miss Dad so much, that's all." He began to cry again. "When I read his letter . . ." He paused and shook his head. "God, sorry, you don't need to have me falling apart."

Caroline reached across and took his hands. "I'll always need you, even when you fall apart. Always, always I'll need you." She was crying now. "And I want you to always need me. That's what being a family is all about."

He nodded and held her hands tightly. "Thanks, Mom."

"Look at us, crying over breakfast." She smiled through her tears, then laughed. "It's been a long time since anyone has made me a meal," she said, picking up her fork, "and this is just too good to waste."

Rob nodded and started eating as well.

While they ate she began to tell him a little about East Hope, the house renovations, and the people she had met. She pointed out Will's house across the bay. All of a sudden she thought that breakfast had never tasted so good.

Later Rob told her about Christmas with Harry's father. "I shot a ninety-six one day," he said. "Granddad said he'd set up some golf lessons for me if I come in the spring. What do you think, Mom? Maybe you and the baby could come down to Florida for my spring break."

Caroline glanced out at the snow. "I think that's a great idea. I have a feeling I'll be ready for some warm weather by then."

When she asked about Melanie his mood grew somber again. He told her that they had broken up.

"I'm so sorry," she said.

"It's okay," he said. "It was really my idea. It was on again, off again. Something wasn't working. She's doing okay. We talked before vacation. I think we're still friends."

"That's good," she said, thinking how hard it must have been for her son this fall. Yet he seemed assured, even confident as he sat there telling her about the breakup.

Later, when they were doing the dishes, they heard the sound of the plow, and Vern's nephew arrived to clear the driveway. Rob said he'd go out and shovel a pathway to the garage. "We may need to get the car out today," he said after an affectionate glance at her belly. She found him an extra sweater to layer under his jacket. She watched from the window as he bent, wielding the shovel and working his way from the house to the driveway. Huge sprays of snow flew up and over his shoulder as he dug.

As Caroline climbed the stairs to get dressed, her belly tightened. It felt harder than usual this morning. She stopped. The baby wasn't moving much. Maybe today would be the day.

❦

In the afternoon Rob made a fire in the living room fireplace. He brought Harry's letter down to her. "Thanks, Mom," he said. "I'm glad you showed me this." He met her gaze and smiled.

She asked him if he wanted to keep it. He said no, that she should have it. Neither of them spoke of the letter again. It was as if they both agreed they needed to quietly savor the calm after a storm.

"Would you mind putting it under the Chinese bowl on the table in the hall?" she said. "I'll put it away later."

He went to the hall. "What's with this clock?" he called out. "Doesn't it work?"

Caroline explained that Hollis had showed her how to wind it, but that the last time it had stuck when she tried to do it. "The directions are in the drawer," she said. At that moment she experienced a sharp pain. The backache had become something else. She got up and walked slowly to the kitchen, needing to move, wanting the pain to go away.

At the sink the pain came again. She gripped the counter and waited. The pain subsided. She glanced at her watch. The minute hand swept full circle. Then several times more. Five minutes went by. Nothing else happened. She filled a glass with water.

Rob called from the hall. "I think I got it to work."

Caroline stood still and listened. The even ticking of the clock once again filled the house.

❦

Within the hour the contractions were less than ten minutes apart. For the third time in her life Caroline was pulled into the all-powerful experience of giving birth. It was as if she were being hurtled into a vast stream with a strong current forcing her along among the rapids, at moments fast and smooth and then, without warning, wrenching and rough, like crashing into jagged rocks. Dr. Carney instructed Caroline to come to the hospital immediately.

Rob wanted to drive her to Ellsworth in the old Volvo. She told him that car was too heavy in front, not great on the snow-covered roads, and that Dottie and Vern were on call to drive her into Ellsworth when she needed them.

"Mom, I've got an idea," he said. "I'll call Will. His Jeep is great in the snow."

Another pain hit. She breathed into it, willing her mind to move outside her body. This was only the beginning. When the contraction was over she nodded and told him where to find Will's number. Rob strode into the kitchen immediately and got on the phone.

She went up to her room and put the items she needed into her overnight bag. Another contraction made her stop and hold her breath. This time she forced herself to breathe deeply while the pain, like an intense heat, tightened her belly. When it subsided she looked again at the bassinet in the corner of her room. Her mother had sent her a soft white blanket and a plush brown bear along with a card that read, *For your Maine baby, With love, Mother.* She opened the drawer where the tiny clothes, clean and soft, lay waiting for the little person who was now, without a doubt, on the way.

At last, she thought. On this cold afternoon, the seventh day of February, her baby was coming. Lila's dear house, silent for so long, would be silent no longer. She went for her coat, but as the next contraction set in she had to lower herself to a chair. The contractions were definitely coming closer. Finally she heard the sound of Will's car. Rob, looking terrified but determined to be brave, carried her bag and walked her out to the car. "Careful, Mom," he said. "Don't slip." He had taken her arm, and she felt his grip firmly on her elbow. If she fell, he would go with her. Will helped her into the front seat and placed a blanket across her lap.

By this time Caroline found it hard to speak. Rob sat behind his mother. He kept his hands on her shoulders during the drive, but soon his kind words, his mumbled phrases intended to soothe her were drowned out in the waves of pain that were coming faster and faster. She was vaguely aware of arriving at the hospital, of a hurried exchange of insurance cards, one more form to sign between contractions.

Rob and Will, with worried smiles and fumbling hugs, turned her over to an efficient nurse. At this moment Caroline was ready to leave them behind. Next came the frantic change into a nightgown, some flimsy piece of printed cotton that hardly mattered, the nurses wheeling the bed, the bright lights, and the cold delivery room. Dr. Carney's encouraging voice felt like a blurred dream. Sounds at a great distance, the smell of disinfectant, the steady beeping of a monitor, the gentle coaxing of the nurse at her side, all became a jumble of annoyances interfering with this force controlling her body. All she wanted was her baby. The months of kicks, the pressure on her spine, the huge belly that blocked the sight of her toes now became her baby. *My baby, my baby,* she thought. Yes, it was right.

Suddenly Caroline was overcome by a feeling of power. She was doing this on her own. Pete was far away, her mother was resting at home waiting for her old bones to knit back together, and Will and Rob were somewhere pacing in a waiting room. And here in the cold Maine winter she was doing this totally amazing thing. Her body was doing its job. A sudden energy surged forth. Her baby was coming and her life was going to change.

Faces flashed into her mind, like quick images on a movie screen. Harry when she first met him. Rob, the infant. Her mother smiling from the old chintz chair in their living room in Connecticut. Her father wiping sweat off his brow in his garden. Will, sitting on the rocky beach behind the bookstore. She saw Lila's house awash in the golden light of a summer afternoon. She pictured the lilacs in bloom in the spring and the sparkle of the bay, and the days growing longer and longer. The light, the shimmering brightness of the world around her, flooded her vision. She closed her eyes, allowing her body to ride the next wave, this one more powerful than the rest.

"Okay. Now, Caroline." Dr. Carney's voice interrupted her dreaming. "Go ahead and push."

Photo by Elizabeth Kupersmith

Katharine Davis is also the author of *Capturing Paris*. She grew up in Europe, taught French for many years, and worked as a docent at the National Gallery of Art. She lives in Alexandria, Virginia, and York Harbor, Maine. She can be reached at www.katharinedavis.com.

CONVERSATION GUIDE

East Hope

KATHARINE DAVIS

This Conversation Guide is intended to enrich the individual reading experience, as well as encourage us to explore these topics together—because books, and life, are meant for sharing.

A CONVERSATION WITH KATHARINE DAVIS

Q. Where did you get the idea for your novel East Hope*?*

A. This novel actually grew out of a short story that I wrote almost ten years ago. For that story a line of dialogue had popped into my head: "How's my favorite redhead?" I envisioned a man saying this to a woman as she enters a house to attend a dinner party. With that image I had the beginning of a character, and I let my imagination go to work. The woman, whom I named Caroline, was ill at ease in that situation. I wondered why she felt uncomfortable, what had brought her to this house, why she was alone. In my story I decided that she was recently widowed, and uneasy with the attention of this man, her husband's best friend. In this early version the reader learns of Caroline's financial difficulties, her loneliness now that her only child is away at college, and her husband's emotional distance and unhappiness in the months before he died. When her husband's friend brings her home in a thunderstorm, she rejects his advances, knowing that a love affair would not be the answer—end of story. Yet over time I kept going back to Caroline and wondering what would happen if she succumbed. What would be the result of that liaison? If it didn't work out, what would she do? Might she want to escape somehow? If so, where? As a writer, I realized I wasn't finished with this character's story. As a reader, I wanted to learn more.

Q. Why did you choose Maine as the place where Caroline would go?

A. Maine is a state with a definite mystique. The coastline is breathtaking, with thousands of islands dotting the shoreline, and a northern light, whose soft angles reflect gloriously off the water. There are forests, rivers, lakes, and mountains, with Mount Katahdin marking the end of the Appalachian Trail. Much of the state is vast and remote, without paved roads. It is a state of great contrasts. A summer retreat for some of the very wealthy, it is also the home of hardworking locals who make their living from fishing the cold waters or farming the rocky ground. The city of Portland offers museums, art galleries, and sophisticated dining, but nearby tiny towns on remote islands, such as Monhegan, with its year-round population of sixty-five, offer few amenities. Long, lightfilled summer days follow long, cold winter nights, when it grows dark by midafternoon. Maine has always attracted adventurers, artists, writers, loners, and eccentrics. Its people are often fiercely independent. I wanted Caroline to attempt to rebuild her life in a place that fostered strength and independence. To my mind, geography deeply affects all of us, and sometimes going to an entirely new place forces us to see with fresh eyes exactly who we are. Also, I love Maine and spend part of each year there, so I was eager to write about it.

Q. Your last book was set in Paris, a world-class, sophisticated city. In comparison, the town of East Hope is a very small, simple one.

A. A small village on the coast of Maine served my characters in *East Hope* by forcing them to confront their problems in a completely new environment, one in which mere physical survival couldn't always be taken for granted. On the one hand, Caroline and Will are more vulnerable, more at risk outside their usual settings, but being totally "away" also frees them. The lack of distractions in East Hope helps them to realize what's really important to them.

Q. You make Aunt Lila's home such an appealing place—describing the light-filled rooms, gleaming wood furniture, the ticking old clock, laundry on lines snapping in the breeze, and all the wonderful scents and tastes of the baking and cooking that Caroline does. Did you deliberately set out to create your idea of a perfect home?

A. Without meaning to I probably did just that. I've always loved houses, though not the large, fancy residences of the very rich. I'm drawn to smaller places, old houses with character and the patina of lives well lived. Simple things can make such a difference: garden flowers on a table, photographs of family and friends, good reading lamps next to comfortable chairs. And, of course, with shelves and shelves of books, you are always in good company.

Q. East Hope *is told from two alternating points of view—Caroline Waverly's and Will Harmon's. Which character is more important to you? Whose story interests you more?*

A. Initially in the writing I was completely focused on Caroline: What happens to a woman when everything she has counted on disappears—husband, home, a happy relationship with her child? Being a woman, I'm drawn to women's stories, but when I considered whom Caroline might encounter in this next phase of her life, I thought it might be interesting to have her meet a man who is also attempting to sort out his life. For a man, losing a job constitutes an immense loss, not only financially but also psychologically, and I decided to further challenge Will by raising serious questions about his marriage. As Will came alive for me, I cared more about him and became more invested in how he would overcome his own difficulties. However, while Will's story is equally important, Caroline's came first.

Q. Your books focus on what some might consider ordinary problems: marriage, relationships, and family—the small, daily struggles in life. Why is that?

A. It's true that there are far greater problems in the world—war, poverty, disease, environmental degradation. These are global problems of immense complexity that affect us all. We need both fiction and nonfiction to illuminate human suffering and inform us about such issues. But there is also a place for fiction that concerns the domestic dramas of everyday life. During a recent visit to the National Gallery in Washington, DC, I was thinking about the different sorts of paintings on the walls. I looked at the huge paintings of historical events, portraits of famous people, and religious art that told stories of faith. Yet my favorite paintings, the ones that most often caused me to pause and reflect, were the small canvases depicting everyday life. In a similar way, we often choose to read about ordinary people whose lives are for various reasons suddenly set off course. We turn to fiction to discover how other people think, feel, and act. We read to expand our understanding of what it means to be human.

Q. Who are your favorite writers? What are you reading today?

A. I tend to read mostly contemporary fiction. It would be impossible to list all my favorite writers, as I would certainly leave some of them out. The first section I reach for in the Sunday paper is the book review. I keep a running list of books I want to read and never go anywhere without a book. On long car trips I listen to books on tape. Some of my old favorites are *Howards End* by E. M. Forster, *Crossing to Safety* by Wallace Stegner, and a French novel, *Thérèse Desqueyroux,* by François Mauriac. In contemporary fiction or classics, I love to sink into another world and enjoy the pure pleasure of a good story.

Q. You taught French for many years. What made you decide to become a writer?

A. I've always been an avid reader. I discovered Daphne du Maurier at the age of fourteen, and since then I've been reading one book after another. Those who like art often try to draw or paint, and as someone who loves to read, I wanted to see what it would be like to write. I quickly learned that writing, while more difficult than I ever imagined, offers up an amazing pleasure all its own.

Q. Can you elaborate on what those pleasures are, and why you weren't scared to death to try writing a novel?

A. What I love most about writing is the creative act. When I am writing time seems to stop and I'm in an entirely different world. I guess it's a form of escape, but it's also a heady experience to create something out of nothing. I have often joked that as an eldest child I'm bossy, and with writing I can be the one who decides how a story will turn out. Of course, I soon discovered that as I began to know my characters, they took on a life all their own. That part is truly magic. I was never scared of writing a novel, but perhaps that was because I was naive about the enormity of the task, and I had no idea how difficult it is to publish fiction.

Q. What's your writing process? How long did it take to finish East Hope*?*

A. I am a morning person and do my best work before noon. After lunch I run errands, do chores, answer e-mail, and tend to the business of life. In the late afternoon I often return to my manuscript and putter a bit, but I rarely accomplish much then. However, even when I'm not writing, I'm thinking about the book. I might get an idea while in line at the grocery store or while driving. I also keep paper beside my bed for ideas in the middle of the night. *East Hope* took about two years.

Q. What do you hope to do in the future?

A. Write more novels. I love reading them, so I will continue to write them. I only wish I had started sooner!

Q. Hmm . . . May I ask how old you were when you started writing? Do you think it helped that you'd already lived a little?

A. I didn't start writing until I was almost fifty. Truly a late bloomer! Soon after I began, I attended a writers' conference and was somewhat intimidated by all the young people there. When

I expressed my doubts to one of the instructors, she told me not to worry and that having life experience was always a good thing. I love examples of other late bloomers. Mary Wesley, a wonderful British writer, published her first work in her seventies.

QUESTIONS FOR DISCUSSION

1. What does Caroline worry about most after Harry's death? What is her greatest concern? What does she yearn for most early in the novel?

2. Caroline and Harry were going through a difficult time in the months before his death. Harry was distant, worried, and caught up in his financial problems. Caroline avoided confronting him and later regrets this. How does this complicate her grieving for him?

3. Caroline goes through many changes in Maine. She learns to manage on her own, to renovate Aunt Lila's house, and, most important, she decides to have a child. How does living in Maine, the place itself, contribute to the person she becomes? Would she have evolved the same way if she'd stayed behind in Chevy Chase?

4. Will Harmon's marriage begins to suffer when his wife moves to New York and she commutes home on weekends. Would their marriage have remained strong without their long-distance relationship? How important is it for the spouses in a marriage to spend time together? Is there no truth to the old adage that absence makes the heart grow fonder?

5. Are Will and Mary Beth ill-suited for each other from the beginning? Or do they grow and mature differently during the course of their marriage?

6. Is Will unrealistic in hoping that Mary Beth will understand his going to Maine for the summer? Does he subconsciously want to end their marriage when he goes ahead to purchase Taunton's without discussing it with her? Is he the one most at fault when their marriage fails? If not, what are the factors that make their life together impossible to salvage?

7. Will and Caroline feel an immediate attraction to each other in spite of all the complications in their personal lives. Beyond the simple rapport that seems to connect them when they first meet, both new and alone in East Hope, what are the qualities that draw them to each other?

8. Is Rob justified in his anger toward his mother? Is he asking too much of her and acting selfish in not wanting to share his life with a sibling? Is he, in his own way, also clinging to their earlier life, the way things were before his father's death?

9. Caroline and Will are both in their forties when circumstances force them to create completely new lives for themselves. Has something similar ever happened to you, or to people you know? In the cases you know, what forced the change, and how did things turn out?

10. Caroline never seriously considers an abortion, but the possibility is raised by her friend. Discuss how unexpected and unwanted pregnancies are handled in the fiction you've read. Do

you think they're written about realistically, or do writers tend to be politically correct? What would you have done in Caroline's situation?

11. Twice, Will is accused of sexual harassment, and in both cases he's entirely innocent. Does the sensitivity to this issue of people in administrative and managerial positions allow women (and men) to take advantage of it, as Will's college student does? Or is Will simply guilty of not having fought hard enough to clear his name? What should he have done when he was first accused, and do you think he handles the situation well when he's accused again in East Hope?

12. Pretend you're writing an epilogue for this novel. What do you envision for Caroline and Will in the future? How will Rob and Pete fit into the picture? What sort of lives will they lead after the birth of this child? Is it a boy or a girl?